"Have you told your husband about me?" Michael asked gently.

Giving a nearly imperceptible shrug, Danica held her breath.

"Why not?" he asked very softly.

"You're *my* friend," she whispered. "He rules the rest of my life. You're *mine*."

Michael closed his eyes and moaned. His hand fell to her neck, and he lightly kneaded the soft skin there. "Oh God," he said, his deep voice trembling, as did his arm, "I'm not sure if I can do this."

"Do what?" she breathed, though she knew.

Framing her face with his hands, he looked at her. "I'm not sure I can just be your friend, Dani. You mean very, very much to me. I need more. I want to hold you, to touch you. Right now, I want to kiss you."

She wanted it, too, more than anything she'd ever have believed possible. Her husband had never stirred her this way, and she felt a sudden anger at what she'd missed. But the anger was fleeting, because Michael was here with her now, making her forget . . . almost.

"We can't," she gasped, feeling torn apart inside . . .

BARBARA DELINSKY

WITHIN REACH

W🌐RLDWIDE

TORONTO · NEW YORK · LONDON · PARIS
AMSTERDAM · STOCKHOLM · HAMBURG
ATHENS · MILAN · TOKYO · SYDNEY

First published May 1986

ISBN 0-373-97018-8

Printed in Canada

To Jayne, Suzanne and Elaine,
for a network of information,
advice and friendship that
defies the miles.

Chapter One

ONE MINUTE THERE WAS NOTHING but a cloud of fog before him; the next she was there, materialized from the mist. Stunned, Michael Buchanan came to an abrupt halt. He hadn't expected to encounter anyone on the beach at such an inhospitable time of year, much less as striking a figure as the one before him.

She was a vision of loneliness standing there, with the March wind tucking her long skirt around her legs, whipping strands of hair across her cheeks. As he watched, she pressed her pocketed hands closer to her body, enveloping herself more snugly within the chic oversized jacket she wore.

He took several steps forward and, still unnoticed, stared. She was lovely. Smooth of skin and with a delicately sculpted profile, she was young enough, old enough, just right. And she was slender. Even the protective folds of her clothing, whose mist-softened hues of hunter green and plum contrasted smartly with her fair skin and the sandy hair that escaped the confines of her stylish wool cloche, couldn't hide that fact.

In her solitariness she was regal; at least that was what he fantasized as he stood, spellbound, studying her. She bore the weight of the world on her shoulders, while at the same time she remained apart, isolated from the masses. Even the fog kept its distance, as though in awe.

Regal...stoic...brave...each thought came to him through the mist; then another. Vulnerable. Body braced against the cold, she shivered from time to time, but she didn't move either to seek warmth or to escape the threat of the pounding surf. She'd fallen victim to the sea, he knew, and he felt an even greater affinity for her. He wondered who she was, this woman who stood alone, tall yet humbled, seeking strength from within. Bidden by a curiosity that went beyond the purely male, he tugged his collar higher and started slowly forward.

Eyes downcast, she didn't see him at first. He paused, hesitant to intrude on whatever thoughts possessed her, but moved on again when his own need nagged. When he came to a halt several feet from her, her head snapped up. With a quick step back, she sucked in a breath and pressed a hand to her heart.

"You startled me!" Her voice was little more than a ragged whisper above the thunder of the tide.

Michael drew in a sharp breath, too, but in amazement rather than alarm. For he found himself looking into the most stunning violet eyes he'd ever seen. It took him a minute to find his tongue.

"I...I'm sorry. I didn't mean to frighten you. It's just that you looked so . . . alone. . . ."

For an instant he thought she was going to cry. Her eyes widened and tears gathered on her lower lids. He saw it then, the haunted cast that fear had momentarily overshadowed, and he wondered what dark thoughts had upset her so. But then they were gone—the torment, the tears—replaced by a composure that suggested he'd simply imagined the cracks.

"My fault," she said in a voice whose tremor might well have been caused by wind. "I was miles away." She gave him a sheepish half-smile by way of apology, and he felt something new and special curl up and glow inside him.

"I hope it was somewhere exotic."

"Exotic? No. Not exactly."

"Exciting, at least?"

Pensive, she searched his face, then shook her head quickly, almost as if in guilt at her admission.

"Your secret's safe with me," he teased on a soft note of conspiracy that ended in a smile, "as long as you're back here now."

"I am." Her whisper was carried away by the wind, but she continued to stare at him. When she finally spoke again, she sounded confused. "I'm not even sure what happened. One minute I was here, and then . . ."

"The ocean has a way of doing that. Of transporting you from one place to another." Tucking his hands in his pockets, he tore his eyes from hers and gazed toward the waves. "It's very sneaky, actually. First you're lured by the sense of freedom of the open beach and the fresh salt air. Before long—you barely know it's happened—your pulse has adjusted to the rhythm of the surf." He looked down at her and was so taken with her rapt expression that his voice thickened. "Some people call it hypnotic, like staring into a flickering fire." He cleared his throat. "I think it's something more. In no time you're caught, laid open, exposed. It's like . . . like nature here is raw and utterly truthful and commands no less from those of us who dare intrude." His voice lowered as he studied the delicate features before him. "Falling victim to the sea means baring one's soul. It can be painful."

For a minute they simply looked at one another. "I'd never thought of it that way," she said at last.

"Neither had I, until it had happened too many times to ignore."

"You've felt the pain?" she asked in a small, surprised voice.

"Many times. Shouldn't I?"

"I don't know. You look so strong."

Dropping his head back, he took a deep breath. "I like to think I am, but that doesn't mean I never suffer. I think strength comes from facing pain, from dealing with it. It's either that or crumble. Pain is part and parcel of being human."

Her expression grew all the more solemn, her voice soft in a wistful way. "I sometimes wonder. It seems...it seems..." When her gaze flicked to his then darted away, he coaxed her gently.

"Go on."

She hesitated for a moment longer, and there was a note of despair in her voice when she spoke. "It seems that some people are immune to it."

"Immune to pain? No," he mused, "I doubt that. There are those who choose to deny it. They're the ones who'd never be caught dead alone with themselves in a room, much less on a deserted expanse of beach." He winked. "It takes a pretty brave person to expose himself this way."

His double entendre wasn't lost on her. She gave a lop-sided smile. "Either that or a dumb one." Then she eyed him cautiously. "Tell me. After this...this baring of the soul takes place, what happens?"

"You go home and cry."

"I'm serious. Does the sea provide answers?"

"Sometimes. Once I stood here in my agony and this little bottle floated ashore with a message inside—" He was interrupted by the audible breath she took. When she simply held it without speaking, though, he prodded. "What's wrong?"

She exhaled slowly. "Your name. I want to scold, but I don't know your name." Then she murmured more to herself than to him, "Isn't that odd?"

Michael understood. There was a warm familiarity about this woman. If he'd believed in reincarnation, he might have suspected he'd known her in another life. Grateful, if that had indeed been the case, that he'd been given a second chance, he held out his hand. "Michael Buchanan." Without breaking eye contact, he tossed his head back in the direction from which he'd come. "I live down the beach." He raised a brow. "And you...?"

She hesitated for just a minute before carefully putting her hand in his. "Danica. Danica Lindsay." As he'd done, she flicked her head, but in the opposite direction. "That's my house."

Instinctively he raised his free hand to seal hers in the cocoon of his palms. When her downward glance drew his attention to the move, he was as surprised as she.

"Your, uh, your fingers are cold," he explained. Though his answer had been an impromptu one, it was apt. He rubbed her hand between his, back and forth, stimulating her circulation and his own. Her fingers were slender, pliant, fitting.

She actually blushed. "I didn't expect it'd still be winter here. It's much milder at home."

"Home?"

"Boston."

"Ah, Boston," he drawled, "the birthplace of liberty."

"Mmmm. That's what they say."

"You don't sound convinced."

She merely shrugged and looked out at the water as she slid her hand from his grasp and tucked it back into her pocket. He'd been right about the ocean, she decided. It had seen through her facade, making her look at things she'd rather have ignored. And, yes, he'd been right about something else; some people simply refused to acknowledge the presence of pain, which was why she was here, alone, today. Was she free? Only in the most literal of senses.

"Liberty is relative, I suppose," she commented, her voice as distant as her expression. But before Michael had a chance to pursue the matter, she tipped up her chin and donned a pert smile. "So. You're a neighbor. Mrs. Sylvester warned me there were some pretty important people up here."

She tipped her head to the side, admiring the man before her. He wore a sheepskin jacket, well-worn cords and hiking boots whose laces were undone. He was tall—she guessed him to be a good six-three to her own respectable five-eight—and sported the faint shadow of a beard, which might have given him a roguish look had it not been for the extreme gentleness of his features. Then, too, there was the healthy rumple of his hair, which was a shade of blond not unlike her own. Dirty blond, they'd always called it, which had never failed to annoy her as a child, since she'd washed her hair every night as ordered.

"You don't look important," she teased softly.

His lips twitched. "How is an important man supposed to look?"

"Oh, he wears a three-piece suit and wing-tipped shoes—"

"On the beach?"

"No. Okay. Make that flannel slacks, a designer sweater and loafers, perhaps with a cashmere topcoat in this kind of weather. He's fresh-shaven all the time—'' she drew out her words in mockery ''—and his hair is perfectly groomed.''

"In this wind? He must use hair spray."

She smiled slyly and shrugged. "He's been known to."

"Sorry, I don't fit that mold, but, then," he chided, "you knew that all along.... Does that mean I'm a nobody?"

"Oh, no. It means you're very refreshing and, in that sense, very definitely a somebody." She'd never spoken truer words. At the moment she'd had it with three-piece suits, wing-tipped shoes, flannel, cashmere and hair spray.

"Ahhhh. That's a relief." Then he thought. "Were you talking about Mrs. Sylvester, as in Judy, the realtor?" When Danica nodded, his pleasure grew. "I assumed you were visiting the Duncans. You mean to say they've sold?" Again she nodded. "And you've bought their house?" Another nod. "That's great!"

"I'm not so sure right about now," she grumbled. "There've been workmen all over the place for a month. I'm beginning to think they'll never finish."

"Tell me about it," Michael mused, remembering all too well the work he'd had done over the years. "New roof, new heating system, thermapanes—"

"Not to mention a total overhaul of the plumbing system." She sighed, but there was a whimsical expression on her face. She'd enjoyed seeing each piece of work done. It had given her something to think on, something to wish on. "And that was before we even discussed decorating. But I do adore the house. It'll be fantastic when it's done." Her eyes scanned the oceanscape as it grew more visible with the slow lifting of the fog. "With a view like this, how can you miss?"

"It's addictive, isn't it?"

"Mmmm." She tugged her jacket closer, aware of being cold but having no desire to return just yet to the house. Strange, the last thing she would have thought she wanted a little while ago was company, but Michael Buchanan was something else. "How long have you owned your house?"

"Nearly ten years."

She arched a brow. "Not bad."

"More the rule than the exception. Kennebunkport has a loyal following. Even the summer swell is largely made up of people making return visits."

Danica thought about that for a minute. It was in keeping with what the realtor had said about the population being stable. "Judy told me this was a quiet area, that people keep to themselves pretty much. That must be why you didn't know about the Duncans moving."

"Actually, I've been away."

She grimaced. "That was stupid of me. You probably have another place."

"No. This is my one and only. But I've been gone since November and just got back last week. I was never that close to the Duncans. We, uh, we moved in different circles." The fact was that the Duncans barely tolerated the presence of a Buchanan nearby, but Michael wasn't about to tell that to Danica. He didn't yet know who she was. Her name hadn't rung a bell, but she obviously came from class, and he knew how much she'd had to have paid for her house. He prayed that her family had somehow managed to steer clear of his. Powerful people—important, to use her word—were natural media targets, and his family was very definitely the media. "I knew they'd sell sooner or later. I guess I thought it would be later."

"Fortunately not." Danica had considered it a stroke of luck that there'd been a house such as this on the market for her to see. She'd also thought it to be a harbinger of good things to come. Once the house was done, it would be a "gem," to quote her decorator. The word she preferred to use was *savior*, but that remained to be seen.

She jumped when warm fingers brushed a strand of hair from her mouth, and her eyes flew to Michael's.

"Your cheeks are getting windburned," he explained, wishing he'd had an excuse to linger at her lips, the lower one of which she now bit. He tried to decide what he saw in her eyes, but he wasn't sure if what he wanted to think was yearning was in fact nothing but surprise. Her eyes were rounded, her lashes long and dark. It was the only tip-off he had that she wore makeup, so skillfully and subtly was it applied.

His attention was drawn again to her mouth when she dragged her lip from beneath her teeth. Almost simultaneously she looked away, and he grew anxious. She was withdrawing. But he couldn't let her go so quickly, not when he'd finally found her. He tucked his hands in his pockets for safekeeping. "It's pretty cold out here. How about a warm drink at my place?"

Hot chocolate, like his eyes, she thought to herself. He was a very attractive man.

She shook her head a little too quickly. "Thanks, but I'd better not. I'm heading home in a couple of hours and I've got to check on a few more things before I leave."

"When will you be back?"

"Next month."

"Not till then?" he asked with such boyish dismay that she laughed. It was lovely to feel wanted. Lovely. . . and new.

"'Fraid not."

"What's so important for you to do in Boston?"

"Oh—" she rolled her eyes "—this and that."

"Do you work?"

"Not . . . in the traditional sense."

"Then, in what sense?"

Danica thought for a minute, wondering exactly what it *was* she did or, more precisely, how to explain it to a man she wanted to impress. It struck her as incredible that she'd never faced such a task before, but she'd always lived and breathed in exclusive circles, and anonymity was something she'd never know. She was rather enjoying it now, even in spite of the urge she had to lie and say that she was a pediatrician or something equally as impressive.

But Michael was expecting the truth. He seemed like that kind of person, different from so many of the people she knew. He made eye contact; that said a lot.

"What do I do?" she finally repeated, then echoed herself, with one strategic change. "What do *you* do?"

He indulged her with a gentle smile. "I'm a writer."

"Oh, God."

"Uh-uh. Nothing threatening. I write about the past. They call me a historian."

"'They'? What do you call yourself?"

He shrugged, eyes twinkling mischievously. "A writer."

"Why not a historian?"

"It sounds too pretentious and I'm not that way."

She could see that. She could also see that he looked nearly as cold as she felt.

"What are you staring at?" he asked.

"Your ears. They're turning red." Though his hair was on the long side and his ears hugged his head nicely, the wind was having a field day.

"That's okay. Between my red ears and your blue lips, I'd say we liven up the scenery. Come on. How about that drink?"

She was smiling now, too. "I can't. Really."

"I've got a fire going. It'd warm you up. Your place is probably like a barn."

"Mmmm...close." With workmen running in and out, there seemed to be a steady draft. "But the heater of my car works fine, and I've got to be back in Boston before dark."

"Your car turns into a pumpkin then, does it?"

She mirrored his grin. "Something like that."

"Then, I guess you'd better go. I wouldn't want you stranded on the highway or anything." He shifted from one foot to another, then cleared his throat. "Well, I guess I'll see you when you come back up next month."

"You'll be here?"

"Should be."

She nodded and took a step back. "Maybe it'll be warmer then."

He nodded but didn't move. "The beach is nice in April."

She took another step. "I'll bet it is.... Well, take care, Michael."

"You, too, Danica." He raised a hand in mock salute as she took a third step. "May the good fairy be with you."

She laughed and shook her head as though to chastise him for his silliness, then realized that she loved it. When he winked, she loved it even more. But she had to leave. She had to.

Michael watched her turn and take several plodding steps through the sand toward her house. She turned back to give him a broad smile and a wave, and he wondered if there was in fact such a thing as love at first sight. Then a gust of wind whipped across the sand and she drew her free hand from her pocket to hold the cloche on her head.

The last thing he saw as she disappeared into the fog was the wide gold wedding band on the ring finger of her left hand.

Chapter Two

SEVERAL DAYS LATER, Danica sat on the edge of the king-sized bed she shared with her husband and watched him pack.

"Is there anything I can do?" she asked, but she already knew the answer. It was the same every time. After all, Blake had been a bachelor for better than thirty-five years. He'd either pack for himself or have Mrs. Hannah, their maid, do it. Danica knew she should be grateful; Blake coddled her, asking of her only the social amenities required of the wife of a man of his position. Any number of women would die to be in her shoes. Yet, rather than privileged or pampered, she felt superfluous.

"All set, I think." He didn't look up; he concentrated on setting his dress shoes at just the right angle in the bottom of the bag.

"Are you going with Harlan?" Harlan Magnuson was the head of the computer division of Eastbridge Electronics, Blake's corporation. He was young, brilliant and aggressive, and often accompanied Blake on business trips. From what Danica could gather, the combination of Harlan's daring and Blake's solid business sense was a potent one.

"Uh-huh."

"How long will you be?"

"No more than three days. I'll be back in time for the cocktail party Friday night."

"That's good. The Donaldsons would never forgive us if we missed it." She absently rubbed the edge of the suitcase. They'd bought it as part of a matching set four years ago when they'd been headed for Italy. She recalled that trip with a smile. Blake had had business in Florence, but from there on they'd simply relaxed, spending several days in Milan en route to the villa they'd rented on Lake Como. It seemed so long since they'd taken a vacation like that. Or rather, she amended, it seemed so long since they'd had *fun* like that. Sighing, she looked at the bag. For all its use—and Blake used it often—it appeared to be wearing better than her marriage. "I wish you didn't have to go."

Taking underwear and socks from the drawer, Blake returned to the bed. "You know I do," he said. She wished she could have said that she heard regret in his tone, but she just wasn't sure, which seemed to be a recurrent problem lately. She couldn't read Blake; perhaps she'd never been able to but had simply deluded herself.

"You do so much traveling. I tell myself that you've got to, but it doesn't help sometimes. . . . You won't reconsider and let me come along?"

He straightened and spoke quietly. "I really have to be free this time, Danica. With the exception of a dinner tomorrow night, it'll be business all the way."

"Mmmm. I know. But . . . it's so quiet here when you're away." Saying the words, she realized that it wasn't the quiet that bothered her but the fact that she felt . . . widowed. Twenty-eight years old and widowed.

Stifling the thought, she watched him carefully coil and pack two leather belts. Her gaze slowly climbed to his face and she was struck, once again and for the umpteenth time, by how handsome a man he was. The very first time she'd been so struck she'd been nineteen and attending a fund-raiser for her father. Blake Lindsay had been impressive then, tall and dark and immaculately groomed. Now, nine years later, he was no less attractive. The years had barely touched him, it seemed. His forty-three-year-old body was firm and well toned, but then, he believed in exercise, jogged regularly, played squash several times a week and watched his weight. That he prided himself on his appearance had been obvious to Danica from the start. Unfortunately, between exercise and work, he seemed to have little time for much else, let alone her.

"You've got plenty to keep you busy, haven't you?" Pivoting, he went to the closet, selected several ties from the rack, then moved toward the window to scrutinize the possibilities in daylight.

"Oh, yes. There's a board meeting at the hospital tomorrow and I have an appointment with the printer on Thursday to order our invitations."

"Plans are going well for the party?" He sounded distracted, which was no wonder, Danica decided, since he faced the monumental task of choosing between two blue and gray silk ties, the stripes of which varied infinitesimally in width. She could no more understand how he could choose one over the other than she could why he owned two such similar ties in the first place, but then, perhaps he felt the same way about her blouses or textured panty hose or belts.

"The caterer's all set. So's the florist, and I've booked the chamber music ensemble from the conservatory. That pretty much does it until after the invitations are printed. Have you decided whether or not to invite the group from SpanTech?"

Having somehow decided between the two ties, Blake put the loser back in the closet and returned to lay the others carefully in his suitcase. "SpanTech? Mmmm... not sure yet." He rubbed his upper lip, then set off for the bathroom. When he returned, he carried a case containing his grooming needs. After fitting it into the space he'd purposely left, he returned to the dresser for shirts.

"It'd be easy enough, Blake. Another ten or twelve people won't make much difference as long as we notify the caterer in time. It certainly won't mean any more work for me, and if you think it'd be worthwhile to invite them..." She knew that Blake had been negotiating to bring in SpanTech, outstanding for its research in microelectronics, as a division of Eastbridge.

He sent her a brilliant smile, which flared, then was gone. "Let me think about it a little more, okay?"

She nodded. When a silence fell between them, she searched for something else to say. "Did I tell you Reggie Nichols called?"

"She's in town?"

"Mmmm. She's seeing some guy, I guess."

"Isn't she playing the circuit?"

Reggie Nichols had been top-rated in women's tennis for more than a decade. She and Danica had been friends since Danica's own tennis-playing days when the two had trained under the same coach.

"Sure. But I guess she needs the break. From what she said on the phone, things have been rough. Every year there are younger faces. I think it's getting her down.... My Lord, Blake, you've got six shirts there." She'd been watching him place them one by one, starched and cardboard-backed, in the suitcases, and couldn't resist teasing him. "Are you sure that's enough?"

"I'd rather have extras, just in case," he answered in dead earnest, which Danica found to be all the more amusing, since Blake Lindsay never spilled, rarely sweated, barely wrinkled.

"Anyway—" she was smiling "—Reggie and I are having lunch on Saturday...uh, unless you want to do something, in which case I'll cancel."

He had finished packing the shirts and was reaching for his suit bag. "No, no. Don't do that. I'll be at the club."

It was either that or at work, so Danica had known she'd be safe making the lunch date with Reggie. Until recently she'd spent her own Saturdays waiting for him to come home. Perhaps in her old age she was wising up. Then again, perhaps not. More than once it had occurred to her that though she'd convinced Blake to buy the house in Kennebunkport as a hideaway for the two of them, it was going to be something else getting him there. Last week was a perfect example. He'd promised he'd take the day off to drive up with her, then had been besieged by a handful of last-minute emergencies, which demanded his attention. She didn't quite understand why a man who headed his own company couldn't get subordinates to do the work.

"Is something wrong, Pook?" he asked gently.

Her head came up. "Hmmm?"

He sent her that same ephemeral flash of a smile as he threaded hangers through the slot at the top of the suit bag. "You look angry."

She realized that she felt it, but the last thing she wanted was to sound like a shrewish wife, so she forced herself to relax and spoke with measured calm. "Nothing's wrong. I was just thinking of Maine."

"Any more word from the decorator?"

"She called yesterday afternoon to say that the cabinets are set to go in." They'd been special-ordered in a white oak that Danica had fallen in love with, but she'd debated the decision for days, since using the white oak had sent a number of other dominoes toppling—namely countertops, ceiling fixtures and flooring, all of which were now in the process of being changed. But Blake had said to go ahead, so she had. "When I was there last week, the kitchen was barren."

Blake laid the suit bag on the bed, straightened the lapel of the tuxedo he'd put in last and drew up the zipper to close the bag.

Taking a breath, she forged cautiously on. "Once the cabinets are in, the refrigerator and stove will be hooked up. At least then we'll be able to have something to eat or drink. I mean, the place won't really be livable until May or June, but it's getting there. I was hoping to go back up next month to check on things. You'll come with me, won't you?"

"If I can."

"You haven't been there since we first looked at it. I'd really like you to see what's been done. If there's anything you don't like—"

He was doubling up the suit bag and fastening the straps. "You've got wonderful taste." His smile was on. "I'll like it."

"But I want you to *see* it, Blake. This was supposed to be a joint venture, a place where we could be alone together."

Blake made a final scan of the room. "All in good time. When it's finished, we'll spend the time you want there. Things must be pretty primitive now. Did the decorator say anything about those kitchen cabinets you wanted?"

Danica opened her mouth in reproach, then shut it tight. He hadn't been listening. That was all. His mind was on other things.

"Next week. They'll be in next week," she murmured, rising from the bed and heading for the door. "I'll send Marcus up for the bags," she called over her shoulder as she started down the stairs. But Blake was soon beside her, putting his hand lightly on her waist. It bobbed as they descended; their steps never quite matched.

"You won't forget to RSVP to the Hagendorfs, will you?" he asked. Danica could almost see his mind's eye going down the list headed Remind Danica. It came right after What to Pack and right before Names (and Wives' Names) of Business Associates in Kansas City, which was where he was headed this week.

"I've already done it," she said evenly. Patience was a virtue; so read the tag on her tea bag that morning.

"And the charity ball at the Institute?"

"They're expecting us."

"Good. You could give Feeno a call and see if my new tux is ready. If it is, have Marcus pick it up." They rounded the second-floor landing and made their way toward the first. Blake dropped his hand from her waist. Danica slid hers along the lustrous mahogany banister. "Oh, and Bert Hammer mentioned something about your serving on the nominating committee."

"For the Institute?"

"Mmmm. They need younger faces. Are you interested?"

"Sure. You know I love art."

Blake chuckled, more the indulgent parent than the amused mate. "This would have very little to do with art, I'm afraid. It'd mean sitting at a table, tossing around names of the most popular and up-and-coming Bostonians. They know you're in the social mainstream. They'd be picking your brain."

Danica shrugged and gave a small smile. "I don't mind. It's nice to feel useful. And besides, I know three women who'd each give her right arm for an entree to the board; two of them would be fantastic."

"Not the third?"

"Uh . . . Marion White?"

"Oh." He cleared his throat and tried not to grin. "Yes, I think you're right." They'd reached the street floor, where Marcus Hannah stood waiting. "The bags are by the bed," Blake instructed in a voice of quiet command, "I'll be in the library when you're ready."

Marcus nodded and headed up the stairs while Blake disappeared, leaving Danica standing alone by the front door. She walked slowly back toward the library, but when she heard Blake talking on the phone, she reconsidered and took refuge in the den.

It hurt that he should be calling the office, which he'd left no more than ninety minutes before, when he might be talking with her. After all, he was going to be away for three days, and though she knew he'd call her at least once or twice during that time, she also knew that he'd call the office much more often. She wished she could say that he worked too hard, but he looked wonderfully healthy and seemed perfectly happy with his life. If he was busy, it was by choice. Perhaps that was what hurt most. He did choose.

At a sound in the hall she looked up to see Marcus, bags in hand, heading back through the lower pantry toward the courtyard where the car was parked. On cue Blake emerged from the library, set his briefcase on the floor by the closet and reached for his topcoat. By the time he'd retrieved the briefcase, Danica was by his side.

"Behave while I'm gone," he said with a bright grin, then leaned forward and kissed her cheek. For an instant she was tempted to throw her arms around his neck and hold him there, but she knew she'd be grasping at straws. Blake would no more be swayed by an emotional appeal than her father would have been. They were so alike, those two, so alike. Disturbed by the thought, she slid her hands into the pockets of her skirt and put on a smile. Her father would have approved.

"I'll behave." She followed Blake to the back door, watched him cross the cobblestone courtyard and climb into the Mercedes's rear seat. It was a scenario that had grown all too familiar to her, as had the accompanying sadness. But the sadness had altered in nature over the years, she realized. It wasn't so much Blake's departure that affected her now, for she saw little enough of him when he was home. Rather, the sadness she felt was a more general one dealing with love and happiness and promise.

Blake looked up once to smile when Marcus backed the car around. She waved, but his head was already lowering. He was opening his briefcase, she knew, and she suspected his mind was miles away by the time the car disappeared from her view.

"AHHH, MRS. LINDSAY. Mrs. Marshall is already seated. If you'll come this way...."

Breathless, Danica smiled. "Thank you, Jules." She was a graceful figure breezing after the maître d', her blond hair looking stunningly windblown, her calf-length silver-fox fur undulating gently as she let herself be led to the corner table the Ritz always held for her when she called.

"Mother!" She leaned down to press her cheek to the woman whose eyes lit up at her approach. "I'm sorry! Have I kept you waiting long?"

"Not more than a minute or two, darling. How are you? You look wonderful! Your cheeks are so pink..." Eleanor Marshall frowned at her only child. "You didn't *walk* here, did you?"

"Sure. I cut through the Public Garden. It'd have been silly to drive, and besides, I love the fresh air."

Eleanor eyed her daughter reprovingly. "Danica, Marcus is *paid* to drive you, silly or not. The Public Garden isn't the safest place in the world...." She paused to place her order for a vermouth cassis to Danica's kir.

"I'm all right, Mother. Here, safe and sound. And you look pretty fine yourself! New earrings?"

"They were a gift from the family we stayed with in Brazil last year. They're topaz, a little too... much for some occasions, but I thought you'd appreciate them."

"I do. You wear them well." Which was one thing Eleanor did do. Though far from being beautiful, she dressed to play up the best of her features. At fifty-two, she was a stylishly attractive woman, though she rarely turned heads unless she was with her husband. "Is it ethical for Daddy to accept gifts like that?"

"Your father says it is," Eleanor answered with quiet assurance. "He usually knows."

Danica wondered, but she said nothing. It wasn't often her mother came in alone for lunch—it wasn't often she'd *ever* had her mother to herself—and she didn't want anything to mar their time together. Shuttling between Connecticut and Washington, not to mention flying off on numerous trips each year, her parents weren't easily accessible.

"I'm so glad you called. This is a treat. Somehow talking on the phone just isn't the same." It never was, though she wondered if her mother agreed. "How's Daddy? You said he was going to Vancouver?"

"He left yesterday morning, just before I called you. It was a last-minute trip; he's filling in for a committee member who took sick. He sends his love, by the way. I told him I was seeing you when he called last night."

"Didn't you want to go with him?"

"I felt—" Eleanor took a breath and let it out with a sheepish grin "—like staying home. It must be the years creeping up. When your father's away, things are quieter. I find I need that from time to time."

Strange, Danica thought, how her mother enjoyed that quiet, while she found it terrifying. It wasn't that she craved her parents' political whirl of a life; that was the *last* thing she wanted, and besides, she was busy enough socially. No, what she wanted... what she wanted was... the noise of a happy home. What frightened her was the thought of a lifetime filled with the silence that too often entombed the Beacon Hill town house she shared with Blake.

She refocused her thoughts on her mother with a hint of concern and good cause. "You're feeling all right, aren't you?"

"Oh, yes. Fine. The doctors' reports are wonderful." Four years earlier Eleanor had had a hysterectomy when a uterine tumor had been detected. Between the surgery and subsequent radiation treatments, it appeared she was cured. "It's just that I get tired of living out of a suitcase. And since your father's going to be at meetings most of the time..."

Danica thought of Blake and wondered how her mother managed to avoid the frustration she felt. It was difficult when a man's work was his mistress, as Blake's seemed to be. "Daddy doesn't mind, does he?"

"What do *you* think?" Eleanor smiled. "He thrives on it. In fact, he's that much more relaxed, since he doesn't have to run for another four years." William Marshall was the senior senator from Connecticut, a twenty-one-year veteran of the United States Congress. "He's as active as ever, but the pressure isn't as intense. When he's up for reelection himself, it's a matter of life or death."

She spoke matter-of-factly and Danica understood, knowing that to her father winning *was* a matter of life and death. What she didn't understand was how her mother could stand it, but Eleanor seemed fully acclimated to that way of thinking.

Not so Danica. More than once over the years she'd wanted to rebel. First she hadn't had the courage; later she'd seen the futility of it. It would have been a losing battle, and very simply, she couldn't afford another loss. More than anything, she'd wanted her father's approval, and to win that, she'd had to follow his rules.

"Campaigning for someone else," Eleanor continued, oblivious to Danica's thoughts, "well, it's easier. By the way, he's come out for Claveling. You know that, don't you?"

Danica knew that her father had been torn between two men, both announced candidates for his party's presidential nomination. With the first of the primaries over, it appeared that Claveling was the one more likely to succeed. "So I read. It's been all over the papers."

Eleanor made a sound that Danica might have called a snort if it had been anyone else making it in any other place. But her mother was impeccably controlled, and the Ritz was exquisitely proper. Therefore there'd been no snort. It had been a nasal moan, she decided, and had reflected the same tempered displeasure which Eleanor proceeded to express.

"Don't mention the papers to me."

"Has something happened?" Over the years William Marshall had had his tiffs with the press.

"Oh, just a small article in the local paper criticizing your father for a speech he gave last week. It didn't bother him, but

I got annoyed. It seems the newspapers are always looking for something to attack. If they can't cry income tax evasion or conflict of interest, they pick on petty little things. The powerful are always targets. If the powerful are well-to-do, so much the worse. You should remember that, Danica.''

"Me? I'm not in the limelight like you and Daddy."

"You may be. After all, Blake is standing right beside your father in support of Claveling."

It was the first Danica had heard about it, and she wasn't sure whether to be shocked, angry or downright depressed. The minute it took for the waiter to set their drinks before them gave her a chance to compose herself.

"I hadn't realized it was definite," she finally managed. When push came to shove, she was embarrassed to admit to her mother that her husband hadn't communicated with her on so important a matter. Blake had to know she wouldn't be thrilled. He had to know that she craved something in life other than parties and rallies and press conferences.

"It's definite. They've spent hours discussing it on the phone."

"Daddy and Blake?" Again Danica hadn't known, though she knew how close the two men were. They'd been friends since long before Danica and Blake had married. Their relationship had always been one of contemporaries, rather than father and son-in-law.

"Your husband has influential contacts in the business world, my dear," Eleanor announced quite unnecessarily, since Danica already knew it, and with a hint of excitement that only increased Danica's dismay. "He's the kind of man who inspires confidence, the kind who can coax people to contribute to a worthy cause. Jason Claveling is a worthy cause. If he wins the nomination, he'll be elected."

"You're sure?"

"I'm sure. And it never hurts to be on the good side of the president of the United States."

Ethical issues aside, Danica couldn't argue with that. Political pull did wonders, particularly when it came from the top. "I'm surprised Daddy's never gone for it."

"For the presidency?" Eleanor laughed softly and grew more pensive. "No. The risk is too great, I think. Over the years your father has made his share of enemies. Any strong figure is bound to, and William has been known to be unbending at times. But he plays to win. He needs to be in full control, and that's not possible in a national election. Besides—" she perked up "—he's enjoying seniority in the Senate."

Danica nodded, still trying to assimilate the fact of Blake's impending political involvement. She should have seen it coming, but she hadn't. And, for whatever his reasons, Blake hadn't seen fit to enlighten her.

"So," she sighed after having ordered a bowl of summer squash soup and a crabmeat salad, "when does the hoopla begin?"

"Soon, I'd imagine.... You don't look wild about the idea."

Danica made a wavering gesture. "We've got plenty of evenings planned as it is. This means there'll be that many more."

"Are there other things you'd rather be doing?" Eleanor asked in surprise. When she'd been Danica's age, she'd been entranced by every aspect of her husband's nascent political career.

"There might be." She was thinking of whimsical things like going to a movie, driving with Blake down to Provincetown for the day or up to Kennebunkport, for that matter. Unfortunately, her mother reached another conclusion.

"Darling," she began, eyes widening in excitement, "are you . . ."

Danica smiled. "No, Mom. Not yet."

"But you'd like to be."

"We've discussed this before. You *know* I'd like to be."

"Is there a problem?"

"Of course not!"

"Don't get defensive, darling," Eleanor said softly. "I was just asking. After all, you've been married for eight years—"

"Which is nothing, when you stop to think how young I was way back then. I don't think I would have made a particularly good mother at twenty or twenty-one or twenty-two. Goodness, you make it sound as though I'm running out of time. I'm only twenty-eight. Nowadays women have babies when they're forty.''

''True, but when you're forty, Blake will be fifty-five, which is exactly the age your father is now, and look at *you*.''

''Daddy was young when he married. There's a difference. If Blake's first concern had been a family, he'd probably have married a lot earlier.''

''Still, I'd think he wouldn't want to wait too long. And besides, think of your father. He's ready to have a grandchild.''

''So you've told me before,'' Danica managed in a dry tone. She didn't like this discussion; never had, never would. She wanted to have a baby very badly. She wanted to make Blake a father, to make William a grandfather, to be a mother herself. Unfortunately, it was easier said than done.

''Will you oblige him?''

''I hope so.''

''Are you . . . are you sure there's no problem?''

If there was a problem, it was that Blake was either out of town or tired, and there was *no way* Danica was going to discuss that with her mother. Sad as it was, she didn't feel close enough.

''I'm sure,'' she said, intent on changing the subject. ''And as to what I'd rather be doing than going to political fundraisers, I'd rather be in Maine with Blake. You should see the house. It's exciting.''

As they ate, Danica filled her mother in on the details of the remodeling work. It was a fairly safe topic until Eleanor raised the issue of physically getting to Maine and back.

''I don't like your driving there alone.''

''Blake will be with me from now on. At least,'' she thought aloud, ''he said he would be, but if the Claveling campaign takes much of his time—''

''It may. You know that. Which means you'll be making the trip by yourself.''

Danica wasn't thrilled with that idea, but her discouragement had nothing to do with the drive. "It's not much of a trip . . . an hour and a half, give or take for traffic."

"That's an hour and a half in a small car that could easily be mashed between two trucks on the highway. If Blake isn't there, Marcus should drive you."

"What in the world would Marcus do up there while I'm checking over all those little details?"

"He can wait. That's his job. Better still, he can familiarize himself with the area so he'll be comfortable when he and his wife go up."

"They won't be going." When her mother stopped midbite to stare at her, Danica explained. "The house is for Blake and me. An escape from the city. A place where we can be alone together. I don't see the need for having one in help there, let alone two. We can drive ourselves wherever we want to go, and there shouldn't be any massive cleaning to do, since we won't be entertaining there."

"What about food?"

"I can cook, Mother."

"I know you *can*, but wouldn't it be easier if Mrs. Hannah did it?"

Danica's mind was set. She'd yielded on many, many things in her life. This was one on which she was determined to hold fast. "No. The Hannahs will watch things in Boston while Blake and I are in Maine." She slanted her mother a grin. "You never can tell. With a little practice, I might just emerge as a competitor to Julia Child. Daddy would love that. . . . You'll both come up when the house is done, won't you?"

Before Eleanor had a chance to answer, a friend of Danica's approached to say a fast hello. Danica graciously made the introductions, then sat back and marveled at the skillful way her mother made conversation. It was as though Eleanor truly, truly cared about this new acquaintance.

"Well?" Danica said softly when they were alone once more.

"She's lovely, darling. You serve on the hospital board with her?"

"Yes. But I wasn't asking about that. You and Daddy will come up to Maine to visit, won't you?" It meant a lot to her; she was hoping to impress her parents with the house, its location and her own abilities to play hostess.

"I thought you weren't entertaining there."

"Family's different."

Eleanor sighed. "Of course we'll come. But I wish you wouldn't be so difficult about things. I still don't like the idea of your driving up there yourself."

"Listen to you, Mother," Danica chided. "You'd think I was sixteen."

"I know you're not. But I do worry.... At least you could take the Mercedes. It's bigger and heavier than the coupe."

"But I love the Audi, and I get so little chance to drive around here. Boston drivers are awful. By comparison, Kennebunkport is a dream." She took a deep breath and gazed down at the people walking briskly along Arlington Street. "There's a sense of freedom you get when you drive by yourself on the open road."

"You *sound* about sixteen. But you never craved freedom then."

"Mmmm." Danica grew momentarily pensive. "Didn't you ever wonder whether I did things behind your back?"

"What kinds of things?"

"Oh . . . you know. Smoke. Drink. Go places I shouldn't."

"You were always well supervised."

"Not every minute. The housemother at the dorm didn't know everything that happened."

"At college I wouldn't expect—"

"I'm not talking about college. I'm talking about boarding school. Even before I left to live at Armand's, there was plenty going on."

"Danica, you were thirteen years old then!"

"Still, I knew what was happening. Some of the girls smuggled stuff into the dorm. Either that or they'd sneak out, and they made it—and back—without being caught. Come on, Mother," she chided at the look of dismay on Eleanor's face, "you had to know that kind of thing happened."

"I suppose...but—" she was slowly shaking her head "—you didn't do any of that . . ." She had effectively answered Danica's question.

Danica smiled. "No. I was too much of a coward."

"A coward? No, no, darling. You simply set higher standards for yourself."

"Daddy set higher standards for me, you mean." She rolled her eyes. "God, I was so innocent that if I'd tried the smallest thing, I'd surely have been caught, and if I'd ever been caught, Daddy never would have forgiven me." Her smile faded. "It was bad enough giving up tennis. He doesn't ever mention that now, does he?"

"He goes to matches whenever he can. You know he's always loved the game. But, no, he doesn't sit there fantasizing that it's you on the court. He accepts things when he has no choice."

Danica idly pushed a forkful of crabmeat around her plate. "I'm sorry—for his sake—that it didn't work out. He would have been proud if I'd been able to make it."

"Are *you* sorry it didn't work out?"

"In terms of the game, no. I just didn't possess that all-fire determination it took to be number one, at least not in that field. And besides," she sighed, "it's over and done. Maybe I'm like Daddy in that respect. I've accepted the fact that I'll never make it to center court at Wimbledon.... Strange to be talking this way ten years after the fact."

Not at all strange, she realized, though sad. There were many things she'd never discussed with her mother, because Eleanor Marshall was first and foremost William Marshall's wife. That Eleanor had a daughter—that *William* had a daughter—had always seemed incidental.

"By the way," Eleanor went on, "I understand that your friend Reggie was given a run for her money at the Virginia Slims tournament in New York."

"How did you know that?"

"Your father was reading an article about young Aaron, uh, Aaron—"

"Krickstein."

"Thank you, darling. Anyway, he was reading that article and the other headline caught my eye. Have you heard from her lately?"

"We had lunch together last Saturday."

"You did! But I thought she was going on to Florida with the rest of the tour."

"They do have time between tournaments, Mom. Reggie was visiting someone here. Actually, she was thinking of skipping Florida altogether."

"Can she do that? Doesn't she have a commitment to the sponsors?"

"Commitments only go so far. If a player is injured, she doesn't play. In Reggie's case, she's mentally exhausted. One season finished and the next began on its heels, and she needs a break."

"From what I read I can understand it. She won by the skin of her teeth. That kind of thing has to be exhausting, both physically *and* mentally." Eleanor arched a brow. "Maybe while she's here she'll get you to play."

"She's got other things on her mind."

"But I'm sure she'd love to play with you—"

"I'm not playing. You know that."

"Mmmm, and I feel badly. You were *good* darling. There was no reason why you had to give it up completely just because you couldn't be number one."

"You make me sound juvenile."

"Well, *aren't* you carrying it a little too far?"

"No."

"Darling, you were the number-four player in this country—in this *country*—when you were sixteen. That was a feat that took quite some doing. And now . . . nothing. How long has it been since you held a racket in your hand?"

Danica met her mother's gaze. "The last time I held a racket was on Saturday, June 2nd, three days before my eighteenth birthday."

"You see?" Eleanor exclaimed. "It's been ten years! Isn't that a little silly?"

"Not to me. I'd had it with tennis—"

"Your shoulder was injured."

"It was much more than that," Danica argued softly. "We discussed it at the time, Mother—Armand and I, you and Daddy and Armand. I wasn't happy. I didn't want to play. My shoulder would have healed enough to continue, but I just wasn't interested." She paused and counted to five. She was sure that if she and her mother were to get into a similar discussion in a week or a month, Eleanor would once again blame the demise of her career on that shoulder injury. To be forced out of competition by a physical injury was somehow all right; after all, one couldn't help that. To willingly withdraw—because of lack of drive, no less—was unacceptable. "Why the talk of tennis all of a sudden?"

Eleanor sighed. "No special reason. It just came up along with talk of Reggie. And I do think about it from time to time. I'm sorry, but I can't help it. I still believe that if you'd wanted, you could have been right up there *with* Reggie." When Danica opened her mouth to argue, Eleanor went right on. "Tennis has come into its own in the past decade. Women are doing much better."

"My Lord, I don't need the money."

"Of course you don't. All right. Forget competing. What about playing for fun? It's wonderful exercise."

Danica smirked. "Mother, are you trying to tell me something?"

"Don't be silly, darling. You're as thin as ever. I'm merely suggesting that exercise is good for you."

"I get exercise. I walk wherever I can."

"I'm talking about *organized* exercise."

"I have ballet class three times a week."

"Hmmph. It's not a particularly social activity."

Finally Danica understood. "You're wrong there too, Mom," she offered gently. "I've met some wonderful people dancing. Granted, they may not be the same type I'd be playing tennis with at the club, but they're every bit as stimulating, if not more so. They're refreshing. I like them."

If she'd been trying to make a statement, it went right over her mother's head. Eleanor had evidently written off that particular subject. "Well, I hope so. By the way, did you know that Hiram Manley's brother died?"

LATER, WALKING BACK across the Public Garden, more slowly this time, Danica thought about the two hours she'd just spent with her mother. She'd looked forward to them as she always did. As always, though, anticipation had exceeded reality. She wished Eleanor was the type of mother with whom she could share her heart and soul, but she wasn't. Eleanor wouldn't understand. As a result, Danica felt the same frustration, the same loneliness she always felt where her parents were concerned.

All her life she'd hoped it would change. When she'd been a young child in the care of hired help, she'd dreamed of the day when she'd be old enough to travel with her parents. But when she'd been old enough, she'd been sent to boarding school, then to live and train at Armand Arroah's tennis academy, then to college. Even now, a grown woman married to a good friend of her father's, she found family warmth to be elusive.

Pausing at the apex of the footbridge over the pond, she was staring into the dark water when a movement at its edge caught her eye. A young child, his mother kneeling beside him, was offering torn bits of bread in jerky thrusts to the congregating pigeons. From time to time he stole a bite himself, then fed one to his mother. Both were bundled against the wind, which ruffled the water in random gusts. Neither seemed to mind the chill.

Danica guessed the little boy to be three and tried to remember what she'd been doing when she was three. She couldn't. But she'd been in nursery school when she was four, and she had vague memories of that. By the time she was five she'd been enrolled in an exclusive private school in the suburbs of Hartford and was spending her summers at a select day camp. Her memory made little differentiation between the two. There were loud groups of children at each and a certain amount of regimentation. She played at friends' houses, had friends home to play at hers. There was a jumble of birthday parties and clowns and magic shows, frilly dresses and Mary Janes.

When it came to memories of specific events, she had very few. She did remember going to Elizabeth Park to feed popcorn to the fish, though. Now she wondered what kind of fish ate popcorn; then she'd simply been overjoyed by the fact. But it hadn't been her mother who'd braved the cold to share her excitement, who'd set aside an afternoon to spend in unrushed play with her child. It had been the housekeeper.

Danica watched the little boy throw the last of his bread to the birds, then bat his mitten against his snowsuit. Moments later, when his mother swept him up into her arms and hugged him tightly before starting off down the path, she felt a pang of envy—envy of the child who had such a loving mother, envy of the mother who had such a warm, cuddling child.

Starting off toward Charles Street, she vowed that if she had a child, things would be very different from the way they'd been when she'd been young. Money didn't buy happiness. Neither did power. She didn't care what obligations she'd have to cancel. She'd spend time with her child.

Just thinking about it brought a lump to her throat. She had so much love to give . . . so much love to give that she sometimes thought she'd burst.

CHILLED BY THE TIME she let herself into the town house, she settled into the leather couch in the den, tucked her legs under an afghan and watched while Marcus built a fire. When Mrs. Hannah brought her a cup of tea, she let it steep while she held it and absorbed its warmth. Only when she removed the tea bag and propped it on the saucer did she examine its tag.

"Happiness is a way station between too much and too little," she read, and smiled her sad agreement.

Chapter Three

DANICA MADE THE TRIP to Kennebunkport in record time. It wasn't that there'd been no traffic, for there had been. It wasn't that she'd been in a hurry, for she hadn't been. But she'd been angry. And much as her better sense told her to slow down, she'd found perverse satisfaction in stepping on the gas.

Even now, having left the highway at Kittery in favor of the shore route, she burned when she thought of Blake. Over and over she replayed the conversations she'd had with him regarding the trip they were to have made together.

"Blake?"

"Mmmm?" He'd been looking in the mirror readjusting the knot of his necktie.

"How does next Wednesday sound for taking a drive to Maine?"

He'd stuck his chin up and tugged some more. "Next Wednesday...uh...next Wednesday's fine."

"It's still a week off. We could make it Tuesday or Thursday if you'd rather."

"Nope." He'd smiled at his image. "Wednesday's okay."

That weekend she'd asked him again. "Blake?"

"Hmmm?" This time he'd been engrossed in the Sunday paper.

"Is Wednesday still okay?"

"Wednesday?"

"...Maine?"

"Oh." He'd noisily turned the page. "As far as I know it's fine."

On Tuesday morning, unable to help herself, she'd raised
it a third time. "Blake?" He'd been in the library making a
fast phone call before leaving for work.

"Yes, Danica."

His slight impatience hadn't deterred her. It wasn't often
she asked things of him, but their driving together to Maine
meant a lot. "I'm counting on you for tomorrow."

"I know," he'd said evenly and had been out the door soon
after.

Late that afternoon, though, he'd called from the office,
announcing that he had to fly to Atlanta in the morning instead. She hadn't argued then or later when he'd come home
to pick her up for a dinner party. She'd been the patient, understanding wife right through the moment when she'd kissed
him goodbye and waved him off to the airport.

Inside she was seething.

Now, approaching the house she'd set such stock in, she felt
the anger finally sweeping away. In its place was an overwhelming hurt, an abject loneliness, a sense of loss. She'd had
a dream—for years and years, it seemed—but it didn't look
like it was going to come true.

Pulling from the main road onto the curving driveway, she
brought the Audi to a halt before the front door of the house.
Either her timing was particularly good, or having turned off
the car, she simply relinquished the taut hold she'd had on
herself. Her eyes suddenly filled with tears, and unable to do
anything else, she draped both hands over the steering wheel,
dropped her head forward and cried.

MICHAEL BUCHANAN HAD QUIETLY KEPT an eye on the
Lindsay house since the day he'd last seen Danica. Oh, yes,
he knew who she was now. A quick call to the realtor had
given him the identities not only of Danica's husband but also
of her father. A more lengthy call to his sister, Cilla, who lived
and worked in Washington, had told him more. Anything else
he'd learned had come from a study of newspaper microfilms
on file at the public library.

Danica Lindsay was very definitely off-limits. Not only was she married, but she was the daughter of a man his father had never seen eye to eye with.

Still, he hadn't been able to forget her, to put from mind the image of her standing so alone on the sand. He hadn't been able to forget the haunted look he'd caught on her face before she'd composed herself. The realtor, his sister, the papers, had given him biographical facts. What they hadn't touched on was whether she was happy.

And he cared. Something had happened that morning on the beach, and he couldn't turn his back on it.

Okay, fine. So he couldn't court her as he would have liked. But she was going to be his neighbor for whatever period of time she chose to spend in Maine. And he intended to be her friend.

For a while all he'd seen when he'd passed her house had been pick-up trucks and vans in the driveway. Lately, though, they'd been there less often. Today there were none.

But there was a car, and on sheer instinct he knew that it was hers. It fit her... a silver Audi coupe... classy... sporty but dignified. Slowly, he saw the red brake lights go off and he knew she was in the car. At the end of her driveway he pulled up and watched, unable to see much more than a shadow in the driver's seat. When the shadow seemed to wither into itself, he frowned. Then, driven as much by confusion as by concern, he climbed from his Blazer and walked up the drive.

The morning's brightness was his ally. With each step he took, the shadow in the front seat of the Audi took on greater color and form. Danica. Wrists dangling over the top of the steering wheel. Blond head fallen against her arms. Shoulders quaking.

He picked up his step, trotting the last few yards, then, as softly as his thudding heart would allow, tapped two fingers against her window.

She looked up with a start and he saw her tears.

"Oh, God!" he murmured, feeling a tightening inside. He tried to open the car door, but it was locked from the inside and Danica had put her head back down on her arms. She was frightened. No, embarrassed. But he didn't want her to hide. Not from him.

Again he rapped softly on the window. "Danica? Are you all right?" Her shoulders lifted. She seemed to be trying to get control of herself. Either that or she was crying all the harder. He didn't know which and spoke with a hint of panic. "Open the door, Danica."

Blotting her eyes with one hand, she opened the door with the other. Then, taking a shuddering breath, she laid her head back against the headrest and closed her eyes.

Michael pulled the door open all the way and hunkered down, facing her. "What's wrong?"

She squeezed her eyes shut and furrowed her brow as if she were in pain.

"Are you sick?"

She shook her head and held up a hand. "Give me...a minute."

On instinct he lifted his hand and closed it around hers. As naturally, her fingers curled around his thumb and held tight.

He spoke very softly. "Right about now I think I'm supposed to whip a neatly folded handkerchief out of my pocket to give you. At least that's what a real gentleman would do." He stuck his hand in his jacket pocket and, even as he drew out a crumpled supermarket check-out slip, knew there was no point in looking further. He'd never been one for neatly folded handkerchiefs. "Guess I'd strike out as a real gentleman. Have you got any Kleenex?"

Sniffling, she released his hand and turned in the seat to fumble in her pocketbook. Moments later she was pressing a tissue under first one eye, then the other.

"I'm sorry," she whispered.

"Don't be silly. We all have our moments. Something's upset you, that's all." He glanced around. Hers was the only car in sight and the house looked deserted. "Is there anyone I can call?" She shook her head. "You're alone." Fresh tears welled in her eyes. "Ahhhh. And that's the problem...or part of it, at least?"

Chin tucked to her chest, eyes closed again, she pressed a finger to the spot between her eyes and nodded. When once more she'd composed herself, she sniffled and looked up. "I was really hoping my husband would come. At the last minute he rushed off to Atlanta on business."

"I'm sure he had to," Michael offered gently. "From what I understand, he's an important man." When Danica looked up in surprise, he smiled. "I do know who your husband is. And your father.... You weren't planning on keeping them a secret forever, were you?"

Helplessly she responded to his gentle teasing. "It was kind of nice to be a nobody for that little while we talked."

Michael wondered if she remembered "that little while we talked" as clearly as he did. He'd spent many an hour thinking about it since she'd gone. "You'd never be a nobody."

"You know what I mean. Not Blake Lindsay's wife. Not William Marshall's daughter. It isn't often that I get to be with people who see me for *me*."

"I will."

Somehow she knew it. Looking into Michael Buchanan's eyes now, she felt the same warmth, the same lightness she'd felt that first day on the beach. "I'd really like that," she said, breaking out into a slow smile, then sniffling and looking down self-consciously. "God, I must look awful."

"You look wonderful." Very gently he brushed a tear from her cheek with his thumb, then pushed himself up and held out his hand. "Come on. Time to go in. That is why you've come—to see the house—isn't it?"

She gave him a sheepish grin. "Right." Putting her hand in his, she let herself be helped from the car. "My decorator's been checking. She says things are nearly done." For the first time she looked around, tipped her head back, took a deep breath—slightly uneven from her recent tears—of the ocean air. "Mmmm. Nice. An improvement over the last time."

"It's warmer. And sunny. No fog." Michael remembered that fog and the way it had given a mystical quality to his meeting Danica. He still felt it—a kismet of sorts. Much as he told himself he was crazy, he couldn't shake the feeling.

As they walked up the flagstone path to the door, Danica admired the landscape around the house. White pines dotted

the yard, standing guard over clusters of bayberry and stag-
horn sumac. Though it was still too early for any of the
flowering shrubs to blossom, the scrubby junipers looked
fresher, in the first stages of rejuvenation.

Unlocking the door, she stepped inside, then walked slowly
from one room to another in silent appraisal of the work that
had been done. Michael followed her, standing in the door-
way of each room she entered.

The house was almost identical to his own, which wasn't
surprising given that the same architect had designed both of
them and the same contractor had built them some twenty
years before. Both were of a modified Cape style, sprawling
and open and fashioned to take advantage of the spectacular
view of the sea. The structural changes Danica had made—
breaking through walls between kitchen and living room and
foyer—only served to enhance the sense of freedom and space.

"What do you think?" he asked when they'd returned to
the living room.

"Not bad," she said, but her smile was spreading. "Not
bad at all. In fact...I think it looks great. Of course, it'll look
that much better once the furniture's in, but I'll appreciate
that all the more for having seen it as it is now."

Michael agreed. "Looks to me like the furniture is the only
thing left to come."

"That and a few area rugs. I thought I'd buy artwork and
pottery, ashtrays and things, up here.... The walls look wonderful. When we decided to strip the paper off, I was worried
about what we'd find underneath. But we did okay." The
walls were painted a soft cream color to blend not only with
the woodwork accenting doors and windows but also with the
refinished planks on the floor. Overtly excited now, she returned to the kitchen. "I love it," she murmured to herself.
When she heard Michael behind her, she tossed him a quick
grin. "I agonized over these cabinets, but I'm thrilled with
the way they look." She studied in turn the ceramic tile un-
derfoot, the Formica countertops—all in off-white shades—
and the newly recessed ceiling fixtures that gave an even more
contemporary look to the room. "Perfect." She was beaming. "I love it!"

Daring to hope, she opened the refrigerator. The light went on; cool air wafted out. Leaving the door to swing shut on its own, she turned to test a burner on the stove. It worked.

"There!" In triumph she turned back to Michael. "I think I'm in business!" Rubbing her hands together, she backtracked to the hall to adjust the thermostat and bring up some heat.

He followed. "Whoa! What are you in business for?"

"Now that I've got a livable home, I think I'll live in it for a while."

"For a while. How long are you up for?"

"The day." When he chuckled, she grew thoughtful. "Come to think of it, though, there's no reason for me to rush back to Boston tonight. Blake's away. Mrs. Hannah can cancel—"

"You're not planning to spend the night *here*."

"Why not?"

"My God, Danica, the place is little more than a shell!"

She shrugged, liking the idea more and more. "I can buy what I need for the night. There are stores up here, aren't there?"

"Sure, but—"

"I was going to have to buy pots and pans sooner or later. I can pick up soup and tea, maybe butter and eggs at the supermarket. I don't need much."

Michael remained silent, watching her as she walked to the window, ran her hand along the newly painted sill, knelt to touch the sanded and polished floor. Her pleasure was contagious—or was it simply the pleasure he felt in seeing her again? Her excitement was pure, refreshing, innocent in its way. "Uh . . . Danica?"

She turned to him with the brightest of smiles. "Uh-huh?"

"Where are you going to sleep?"

For an instant she frowned, but only for an instant. "Mmmm. I hadn't thought about that."

"You can't exactly curl up on the bare floor."

"Uh . . ." Somehow curling up on the floor did seem to be above and beyond the call of duty. On the other hand, with a little ingenuity . . . "How about an air mattress and some blankets, maybe even a down sleeping bag . . . mmmm, that's a nice idea." She looked up to find Michael slowly shaking his head. "You think I'm crazy."

"No, no. It's not that at all. I'm just . . . amazed. I wouldn't have imagined you'd want to camp out."

"You mean you wouldn't have imagined I'd be the *type* to camp out," she quipped, but there was no censure in her voice, because Michael's gentle manner precluded it. Besides, he was right. Her sheepish expression told him so. "There's always a first time for everything," she said, her voice soft, her gaze suddenly bound to his. He had such remarkable brown eyes, she thought. They were clear, warm, genuine, and made her feel very special. She needed that right now, when she felt incidental to so much of the rest of her life. She needed to be valued, and Michael did that. Basking in his approval, she glowed.

"Danica . . . ?" he whispered, then swallowed hard. When she looked at him that way, it was all he could do not to take her in his arms.

Her voice was scarcely louder than his whisper. "You shaved today." His jaw was square, strong, smooth now where she recalled it had been rough. "Last time you hadn't."

"I hadn't expected to see anyone last time."

"But you couldn't have been expecting—"

"No. I didn't know you were coming today. I was passing by on my way into town and I saw the car. But I always look to see who's here. I was wondering when you'd be back." He'd been speaking very quietly. Now he swallowed again. "Does that bother you?"

Danica shook her head. How could it bother her when she felt better than she had in weeks? "It's kind of nice to know there's someone here."

"We can be friends, then?"

She burst into a smile. "I thought we already were."

"Do you want that?"

"Very much."

"I'm glad." He couldn't seem to tear his gaze from hers but realized that he'd better do something if he hoped to behave himself. And he had to. She was off-limits . . . off-limits . . . off-limits . . . "Wanna go shopping?"

"Shopping?"

"For pots and pans and a sleeping bag and—"

"Ah. Shopping. Sure. But you don't have to—"

"I'm your friend, aren't I? What kind of a friend would let you wander around a strange town alone?"

"I've been here before," she chided, but she felt very, very pleased.

"*Being* here has little to do with *shopping* here. Come." His hand swallowed hers before she could refuse, and he was heading for the front door. "There are stores and there are stores. I know exactly where to find what you need. It'll save time for both of us."

"Both of us?"

At the door he turned. "If you refuse my offer, I'll only spend the day worrying that you've been ripped off."

"But, Michael, I can't take your time this way."

"Why not? I'm not complaining."

"What about your work? You said you were a writer."

"I am. But one of the nice things about being a writer is that my time is my own to apportion as I wish. I was going into town anyway. Now I'll have company."

She held more tightly to his hand when he would have tugged her forward. "Are you sure?"

He grinned. "I'm sure.... Let's go." He had started to turn when she drew him back a final time.

"Michael?" He was looking down at her, one brow arched as though prepared to do further battle if she resisted his offer. "Thank you."

The brow lowered and he seemed to melt. "For what?"

"For stopping." She tossed her head toward where her car sat, but the motion came out like a half-shrug and she lowered her eyes self-consciously. She couldn't forget that not an hour before she'd been slumped over her steering wheel, crying her heart out. It still hurt when she thought of Blake, but she didn't feel quite as alone. "For helping me over that."

"I didn't do anything."

"You were here."

He cleared his throat and studied the slow movement of his thumb over her fingers. "Well, let's just say we're even then."

"Even?"

"Mmmm. I was feeling pretty lonely myself." The smile he produced was boyishly honest. "It's nice to have a friend to play hooky with."

On impulse Danica threaded her arm through his and squeezed tight. She was in a new place with a new home and a new friend. If Blake had chosen not to come, that was *his* problem. *She* was going to enjoy herself!

Taking Michael's Blazer, which would more easily hold Danica's purchases, they spent the next hours shopping for the things she'd need if she intended to spend the night at her house.

"Are you sure you want to go through with this?" he growled out of the side of his mouth as she stood debating between two particularly beautiful handmade quilts they'd found at a small shop in the Union Square group. He had set one arm straight against the counter she faced and had the other tucked in his pocket. His body was angled toward hers in a way that reflected the protectiveness she inspired. "It seems sacrilegious to be throwing one of these on the floor." In truth, he didn't like the idea of *her* spending the night on the floor—or spending the night alone, for that matter. Taking it one step further, what he really wanted was for her to stay with him, but he knew that was impossible.

"No, no, Michael. It'll be fine. This is something I'll be able to use in the spare room once the beds are in. Much better than wasting money now on a sleeping bag or a bunch of blankets. In fact," she thought aloud, "I think I'll buy matching quilts while I'm at it. And throw pillows. Since we're here now . . ." Her words trailed off as she sent him an apologetic glance. "Are you bored to tears?"

"Are you kidding? It's a joy to watch you shop. You're so enthusiastic about it."

"But still . . ."

"Listen," he said softly, putting an arm around her shoulder, "I've shopped with women before and I swore I'd never do it again. They pick things up, put them down, pick up something else, go back to the first, leave the store, return two minutes later, having changed their minds again . . . but this is different. You're having fun and it's catching. Do I look like I'm suffering?''

He looked positively gorgeous. Suffering? "No. But I feel guilty."

"That's *your* problem." He flashed her a grin, gave her shoulder a squeeze and crooked a finger toward the saleswoman, who'd been timidly hovering in the background, trying to busy herself by working on a new quilt while at the same time remaining accessible. "Have you got matching quilts to either of these two?"

It happened that only one of the quilts had a mate, but it was the one Danica favored, so she was thrilled. After purchasing six coordinating throw pillows—three for each bed when the guest room was furnished, plenty for Danica to choose from tonight—they moved on.

True to his word, Michael knew where to find what. Though he preferred to patronize local shops wherever possible—as had been the case with the quilts—he also knew of more practical places to shop for less esoteric things such as pots and pans. And he knew of the best place to stop for lunch, which happened to be an intimate chowder-and-salad house at the edge of Dock Square.

"This is a sight more than I expected when I left Boston this morning," Danica commented, knowing it was an understatement. When she'd left Boston, her spirits had just about hit rock bottom. Now she felt distinctly renewed.

Michael reveled in her pleasure. "Me, too. I'd expected just another ho-hum day."

"I can't believe your days are ho-hum. You can write. You can pick up and . . . and play hooky. You can come and go as you please."

He saw her frown. "What's wrong?"

"I was just envying you your lack of commitments but . . . I'm just assuming that. I've never asked whether you're married or anything." Her voice dropped to a self-deprecating whisper. "That was dumb of me."

"No. You've never asked because you didn't have to. You know the answer."

She looked at him then for a long time, then slowly nodded. "But why, Michael? Why no wife?"

He shrugged. "There was never any need to get married. I've had intense relationships, but thanks to the women's movement, none of them have ended in marriage."

"What do you mean?"

His cheeks reddened for a minute, a sensitivity that took the edge off what might otherwise have sounded chauvinistic. "The liberated woman is less apt to require a commitment."

She nodded. "You sound relieved."

He thought about that for a while, finally choosing his words with care. "I haven't been ready for marriage. I travel—doing research and all—and I enjoy that. When I'm home, there's my writing to do and God knows writing is a solitary profession. I do have friends, so when I get lonely, I pick up the phone." His voice lowered on a sadder vein. "There are times though . . . there are times when I wish . . ."

"Wish what?"

He fiddled with the saltshaker, turning it clockwise, then counterclockwise, and spoke slowly as the thoughts came. "There are times when I wish I did have a wife and children . . . times when my house is too quiet, when I'd give just about everything to have a family materialize and be there with me. *My* family. A wife who'd sit talking softly with me late at night. Children who'd look a little like each of us, who'd be half angel and half devil but thoroughly lovable." He paused for breath, then gathered the courage to look up. Danica sat staring at him, her eyes large and moist. ". . . Danica?"

She blinked once and tried to smile, but it took her a minute to garner that control. It frightened her that he should share her dreams. "I can understand why you're a writer," she finally managed. "You express yourself well."

"Yeah, well, I'm not sure I like what I express sometimes."

"Your thoughts are beautiful."

"I don't know about that. They're pretty selfish. I'm not sure I deserve a family. It'd be like having my cake and eating it too. If I'd wanted children now, I should have made a commitment before."

Danica thought of Blake and of a similar conversation she'd had with her mother. But Michael seemed so much younger than Blake, both in years and behavior. He was spontaneous where Blake was disciplined, casual where Blake was formal. She couldn't ever remember Blake's hair falling across his brow as Michael's did now. "Things aren't that simple sometimes. You said it yourself. You've wanted to travel. And write." She paused. "We all make choices at certain points in our lives. That doesn't mean we never have second thoughts."

Michael knew she was speaking personally. Her voice held sadness and there was the same haunted cast to her eyes that he'd seen when she'd been on the beach a month before. "Do you?"

"Do I what?"

"Ever have second thoughts about the choices you've made."

She crinkled up her nose and forced a smile. "I'm like anyone else. I have moments when everything seems wrong." They were both remembering the moments she'd spent that morning sitting in her car in tears. "But," she went on in a tone that reminded Michael of the stoicism he'd detected in her on the beach that first day, "I've got an awful lot that most people don't have."

He wanted to go back, to talk about what had seemed wrong to her before, but the waitress chose that moment to bring their lunch, and needing to see Danica smile some more, he redirected the conversation to more chatty topics involving Kennebunkport. Later, though, in the supermarket, he sought to appease his curiosity.

"Tell me what you've got, Danica."

"I've got tea bags, half a dozen eggs, a quart of orange—"

"Not that, imp," he chided, widening his eyes in emphasis. "I can *see* what's in the cart." They were leisurely strolling down the aisle with paper supplies, Michael wheeling,

Danica ambling beside. "When we were in the restaurant, you mentioned that you have more in life than most people. Tell me. I want to know."

She reached out to remove a roll of paper towels from the shelf and set it in the cart. "I suppose I've got the usual, just more of it."

He sensed a modesty in her and respected it even as he needed to know more. "Nice home?"

"You've seen it."

"Not here." Again he was scolding, again, though, in the most gentle of tones. "Tell me about Boston."

She took a deep breath and grasped the edge of the cart as they walked. "I . . . we live on Beacon Hill."

"A town house?"

"Uh-huh. It's three stories high, with a charming front walk and a courtyard in back. We share the courtyard with our neighbors."

"The only town house I was ever in on the Hill was weird. It had the kitchen and living room—"

"On the second floor, with the bedrooms above and the family rooms below?" She laughed at his expression, which clearly said he thought the arrangement was awful. "That's how ours is. It's really the most practical setup. We've got good space front to back and top to bottom, with next to none side to side. The stairs are steep and long. It makes sense to have the kitchen and living room in the middle."

"I guess." They'd stopped at the end of the aisle, moving on only when the approach of another shopper necessitated it. "Still, it must be hard to get used to."

"Not really. The rooms may be narrow, but they're big. We entertain on the first and second floors. Anyway, my dad's place in Washington isn't that much different."

"You lived in Washington rather than Connecticut?"

She shook her head but had no desire to elaborate. "Do you have a dog?"

"Excuse me?"

"A dog. Do you have one?" She pointed to the shelf lined with dog food, but she was eyeing Michael speculatively. "I can picture you running along the beach with a beautiful Irish setter at your heels.''

"I had one," he said, stunned. "It died last year.... You had to know." But she simply shook her head. "That's uncanny." After a minute he took a breath. "One part of me wants to get another. I look in the papers every week. The other part still mourns Hunter. He was a beauty."

"How long did you have him?"

"Nine years. I bought him when I moved up here. It seemed a great place to have a dog."

"Get another," she urged, suddenly animated.

"I think *you* want one."

The animation waned. "I do, but it's out of the question."

"I'm sure lots of people on Beacon Hill own dogs, for protection if nothing else."

"Mmmm, I often see them out walking. But it's cruel. A dog needs room to run."

"You could have one up here."

"Blake hates dogs," she stated quietly.

"But if the dog is here and he's there . . ."

"The house up here is for the two of us." She gave a rueful laugh. "If he ever makes it. And anyway, the dog would still have to live in the city. It's not like we'll be here full-time."

They moved on toward the check-out counter then, with Danica wishing she could live here full-time and Michael wishing she had the dog and no Blake. Both knew they were dreaming, but dreams were fun from time to time. And Danica knew for a fact that she was having fun.

Later, after they'd stowed her purchases in her house, they headed for the beach. It was breezy but comfortable, as it hadn't been that day a month before. Though she wore the same stylish jacket she'd worn then, now it lay open over her soft, moss-green sweater and winter-white slacks. Michael, too, was more at ease with the elements than he'd been then. They walked slowly, pausing occasionally to look at a cluster of seaweed that had washed up, moving on by mutual and unspoken consent.

"What are you writing now?" Danica asked, pushing her hair behind one ear so that it wouldn't blow in her face when she looked up at him. He was tall and sturdy. She liked that.

"Now?" He grinned. "A short history of professional sports in America. It's something light, something I was in the mood to do."

"Doesn't sound all that light to me," she said tightly. She wondered if he knew she'd played tennis, wondered if he'd say anything about it. She hoped not. She didn't want her past to intrude. Not just now. "There must be a whole lot of research to do."

"Yeah, but it's fun research, especially the interviews. I've talked with some of the old-time greats. Hockey, baseball, boxing—you name it. I needed a change of pace after last year."

"Last year?"

"Ummm. Then it was an analysis of religious and racial bigotry as a function of economic depressions and recessions."

"A mouthful. But fascinating." And a wonderful diversion. "Is the book out yet?"

"Next month."

She grinned. "Congratulations."

He grinned back. "Thanks."

It took her a minute to catch her breath. "What was your theory?"

"That bigotry is heightened by economic crises. It's nothing people haven't known for years, but few have taken the time to document it."

"You were able to?"

"Easily. History speaks bluntly. In times of economic stress people look out for themselves. They blame their woes on the next guy, particularly if he's weaker or less able to defend himself."

"Even if he's stronger, I'd think. There's many an ethnic or religious group that's been *superior* in one field or another and because of that has become the bigot's target."

Michael beamed. Somehow he'd known she'd be politically astute. "I discussed that at length in the book. I'll give you a copy as soon as I get mine."

"I can buy one—"

"Don't be silly. It'll be my pleasure."

They'd come to an outcropping of rocks. Michael jumped up on the first, held out his hand to Danica, who readily followed him. When they'd reached the top, they perched on adjacent boulders.

"How many books have you written?"

"Four."

"All published?" When he nodded, she grinned. "Then it must be old hat to you, having another book appear on the shelves."

"It's never old hat. There's always the excitement and the pride. And the fear."

"Of how it'll do?"

"You bet. As it is, the books I write aren't blockbuster material."

"They're nonfiction. You can't compare apples and oranges."

"Still, we're talking another ball game." He laughed softly and added an aside. "Sorry about that. This new thing is in my blood."

"How *did* it get in your blood—writing, that is? Did you specialize in school? Did you always know you wanted to write?"

Michael gazed out across the sand and shifted one long leg to the side. "For a while I thought it was the last thing I wanted to do. Writing runs in my family. I wanted to be different."

"I can buy that," she said softly. "Did you try?"

"Oh, yeah." He looked down at his hands. "When I was in high school, I worked afternoons for a landscape architect. I was a lousy gardener, but I prepared a terrific PR brochure for my boss. During the year I took off after high school to bike across country, I did everything from short-order cooking to computer repairs to support myself; the real money came months later when my father had the letters I'd sent home serialized in a magazine." Propping his elbows on his knees, he looked seaward again. "By the time I got to college I thought I was headed for law school and the diplomatic corps; I spent most of my senior year collaborating with one of my professors on a book about the Russian Revolution. Even my stint in Vietnam backfired; the things that kept me going were the editorials I was sending back home."

When he looked back at her, the frustration she'd seen on his face had vanished. "Everything seemed to be pointing toward a writing career. I could only fight it so far."

"Is your family that overbearing?"

"Overbearing?" He chuckled. "That's one way of putting it. But wait. I'm being unfair. My father is the only real villain there," he decreed, but he was grinning. "Everyone else is okay."

"How many are there?"

"Four of us kids, plus Mom and, of course, Dad."

Danica's eyes lit up. "Four kids? You must have had fun growing up."

"We did, thanks to Mom. She's a free spirit, as easygoing as Dad is demanding. She kept a handle on him as much as she could, at least until we were old enough to speak up to him. Poor woman," he mused fondly, "after all her struggles to offer us the world, we've *all* ended up doing one sort of writing or another."

"Really?"

"Mmmm. The oldest, Brice, works with my father in New York. The youngest, Corey, edits his own magazine in Phillie. Cilla writes feature articles for one of the papers in D.C."

"Cilla?"

"Priscilla. My sister."

"Is she older or younger?"

"Older by six minutes."

"Twins! I don't believe it! Are there *two* people like you in the world?"

He laughed. "She's a she, which means we're fraternal twins, which means we're no more alike than any brother and sister. She's very different from me—more outgoing, aggressive. She loves the rough and tumble of newspaper report-ing; I'd be a basket case in a matter of months."

"Everyone has his strengths. And since you do what you do so well—"

"Now, you don't know that," he teased with a lopsided grin.

"I know," she vowed softly, guided by instinct. "And I think it's great that you're doing what you enjoy. And that you're so successful at it. The other Buchanans must be proud."

Michael hesitated for a moment, but not because he had doubts about his family's pride. Rather, he was wondering when Danica would begin to put two and two together. The mention of the name Buchanan, the talk round and about newspapers and magazines . . .

" . . . Michael?"

"Hmmm?"

Her face was a study in dawning awareness, a showcase for dismay and apprehension. "You...haven't said exactly what it is your father does." Her voice was very, very quiet.

"No, I haven't. I think you've just guessed."

She closed her eyes and dropped her chin to her chest, then suddenly threw her head back and laughed. "I don't believe it." Her gaze met Michael's. "I don't believe it! Do you know how much my father hates yours?" But she was grinning. It had suddenly occurred to her that it wasn't her war.

Michael agreed. "I can imagine. I'm not sure if the two of them have ever actually met, but I'd hate to be around when that happened. Our papers haven't been kind to your father over the years."

"My father hasn't exactly inspired kindness." She shook her head in amazement, trying to assimilate what she'd learned. "The Buchanan Corporation. Unbelievable." Then a thought struck and her knuckles grew white on the rock by her hip. She'd come to trust Michael completely; it would be a blow to find she'd misplaced that trust. "You've known all along?"

But he was already shaking his head. He'd anticipated her apprehension and had prepared his defense. "I had no idea who you were that first day. It wasn't until I spoke with Judy that I learned you were the senator's daughter, and since then I've been wishing I belonged to any other family but my own.'' He swiveled on his rock to more fully face her. ''You could hate me for some of the things our papers have said about your father, but please believe me when I say that I've never condoned that kind of attack. That's one of the reasons I'd never have made it with the Corporation. I meant what I said on the beach last time about my writing not being threatening. I would never do anything to hurt you, Danica. You know that, don't you?''

She searched his face then, seeing the things she'd seen all day and more. It was a handsome face, with its melting brown eyes and its windblown cap of sandy hair, and it held warmth and strength and affection. It also held desperation, and that she understood.

Slowly she nodded, thinking how very lucky she was to have found a friend who wanted her friendship every bit as badly as she wanted his.

Danica took her time driving back to Boston the following day. She felt relaxed and refreshed, free of the anger that had been her companion the morning before. She knew that Blake would be home that night, that she'd tell him about the house, what she'd bought, how she'd slept on the living-room floor.

She wouldn't tell him about Michael, though. Not yet. Michael was her own friend, neither a businessman nor a politician. Perhaps it was defiance she felt: after all, Blake had been too busy to make the trip; therefore he had no claim to what he'd missed. Besides, she reasoned, she had a right to a friend, particularly one who was as easy to talk with and as easy to be with as Michael Buchanan. If there was something naughty about her associating with a Buchanan, so be it. She admired Michael. She enjoyed him. And she was thoroughly looking forward to seeing him again when she returned to Maine.

Chapter Four

BLAKE WAS with Danica the next time she drove north.

"I still don't believe it," she teased in the car, hoping to cajole her husband into a better mood. She knew that he'd had second thoughts about making the trip but had yielded for her sake, and she was grateful. She firmly believed that given time alone in a place far removed from the maelstrom of the city, she and Blake could recapture the spark their marriage had had once upon a time.

"I shouldn't be here," he stated with the same quiet conviction that characterized his every move. "My desk will be piled high by the time I get back."

"We'll only be away for three days," she scolded gently. "Besides, you owe it to yourself. You're always working. It's been so long since you took time off just to relax."

"A weekend would have been better."

"But it's impossible to get away on a weekend, Blake. We've been busy every one of the past six, with more to come in June. It's the pre-summer rush of dinner parties, I guess, not to mention the fund-raising you're doing."

"You aren't still bothered by that, are you?"

"No, no." Slowly, very slowly, she'd acclimated herself to Blake's active support of Jason Claveling. There had been no argument. She and Blake never argued. They *discussed*. And with Blake his usual eloquent self when he wanted to make a point, she'd never really had a chance. So, in time, the hurt had simply faded, then disappeared, as it always did. After all, she did want to be a good wife to him. "I can stand it as long as you can.... Doesn't it ever get to you, the backslapping and handshaking?"

He smiled and shot her a fast glance. "It's business. You should know that. What does Bill say when you ask him?"

"I've never asked. With him, it's a way of life. From the earliest I can remember, he was going to political functions of one sort or another, and Mom accepts them, trouper that she is. You, well, I guess I didn't expect you'd become so involved."

"I was involved when you met me. Then I was raising money for Bill."

"Mmmm. For the longest time I wondered about that. After all, you were a resident of Massachusetts while Dad was the senator from Connecticut."

"Bill was a friend. I also happened to approve of his stands in the Senate, especially those affecting big business."

"You were buying an insurance policy."

His lips twitched in amusement at her subtle sarcasm. "It's done every day of the week. In Bill's case, it was easy. I liked him personally. And I liked you. With Claveling, it's business all the way."

They drove on for a while in silence before Danica spoke again. "If Claveling's elected, what will it mean to you?"

Blake's answer was on the tip of his tongue, suggesting where his own thoughts had been. "Import quotas. Favorable trade agreements. Tax benefits. Who knows . . . maybe a cabinet appointment."

She saw his grin when she darted a look his way. "Fun-ny," she murmured, and relaxed back in her seat as the Mercedes crossed the Piscataqua River and entered Maine.

In her very biased opinion, the house was stupendous. Since Blake had insisted she let the decorator supervise all the furniture deliveries—and since she'd been unable to get away to do so herself—she was seeing the finished product for the first time alongside Blake.

He seemed to approve, though whether he was simply indulging her she wasn't sure. He walked from room to room, hands buried deep in the pockets of his slacks, and nodded from time to time.

"Well?" she finally asked. Her own excitement was tempered only by the suspense of not knowing what he thought.

"It's very nice."

He'd said the words, but without passion. Her shoulders sagged. "You don't like it," she murmured.

"I do. It's perfect. You've done a wonderful job, Pook." He gave her a broad smile, then turned. "I'll get the bags."

Very diligently, given the fact that they'd only brought clothes for two days, and strictly casual ones at that, Blake unpacked while Danica went through the house a second, then a third time. Determinedly overlooking her husband's apparent indifference, she enthusiastically examined every piece of furniture that had been delivered. It was the antithesis of the Beacon Hill town house, which, in keeping with its structure, had been decorated in a more classical style. Here, newly installed skylights illumined modular sofa clusters, low swirling coffee tables, custom-made wall units. The feeling was one of openness and lack of clutter and was precisely what Danica had wanted.

Blake returned from the bedroom to wander around the living room. He didn't touch anything, simply... wandered.

"Uh—" she rubbed her hands together "—what would you like to do?"

He shrugged and looked toward the deck. "Walk out there."

He stood on the deck for no less than ten minutes, staring in the direction of the waves. When Danica had grown tired of waiting, she came to stand several feet from him. "Pretty, isn't it," she offered with a smile, hoping to get him talking. She hated the lengthy silences that so often existed between them, because she could never tell what he was thinking. His face was always composed, his manner invariably as unruffled as his hair. But she knew that he *felt*, that he *thought*. What she didn't know was why he couldn't share those thoughts and feelings with her.

This day, this setting, apparently was going to make no difference. He simply nodded.

"It's been interesting watching the changes since I've been here," she went on, trying to sound as nonchalant as possible when in fact she was forcing conversation. Normally she would have been perfectly happy just to quietly appreciate the scene. Somehow now, beside Blake, she felt impelled to chatter. "When I came up in March, it was really cold. The ocean was a mass of whitecaps. You couldn't smell much of anything because your nose was frozen. Then last month it was warmer. The air was moist and the wind didn't bowl you over." She inhaled deeply. "This is nice, though. May. You can smell the beach grass...feel the sun." Tipping her head back, she closed her eyes and basked, momentarily forgetting Blake's presence until he made it known.

"You said something about wanting to pick up paintings?"

Righting her head, she looked at him. "By local artists. Maybe a sculpture or two, also."

"Why don't we go now? I want to explore the streets and plot out a route to run."

"You're going to run up here? I...I kind of thought you'd take a break from all that." When he shook his head, she felt another tiny bit of hope die. "I suppose it would be nice for you to run along the shore," she rationalized, then sighed and forced a smile. "I'll get my purse."

THEY SPENT the next few hours idling through shops, looking unsuccessfully for artwork, then lunching at Cape Porpoise, buying groceries at the market, driving round and about the local streets while Blake calculated the best eight-mile route for him to run. In theory, it was an easygoing afternoon, just the two of them doing things together as Danica had dreamed.

In fact, it was a letdown.

To Danica, who was ever watchful, Blake seemed uncomfortable. It was as though he felt out of place, which she couldn't understand since Kennebunkport was sophisticated, certainly enough so to satisfy his tastes. But he kept looking around, restless, as if waiting for someone to talk to. Evidently Danica wasn't that someone, for he seemed disinclined to carry on more than the most superficial conversation with her.

Between her watchfulness and those attempts at conversation, she felt drained by the time they returned to the house.

Once there, things were no better. Blake wandered around like a lost soul, looking more frustrated than pensive, more awkward than unsure. She was half relieved when he disappeared into the den with the briefcase he'd smuggled into the house. When she peeked in on him an hour later, he was talking on the phone and looking happy for the first time all day.

Busying herself in the kitchen, Danica studied the cookbooks she'd brought, then painstakingly prepared a meal she felt sure would impress him. Indeed, he complimented her when he finally emerged for dinner, but no sooner had she brewed his coffee than he escaped back into the den, leaving her alone with her tea and her thoughts.

Idly she lifted the tea bag tag. "Love is the magic that makes one and one far more than two," she read silently, dropped the tag and wondered what had gone wrong. She and Blake were very definitely two. No more, no less. Two individuals, wanting, it appeared, increasingly different things in life.

She went to sleep thinking about that, awoke early the next morning thinking of it. Blake lay on his side of the large bed, his back to her, distant even in sleep. She wondered what time it had been when he'd come to bed, wondered if it had even occurred to him that she might be waiting. Not that she had been; by now she was used to being alone. But still, he was a man. Surely he thought of sex *once* in a while.

Studying his sleeping form, she reflected on the early days of their marriage. She'd been attracted to Blake for his sureness, his social grace, his maturity. Sex had never held a high priority in their relationship, and she'd never minded it, since she'd never seen herself as being a highly passionate person. In that, she and Blake had seemed well matched. Still, she couldn't help wondering whether he found her attractive. He rarely reached out for her, and even then she felt he did so more out of obligation than real need. Even now he looked untouchable.

The sound of a buzz jolted her from her thoughts. Blake stirred, pushed himself up on an elbow, reached over to turn off the travel alarm Danica hadn't known he'd brought. She'd assumed they'd sleep late, awaken leisurely, break the pattern that dominated their everyday lives.

Clearly, she'd assumed too much, a point the events of that day drove home. Bounding from the bed, Blake put on his fashionable navy running suit and left the house. She had a big breakfast ready by the time he'd returned and showered, but he ate only the amount he apportioned himself every other morning of the week, so the bulk of her efforts went down the drain.

At her gentle request, they drove up the coast toward Boothbay Harbor, stopping along the way to browse in craft shops and galleries, purchasing a ceramic sculpture and several planters for the deck. Blake was agreeable, if otherwise passive. Again she felt he was merely indulging her whim rather than finding enjoyment in the day himself. Again he disappeared into the den when they returned, and again she felt vaguely relieved. She also felt discouraged, though, and, with a quick word to him, headed out for the beach.

Feeling strangely and suddenly freer than she had since she'd arrived, she wandered over sand and pebbles, around fingers of rocks, heading almost by instinct for the boulders she and Michael had shared a month before.

Michael. The mere sound of his name sparked thoughts of relaxation and fun and excitement. Just thinking about him, she felt better. He was different, so different. And he was her friend.

"Yeo!"

She looked up and started to smile, then, without thinking, broke into a jog, coming to a halt not six feet from him. "Michael!"

He looked as roguish, as bold, as welcoming as ever. He wore an open-necked plaid shirt with the sleeves rolled to the elbow, a pair of jeans that had seen better days, sneakers in a like state, and he was smiling from ear to ear. With his hair lightly mussed and his jaw faintly shadowed, he had to be the most stimulating sight she'd seen in days.

When he opened his arms, she ran forward, tightly clasping his neck while he swung her gently from side to side. He smelled clean and felt strong, and she reveled in his obvious affection.

Finally, he set her back to study each of her features in turn. "You look great!" he said at last, then swooped down to give her another fast hug. "It's good to see you, Danica."

"And you," she managed, breathless and flushed. "How are you?"

"Better now. I saw the car in the driveway last night and was wondering if I'd get a chance to see you." It had been the Mercedes rather than the Audi. Her next words confirmed his suspicion.

"Blake's up with me, but he's doing some work, so I thought I'd come out for a walk." She couldn't seem to stop smiling.

Neither could Michael. "I noticed that your furniture arrived."

She laughed. "Lots of trucks lately?"

"Lots of trucks lately. How does it all look?"

"Great."

"No more sleeping on the floor?"

"Nope."

Michael was about to express his satisfaction until he realized that the arrival of beds meant she'd have slept with Blake last night, and he didn't care for that idea at all. Pushing it from mind, he reached for her hand. "Can you stay and talk for a while?"

She nodded and let herself be led to the same granite seat she'd occupied last time, thinking that though there was many a higher spot, she felt on top of the world.

"I read your book," she ventured shyly when they were perched on the rocks facing each other.

"You *did*?"

"Uh-huh. It was wonderful."

"You must have gotten one of the first copies out."

She laughed. "I pestered the manager of the bookstore so often that he called me the minute it came in. It was really good, Michael. Interesting and informative. Your writing style makes the reading fun."

"You really think so?"

She could see that he was pleased because he was grinning and his voice was higher than usual. In response to his question she nodded, then asked several questions about the things she'd read. Michael answered them enthusiastically, though his modesty was apparent when, as quickly and comfortably as possible, he changed the subject.

"How have you been?" he asked more soberly.

His tone suggested that he knew there were things that bothered her, things that had been bothering her for a long time. She accepted his perceptivity without question. "All right."

When she seemed loath to elaborate, he took the gentler course. "Tell me what you've been up to."

She gave a shy smile and hesitated until his gentle prodding coaxed from her a cursory account of what she'd done since she'd seen him last. When she'd finished, she looked off toward the waves.

"What is it?"

"Oh—" she darted him a glance and smiled self-consciously "—I sometimes feel . . . silly, telling you all this. Nothing I do is earth-shattering. I mean, it's not as if I have a real profession."

"I wouldn't say that. You may not get paid for what you do, but you're certainly performing a service that needs to be performed."

She gave a dry laugh. "By going to luncheons?"

"By going to luncheon *meetings*, at which you plot out the futures of some very worthwhile institutions."

"I'm one of many—"

"That doesn't matter. Every voice counts. If no one took the time to do what you do, many a charitable institution would fall apart. Besides, you care, and that makes your voice all the more valuable."

"Still, there are times when I wish I had a regular job."

"Is it a matter of your own self-image?"

"Maybe . . . in part. Also because I'd like to be busy."

"You're bored."

"Mmmm." She threw up her hands. "It's ridiculous. My days are filled with one thing or another and it's not like I've got time on my hands, but . . . but . . ."

"Your mind's not occupied."

She gave him a helpless look that confirmed what he'd said, then smiled sheepishly. "Maybe that's why you can read it so easily. You do, you know." Playfully she narrowed her gaze. "What am I thinking right now?"

He grinned. "You're thinking that I'm a handsome devil who should have caught you before Blake Lindsay did."

"Well, you are a handsome devil, that's for sure." Her gaze fell to his arm, propped straight on the rock. Golden hair dusted his skin, which in turn was stretched taut over the twist of firm muscle. "You are . . ." she began, but her words trailed off.

With that very same arm Michael collared her and tugged her close. The gentle gesture brought her temple to his jaw. When he spoke, his breath warmed her brow. "I wish I had caught you first, y' know."

Danica melted against him, feeling very, very good. She'd never been a physically demonstrative person, but Michael obviously was, and she found that she loved it. In hindsight, the way she'd earlier run into his arms startled her, yet it had seemed the most natural, most desirable thing to do. She felt wanted, protected, valued. But more, she felt stronger, as if this long-denied human touch had renewed a certain faith in herself.

"You're very special," she murmured, luxuriating in his touch for a moment longer. In the end, it was he who set her back.

"Not special. Just concerned." His voice was husky. He cleared his throat. "And we were talking about what you can do to keep your mind occupied."

"We were?" She felt slightly dazed. It took her a minute to get her bearings.

Michael's recovery was that much faster, but then, he had the advantage of knowing precisely how and what he felt. Not that knowing made things easier; to be wild about a woman who was married to another man was insanity, sheer insanity.

"If you want a job, why not get one?"

She took a long, unsteady breath. "I . . . uh . . . I'm not exactly trained for anything."

"You have a degree, don't you?"

She was finally focusing. "In English. Not very practical in this day and age. But I never expected to do anything with it."

"What *did* you expect?" he asked without censure.

"Oh, much of what I got. A husband. A home—two, now. A life similar in many ways to my mother's."

"But that's not what you want."

She looked down at her hand and nervously twisted her wedding band around. "I feel . . . I feel frustrated."

"What is it you do want from life?"

"Love," she blurted out, then realized what she'd said and colored. "I want children, but they haven't come. Maybe that's why I feel at loose ends. Maybe that's why I feel I have to work." Her laugh was brittle. "I mean, I don't *have* to work. I just—" she widened her eyes in emphasis "—*have* to work."

"I hear you." He'd heard every word, including that one she'd regretted saying but which had told him a great deal, not the least of which accounted for the sadness he'd seen in her from time to time. He wanted to ask about her marriage but didn't quite dare as yet. "I think you should look for a job if that's what you want."

"Oh, I don't know, Michael." She was torn. "Yes, it's what I want. But there are so many factors involved. A job is a commitment. I'd have to shift everything else around. And then there's Blake. I'm not sure how he'd feel about my working. I've always been there when he's needed me."

"He's a big boy."

"I know, and I didn't mean 'need' in that sense. When push comes to shove, Blake doesn't *need* me at all. It's just that he expects me to be there when he gets home. I always have been . . . looking just right, dressed to go out if he wants. But if I work all day, I'll be tired at night . . ."

"He works all day. Doesn't he tire of the game?"

"He loves it."

Some guys did. Michael knew the type. They were driven by forces from without and were not, first and foremost, family men. "Okay. But...wouldn't he be able to understand why you want to work?"

"I don't know. He's of a different generation in many ways. He's so like my father, and I *know* my father would resist the idea of my working."

"Would that bother you?"

A lone herring gull screeched overhead, drawing her attention. She watched it career along an air wave and envied it its smooth ride. "Yes," she said at last in a tone filled with resignation, "it would bother me. I've always wanted to please him."

"Wouldn't it please him to know that you're happy? Wouldn't it please him to know that you'd seen something wrong in your life and tried to fix it? If nothing else, Senator Marshall is a doer. When he sees something he thinks is wrong, he works to change it. I may not have always agreed with his stands, but I'm convinced that he truly believes in each and every one of them."

Danica chuckled dryly. "You must be the only Buchanan who has that faith, at least where it concerns either defense spending or foreign policy. The papers have alternately claimed that he was being bought, that he was carrying out a vendetta or that he was parrying for votes in an election year."

"Well," Michael sighed, "I'm not my family, and my argument is that your father might well be sympathetic to your cause."

"You don't know him, Michael," she murmured. "Oh, yes, he'd be sympathetic to my cause if he believed in it. But he doesn't."

"*You* believe in your cause. Wouldn't that be enough for him?"

"If only. Don't you see? It's not that in theory he'd have any objection to his daughter working. It's that he sees his daughter as already employed, and he's not particularly open to another view. He sees things one way and is terribly narrow-minded when it comes to those who think differently. I guess that's it. But isn't your father the same way?'' From what she'd heard, from what Michael had himself intimated, John Buchanan was a dictator in his own right.

''Sure. I was lucky, though. My mother goes to the other extreme.'' He thought for a minute. ''Have you discussed all this with *your* mother?''

''God, no. She's an extension of my father. Not that I'm criticizing, mind you. She's been the perfect politician's wife. She's always enjoyed the pomp and circumstance. Apparently, it was all she's ever needed.''

''Then, she'd agree with your father.''

''Mmmm. And as far as he's concerned, my place is by Blake's side. In his mind, everything I do should have some bearing on Blake and his career and, therein, my future security.''

''You don't believe that.''

''No. I've just never had cause to fight it.''

''Before.''

She nodded.

''Why the change now?''

She pondered his question. ''I guess I'm getting older. I'm twenty-eight. I've been married for eight years. I'm beginning to sit back and take stock of things.''

''And you want more.''

Again she nodded, but her attention had focused on Michael's lips as he spoke. They were firm lips, with a hint of softness in the lower one that took masculinity into the modern age. He was a man to talk with, to understand. She wondered if he was that much less critical and more open-minded than the other men she'd known or if it was simply that he shared her views.

When those lips moved to speak again, she dragged her gaze back to his eyes. They were more heated now, filled with a passion she'd never seen directed toward her. If only Blake looked at her that way from time to time, things might be different.

''Would a job solve your problems?'' he asked softly.

No, she knew. The problem went far deeper than a simple filling of time. Taking a job would be a stopgap measure. What she needed was love and the warm home she'd always craved but never had. Financial security, social position—they weren't enough. What she needed was to be needed, to be respected as an individual in her own right.

"Well—" she looked down "—it would be a start, I suppose."

"Then, go for it."

Tossing back her head, she shook it, as if by doing so she could dislodge every stumbling block to her happiness. "Which brings us back to square one. If only things weren't so complicated. If only there weren't these other expectations."

"They're other people's expectations, not your own."

"That's what's so muddled. They've been my own for a long, long time—"

"Even though, deep down inside, you've probably always wanted something else?"

"Yes," she confirmed in a tiny voice. "Even then. I'm just not that courageous a person, I guess. I'm afraid of upsetting the applecart."

Michael reached for her hand then and held it in his. His thumb brushed her knuckles, gently caressed her fingers. "You're very hard on yourself, your own worst enemy, I think. Do you remember once we talked of choices?" When she nodded, he went on. "Life is filled with them, and they keep on coming. So many of the choices you've made in the past have been dictated by your desire to please. Now you're discovering that while you may be pleasing others, you're not pleasing yourself." He pressed her hand between both of his and searched her features. She looked so very vulnerable that he ached.

"There'll be other choices, Dani, other choices to be made. At some point you'll venture down a different road, and when that happens, you'll feel comfortable with the decision."

She brushed her free fingers over the soft sprinkling of hair on the back of his hand, then spread her palm there. His warmth seeped into her. His strength was contagious. "You sound so sure that I almost believe it."

"Come 'ere," he growled and hugged her to him again. *I know it,* he thought. *I have faith in you.*

I wish I could package you up, she mused, *and keep you in my pocket all the time. You make me feel so good. You give me such confidence.*

You've never been given a chance. There's so much inside you, so much just begging to be freed.

Why aren't the others like you? Why don't they understand?

They all take you for granted. I never could. But then, you're not mine, are you?

"Oh, Michael . . ." she whispered.

Reluctantly he set her back, but his gaze continued to embrace her a moment longer. "You're apt to be missed," he murmured thickly. "Maybe you'd better head back." *Before I do something that will complicate your life all the more.*

She nodded and, holding his steadying hand, climbed down from the rocks. When once again she stood on the sand, she focused on the horizon. "We'll be leaving tomorrow. The next few weeks will be busy. Then I'll be back. Will you...will you be here?"

"I'll be here."

She looked up at him. "Writing?"

"That, and relaxing. The summer's beautiful up here. There's lots to do."

She smiled, but tears had gathered on her lower lids. On impulse she stretched to lightly kiss his cheek. Then, before she made an utter fool of herself, she quickly set off down the beach.

She didn't look back. She didn't have to. Michael's image was firmly planted in her mind, where it remained for the rest of the day. Much as she tried, given the fact that she was back in her own house with her husband, she couldn't forget those lips, so warm and firm; that arm, corded and strong; the masculine set of that body, which had hugged her, held her, made her feel special. And feminine. She'd never felt so very feminine before. She tingled in secret places when she thought of the curling hairs that had edged through the open neck of

Michael's shirt, when she thought of the roughness of his cheek when she'd pressed her lips there. She grew warm all over again when she thought of the clean, fresh smell of his skin.

And she was terrified.

THAT NIGHT, Danica Lindsay seduced her husband. It was a deliberate act, one born of desperation. And it was a first.

The woman who'd always waited for her husband to reach out now did the reaching. She who'd been shy undressed openly. She who'd been silent whispered an urgent "Make love to me, Blake." She who'd always been in control of herself was now controlled by a greater force.

Aroused as she'd never been, she demanded a fierce pace. Selfish as she'd never been, she concentrated solely on the fire that raged in her straining body. When she reached a heart-stopping climax, she kept her eyes shut and bit her lip to keep from crying out. And when it was over, she curled in a ball and yielded to silent tears of anguish.

For in her heart she knew she'd made love to another man. And she wasn't sure how she was going to handle that fact.

"YOU'RE AWFULLY QUIET." Hand on the banister post, Greta McCabe stopped at the bottom of the stairs to study Michael, who sat sprawled in the shabby armchair he'd occupied since dinner. His eyes had been glued to the rug, but when she spoke, he glanced up and smiled.

"Pat ran out to get more beer. You ran up to put Meggie to bed. There was no one to talk with."

"All night, Mike. You've been quiet all night." She perched on the arm of his chair and squeezed his shoulder. "Is something bothering you?"

Michael took a weary breath and leaned his head against the back of the chair. Pat and Greta were two of his closest friends; he'd known them for years and years. It didn't surprise him that he'd sought out their company tonight, any more than that Greta had sensed something on his mind.

"I think," he began, emphasizing each word in a way that would have been comical if Greta hadn't known better, "that I'm in trouble."

"Work problems?"

He shook his head.

"Family problems?"

Again he shook his head.

"Uh-oh. Michael Buchanan, what have you done this time?"

He knew precisely what that tone of voice suggested and suppressed a groan. "Nothing. I swear to God—"

"You haven't taken up with Monica again, have you? She was trouble from the start."

"No, I haven't seen or heard—"

"Then, you left another one waiting for you at La-Guardia."

"Of course not. That happened four years ago and if I hadn't been so damned preoccupied trying to straighten out the manuscript that got screwed up—"

"You didn't get a girl pregnant, did you?" Greta said with such stoical calm that he could only grab her hand and squeeze it tight.

"No, Greta. I did not get a girl pregnant. Give me a little credit, will ya?"

"Then what is it?"

"I'm in love."

The back door slammed coincidentally with Greta's going perfectly still. "I've known you for a long time, Michael, but I don't believe I've ever heard you say that."

"Say what?" Pat asked, sauntering in with a six-pack under his arm.

"Michael's in love."

"Ahhhh. New book idea?"

Michael smirked. "Not exactly."

"No? Gee, it would be interesting. Taking participatory research to its limits."

"Pat," Greta scolded, "he's serious."

"He can't be serious. He told me once that he'd *never* fall in love."

"I was ten years old at the time," Michael muttered, more for Greta's information than in self-defense.

"And one hell of a ladies' man even then. But cool. Real cool. Babe, you shoulda seem him—"

Michael dropped his chin to his chest in an exaggerated gesture of defeat, but he was grinning. "I taught you everything you know, didn't I, pal?"

"Welllll, I don't know if that's an accurate—"

"Okay, you two. Pat, give Michael his beer and go sit down. Michael, tell me. Who is she?"

"She's . . . a super lady."

"No name?"

"Not . . . yet. I mean—" he looked from one to the other of his friends "—I trust you guys completely, but it's just that . . . well . . . she's very special and very vulnerable and the situation is really . . . awful . . ."

Greta could only imagine one really awful situation. "She's married."

"You got it."

"Oh, Mike, I'm sorry."

Michael snorted. "Not half as sorry as I am."

Pat was leaning forward, rolling his beer can between his hands. "How'd you meet her?"

"Very innocently. On the beach. She was just standing there and I went up to her. She looked very sad and alone. We started talking. God, she's beautiful. I mean, not in the physical sense—well, she is that, too—but from the inside out. She's gentle and bright. She looks at you and you want to melt because there's something there that's afraid and shy but so generous and . . . and in need of a friend." He wore a look of despair. "I swear I was half in love with her even before I saw the damn ring."

The room was filled with silence in the aftermath of Michael's confession. Finally Pat, who'd been staring intently at his friend, sat back in his seat. "Whew. It sounds like you've got it bad."

"Do you see her often?" Greta asked.

"No. But every time I do it's worse."

"What's the state of her marriage?"

"I think it's got problems, but I'm really only guessing. Once in a while she lets something slip."

"Does she know how you feel?"

"She knows that I like her, but I doubt she knows the extent of it. At least she hasn't put a name to it. She's down on herself right about now and I think the last thing she'd dare guess was that a man she'd just met was in love with her."

"How does she feel about you?"

"Right about now I think she feels confused. She's so innocent; that's one of the incredible things, Greta. We've just kind of fallen into this thing and she's so unsuspecting that it goes on and on and we fall deeper and deeper. The excitement is there for both of us when we see each other after being apart. She holds my hand. She lets me hug her. Very innocently, I think. She trusts me as a friend. But I'm afraid...because lately..." He grew quiet, absently rubbing the moisture that had collected on the side of the beer can.

"Geez, don't stop now."

"Pat, pleeeze. What, Mike? What's happened?"

He took a swig of beer. "Well, I think she's beginning to feel physical things that she doesn't expect...or want. It probably frightens her. Hell, it frightens me. And I'm not sure just where it's going to end."

"She's married, Mike. You'd never do anything..." Greta began, only to be silenced by Michael's pained expression.

"You both know me as well as anyone does. You know where I've come from. You know how I feel about homewreckers. I saw what happened to my mother when Dad took up with Deborah; I'd never want to cause that kind of hurt. But, God, I've never seen it from this side before. I mean, if the woman is unhappy and we can give something to each other..."

"You're right," Greta declared, "you are in trouble."

"I feel—" he threw a hand in the air, continuing his outpouring of thoughts as though Greta had never spoken "—torn by the whole thing. Oh, not when I'm with her. When we're together I can't think of anything but the pleasure I feel, the pleasure *she* seems to feel. But when she's gone and I stand back and see the whole situation, it scares the hell out of me. I don't want to come between her husband and her, but I'm not sure that there's that much of substance between them. It seems more like a marriage of convenience, which, good soul that she is, she's trying to make work.''

"How long has she been married?" Pat asked.

"Eight years."

"Any kids?"

"No."

"Statistically speaking, if there are problems, she'd be ripe for divorce."

"Perhaps statistically, but there are other factors at work here. Her family is very strong . . . and prominent."

Greta groaned.

Michael shot her a knowing glance. "Right. To make matters worse, her father and mine aren't exactly admirers."

Pat grimaced. "You do pick 'em."

"No, no, Pat. She's different from any woman I've ever known." He gave a sheepish grin. "I could elaborate, but I've already said enough. I'll be boring you pretty soon."

"You won't bore us," Greta soothed. "I just wish there were something we could do to help."

"There is," he responded, realizing that the idea was coming only as he spoke but instantly liking it. "You can be her friend."

"Will we meet her?"

"I think she'll be here on and off through the summer. I'd like to bring her over one day. She'd enjoy it here."

"Here?" Pat scanned the room. "This place isn't exactly the natural habitat for people from prominent families."

Michael didn't need to look around. He knew that the two-bedroom house was small, that the furniture was worn, the decor plain. He also knew that neither Greta nor Pat came from prominence, that Pat worked his tail off as a tuna fisherman, that the McCabes would never be wealthy, nor did they want to be. "She's had the other, Pat, and something's missing. I'm not sure she's ever been in a home. A real home. And that's what you've got here."

Greta took a deep breath. "So you want to make a point. Isn't that playing a little dirty?"

They were too close friends for Michael to be offended. "I'm not out for points. I just want to . . . to see her smile. I want to share something with her. I want her to relax and have fun."

"What about her husband?" Pat injected. "Won't he question where she's going and why?"

"He's a busy man in the city. If his past behavior is any clue, I have a feeling she may be up here alone more often than not."

"I feel a little like a conspirator in crime," Greta moaned.

"Is it a crime to make someone happy?" Michael asked with such poignancy that neither McCabe could hold out against him.

"Of course not. And of course you can bring her here."

Pat agreed. "Hell, I'm curious to see the woman who's finally brought you to your knees."

"Mmmm," Michael mused, "she has done that. The question is whether I'll ever be able to stand again."

Chapter Five

DANICA CHOSE HER TIME WELL, waiting for a moment when Blake was relaxed and in as good a mood as possible. It came when Marcus was driving them home from a cocktail reception they'd attended in Concord. The reception, a gathering to honor one of Blake's prominent friends in the business community, had been successful. Blake was seated beside her in the back of the Mercedes. He had no briefcase with him, no papers to read, and the drive home was going to take a good thirty minutes.

"Blake?"

"Hmmm?"

She knew his mind was elsewhere, but then, she couldn't ask for miracles. "I've been thinking." He said nothing, so she went on, schooling her tone to one of quiet conviction. "I've decided to spend the summer in Maine."

She looked over at him, but his expression was hidden by the night. So much the better, she mused. She wanted nothing to rob her of her confidence. And she did feel confident on this matter. She'd given it much thought, *much* thought since they'd returned from Kennebunkport three weeks before.

"The entire summer?"

"Uh-huh. It seems to make sense. July and August are always quieter around here. Everyone is away."

"*I* can't spend the entire summer in Maine. July and August will be hectic for me. The convention's coming up."

If it hadn't been the convention, she felt sure it would be something else. She'd been through summers in Boston before, and had been discouraged. Blake kept himself occupied, leaving her to wither, to suffer the heat or to frequent the country club. Neither option appealed to her. She would have loved to go to the beach, but Blake disliked public crowds. The same applied to a stroll through the Marketplace, a cruise in the harbor or an evening on the Esplanade listening to the Boston Pops.

When she'd pushed for the house in Maine, she'd hoped she and Blake would *both* escape there. His initial reaction to the place, though, hadn't been promising. And then there'd been this political campaign, which would complicate things all the more. "I haven't forgotten the convention. And it's another reason why it'd be silly for me to stay around. You'll be busy, but what will I do?"

"There are certain times when I'll want you with me."

She knew about those and had allowed for them. "I'll drive back whenever you want. And you can come up when you're free."

She held her breath, half expecting him to object. After all, it would mean that they'd be separated for the bulk of two months. Deep down inside, she half *hoped* he'd object. It would be nice to know that he'd miss her.

"Is that what you want?" he asked evenly.

"It's not what I want," she returned, unable to hide her frustration. "What I want is for the two of us to spend the summer there together. But you can't do that, can you?"

"You know I can't."

It occurred to her that he did that a lot—said "you know" this or "you know" that—and it annoyed her. It was a way of shifting blame, of evoking guilt, of putting her down. Too often that you-should-know-better tone of his made her feel like a child being chastised, and she resented it.

"You know, Blake," she began, purposely copying his tone, "if you really wanted to, you could. Many a man does, particularly one in as secure a position as you."

"This summer's different."

"Is it?" She listened to herself and realized that it wasn't often she spoke up to him. Once started, she couldn't help herself, though she kept her voice low. "You don't like it up there, do you?"

"Of course I do. It's a lovely place."

She knew he was patronizing her. "You were bored the whole time we were there. You were happiest when you were in the den going through papers or talking on the phone."

He didn't deny it and she wondered, as she had so often since they'd returned, what he'd though of their lovemaking that night. He hadn't touched her since, which wasn't unusual for him. Nor had he said anything immediately after. He'd rolled onto his side of the bed and gone to sleep.

"I love my work. You should be grateful. If I was bored and frustrated, I'd be impossible to live with."

"I sometimes wish that would happen. Maybe then we'd fight at least. It's so hard to get a rise from you, Blake. Does *anything* upset you?"

He gave a dry laugh. "If I let every little thing upset me, I'd never have gotten to where I am today."

"Not every little thing. How about one *big* thing?"

He seemed to hesitate longer than usual. "Yes, there have been *big* things that have upset me, but not for long. Nothing's accomplished by getting upset. You have to think clearly. You have to analyze the facts and your options. You have to make decisions and see them through."

"Spoken like the successful businessman you are," she murmured. In truth, she'd been thinking about their relationship when she'd asked if anything ever upset him. He'd chosen to respond in terms of work. It was typical.

"Danica," he sighed, "is something bothering you?"

"Why would you think that?" Her sarcasm sailed over his head.

"You sound as though you resent my work." Still he didn't raise his voice. She wished she could have attributed that fact to Marcus's silent presence in the front seat, but she knew better. Marcus was the perfect chauffeur, trained to be blind and deaf as the situation demanded. Besides, it was raining, and the steady patter on the roof served as static to further diffuse their low-spoken words. "I've worked hard to get where I am. You, of all people, should understand that."

There it was again. She gritted her teeth. "Why me, of all people?"

"You come from a family where achievement is highly prized. Your father has worked hard for years to cement his position."

"That's right. And in doing so, he's sacrificed a good many of the finer things in life."

"I don't know about that. It seems to me he's got pretty much everything he wants."

That, in a nutshell, was what was wrong, Danica realized. It had less to do with William Marshall being satisfied than with Blake Lindsay identifying with the components of that satisfaction. She seemed to be the one marching out of step in the parade.

"Power," she sighed in defeat. "He's got power."

"Isn't that what it's all about?"

Staring at her husband's smug profile in the darkness, she knew there was no point in continuing the discussion. He didn't see the way she did; it was as simple as that. Perhaps it was her own fault, she mused. She'd married a man so like her father that she was *bound* to suffer the same frustrations she'd known growing up. A psychiatrist would have a field day. On the other hand, it didn't take a psychiatrist to explain why she'd done it. All her life she'd wanted her father's approval. Marrying Blake and being the perfect corporate wife had fallen within that realm.

How to cope. That was the issue she faced. In actuality, she'd followed Blake's formula to the letter. "You have to think clearly. You have to analyze the facts and your options. You have to make decisions and see them through."

The fact was very simply that she was involved in a marriage that gave her little reward or pleasure. The options were also simple, since she couldn't quite abide by the concept of divorce. The decisions, ah, those were harder to reach.

She rose to the occasion. First, she realized that she had to accept Blake for both his strengths and his weaknesses. What he lacked on the human side of the scale he made up for as a provider, as a man well-known and respected among his peers.

Second, she realized that she was, at some point, going to have to look for work. It might take time, both to secure a job that would conform to her life-style and then to garner the courage to confront Blake with her decision, but she was increasingly convinced as each day passed that it was the wisest course open to her.

Third and finally, she *was* going to Maine. She'd thought it all out. She wanted to be away from the city, away from the emptiness that seemed to characterize her life there. She wanted fresh air, open space, time to herself in a less prescribed environment.

She'd also thought a great deal about Michael, and specifically, her attraction to him. In the weeks since she'd seen him, she'd been able to put into perspective what she'd felt that day on the beach. She liked him very, very much. He stirred her in ways that might have been wrong if she hadn't been so committed to her marriage. True, she fantasized about him, but that was okay. The reading she'd done—and she'd done a great deal of it on the subject since that last trip north—had said that fantasizing was normal and, in its way, healthy. Put in its proper place, it could do her no harm.

Michael knew the facts of her life, that she was married, that she could never offer him more than a friendly hug or companionable hand-holding. God only knew she needed both of those things. Should she deprive herself of a very lovely, very warm, close relationship?

Her real source of protection, though, came from something that was as yet only the merest suspicion, the faintest hope. She was overdue for her period, and she'd always been punctual to the day. If she was pregnant, her problems might be solved. Not that she set great stock in Blake's attentiveness as a father—nothing he'd done in recent years as a husband had warranted such faith. But she'd be a mother, and a whole new world would be open to her.

Thus fortified, she headed for Maine on the twenty-third of June. It was a Friday morning. Blake, surprisingly enough, was accompanying her, taking the Mercedes while she drove the Audi so that he could return to Boston the following day. He'd said that he wanted to see her settled, and indeed, she'd brought along several cartons of things—clothes, a stereo, records, books—so his help was appreciated. He hadn't even suggested that Marcus do the dirty work; perhaps he'd known she'd have insisted on doing it herself given that particular choice. Then again, perhaps he felt guilty.

He was a fine caretaker; she had to say that much. And though she sensed his accompanying her was more a conciliatory gesture than anything else, she couldn't look a gift horse in the mouth.

Ironically, Blake was more satisfied than she'd ever seen him in Maine. He patiently helped her unload what she'd brought, spent several hours out on the deck with her explaining all he'd be doing back home that would keep him from joining her for several weeks at least, took her into Ogunquit for dinner, and was perfectly amiable the whole time. He made no attempt to touch her that night, and she felt no urge for him to do so, but he did kiss her sweetly before he set off the next day, and he did promise to call every few days.

For the first time his departure didn't bother her. He was going home. She felt she *was* home. This place was hers as no other house she'd ever lived in had been. In part it was because the responsibility of its care rested on her shoulders, in part because here she was fully responsible for herself. There was no maid to cook or clean or make the bed, no handyman/chauffeur to open and close windows, to bring deck chairs in from the rain, to lock up at night. She did everything herself, when and how she wanted, and she loved it. She felt confident and capable and thoroughly self-satisfied. She felt free.

The first thing she did after Blake left was to drive into town to buy food, then to stop at a local shop and pick up several pairs of jeans and some T-shirts. There was a certain perverse pleasure in wearing Kennebunkport plastered across her chest; she'd never done anything as…as plebeian before, but then, she'd never wanted to be a part of the crowd before. The chic shops she patronized in Boston and New York would never have dreamed of carrying either the knockabout sandals or no-name sneakers she bought, a fact that made these items all the more valuable to her. Moreover, she totally enjoyed the salespeople who helped her and spent a startling amount of time talking with them, such that it was nearly dark when she finally returned to the house.

Too dark to seek Michael out. And on a Saturday night…not right. After all, the man might not be married or otherwise attached, but he still had to date. He was human. Very male. Certainly sought after by any number of local women.

Hence, it was midday Sunday when she finally felt it fair to intrude upon his weekend. Donning one of her new T-shirts, the sneakers and a pair of the jeans she'd spent the previous night washing and drying no less than three times, she set out across the beach. She'd never seen his house. It was time she did.

Set at the end of a winding road in a way hers was not, the house was perched above the rocks and was sheltered by numerous clumps of pitch pines that kept it hidden from view until well after she'd passed the familiar boulders. A stairway of stone, guarded by a weathered handrail, had been etched from the rocks and led to the deck. There wasn't a back door, only a screen where the glass slider had been opened. Given the brightness of the day, she couldn't see inside.

She started across the deck, then, unsure for the first time, moistened her lips and wondered if she was being too forward. Previously Michael had done the approaching and it had been on the beach, a casual enough place for an encounter with a friend.

Then she caught herself. He *was* a friend, and had *he* been a *she*, Danica doubted she'd feel any of the hesitancy she did now. It was just going to take some getting used to—this close friendship with a man—she told herself.

Bolstered by that understanding and by the sheer excitement of seeing him again, she approached the screen, shaded her eyes from the outside glare with one hand and peered inside.

"Michael?" she called softly. She heard voices, but it was too late to turn back. "Michael?" Slightly louder. She still couldn't see a thing.

Then she did. The man himself. Approaching the screen, sliding it back, surprise and pleasure lighting his face.

"Danica!"

She smiled, feeling as pleased as he looked. "I just, uh, just wanted to say hello."

He took a caressive hold of her shoulder. "You're back."

She couldn't help but laugh. "Looks that way."

"That's great," he said softly, taking in every one of her features before slowly lowering his gaze and arching a brow in amusement. "You've been shopping."

"Uh-huh." She glanced down. "What do you think? Will I fit in?"

"You would fit in anywhere. God, you look great!" The sound came from deep in his throat, a near growl that made her believe every word contained therein.

"So do you."

He was wearing a velour robe that reached mid-thigh, and nothing else. Danica couldn't seem to drag her eyes from his legs, which were long and lean and spattered with the same tawny hair that escaped the robe at his chest.

Her appraisal was enough to startle him into realization of his disheveled state, and he swore under his breath. "Hell, I'm a mess!" Before she could argue, he held up a hand and commanded, "Wait here." He was halfway through the living room before he turned and hurried back to grab her hand and draw her into the house. When at his urging she slid into a chair, he popped a kiss on the top of her head. "I'll be right back." Then he was gone, leaving her grinning, which seemed to be a common affliction when she was with him, she mused.

His brief absence gave Danica time to look around, which she did with interest. The armchair she sat on, its mate and a matching sofa were of leather, soft, aged leather that looked rich and well-worn, and wore the haphazardly strewn Sunday paper with flair. In the center of the room stood a low table of slate that matched both the fireplace and the floor. The latter was softened by a large and handsome area rug of Scandinavian design.

Very clearly, there had been a method to the basic decor, but basic was where the method stopped. For on every table, every wall, every shelf and the mantel were diverse assort-

ments of plaques, masks, pieces of art and other memora-
bilia she guessed to have come from his travels.

Those that were within her reach she studied closely—a
limestone burial jar, an ancient elephant tusk, a copper fish
she guessed to be of Mayan design. Then she sat back and
scanned the room again, marveling that one man could have
amassed such an exotic collection.

By contrast, the small television, which rested atop the
counter separating living room from kitchen, seemed mundane. It was, she realized, the source of the voices she'd heard
when she'd first crossed the deck. But there was nothing
mundane—or so the indoctrination went—about the program that was on.

Just then Michael reappeared wearing jeans and a short-
sleeved shirt. He looked freshly showered and shaven, and his
hair was damp but combed. He looked wonderful.

"That was fast," she breathed. "I always thought it took
at least fifteen minutes for a man to shave, but I haven't been
here more than five."

"I'm sorry to have kept you waiting even that long. If I'd
known you were coming..." He grew hesitant. "I saw both
cars in the driveway and thought you'd be busy at least till
tonight."

"Blake had to be back in Boston last night. I would have
come by sooner, but I wasn't sure if you'd be free."

Her suggestion was subtle but too obvious to ignore. "I did
go out last night, but it was an early evening." He'd tried; oh,
yes, he'd tried. But no other woman seemed to measure up to
the one before him now.

Danica cast a glance at the television, which was still on. "It
looks like I've disturbed you anyway."

"Are you kidding?" Padding barefoot across the stone
floor, he flipped off the set. "I turn this on more out of habit
than anything."

"*Face the Nation*? Shame on you. No Sunday is complete
without it."

At her lightly mocking tone, he felt instant sympathy.
"That's how it is?"

"You bet. Nothing, and I do mean *nothing*, comes between my men and *Face the Nation*."

"We're not all like that," Michael said, pushing aside the business section to sit on the sofa not far from her. Then he looked back down at the paper, gathered it and several nearby sections and tossed them onto another pile on the table. "Sorry about this. Living alone and all, I get carried away."

"Don't apologize. I love the way things look."

"Now you *are* kidding."

"Uh-uh. It's refreshing." How often she used that word to describe things to do with Michael! "In my house the paper never gets a chance to be scattered. Blake keeps everything in neat piles, and if something by chance does get out of order, Mrs. Hannah is right there to straighten it." Another dig at Blake, and she felt quickly contrite. Yet she could neither apologize nor take the words back. Michael inspired an honesty in her, an impulsiveness she couldn't deny. She was just going to have to be more careful. After all, she really didn't want to malign Blake. He was her husband.

"Anyway," she sighed, looking around her, "I love your house. I've never seen it before."

"It's not that much different in design from yours."

"No, but it looks lived in."

"It looks messy, is what it does."

She shook her head. There was so much to see here; by comparison, her own house seemed stark. "Lived in, and very happily so. These are all souvenirs of your escapades?"

"Yup." When she rose from the chair and crossed the room to gently finger one of a pair of unusually shaped iron candlesticks that stood on the mantel, he explained that they were from Portugal and that he'd been studying emigration patterns when he'd found them. When she moved on to examine a hand-carved Mexican lava ball, then a pair of Majorcan grinding rollers, he told of their acquisitions, as well.

What he really wanted was to learn more about her home life, her husband, the frustrations she felt. But she was so enthused about the collection of hats on the wall, the cluster of baskets in the corner, the bronze Japanese vase on the table, that he found himself wrapped up in telling her one story, then another and another.

"You lead such an exciting life," she breathed, returning to sink down into the chair at last. Her face was glowing, as though for that little bit of time she'd lived the excitement with him.

He knew then that that was what he wanted her to do, though he knew that life with her would be exciting in very different kinds of ways.

"It looks like you've been all around the world!" she exclaimed.

"Almost. There are still some places I'd like to see." He paused. "You must have done your own share of traveling."

She shrugged. "Some, but to none of the out-of-the-way places you've been."

"You didn't travel with your parents?"

"Only to vacation spots—the Caribbean, Hawaii, Hilton Head." Once a year, the mandatory family jaunt. "When it came to the truly exotic places, they went alone."

"Why? Surely it would have been educational for you."

"You'd think so," she mused, "but they kept me involved in other activities and assumed I wouldn't mind."

"What other activities?"

"School." She didn't yet want to go into her tennis years, when every free minute had been spent on the court. She'd failed her parents' expectations there, and to a certain extent, she believed in that failure herself.

Her answer had been pat and was theoretically without argument, yet Michael wasn't ready to let the subject of her past drop. "Do you travel much with your husband?"

Her eyes clouded then. "I used to. He'd take me on business trips—in this country and abroad—and we'd have a few days to ourselves when the business was done. Lately, though, he's been so busy that it's just as well he goes alone."

"He doesn't have time for you," Michael stated quietly.

Danica opened her mouth to disagree, then closed it. "You have a way of hitting home, Michael Buchanan," she murmured.

He reached over to lightly stroke her cheek. "I don't mean to hurt, but something's obviously not right." They both knew they were dealing with the present now. "What man in his right mind would leave his wife on a Saturday night."

"It was another political thing, and I'm very much in overload when it comes to those. So it was my fault as much as his. If I'd been agreeable, I'd have waited for Monday to drive up."

"Then he wouldn't have come at all."

She didn't deny that possibility. "He really was helpful. I wanted to bring lots of things with me. He helped carry them in and put them away."

Michael swallowed the sarcastic remark that was on the tip of his tongue. He knew that to openly criticize Blake at this point might endanger his relationship with Danica. As it was, Blake was the major obstacle standing between them. If that was ever to change, Danica had to be the instigator, not Michael.

Besides, something else interested him, something written between the lines. "How long are you up for this time?" he asked with studied nonchalance. He'd had dreams, and in those dreams he'd made plans. He was tired of being alone. There was lots to do during a summer in Maine. He'd settle, albeit regretfully, for a platonic friendship if it meant he might spend more time with Danica.

Her smile sent his hopes soaring. "The summer. The whole summer."

"The *whole* summer?"

"Uh-huh. I promised Blake that I'd go back for a day or two now and again, but otherwise I'm here to stay."

"Will he be up much?"

"He's very involved with the convention—he and my father, both. It's important that he be around. He said he'd make it whenever he could, but—" she rolled her eyes "—I'm not sure how often that will be."

"Was he upset with your coming?"

She crinkled her nose in a gesture that might have answered his question either way. "I think it'll be easier for him with me up here. He knows that I'm not as enamored with politics as he is.''

"Strange, given who you are." He thought. "Then again, not strange at all. Rebelling at last?"

She grinned. "It's about time, don't you think?"

"I think," he stated with care, "that it's good you're beginning to think of yourself. I also think that I couldn't be happier." He paused. "Will Blake mind if I draft his wife to go to the flea market with me today?"

Danica answered his roundabout invitation by beaming. "The flea market! Fun! Are you looking for something special?"

"Just a few hours of relaxation, and it wouldn't be the same alone."

"You may not believe this, but I've never been to a flea market."

She was right; he didn't believe it. *"Never?"*

"Well, maybe an open-air market in London or Venice. But those were different, and they were very much souvenir-hunting excursions. I've never been to a real country flea market, and certainly never just for the sake of enjoyment."

"Well, pretty lady," Michael drawled, rolling to his feet and drawing her up with him, "you're in for an afternoon to remember." He was holding her hand, looking down at her, and suddenly he paused, all amusement gone. Her cheeks were flushed, her violet eyes filled with excitement and softness and warmth. He swallowed hard and squeezed her hand. "Danica, *will* Blake mind?"

"Blake doesn't know."

"You haven't told him about me?" Unable to resist the lure of flaxen silk, he stroked her hair. It was soft and shimmering beneath his fingers.

Giving a nearly imperceptible head shake, she held her breath. She was totally aware of the man before her and knew she should turn and run but was rooted to the spot.

"Why not?" he asked very softly.

"You're *my* friend," she whispered. "Blake rules the rest of my life. You're *mine*."

Michael closed his eyes and moaned. His hand fell to her neck, and he lightly kneaded the soft skin there. "Oh, God—" his deep voice trembled, as did his arm "—I'm not sure if I can do this."

"Do what?" she breathed, though she knew. She felt; she needed; she wanted. And she feared. She feared because what she craved was wrong, forbidden. Still, one part of her had to hear the words. She had to hear that she was wanted, needed in return.

Framing her face with both hands, he looked at her then. She felt the touch of his gaze flow through her like sweet honey, momentarily healing all those bruised and lonely spots left by a lifetime of need. "I'm not sure I can be just your friend, Dani. You mean very, very much to me."

She was thrilled; she was scared. Her eyes told of her dilemma, but before she could speak, Michael did.

"I need more. I want to hold you, to touch you. Right now, I want to kiss you."

She wanted it, too, more than she'd ever have believed possible. Blake had never stirred her this way, and she felt a sudden anger at what she'd missed. But the anger was fleeting because Michael was here with her now, making her forget . . . almost.

"We can't," she gasped, feeling torn apart inside.

"I know. Which is what makes it so unbearable." Swearing softly, he strode away from her, pausing before the slider, propping his hands low on his hips and dropping his head forward. He was the image of dejection, and Danica felt a new kind of pain.

She started to approach. "Michael . . ."

He held up a hand, though he didn't turn. "I have to ask you something." The hand that had held her off now rubbed the back of his neck. "Why did you come here today?"

"I . . . I wanted to see you?"

"Did you know how I felt?"

"I thought . . . I thought . . ."

He whirled around, jaw tight. "Didn't you know after last time that I wanted more? Didn't you feel it yourself?" Her eyes held the guilt that was answer in itself. "What did you think was going to happen?"

Insides churning, she tried to gather her thoughts. "I was looking forward to seeing you. I thought we . . . we could talk like we did before, maybe . . . see each other from time to time." She wrapped her arms around her waist in a gesture of self-defense. It hurt when Michael spoke to her this way, even though she knew he was justified in doing so.

He persisted, his ultimate need at the moment being to air all that had been festering in his mind for weeks. "But what did you think would come of it all? Didn't you wonder how long I'd be able to take being with you without . . . without . . ." He didn't need to finish. He'd said it before, and the words only made the wanting that much greater.

"No," she whispered, frowning in faint surprise. "I never wondered that. I guess I assumed that the fact of my marriage to Blake would be enough to keep us both in line." She paused, then heard herself go on. She needed to air things, too. "I guess I was thinking of myself. You're something new to me, Michael. With you I act differently, feel differently." Unable to face him, she lowered her gaze. "I felt something last time. I think I've felt things from the beginning." She looked up and went on with more urgency. "But there's so much more. I can talk to you. I can relax, be myself. You don't expect; you simply accept. And I need that." Her eyes filled with tears. "I've never had it, and I want it so badly. I suppose, after last time, one part of me knew I was playing with fire by coming up here for the summer, by coming over here today. But I couldn't help myself! I swear I couldn't! You have to believe that! I couldn't help . . . myself . . ."

He was before her in two strides, brushing away the tears that trickled slowly down her cheeks. "Shhhh. Don't cry. Oh, sweetheart, don't cry."

Somehow she was in his arms then, and he was holding her tightly, rocking her gently from side to side while she clung to his neck. Her silent sobs cut through him, paining him nearly as much as her closeness did, but differently.

"Shhhh. I believe you. I believe you, and I feel the same. If I was smart, I'd stay away from you, but I can't. Do you understand that?'' He held her back only enough so that he could see her face. ''I can't, Dani. As God is my witness, I need you.'' He hauled her back against him, pressing her face to his throat. His own was tight. It was a minute before he could speak. ''I don't want to do anything to destroy your marriage, but I can't leave you alone. I guess that puts us back where we started…. Except—'' he pressed his lips to her hair ''—now you know how I feel. Does that scare you?''

She nodded, but all the while she was savoring the clean male scent of his skin. ''It also makes me feel very good,'' she confessed in a tiny voice. ''I'm being selfish again.''

''Not selfish,'' he murmured against her hair, ''just realistic. And honest. I want you to be that with me. Always. And I may be condemning myself to a hell of sorts, but I'm glad you feel the way you do. At least you'll understand when I need to touch you from time to time.'' His voice grew gruff with determination. ''I'll be damned if I'm going to deny either of us the other's company. Not when that son of a bitch could care less.''

Danica was the one to draw back then. ''That's unfair. He doesn't know.''

''*Would* he care?''

She took a quick breath to respond with what would have been an easy lie, then held it. Michael had asked for honesty. This she could give him, when there was so much she couldn't. Slowly she released her breath. ''I…I'm really not sure. There are an awful lot of things about Blake that I'm not sure of anymore. But I married him willingly, and he's got many strong points. He's never been the jealous type—''

''Has he ever had reason before?''

''No, but—''

''I think you should tell him about us.''

''About *us*? You make it sound like we're having an affair, when—''

''That could be the case if we're not careful. Knowing that Blake knows we're friends, knowing that he knows we spend time together, might just help us be careful. Hell, Dani, we've got to do *something*.''

His look of helplessness was so endearing that it gave her a measure of strength. She couldn't help but smile. "Self-control. That's all it takes. Self-control. As the tea bag says, self-control is the magic carpet to salvation."

"I drink coffee," he grumped, then tossed his head toward the door. "Come on. If we don't leave now, we'll miss the best buys."

AS IT HAPPENED, they bought nothing but ice-cream cones and time, the former to satisfy one appetite, the latter to put others on hold. It was evening by the time they returned, and they were both pleasantly tired.

Danica, for one, felt more at peace with herself than she had in a while. "Michael?" She'd just opened her front door. "There was a reason why I decided to spend the whole summer here."

"You mean aside from wanting me to distraction?" he teased over her shoulder.

She elbowed his ribs, then turned to face him. "I need to think. The last few years have been frustrating for me in many ways, and I'm not sure it all has to do with Blake." She was giving Blake the benefit of the doubt. After all, it took two to make a marriage work. Avoiding his gaze, she continued softly. "I need a break from my life as it's been. I have to think about where I'm going. There's always the possibility of my getting a job; we've talked about that before. But—" she hesitated for just a minute, then knew she had to go on "—there's also the possibility that I might be pregnant."

Almost timidly she raised her eyes, but Michael's face was shadowed, his expression hidden by the night.

"Pregnant." He breathed the word in near awe and reached out to touch her, then stilled his hands in midair and gave a short laugh.

"Michael?"

He shook his head. "Absurd. I swear I'm losing my marbles. My first reaction was pure joy, until I realized it's not even my kid."

"You can still be excited."

The hurt in her voice brought him to his senses. He did touch her then, taking both of her shoulders, smoothing his hands over her back. "I am, Dani, I am." Dipping his head, he kissed her softly on the mouth. "It's what you want, isn't it?"

"Very much."

"Then I'm happy, no, thrilled for you. But jealous. I have to say that.... You don't know for sure?"

"It's too early. I'll see a doctor in another couple of weeks."

"Are you feeling all right?"

"Fine. I mean, it's too early to feel sick or anything. The calendar is the only thing that says it might be so."

"Blake must be pleased."

"Blake doesn't know." It was the second time she'd said those words that day, and she felt slightly sheepish. "I didn't want to get his hopes up. We've waited too long." From sheepish to guilty. She'd implied that Blake *would* be pleased, when, in truth, she wasn't sure. No, she amended, he would be pleased, but in his own inimitably dispassionate way.

"Then, I'm really pleased, on his behalf and my own. And I'm glad you told me, Dani." *Before* Blake. It was the little boy in him being perverse. "Now I'll know to be careful with you. No wrestling, no tackle football..."

She gave a soft laugh. "Thank you. I'd appreciate that." What she appreciated was the sentiment behind his teasing. Though she knew she was healthy and strong, and that nothing could dislodge a healthy baby, if indeed one grew within her, Michael made her feel special. But then, he always did. It was one of the reasons she was so drawn to him. "Well," she sighed, "on that note I'd better get in. It's been a wonderful day, Michael. Thank you."

"Thank *you*. I'll see you later in the week?"

She smiled. They'd already talked about the work he had to do, as well as about the reading and sunning and relaxing she intended to do. "I'd like that." She stepped into the house. "Get a lot of writing done, you hear?"

"I hear. Lock that door good, you hear?"

"I hear. Good night, Michael."

"'Night, Dani." He was halfway down the path when he couldn't resist a final note. "Sweet dreams!" he called, wishing the same for himself but somehow fearing it would be a different kind of dream he'd have.

Oblivious to his lascivious thoughts, Danica watched him back from the drive, then closed the door softly and locked it tight.

BLAKE CALLED on Wednesday night. "Danica?"

"Blake! Hi!"

"Did I get you from somewhere? The phone rang eight times before you picked it up."

"I was on the deck. The surf is wilder than usual and I didn't hear the ring at first."

"Bad weather?"

"Not yet. But it looks like it's going to pour. How is everything?"

"Just fine."

". . . Anything new at the office?"

"Not that I can think of."

". . . I assume the party went well on Saturday."

"Uh-huh. They were asking for you."

"Oh?"

"You sound surprised."

"A little. I never thought I was noticed at those things."

"Come on. There are always women there for you to talk with."

". . . Yes. Right. Well, I'm sure they had each other."

There was a brief silence from the other end of the line. Then: "So, how are you doing?"

"Really well. I finished Vidal's *Lincoln.* It was interesting." She paused to give Blake an opportunity to ask her about it. When he didn't, she went on. "And I've started Ludlum's latest. I'm not sure I like it as well as some of his others, but it may just be that I'm having trouble getting into it."

"So, you've been spending your time reading."

"Not all of it. I drive into town every morning. I'm thinking of getting a bike."

"Isn't it awfully hilly there for a bike?"

"Nah. It'd be great exercise."

"I suppose. And since you're not dancing—"

"But I am! I put music on and go through the routine from my class once a day. That was one of the reasons I wanted a stereo up here. Regarding the bike, though, it'd be fun as well as practical. With the summer crowds here, it's sometimes hard to find a parking space in town. I feel guilty taking the car when it's so close. It can't be more than five miles into town and back."

"What do you do in town? The shops don't change that much from day to day, do they?"

"No. But the people are lovely. I got to talking with a woman who owns the sportswear shop. She's fascinating. She's got a Ph.D. in biology and worked in research for six years before deciding to chuck it all and move up here. Her husband is an artist and has a gallery down the block from her shop. I bought one of his paintings, by the way. It's a sea-scape, but very modern. It looks great in the bedroom."

"Sounds good."

" . . . Anyway, Sara and I had lunch together today. It was nice. Oh, and I'm working up the beginnings of a tan."

"Be careful with that. Too much sun is bad for the skin."

"I use lotion."

"Make sure it's Factor 15. I wouldn't want you to be all wrinkled and leathery by the end of the summer."

"I won't be all wrinkled and leathery. I just may look healthy."

"Good. Listen, Pook, I've got to run. We're meeting to-night with a new account. Harlan's giving me the high sign."

"You're still at the office?" It was seven o'clock. Some-how she'd assumed he'd be calling from home.

"Not for long. I'm on my way." His words were directed as much to the man standing in the room, Danica guessed, as to her.

"Go ahead. Good luck with your meeting. And give Har-lan my best." She couldn't stand Harlan Magnusson, with his French-cut suits, dark curly hair and wire-rimmed glasses. He was always moving and he made her nervous. Still, he was her husband's right-hand man.

"Will do. We'll talk more another time. Bye-bye."

IT WASN'T UNTIL the following Tuesday that he called again, and the conversation opened along similar lines. Yes, he was fine. No, there was nothing new at the office. Yes, she was fine. No, she wasn't bored.

"The Fourth of July was fun up here, Blake. I'm sorry you couldn't make it."

"You know that I had to be in Philadelphia. We discussed it when I drove you up there."

"Yes. Did everything go well?"

"Just fine."

"I'm glad.... There was a fireworks display here. I went with one of our neighbors." She broached the subject with a nonchalance she didn't feel, but she realized that Michael had been right that she tell Blake of their friendship. It wasn't so much that she saw it as a deterrent to physical involvement; since she and Michael had aired their feelings, they'd seemed able to keep things well under control. It was more a matter of accounting for her time, a good deal of which was spent with him. It was also a matter of being covered should she run into someone she knew when she was with Michael. It seemed only fair that if Blake was to get a report back that his wife was seen with another man, he'd be able to say with confidence, "Oh, yes. I know. He's a good friend."

"You've met the neighbors?" Blake asked now.

"Several." It was the truth. She'd taken walks by herself on the roads near the house and had encountered various of the homeowners nearby. "There's a retired banker and his wife— Kilsythe?"

"City Trust. I've heard of him."

"And an anesthesiologist and his family. The one I went to the fireworks display with is a writer."

"Oh?"

"A historian. You'll know his family. Buchanan."

There was a moment's silence. "Mmmm. Watch out for him."

"Oh, he's safe. He doesn't have anything to do with his family's papers."

"Still, you can never be too careful."

She paused, about to argue more until she realized the futility of it. "I'll be careful.... Blake? We're still on for Saturday night, aren't we?" They had a long-standing commitment to attend a movie premiere, a benefit for the Heart Association.

"Of course. When can I expect you?"

"I thought I'd come in on Friday." She had made a doctor's appointment for that afternoon, though as yet she didn't want to say anything to Blake. "I'll drive back Sunday. Is that okay?"

"Sounds fine. I'll see you then."

"Okay. Bye-bye."

FRIDAY AFTERNOON Danica learned that she was indeed pregnant.

Chapter Six

DANICA GAVE BLAKE the good word shortly after he arrived home from work on Friday evening. He was surprised, then pleased, and insisted on calling her parents immediately. It was easier said than done, though Danica might have predicted that. It seemed the Marshalls had left their Connecticut home, where Blake had expected they'd be, to spend the weekend with a congressman friend of William's at a horse farm in Kentucky. After a series of forwarding calls, which Blake endured with characteristic patience, he eventually got through and passed on the news with a pride suggesting that he'd accomplished the deed on his own.

For the most part, Danica let him do the talking. She couldn't help but feel that he was more pleased with the enhancement of his own image than with the fact itself. But she was loathe to criticize, when she, too, felt a little of the same. Her father was gratified; in his eyes, her status soared, and that mattered to her. Still, deep down inside, her greatest joy was in the prospect of holding a baby in her arms, of being needed by a helpless infant, of loving it and having it love her in return.

It was on the drive back to Maine on Sunday afternoon that the joy emerged full force. She couldn't keep from smiling. The prospect of her future had, with the doctor's pronouncement, taken a turn for the better. For the first time in months she felt optimistic. And she couldn't wait to tell Michael.

Unfortunately, he wasn't home. She let the phone ring for a while, dialed right back on the chance that she might have misdialed the first time, then tried again five minutes later, thinking that he might have been in the shower.

Undaunted, she changed from her city sundress into a tank top and shorts and walked the beach for a while, grinning, sighing happily, edging closer and closer to Michael's house in the hope that he'd return and saunter out on the deck. In time she stationed herself on the boulder she'd come to think of as theirs, with the confidence that Michael would find her.

Sure enough, not long after, as the sun dipped low behind her, she heard his call and saw him trotting toward her down the beach. He came to a prolonged halt on the sand beneath her.

"You look like the cat that swallowed the canary," he said, eyes narrowed in speculation.

Beaming from ear to ear, she nodded. "I saw the doctor on Friday." She didn't have to explain.

"And...it's true?"

She could only grin and nod again.

"Hey, Dani, that's great!" He made his way up the rocks to where she sat and hugged her soundly. "That's great!" Fortunately, he'd had time to get used to the idea. While on the one hand he regretted that a child would be another tie binding Danica to Blake Lindsay, on the other he was thrilled for her. He knew how much she wanted a baby. "When's it due?"

"In February. I'm just six weeks pregnant."

"And the doctor gave you a clean bill of health?"

"Yup. I've got vitamins to take, but that's it."

"How about Blake?"

She grinned. "No vitamins. His job is done."

"Not a very modern view, but that wasn't what I meant anyway. How did he take the news?"

"Happily. He called my folks, then his." He'd done the latter only reluctantly, and then, not until Sunday morning. Danica had never been able to understand his relationship with his family. His parents and only sibling, a brother, were of solid middle-class stock living and working in Detroit. Though Blake sent them money from time to time, he seemed to want little else to do with them. Danica was the one to send birthday and anniversary cards, not to mention keeping after

Blake to call them. She felt badly; she'd only seen them four times in the eight years of her marriage.

"I assume they were all duly excited," Michael speculated.

"Uh-huh. It was amazing. My mother grew really concerned. She went on and on about what I should and shouldn't do and how to take care of myself.... She never did that when I was a child."

"You knew all the answers then?" he teased.

"Not quite. I had to find them for myself, though. Mom was never there."

"Of course she was. You're exaggerating."

"Don't I wish. In fact, as I remember, I did an awful *lot* of wishing back then on this very topic. Mom was always in and out as my father's schedule demanded. She never seemed to be there when I needed her." She grew more pensive. "I remember when I had the chicken pox. I was seven at the time and my father was running for his first term. God, was I sick. The only thing I wanted was for her to hold me. She was campaigning with him, of course. So I just burrowed under the covers and . . . and itched."

Michael ached for her. "There must have been someone with you."

"Oh, yes. We had a housekeeper. She was very efficient, a good cook, and she cleaned beautifully. Unfortunately, at the time I couldn't bear the thought of food and I could have cared less about a clean house. What I wanted was my mother."

He could understand it. He remembered being sick himself, having his mother sit with him, read to him, dote on him. There had been times when he'd actually welcomed a cold, just to have that time alone with her. It had been very special, something he'd always remember.

Thinking of the very different experience Danica had had, he had to struggle to curb his anger. "I'm sorry," he said at last.

She flashed him a sad smile. "It wasn't your fault."

"I know, but still, you're right. A mother should be there. I'm sorry you had to weather the storm alone."

"Well, I suppose it was good training. I got used to it, even though I always wished things were different. They will be for my child, that's for sure." She sighed. "Which brings us back to what I was saying. Among other things, my mother told me to stay put in Boston. She thinks I'm crazy to be coming up here."

Michael rolled his eyes. "How did you answer that?"

"I *wanted* to say that it was none of her business, that she had no right to tell me what to do at this late date."

"But you didn't."

"No, I didn't. In her own rather bizarre way, she does love me. I'm sure she's legitimately concerned, and I suppose I should be grateful after so many years of going without. I told her that the doctor recommended fresh air and exercise. I also told her that I wanted the baby very badly and that she'd have to trust that I wouldn't do anything to endanger its health."

"How about Blake? Does he have any second thoughts about your being alone up here now?"

"Blake? Oh, Blake echoed Mom's sentiments after I'd hung up, but I don't think he's really worried. I'm not an invalid, for heaven's sake."

"Still, I can understand his concern. You are alone here."

"I have you," she said with a teasing glint in her eye.

He returned the look, though his own teasing was strictly on the surface. "True. . . . Is this new?" He fingered the gold necklace at her neck; it was a delicate serpentine chain with a diamond embedded at its center. Of course, her skin fascinated him even more, warm and soft where his fingers brushed it.

"Blake gave it to me on Saturday. He . . . felt the occasion called for something." Blake was very good at that, she knew, very proper. As forgetful as he was when it came to his family in Detroit, he had a set image in his mind of how he should treat his wife. There was jewelry on each anniversary, a fur or other piece of expensive clothing on each birthday, a bouquet of flowers on Valentine's Day. Of course, Danica would have been just as happy with a quiet dinner for the two of them on any of those occasions, but she was never consulted.

"Not bad," Michael mused.

"Not necessary," she argued but left it at that.

He accepted her curtness, which was a statement in itself, and leaned back. "Funny, you don't look pregnant." Given good excuse, he raked her length, admiring the firm thrust of her small breasts, the slimness of her waist and hips, the shapeliness of her legs.

"Thank God for that! If I looked pregnant at this early stage, just imagine how I'd look six months down the road."

"You'll look wonderful." He met her gaze without hesitation. "You'll be a beautiful mother."

She smiled, feeling self-conscious but pleased that Michael had thought to say such words. "Thank you," she murmured. "You're very good for my ego."

"Blake doesn't say things like that?"

"Oh, he does. But . . . he's big on physical fitness and I'm going to be pretty fat in a while." It had occurred to her that Blake might not be terribly attracted to a whale, but then he didn't seem to be terribly attracted to her now. She sensed he would use her pregnancy to keep his distance, sensed he'd probably be relieved to have the excuse. When she'd not so subtly informed him that the doctor hadn't ruled out any activity, he'd simply nodded.

"Pregnant women have an aura about them," Michael said softly. "They glow from within. My sister-in-law says that she loves being pregnant, that she feels she's doing what God intended, that she's always proud as punch of her belly."

Danica grinned. "No wonder she and Brice have five kids."

"They should. They're wonderful parents. Brice may work with my father, but before he agreed to do it, he set down certain rules. He wants to be home most nights and weekends, and he is."

"Your father accepted that?"

"He had no choice. The options were either that or have none of his children there to take over when he decides to retire. He may be a tyrant, but he does love us. I guess he's finally accepted that we're adults."

"I wish my parents could do that," she murmured.

"It took a while, Dani, and lots of fights. In Brice's case, he knew what he wanted and he stood firm. Some day you'll be able to do that."

MICHAEL'S WORDS ECHOED in Danica's mind long after she and Michael had gone their separate ways that night. She wondered if the day would come when she'd have the courage she sought. She was proud that she'd stuck to her guns about spending the summer in Maine; it was a step in the right direction. Then again, perhaps it had been a matter of options after all. The alternative to being in Maine had simply become unacceptable to her; hence she'd held her ground. Perhaps in the future other choices would be as clear-cut. Now that she was expecting a child, the issue of working was temporarily on hold. She prayed that once she was a mother herself, she'd find the strength to stand up for other things, to put her father's approval in perspective, to make the best decisions for both herself and her child.

Her child. Not Blake's. Strange that she should be thinking of it that way. Strange, and sad, but realistic. If Blake was going to prove to be the same kind of father her own had been, she'd just have to be that much more attentive a mother. *That* was something to which she was fully committed.

"DANICA, MAYBE THIS ISN'T such a good idea..."

"Why ever not?"

"Well, you could fall or... or be hit by a passing car. The roads around here are pretty rutted at spots."

"Come on, Michael. You were so excited last week. You agreed yourself that it'd be good exercise."

"That was before your pregnancy was confirmed."

"And the doctor wants me to exercise."

"So dance." He'd dropped by her house unannounced one day and had caught her in leotard and tights. Shyly she'd explained what she'd been doing, and though she'd staunchly refused to give him a demonstration, he knew that in action she'd be as graceful as a prima ballerina. As it was, he couldn't shake the image of how gorgeous she'd looked with her hair stuck behind her ears and the finest sheen of moisture on her skin.

"I do dance, but I want to be outside. You bike all the time. Are the roads too rutted for you?"

"I'm a man."

She scowled. "You're a chauvinist." Strangely, though, she wasn't angry. Similar words coming from Blake would have riled her, for she would have felt he was being condescending. There was none of that feeling with Michael. Rather, he seemed to be genuinely concerned for her well-being.

She waved toward the young man who worked at the bike store, then turned a bright smile on Michael. "I've made up my mind. Now, is this the right one, or do you think the blue one would be better?"

"Red. By all means. You'll be more visible."

"That's not what I—"

"For safety's sake, Dani. Please. And you've got to get a helmet and a reflective vest."

"I hadn't planned on riding at night."

"Indulge me," he pleaded with a sigh.

It did the trick. She bought the best helmet the store carried, a reflective vest that she doubted she'd ever wear, and a T-shirt with the name of the bicycle she'd bought emblazoned on its front. The last she purchased with glee, finding as much pleasure in Michael's heavenward glance as in the prospect of wearing the shirt itself. In truth, Michael savored her glee nearly as much as he looked forward to biking with her.

Little did he know what the sight of her riding directly ahead of him would do. Her lithe body, back bent against the wind, hands propped low on the handlebars, firm bottom rocking gently from side to side as she pedaled, shook him. More than once he missed a rut in the road himself and nearly fell. It was sweet, sweet torture.

He had no way of knowing that the torture wasn't one-sided. Danica was as aware of him when they rode together, of the way his shoulders bunched when he leaned forward, of the way the veins in his forearms stood out, of the way his skin-tight pants molded his muscled thighs to perfection. She was

grateful that she most often rode ahead where she didn't have
to be constantly tempted. And she was grateful, in wholly new
ways as the week passed, that she was pregnant.

It was too easy to pretend that she and Michael were together in every sense of the word. The fetus within her was a
reminder of the man who had sired it. And Lord knew she
needed reminders. In the six days since she'd left Boston,
Blake hadn't called once.

ON SUNDAY EVENING she phoned home only to learn from
Mrs. Hannah that Blake was in Toronto and was expected
back the following day. She was hurt that she'd had to learn
this from the housekeeper and embarrassed when Mrs. Hannah had seemed surprised that she hadn't known. Covering
as best she could, she hung up the phone and stewed.

Fortunately, Michael was working all day Monday; otherwise she feared he'd sense her mood and that, with little
coaxing, she'd spill her marital woes in his lap. Instinct told
her not to do that. Instinct . . . and loyalty to Blake.

When Blake did call on Monday night, she couldn't hide
her frustration. "I didn't know you were going to Toronto."

"I thought I'd mentioned it."

"No. And I felt like a fool learning it from Mrs. Hannah.
She must have some great idea of how close we are."

"She's the housekeeper. It's not her place to pass judgment. Besides, she and Marcus have been with me for more
than ten years. She knows that I travel a lot."

He had deftly avoided the issue, Danica mused. "Still, I'm
your wife," she argued quietly. "I should have known."

"At the time *I* found out, I wasn't sure you'd be in."

"You could have had your secretary call and give me the
message. Would that have been so difficult?"

"Honestly, Danica, you're making too much of this. It was
a last-minute trip."

"It's always a last-minute trip."

"You know that it's business."

"It's always business," she murmured, but she was beginning to feel like a shrew. Determinedly she gentled her voice.
"When will it be pleasure, Blake? I'd really like you to come

up. In another two weeks you'll be off to St. Louis for the convention. Won't I see you before then?''

There was a pause and a shuffling of papers in the background. ''I could try to make it this weekend.''

She had the strangest feeling that she was being shuffled along with the papers, categorized, slotted, finally and reluctantly squeezed into her husband's tight schedule. It wasn't the nicest of feelings. For that matter, though, it wasn't totally new.

''I'd like that,'' she said in an even tone.

''I'll have to do some work while I'm there,'' he cautioned.

''Of course. I understand.''

''Okay. Then I'll plan on it. Saturday and Sunday.''

Friday through Sunday was too much to ask. ''Great. I'll see you then?''

He confirmed it once more and neatly wound up the conversation. Only after she'd hung up the phone did Danica realize that he hadn't even asked if she felt well.

MICHAEL WAS EXACTLY what she needed when he breezed in excitedly the next morning. ''Are you busy?''

She cast a glance back at the kitchen table where she'd been seated before the doorbell had rung. ''Just writing a letter.'' To Reggie at the hotel where her itinerary said she'd be staying.

''Can it wait?''

''Sure. What's—'' He had her arm and was propelling her through the door. ''Michael, I'm not dressed!''

''What do you mean, you're not dressed?'' He darted a look—darting was all he dared allow himself—at her T-shirt and cutoffs. ''You look great!''

''But these shorts are . . . are too tight . . .''

He did take a look then and grinned. ''They're fantastic. You're as slim as ever.''

She blushed. ''I washed them so many times to make them look faded that they shrank more than I expected they would.'' He couldn't see that the snap was undone since it was hidden beneath her shirt, but she felt uncomfortable. ''Give

me a second.'' Dashing back into the house before he could
object, she quickly changed into a more comfortable pair of
pleated shorts and a stylish jersey. ''Where are we going,
anyway?'' she asked with a smile as she rejoined him on the
front walk.

He was smiling, too. ''You'll see.''

Throughout the fifteen-minute drive she tried repeatedly
to wheedle their destination from him, but he was clearly enjoying his secret. He was excited about something, and she
sensed it went beyond the mere fact of the mystery.

When he pulled into the drive of an old Victorian house in
Wells, she was no closer to an answer. When a large Labrador retriever bounded out to greet them, she was still
stumped. Moments later, though, after they'd shaken hands
with a gentle-faced woman who led them to the rear of the
house, she understood. There in the backyard, toddling round
and about two towheaded children, were four of the sweetest
strawberry-blond puppies she'd ever seen.

''Michael,'' Danica breathed, ''*look* at them.''

''I am. I am. Are they wonderful?''

''Oh, yes.'' Slipping to her knees beside the children, she
reached out to touch the small, trembling body of one of the
puppies. ''Are these yours?'' she asked the child nearest her,
a little girl, who, though shy, managed to nod. ''How old are
they?''

''Six weeks,'' her brother answered, clearly the older and
bolder of the two. ''My mom says it's time to find homes for
them. We're keeping one, though.''

''Jasper,'' the little girl murmured.

Danica leaned closer to her. ''Jasper?''

''That one.'' The child pointed to one of the puppies,
amazing Danica with her ability to differentiate one tawny
bundle from the next.

''He's a sweetheart,'' Danica said. ''You've made a good
choice.''

''What about *you*?'' Michael asked with soft excitement,
coming to squat by Danica's side. ''Any preference?''

''They're all precious, Michael. I couldn't possibly choose
between them, much less tell them apart.'' The last was mut-

tered out of the corner of her mouth, lest she offend the children.

"Well, I can." Leaning forward, Michael scooped up one of the puppies and held him at eye level. "This is the one I want."

"How do you know?"

He shrugged. "Instinct. Something tells me he'll love to run along the beach when he gets bigger." He winked at Danica, then turned to the children. "Does this one have a name?"

"Magpie," the little girl announced in a wispy voice that trembled. Large, sad eyes darted from the puppy to Michael and back.

Michael knelt again, shifting the puppy to lie snugly on his arm. "Magpie," he repeated in a gentle tone. "That's an unusual name for a dog."

The little girl thrust out her chin. It trembled, too. "I have a doll named Magpie."

"You do?"

"And a duck," her brother injected with a hint of disgust.

"He's stuffed," the little girl added, ignoring her brother.

"Ahhhhh. So you like the name Magpie."

The child nodded with such solemnity that Michael had to force himself not to grin. He sensed she wasn't looking forward to parting with any one of the dogs.

Settling down on the lawn cross-legged before her, he rested his elbows on his knees and spoke softly, confidentially. "I have a favorite name, too. Y' see, when I was a little boy, I had this monkey." When the child's eyes widened, he quickly explained. "Not a real one, mind you. I don't think my mother would have cared for that. This one was like your duck. I called him Rusty because of his color."

The little girl thought about that for a minute. "Rusty's a nice name," she said at last. "What happened to him?"

"He was my best friend for years. After a while he got so worn-looking that my mom started patching him up."

"Then what happened."

"After a while you couldn't really tell he was a monkey anymore. Y' know what he looked like?" The child shook her head. Michael lowered his voice even more. "He looked like a puppy. At least that's what I thought, but maybe that was because I wanted a puppy so badly."

"Did you ever get one?"

"Yup. I loved him to pieces, too. But now I'm grown up and I live by myself, and I could really use a dog to keep me company." He gently scratched the warm ears of the puppy on his arm. "Do you think this little fellow would do that?"

The little girl gave a one-shouldered shrug. Her lip began to quiver.

"What if I promised to bring him back to see you from time to time?"

Again the child gave his question thought, finally whispering with the most tenative of hopes, "Would you do that?"

"If you'd like. That way you'd know he's happy and well."

Danica, who'd been watching and listening to the exchange, felt her throat grow tight. She'd never seen Michael with a child before, but he was wonderful. He'd been attuned to the little girl's sadness and, without patronizing her in any way, had managed to ease it somewhat. It was but another thing to add to the list of qualities she admired in the man.

An hour later, with the back of the Blazer loaded with puppy supplies and the object of their use lying asleep in Danica's lap, she mentioned it. "You were terrific with that little girl, Michael."

"It was easy. She was sweet."

"Still, you handled her well.... Did you really have a monkey named Rusty?"

Michael's neck grew pink. "Ummm."

"And it got worn out?"

"Ummm."

"What did finally happen to it?"

There was a pause, then: "My mother threw him out." When Danica made a sympathetic sound, he rushed on. "It was only a toy. I'd outgrown it."

"I sometimes wonder if we ever outgrow toys like that. They represent an important part of our childhood. It's sad...the parting."

He shot her a curious glance. "You sound like you've had the experience."

"Mine wasn't the same as yours, but yes. I had a doll. I was probably closer to her than to my mother. I had to leave her when I went off to boarding school."

"Wasn't she waiting for you when you got home?"

Danica shook her head and gently stroked the puppy's soft fur. "My room had been done over into a teenager's room. Mom discarded her along with the canopy bed, the candy-cane wallpaper and the lollipop mirror. She had wanted to surprise me with what had been done to the room. Fortunately, she wasn't there when I saw it. I cried for hours." She laughed. "Maybe it's best that way. You know, zip, gone. Brief period of mourning. Done."

"Will you do it that way for your child?"

"No!" Her response had been instant. Now she softened her voice. "No. I think I'd like decisions like that to be joint ones. In any event, I hope I'll be a little more sensitive to my child's needs. Childhood is short. Often it's rushed all the more. I don't want to do that."

Looking over at her, Michael felt a sudden swell of sadness, and love. Sadness for all she'd missed in life, love for what she was in spite of it. She was going to make a wonderful mother. He only wished it was his child she'd be mothering.

As PROMISED, Blake came on Saturday morning. As warned, he brought work with him. By Sunday afternoon when he pulled out of the drive, Danica wondered why he'd even bothered making the trip. They'd had little to say to each other beyond the mandatory surface conversation and had spent most of their time at the house, each on his own.

That the silence, the lack of communication, bothered Danica much more than usual was no surprise. For the first time in her life she had a source of comparison. *Don't do it. It's not fair. Blake's your husband. Michael's your friend.* But she couldn't help herself. The differences were glaring. The more she fought them, the more pronounced they became, and in consequence, the sadder she felt.

As always, though, Michael came through. She was feeling particularly low when he called on Wednesday afternoon. They'd been out biking together the day before, but she'd expected he'd be working.

"Can you come over, Dani?"

"Uh, sure. Is . . . is everything okay?"

"Great! I want you to meet someone."

"Someone? Who?"

"Come on over and see."

He was the mysterious Michael again, and she could hear his smile. But . . . why not? She was in the mood for another mystery. Lord knew she needed *something* to pick her up.

Forewarned was forearmed. Dressing in a pair of casual linen slacks and a matching short-sleeved sweater, Danica dabbed blusher on her cheeks, stroked a touch of mascara on her lashes and brushed her hair to a high sheen. Strapping on a pair of chic sandals, she set out across the sand.

Michael was waiting for her on the deck with a woman by his side. She wore a calf-length skirt of a soft cotton fabric that swirled about her legs in the gentle breeze, a loose shirt and a vest. A soft scarf was wrapped around the top of her head and knotted above one ear; its ends flowed into the dark hair that curled gently about her shoulders. Her stance was feminine, but somehow familiar. She was as slender as Michael was lean.

Michael met Danica halfway up the steps and took her hand to draw her the rest of the way. Danica smiled at him, but her curious gaze quickly returned to the woman who waited.

"Dani, I'd like you to meet—"

"Priscilla," Danica finished, her smile widening as she held out her hand to Michael's sister. "You may not look like twins, but the family resemblance is marked." It was there in the strong line of the jaw, the firm lips, the open smile.

Cilla Buchanan offered a handshake, which was filled with confidence. "You're more observant than most. I usually try to pass myself off as his date. He looks more gorgeous every time I see him."

Unable to argue, Danica simply arched a mischievous brow Michael's way. Michael, who was thoroughly enjoying himself, completed the introductions. "Cilla, this is my neighbor, Danica Lindsay."

"Obviously," Cilla drawled, "since she came in across the sand. Well, Danica, I'm glad to meet you. Michael's been grinning in anticipation of something from the minute I arrived this morning. I was beginning to think he was going to keep his secret to himself all day."

"It's that element of mystery," Danica said softly. "He leans toward it, I've noticed."

"He should have been a mystery writer, not a historian."

"There's mystery in history," Michael argued. "That's the whole point in writing about it. It's the unraveling that's a—"

"Challenge," Cilla cut in to finish. "So you've told me many times. I still think you should work for the paper. There's nothing like smelling a story, sniffing out its details one by one and solving a true puzzle."

"You sound like a bloodhound," Michael retorted, but without malice. "Come on. Let's sit down. Lemonade, Dani?"

She shook her head.

"I'll have one, Mike," Cilla said, sinking down into one of the deck chairs and crossing her legs. "Make it tart."

Michael gave her a tart look before disappearing.

"He's a nice brother. I really wish he did work for the paper. Then, we'd be able to see each other more often."

Danica drew over a nearby chair. "He didn't mention you were coming."

"He didn't know." She flipped the ends of her scarf back over her shoulder and shot Danica a buoyant smile. "*I* didn't know until last night. The city room's been a madhouse with the convention going on. Now that we're between the two, there was a sudden lull. I figured that I'd better grab the chance while I had it. Once I get back, it'll be off to St. Louis and pandemonium all over again."

"I didn't realize you did political reporting," Danica remarked with caution.

"Mostly I do investigative journalism, special assignments for the paper. When it comes to national elections, though, just about everyone gets involved in one way or another. I don't mind it; the excitement is contagious."

"Was there all that much excitement in San Francisco? I got the impression that Picard's renomination came off without a fuss."

"To an extent, but then, he's the incumbent. Still, there were some interesting floor battles waged. A vocal contingent of delegates wanted modifications in the platform. They're more moderate than the President and have been uncomfortable with his stands on the economy and foreign trade."

Danica could understand that. Blake and her father were supporting Jason Claveling for those very differences with the President, among other reasons. "They didn't get very far, did they?"

"Nope. Ahh, my lemonade." She reached for the tall glass Michael handed her. He offered a second to Danica on the chance she'd changed her mind. When she shook her head again, he kept the glass for himself and sat down facing the two women.

"You're not talking politics, are you?"

"As a matter of fact," Cilla began without remorse, only to be interrupted by her brother.

"I'd better warn you that Danica's no innocent on that score." He was also warning her to be careful. He knew Cilla to be quick-tongued and opinionated in a way that had never bothered him but might bother another. He wouldn't have put it past her to inadvertently blurt out something that would offend Danica. "Her father is William Marshall."

Cilla's lemonade took a wrong turn in her throat. She coughed, pressing a hand to her chest. "William Marshall? Are you serious?" She was looking at Danica, who smiled apologetically and nodded. "Michael, you're courting the enemy!" she exclaimed, but the thread of humor in her voice echoed Danica's own upon first learning of Michael's family connections.

"I'm not courting her. In case you hadn't noticed, she's married. We're friends. Dani's keeping me sane."

"Fat chance," Cilla murmured with affection. Then she grew thoughtful. "Danica Lindsay. Danica Marshall. Why does that last sound familiar?"

"Probably because you've written so much over the years about Danica's father," Michael suggested. He was closely enough attuned to everything about Danica to sense the faint unease she was feeling at that moment, despite the perfect outer calm she projected. "Maybe you'd better quit while you're ahead, Cilla."

But Cilla would have no part of it. As her brother loved his little surprises, so she loved intrigue. She was smelling a story, and as always when that happened, her inquisitive nature took command. "What does *he* think about your living next to a Buchanan?" she asked Danica.

"I'm not sure he knows. Blake and I just bought the house a few months ago and my parents haven't been up yet."

The gears in Cilla's mind were turning. "Blake Lindsay. . . uh, Eastbridge Electronics out of . . . Boston?"

"Cilla's got a photographic memory, Dani. She's probably seen some caption along the way."

"He's supporting Claveling, isn't he?" Cilla went on, recalling more and more.

"That's right," Danica answered. It was public knowledge. And besides, she wasn't ashamed of it. If Jason Claveling won the nomination, she'd be voting for him herself. No, the only thing that bothered her about the man was the fact that he commanded so much of Blake's time and effort.

"Your father's a big Claveling man." She frowned, struggling to organize fragments of memory. "I'm trying to . . . there's been so much written about William Marshall . . . but . . . I hadn't realized he had a daughter."

"My parents kept me well-protected," Danica murmured.

Michael, who was growing uneasy himself, promptly made a move to shift the conversation. "Slightly different from our situation, but I don't think *anyone* could have kept *you* well protected, Cilla. You were an agressive twerp... speaking of which, how's work going, aside from the conventions?''

Cilla accepted the diversion with grace, Danica with relief. In truth, Danica found herself fascinated with the ensuing talk, which centered on the daily rigor of the newspaper journalist. She'd always viewed the papers from the outside; glimpsing them from the inside now was enlightening.

"You really do all that checking?" she asked when Cilla was describing the work she'd recently done on a bribery report.

"Of our sources? If we didn't, we'd be risking lawsuits every day. Some papers take more chances than others, and of course, public figures are usually fair game. But sources of information can sometimes be pretty sleazy characters. It's in our interest to check them out before we make fools of ourselves. The headline that's slapped on a story can be misleading enough, but then—" she held up a hand "—I don't have any part in that." She glanced toward the sliding screen. "I think your baby wants out, Mike."

Michael twisted around to see the puppy standing forlornly at the screen. In an instant he had freed it from its cage and was gently placing it into Danica's outstretched arms. Quite appropriately, the talk turned to dogs, then, comfortably, to fond childhood remembrances, then old friends, then, as the minutes turned into hours, the novel written by one of Michael's old friends, which he and Danica had been reading simultaneously, then back to the puppy, who, having been romping by their feet after taking a nap in Danica's lap, had proceeded to pee on Michael's sneaker.

"That's it," Michael exclaimed in clipped words, "the final straw!" Scooping up the little dog, he stared it in the eye. "I've been up every damn night this week with you, you fool pooch. I've spoon-fed you, cleaned you, toted you to the vet, held your paw when you cried for your mama. And what do I get for all this love?" He glared at his sneaker and muttered a brief obscenity, which Danica was fast to contradict through her laughter.

"Not that, Michael. At least not yet. Maybe you'd better take him in." When Michael moved to do so, she looked at Cilla, who had shared her appreciation of the puppy's unique, if misplaced, demonstration of love. "How about you and Michael coming to my place for dinner?" She'd already learned that Cilla was up for several days. Cilla, in turn, had already learned that Blake had returned to Boston the Sunday before.

"No way." Cilla stood alongside Danica. "I'm taking *you* both *out*."

"That's silly, Cilla. You probably eat out five or six nights a week."

"Now, how did you know that?"

"You're a working woman. You've got a hectic schedule."

Cilla lowered her voice as the two women entered the house. "The truth of it is I'm a lousy cook. Either I burn the butter or curdle the sauce or cut my finger instead of the tomato. I have this wonderful guy, though—"

"That you're seeing?"

"No, no. This guy cooks. When I'm planning to have a *guy* guy in for dinner, I give Fred the key to my apartment. He comes in during the afternoon and prepares everything, then leaves simplified instructions on what I have to do to make sure things are hot. My dates rarely know the difference."

"Pretty tricky."

"Tell me you think I'm awful. Are you a gourmet cook?"

Danica laughed. "Not quite. I've never had much of a chance to cook. The kitchen's always been, uh, occupied. What it boils down to is that I'm learning how to cook up here. If I do say so myself, I'm not too bad."

"Two women after my own heart," Michael hummed, catching talk of food as he passed them on his way from kitchen to bedroom. "Let's go, ladies. I'll just change my shoes and then I'm taking you both out to dinner."

"*I'm* taking us out to dinner!" Cilla called.

"No, you're not," Michael bellowed back from what Danica guessed to be the bottom of his closet. "I've never been a kept man and I don't intend to start now. Be gracious in defeat, Cilla. A docile woman is a thing to behold."

Cilla wasn't about to be either gracious or docile. "Try writing *that* in a book, Michael, and they'll boo you off the shelves. 'A docile woman is a thing to behold,' my foot.

Modern men don't say things like that. They don't even *think* things like that.'' She lowered her voice so that only Danica could hear. ''At least, if we keep telling them they don't, maybe they won't. I sometimes wonder if it isn't a losing battle.'' A momentary frown creased her brow, as though mirroring the passage of a brief pain through her mind.

Danica was intrigued. Until that moment she hadn't see a single dent in Cilla Buchanan. She'd seemed confident, optimistic, indeed a tiny bit intimidating to Danica. But with that fleeting frown something had emerged. Vulnerability? Sadness? Danica couldn't quite pin it down because it was already gone, but she sensed that Cilla's pain was very personal.

Over dinner she kept an ear out for anything that might lend credence to her suspicion. Once, in passing, Cilla spoke of her ex-husband, Jeffrey, but her tone remained even. Danica wondered whether she was well controlled, legitimately neutral or simply preoccupied. She kept giving Danica the most pensive looks from time to time.

The three were enjoying dessert when Cilla abruptly put down her fork. ''I remember now,'' she said, her tone one of dawning recognition. ''Danica Marshall. Of *course* I've heard that name. Didn't you play tennis at one point?''

In the instant Danica realized that it would have been foolish to feign innocence. ''Yes. A long time ago.'' She dared glance at Michael and caught the discomfort in his eyes. It was enough to tell her that he'd known all along, that he'd been waiting for her to raise the subject herself, that he hadn't wanted to dredge up something she'd rather not have mentioned. Ironically, this knowledge gave her strength.

''You were good, as I recall. You made it to the top.''

''I was ranked fourth in the country.''

''But—'' again Cilla tugged at her memory bank ''—you stopped. Very suddenly.''

''Cilla, I'm not sure Dani wants to discuss—''

''It's okay, Michael,'' Danica said softly, giving his hand a reassuring squeeze. ''I don't mind talking about it.'' Maybe it was that, given the success of Cilla's career, she wanted to share her own, albeit defunct one. Maybe it was that she liked

Cilla. Maybe it was that she needed Michael to hear. Then again, maybe it was the wine she'd drunk.

"I was eight when I first started playing at our club. Our pro believed I had talent, and my parents jumped at the thought. They gave me lessons, twice a week during winters, every day during summers. When I began entering tournaments, and winning, they were thrilled." She paused and looked down, momentarily unsure as to how much to say, then, with the sudden confidence that she was in the right, raised her eyes and went on.

"My father has always been a competitor. He imposed that drive on me. He was convinced that I could be the country's top-ranked female player. He was proud of what I was doing and that motivated me to work harder. I was twelve when I went off to boarding school. I had a private coach there." She arched a brow. "I had a special schedule and was excused from classes whenever there was a tournament. Not great for winning friends in school. Anyway, by the time I was fifteen, my parents decided to enroll me in a full-time tennis academy in Florida."

"Arroah's," Cilla prompted, recalling the association of the two names.

Danica nodded. "Armand was wonderful. He was just starting the academy. I lived in his house, along with several other players." She looked at Michael, who'd been listening quietly. "Reggie Nichols was one of them. We'd met before, but that was where we became close friends. Eventually the school expanded enough to warrant a dorm, but Reggie and I stayed close."

"That's understandable," Cilla remarked. "You were well matched in skill."

"We liked each other. Reggie could usually beat me on the court, but I never felt myself in competition with her. That was where the trouble began, I guess."

"Trouble?" Michael asked.

"I just wasn't that competitive, at least not enough so to take me to the top."

"You had an injury," he argued, revealing exactly how much he had known about her career before she'd ever said a word.

Danica eyed him sadly. "The papers don't tell everything, and what they don't know they can't report. I'd been agonizing for months. I'd reached a point where I just didn't enjoy what I was doing. I mean, I'd been living and breathing tennis for so long, and suddenly I just didn't see the point. It was supposed to be fun, but it wasn't. Winning didn't mean enough to me. I didn't have the drive it took to get to the top. And I couldn't stand the pressure."

"From home?"

She hesitated, then nodded. "Hurting my shoulder was the best thing that could have happened. It brought things to a head. If I'd wanted, I'm sure I could have played once the shoulder healed. I chose not to."

"Your father must have loved that," Cilla speculated dryly.

"Don't you know it. He tried to blame things on Armand, then on the doctor who was treating my shoulder, then, inevitably, on me."

Michael felt her hurt, and a pride of his own. "You held your ground, though."

"For what it was worth. I'd become convinced I didn't have it in me to hit that top spot, and being second or third or fourth just wasn't acceptable where I came from. I was relieved when I bowed out, but I was also more than a little disappointed in myself. When you fail to come up to standards that have been solidly ingrained in you, it's hard."

"My God," Michael gritted, "as if you don't have enough going for you without having to be a superstar. You were fourth in the country! Wasn't that good enough for him?"

"I wasn't number one," Danica murmured.

Cilla, who'd been momentarily taken aback by Michael's vehemence, grew thoughtful. "There's a fantastic story here."

Michael pinned his sister with a glare that went far beyond vehemence. "You wouldn't," he growled.

"Of course I wouldn't," Cilla said without a flurry. "I just think that one day Danica might want to write it all down.

Hell, there are books galore on the shelves by one career athlete or another. It'd be refreshing to have the other side told.''

''It's...too personal,'' Danica argued. She suddenly feared she'd said too much and wondered why she'd done it. Cilla was media, *real* media. If she ever pursued the story she smelled, Danica would be appalled. And embarrassed. And hurt. For once, she wished she'd listened to her mother's advice, and Blake's. They'd said to be careful. She'd blown it again!

Chapter Seven

DANICA'S FEARS lurked strongly in her mind. Later that night, as he walked her back to her house, Michael, who'd known precisely what she was feeling, addressed them head-on.

"She won't say a thing, Dani. I know her as well as anyone does. She won't betray your trust."

Danica clutched his arm more tightly. "I keep asking myself why I said all that. It's a part of my life I don't usually talk about."

"It's good to talk about it. You've got nothing to be ashamed of."

"That's debatable but beside the fact. I barely know Cilla. If I hadn't told *you* about it before, why did it all come out tonight?"

"Maybe because Cilla had the courage I lacked. I thought I was being thoughtful by not raising it. Maybe I was just frightened."

"Frightened? Of what?"

"Of crossing that little line between what's my business and what isn't."

"Anything's your business. You should know that by now." She'd been with Blake too long, she realized. She was using his words. But she'd barely begun to admonish herself when Michael disagreed.

"Not anything, Dani. There are some things I can't ask."

"Like what?"

"Like what goes on between you and Blake."

She gave a harsh laugh. "Practically nothing, if you really want to know."

"I don't. Oh, God, that makes it harder." He closed his eyes for a minute, then went on, desperately needing to steer away from what she'd implied. "Why didn't you tell me about your tennis before?"

"Because I didn't want you to see me as a quitter."

"A quitter? Come on. You reached a point in your life where a decision was called for. You made it."

"I could have kept playing. I could have worked harder. I could have pushed myself on and on."

"And you would have been a basket case before you were twenty." They'd reached her door and he put an arm around her waist. "You made the right decision, Danica. You did what was best for *you*."

"That was what I told myself at the time, but I've had my doubts since. I took the easy way out. That's all there is to it."

"That's what he thinks, isn't it?" They both knew Michael referred to her father.

"Sometimes there's not much difference between what he thinks and what I think."

Michael turned to firmly grip her shoulders. "There you're wrong. You think very differently from him. You *are* very different from him. You can't lead your life in his footsteps. You're your own person!"

Looking up at him, Danica smiled softly. "You always say the right things."

"I believe them, sweetheart. I believe in you. I just wish you did yourself."

Touched in the most beautiful of ways by his words, his look, his faith, she stood on tiptoe and wrapped her arms around his neck. "Oh, Michael," she whispered, holding tighter when he enclosed her in a hug.

With a soft moan, he began to caress her back, and she could only close her eyes and enjoy his warmth. It was a physical thing, but emotional, too. She needed it. God, how she needed it.

She felt his lips on her hair, pressing small kisses against its silk, but she needed that, too. He prized her. She had nothing to offer him, but still he prized her. With him she was herself and more of a person than she'd ever been before.

His lips moved lower, whispering her name with each small kiss he planted on her forehead, her eyes, her nose. Entranced by a new and unfamiliar joy, she tipped her head to ease his access. When his lips touched hers, she caught her breath. His was sweet, warm, wafting over her as his mouth hovered, close, so close, so tempting, so ready.

She couldn't think, could only feel and enjoy and live a dream. Her lips were open when his finally closed over them, and she gave him everything that the pent-up woman in her demanded. She'd never kissed a man this way, with this hunger, this force. But sweet. It was so, so sweet. Their lips caressed and explored. Their tongues met and mated.

Then there was a quivering, from his legs to hers, her stomach to his, his chest to her breasts. And suddenly, as each realized that their bodies were taking command in a way that was forbidden, they parted.

Forehead to forehead, they breathed shallowly.

"Ahh, Dani. I've wanted to do that for so long."

She'd wanted it, too, but she couldn't admit it. She couldn't admit anything, because her throat was a tight knot preventing sound.

"Don't be angry," he pleaded in a whisper. "I couldn't help myself. I love you, Dani, and I don't know what in the hell to do about it."

She swallowed hard, then whispered his name and buried her face against the warm column of his throat. *I love you, too,* she wanted to say, but she couldn't. It wasn't fair to either of them. And it wasn't fair to Blake.

"Maybe," she breathed unsteadily, "maybe we shouldn't see each other."

"Don't say that! Please don't say that. I need you too much. And you need me. We'll just...just have to keep things under control."

"Seems to me we said the same thing once before."

"We'll just have to say it again and louder." His tone echoed that determination, but when he held her back and took her face in his hands, his expression was exquisitely gentle. "There are times when I hate Blake, when I wish you could...you would leave him.... Do you love him, Dani?"

"I'm married to him," she whispered even as her body was yearning for closer contact with this man to whom she wasn't married.

"But do you love him?"

"There are... there are different kinds of love."

"Do you *love* him?

She closed her eyes and took a pained breath. *Not as I love you, Michael Buchanan.* "Please... I..."

"I want you to love him, Dani. I want you to say that what we have together is just an... an aberration. Maybe if I know that, I'll be able to keep my distance. Say it.... Say it!"

"I can't!" she cried, opening her eyes and returning the same look of helplessness Michael wore. She couldn't lie. Either to him *or* herself. She didn't know if she loved Blake. Certainly what she felt for him was very different from what she felt for Michael. Maybe what she felt for Michael was an aberration, but it had been building for far too long and there was no end in sight. "I can't. And there's really no point." Her voice held defeat. "I'm married to Blake; I bear his name, wear his wedding band, and... and..."

"You've got his child in your belly." Michael let out the breath he was holding. His hands dropped to her elbows, then her hands. He released one to lightly touch her stomach. "I wish it was mine," he whispered, his voice cracking at the end. Then he turned and started down the path, knowing that he'd only make things worse the longer he stayed. By the time he reached his house, though, he was regretting having left her so abruptly. She'd been upset, too. And she was alone.

Bypassing Cilla's watchful presence in the living room, he went into his den and called her. "Dani?"

"... Yes?"

He kept his voice low, very low. "I'm sorry. I shouldn't have pushed you."

"... You didn't say... anything I... haven't said to myself." Her words were broken.

"Are you all right?"

"... Yes."

He shut his eyes tight. "You've been crying."

"I'm okay now."

"Oh, Dani," he whispered, "I'm so sorry."

"Damn it, Michael, stop saying that!" Frustrated and angered by the entire situation, she found a sudden strength. "If you're sorry you kissed me, remember that...that I kissed you back. So it's just as much my fault as yours. More so, even. I'm...I'm the one who should be thinking about Blake. I'm the one who's betrayed him. And I'm *not* sorry!"

There was a lengthy pause on both ends of the line.

"You're not?" Michael asked at last.

"No," she answered very softly.

"Why not?"

"Because...because...I enjoyed your kiss. I'd been wondering what it would be like. Now I know. But we can't let it happen again. It's too tempting."

Relieved that she hadn't tried to deny what she'd so clearly felt, Michael smiled. "Damn right about that. Listen, Dani, don't be too hard on yourself. If I know you, you'll sit there feeling guilty. It happened. Now we *both* know how careful we've got to be. Okay?"

"Okay.... Michael?"

"Mmmm?"

"I like Cilla."

"I'm glad. So do I."

"Will I see her again before I leave?"

"I'll send her over to visit. How's that?"

"Great...as long as she promises to forget everything she's heard."

"I'll make sure of it. 'Night, Dani."

"Good night, Michael."

He replaced the receiver with a smile on his face and a feeling of fullness in the region of his heart. His momentary serenity was shattered, though, when a quiet voice came from the door.

"What are you doing, Michael?"

He whirled around, stared at his sister, then scowled. "How long have you been standing there?"

Arms comfortably crossed over her chest, Cilla was lounging against the doorjamb. "Long enough. Not that I really needed to hear anything. The vibes passing between you two were obvious."

"Funny, I thought we were pretty subtle."

"What's going on?"

"I'm not sure that's any of your business."

"Come on, Mike. This is Cilla. Your sister. Your twin. Your better half?"

"Good thing you made that last a question. It's always been up for grabs."

"You're avoiding my first question. What in the devil are you doing with her?"

"Don't you like her?"

"You know I do. She's lovely. She's poised and intelligent and pretty—"

"Beautiful. She's beautiful. Inside and out."

"She's also married."

He glared. "I know that."

"You seem to forget it from time to time. Michael, *what are you doing?*"

He gave her another long, hard stare, then turned and propped himself against the edge of his desk. "I'm trying to survive, Cilla."

"What are you talking about? You've been surviving very well all these years."

"That's the whole point. All these years passing and where am I? Sure, I've got a career and financial security. Sure, I've got friends. But I want something else."

"I hadn't realized you felt something was missing." She came to perch by his side against the desk. "You've been with lots of women. How long have you wanted this 'something else'?"

"Since I met Danica. I hadn't realized it was there. No one's ever inspired the feelings she does."

"You're not talking survival. You're talking suicide. Mike, she's out of reach. You can't have her."

"Maybe not all of her. But I can have some of it." He turned to his sister in earnest. "Look, things aren't right with her marriage. That was one of the reasons she bought the house up here. She thought she and Blake would be able to patch things up if they got away from the city. But he doesn't come. Not often, at least. And I have a feeling that things aren't great when he's there. After he left last Sunday, she was in a blue funk. She tried to hide it, but I saw.''

''Maybe you *wanted* to see.''

''I *saw*.''

''So what are you saying? That you're going to sit around and hope that her marriage falls through?''

''Damn it, Cilla, you make me sound like a monster.'' He raked a hand through his hair, ruffling it more than the night breeze already had. ''I'd give anything to see Danica happy, even if that means the recovery of her marriage. But regardless of what happens, we're friends. We were from the first, when we saw each other on the beach last March. It's something I can't change, something that's as much a part of me as a hand or a leg—''

''Or a heart?''

''Or a heart.'' He sighed. ''Which is why I tell you that I'm only trying to survive. I can't live with her. I can't live without her. So I guess I'll have to take whatever I can get.''

''Oh, Mike,'' Cilla murmured sadly, ''it hurts me to hear you say that. You deserve so much more. Maybe you should be out there looking. Maybe now that you've realized what you want...'' She let the thought lapse when Michael's expression grew hard. ''Okay, I know. *She*'s what you want. But there may never be a future for the two of you. Have you thought of that?''

''I try not to.''

''Then you're a fool.'' She threw a hand in the air. ''Hell, we're *all* fools. Love is a bitch. Do you know that?''

For the first time since he'd encountered Cilla in his den, Michael smiled. ''What's doing with you? Still seeing that guy... what was his name... Waldo?''

''Wally, please. And no, I'm not seeing him.''

''What happened?''

''He started getting serious, so I called it off.''

''I thought you liked him.''

''I did. Just not enough to consider marriage.''

''Would you ever consider it again?''

"If the right guy came along."

"But you're still bumping into Jeff?"

"It's inevitable, isn't it? Washington's not *that* big. He asked for you, by the way. He was wondering when you'd be getting down. He misses the talks you two used to have."

"I miss them, too," Michael mused. "We go way back, Jeff and I. Talking shop with him is fun."

"Whose shop . . . yours or his?"

"Either. Both. We pick each other's brains. He's one hell of a bright guy."

"I think the Defense Department's finally realized that. They've given him a promotion. From what he inferred, he's working on some pretty sensitive investigations."

"Really? Who's he investigating?"

Cilla gave a rueful frown. "If he'd been able to tell me that—if he'd been able to tell me *anything*—maybe we'd still be married. I doubt he trusts me any more now than he did then. I'm the *press*. Never forget that."

"Cilla . . . speaking of that . . . you won't blab about anything Dani said, will you?"

"Blab? Of course not. I wouldn't do that to her *or* to you."

"Good. Because I don't want her hurt. I'd never forgive you if—"

"Trust me, Michael. Please? Trust me." She wouldn't write about Danica; she wouldn't gossip. What she *would* do, she vowed, was to keep her eyes and ears open. There was a better than even chance that at one point or another she'd run into Blake Lindsay. And she had every intention of finding out why a guy as good-looking and as successful as he was would all but abandon his lovely, lonely, pregnant wife.

DURING THE NEXT FEW WEEKS, Michael and Danica were very careful. While neither could not not see the other, they kept just enough distance between them to preclude a repeat of what had happened on her doorstep that night. They biked together, ate out from time to time, sat on the beach at sunset talking about a book, a TV documentary or some aspect of Michael's work that troubled him. For his part, he enjoyed running things past Danica. Often she was able to summarize a thought or a theory more succinctly than he could, given his closeness to the subject matter. For her part, she was intrigued by his work, by the intense research he'd done, by the different slant he was trying to convey. Now that he knew about her tennis involvement, she felt totally comfortable discussing sports, though when he popped over one day suggesting that they play a game or two on the local court, she quickly refused. He tried to talk her into it, and to her surprise, she nearly yielded. But she needed more time; thoughts of tennis still evoked vivid memories of drudgery and exhaustion . . . and failure. In the end, they agreed to put it off for another time. Michael was determined to get her playing one day, though. He felt that it would be good for her, that she had to face the past in order to finally accept it. Moreover, he knew she'd loved tennis once, and he desperately wanted her to share that love with him.

During the second week of August Danica drove back to Boston to see the doctor as ordered on a monthly basis. His report was good, and that pleased her. What didn't please her was the fact that Blake wasn't there. He'd left several days earlier to spend time in Washington before going on to the convention in St. Louis. It hurt her that he hadn't wanted to meet her doctor, much less ask him questions that most prospective fathers would have. While Danica had read any number of books on the subject of pregnancy and childbirth since her pregnancy had been confirmed, Blake, to her knowledge, had read nothing. When she'd asked him if he wasn't even the slightest bit curious about what his child looked like at that moment or would look like a month, two, three months hence, he'd simply smiled that winning smile of his and said that nature would take its course whether he knew its intimate details or not. She realized that it was clearly her baby, literally and figuratively.

What bothered Danica most, though, was that during the two days she spent in the Beacon Hill town house, she missed Michael more than she did Blake. It was with relief that she finally returned to Maine and to the man whose excitement at seeing her again warmed her heart.

The convention began, and since she hadn't wanted a television in her own house, she spent every evening watching the proceedings with Michael. On the one hand, she didn't want to watch; on the other, she couldn't help herself. She sensed a part of her future lay in the outcome, and she was tense. Though Michael did what he could to alleviate that tension, it was never more apparent than at the moment that Jason Claveling mustered enough votes to secure the nomination.

When the floor erupted with sign-waving and cheering, she closed her eyes and let out a long sigh.

"Well, that's it, sweetheart," Michael announced. "Looks like your men are going to be a happy lot tonight."

"Are *you* pleased?" she returned. She'd certainly classify him as one of "her men."

"We could have done worse. Claveling's the one who stands a good chance of unseating Picard, and I'm all for that."

"*You* won't be running around during the next three months trying to get the deed done." She moaned. "And I thought the *past* three months were bad."

Michael understood. He knew how much she'd resented the time Blake had spent on the campaign. "Maybe it won't be as bad as it's been. The nomination was the hardest part, given four contenders. In a two-man race, things are simplified."

"I know you're trying to make me feel better, but you're talking through your hat, Michael Buchanan. I've seen my father in situations like these. More accurately, I've read about him in the papers, which was about as close as I was able to get. If he's busy under normal circumstances, during a campaign—be it his own or that of someone he's supporting—he's *doubly* busy. And this time around, Blake will be busy right with him."

"Then that's all the more time you'll have for me," Michael teased, eyes glinting in response to the scowl Danica threw him. "Come on, sweetheart, it won't be so bad. I'll keep you busy."

They both knew that she'd be returning to Boston in September, but Michael was determined to make good on his

word at least until then. When she remained mildly depressed over the next few days—in some part due to the bla-
tantly hurried phone call she received from Blake upon his
return from St. Louis—he set a date with the McCabes.

The Sunday they all spent together was a smashing success. Without any of the initial trepidation Danica had felt
upon meeting the media-minded Cilla, she found Greta and
Pat to be equally as likable. They were fun, unpretentious,
and took great joy in relating stories of Michael in his younger days. The baby—well, the baby stole her heart. By the
time she and Michael left with promises of a return engage-
ment, Danica was looking all the more forward to having a
child of her own.

Four days later, though, she wasn't feeling quite as well.
She'd had an uncomfortable night and was dozing on the sofa
when Michael rang the doorbell. Groggy, she pushed herself
to a sitting position, then up to her feet. When she opened the
door, Michael was quickly alarmed.

"What is it, Dani? Aren't you feeling well?" She was
wearing her long robe and looked frighteningly pale.

She grasped the doorknob and leaned against the door. "I
didn't sleep well. I'm sorry, Michael. Do you think we could
drive to Freeport another time?"

"Of course! L. L. Bean isn't going anywhere!" He took her
arm and guided her back to the sofa. "Here. Sit." When
she'd done so, he propped a hip beside her. "Morning sickness?"

She shook her head. "I haven't had any of that. I've really
felt terrific until now."

He put a hand on her forehead. "Maybe you've got the flu.
You feel warm."

"No. I'll be okay." Slipping her legs behind him, she curled
into the corner of the sofa. When she closed her eyes, Michael worried all the more.

"You didn't get a call from Blake, did you?" That seemed
a sure thing to upset her. But she shook her head. "From your
parents?" Again she shook her head.

"I'll be okay. I think I'll just rest."

It wasn't like her, he knew. There was something she wasn't saying. He gently rubbed her thigh. "Can I get you anything?"

"No. I'll just . . . lie here for a while."

Michael studied her for a long time, then finally got up and wandered through the house. The sheets on her bed were in a tangle. He made the bed, then returned to living room to find her lying with her arms crossed over her stomach and her knees drawn up close. Sitting down by her side, he smoothed the hair from her cheeks. She opened her eyes, but she didn't smile.

"What is it?" he pleaded. "I want to do *something*."

"Just . . . stay around," she said. Her voice was as weak as the rest of her looked, he decided, and the knowledge added to his concern.

He spent the morning with a book in his lap, though he hardly read a word. His eyes wouldn't focus on the open page but kept going to Danica's face. By noontime she was looking more pale than ever.

"Maybe I should call a doctor," he suggested quietly. He knew she wasn't sleeping. She shifted from time to time, gingerly, he thought, and when her eyes weren't closed they focused blindly on the rug, the coffee table, the glass slider.

"Wait a little longer," she murmured. "I'm sure I'll pick up pretty soon."

She didn't. In fact she grew more uncomfortable. Michael reached his limit when she opened her eyes once again and they were filled with tears. He was up like a bolt and on his haunches close before her.

"Damn it, Dani, tell me. Is it the baby? Do you think something's wrong?"

The tears hovered on her lids and she swallowed hard. "I . . . I don't know. I've felt weird since last night. I woke up with a backache."

"I have a heating pad at my place. Should I get it?"

"I feel . . . I feel cramps every so often. They were mild at first and I hoped they'd just go away, but they're not doing that."

Michael forced himself to remain calm. "Are they getting worse?" She nodded and met his gaze and he realized that she was terrified. "It's okay, sweetheart." He pressed a warm kiss to her forehead. "You stay put. I'm going to call the doctor."

"He's in Boston. I can't drive—"

"I've got one here."

"Not an obstetrician."

"He'll give me the name of one. The best in the area." With a squeeze of her arm, he headed for the phone. When he returned, he squatted down. "A Dr. Masconi is waiting for us in Portland. Do you want to put on some clothes?"

Nodding, Danica tried to push herself up, but Michael was quickly lifting her and carrying her into the bedroom, where he set her very gently on her feet. He turned toward the dresser. "Tell me what you want."

"I can do it," she breathed shakily. "You go wait for me. I'll be right out."

"Are you sure? Will you yell if you need me?" When she nodded, he left, but he was right outside her door waiting when she appeared moments later. She'd thrown on a pair of jeans and a long-sleeved summer sweater. But she was crying. When he reached for her, she grabbed his arm. "I'm bleeding, Michael. I think I'm losing it. Dear God, I don't want that!"

Trying to contain the fear he felt, he lifted her up and made for the door. "I don't want it, either, sweetheart. Neither does the doctor. He's an expert. He'll do everything he can." Her arms were around his neck and she was holding him tightly, as if that might help save her baby. He felt more helpless than he ever had before. All he could do was to try to keep her calm and get her to the hospital as soon as possible.

The drive was an agony for them both. Danica sat curled beside Michael, holding his hand, wondering if she was being punished for feeling so much for him but needing his strength nonetheless. Michael tried to soothe her fears with gentle words of encouragement, praying that the baby would be all right, praying that she'd be all right, that she wouldn't blame herself if something did happen.

The hospital wasn't the most efficient of places. The doctor had to be paged from somewhere in its labyrinthine midst, and in the meantime Danica was left on an examining table in one of the emergency room's small cubicles. Once she'd undressed, Michael stayed with her for all but those moments when he angrily stalked to the nurse's station to demand to know what was keeping the doctor.

When the doctor finally arrived, Michael was relegated to pacing the emergency-room floor. He was allowed to see Danica for a brief minute as they were wheeling her upstairs. She'd been sedated, but she saw him clearly. He had to be content with that until the time, much later that evening, when she was wheeled back to the private room she'd been assigned.

He rose quickly from the chair in which he'd been seated, it seemed for days, and waited until she'd been settled in bed. She was still pale, but she was awake. He took her hand and smiled gently.

"Hi. How're you doin'?"

"Okay, I guess," she whispered. Her lower lip quivered. She bit down on it.

Settling his hip by hers, he brought her hand to his mouth and kissed it. Her fingers were limp, her skin chilled. He lowered her hand to his chest and pressed it there in an offer of warmth.

"I feel so tired," she murmured.

"It's the anesthesia. It'll take a while to wear off. Why don't you try to sleep. I'll be right here when you wake up."

Without argument, she closed her eyes. He watched her until he was sure she was asleep, then carefully left the bed and stood staring out the window until he heard her stir. He was back at her side by the time she opened her eyes.

"What time is it?" she whispered.

"Nearly midnight."

She nodded and closed her eyes again, but he knew she wasn't sleeping. He took her hand and held it gently between both of his, sensing that she was mourning, wishing there was something he could do. If that small part of him had once upon a time regretted she'd been pregnant, it now felt her sorrow with the rest of him.

"Michael?" She didn't open her eyes. "It hurts so much up here." She raised her free hand to her head and he knew just what she meant.

"I know, Dani. I know."

"I wanted the baby so badly. It was going to open up new doors for me." A single tear, then another, trickled down her cheeks.

Unable to keep any distance when he felt her pain so intimately, Michael gently lifted her into his arms, holding her while she cried quietly, knowing she needed the outlet.

"I wanted . . . the baby . . ."

"I know. Shhhh. It'll be all right."

"But I don't . . . know what went . . . wrong," she sobbed. "The doctor couldn't . . . say."

"He doesn't know. Nobody knows. The only thing we can guess is that the baby wasn't well. Something may have been wrong right from the start."

"But why? Why me? Everyone . . . else has healthy babies."

"Shhhh. It's okay, sweetheart. Shhhh. There'll be other ones coming along."

"I don't think . . . so. Oh, Michael, I don't think so."

"Don't say that. The doctor saw nothing at all wrong that would prevent you from conceiving again and carrying the baby to term."

"That's not the point! Oh, God . . ."

She was crying again. He held her until the tears slowly eased, thinking all the while about what she'd said, wondering exactly how bad things were between Blake and her.

"Dani . . . ? I called Blake when the doctor gave me the news."

Her body went very still. "You called him?" she whispered against his chest.

"I had to." It had taken three calls, one to the town house, one to Blake's office, finally one to the men's club where he'd met with success.

"What did he . . . did he say anything?"

"He was upset." He was actually relatively calm, perhaps stoic, or simply well controlled, but Michael saw no need in telling Danica that. "He wanted to know how you were. When I told him that the doctor said you'd be fine, he was relieved. He said to tell you that he'd be up tomorrow... uh, today."

If he'd hoped the news would cheer her, he'd miscalculated. She started to cry again, making soft, grieving sounds that tore at his gut, and he could only hold her, rock her gently, smooth back her hair. Eventually, inevitably, exhaustion crept up. She quieted but made no move to free herself from his arms.

"I wanted... our baby," she murmured as she drifted off. "Oh, Michael, I wanted our baby..."

Perhaps because he'd wanted the baby to be his from the start, Michael could have sworn from her words that she implied it had been so. But she was simply doped up and had spoken ambiguously, he reasoned; of course, the "our" she spoke of referred to herself and Blake.

He had no way of knowing that she hadn't been that far gone. He had no way of knowing that, in her way, Danica had thought of the baby she'd lost as hers and Michael's. He had no way of knowing that on the night the baby had been conceived, she'd been loving him—not Blake, but him.

BLAKE ARRIVED from Boston late that afternoon. Danica, who'd been discharged from the hospital in the morning and had slept most of the time since then, was sitting on the sofa in her robe, covered by the light shawl Michael had insisted on, drinking the tea Michael had steeped. She was pondering the tag in her hand which read, "The human spirit is stronger than anything that can happen to it," when the sound of a key in the lock caught her ear.

Her gaze flew to Michael, who was already headed for the door. Heart thudding, she held her breath. The meeting of these two men was something she'd assumed would have happened eventually. She'd never anticipated it taking place quite this way.

She watched them shake hands and exchange brief words, Blake's in appreciation of Michael's help, Michael's in gentle praise of Danica. As unobtrusively as possible, Michael excused himself then, leaving Danica alone with Blake.

He approached and pressed a light kiss on her head before taking a seat across from her. Having come straight from the office, he was wearing a suit. It added to the formality that seemed to yawn glaringly between them.

"How are you feeling?" he asked quietly.

"Pretty good."

"I spoke with your doctor this morning." He proceeded to outline the conversation, which told Danica nothing more than the doctor had already told her himself, nothing more than she and Michael had already discussed. "He says that you shouldn't be worried."

"I'm not."

"He wants you to get lots of rest over the next few days."

"I haven't been able to do much else. Michael wouldn't let me move."

"He seems like a nice fellow."

"He is. I'm grateful he was here yesterday. I wasn't sure what to do."

"I knew you shouldn't have been alone here," Blake charged. "If Mrs. Hannah had been with you—"

"It's all right, Blake. I've survived." *Not my baby, though. Are you sorry?*

"The doctor said that the problem started the night before. What took you so long to get to the hospital?"

She closed her eyes, then opened them with a sigh. "It wouldn't have helped, Blake. Even if I'd gotten there sooner. I didn't do anything here that they wouldn't have had me do there. According to the doctor, it was just . . . just destined."

"I know. And I didn't mean that as criticism."

Then why did you say it? she argued silently. "I'm sorry. I guess I'm just sensitive."

"That's to be expected. You've been through an ordeal."

Not you, though, she thought. Still not a single word of regret that she'd miscarried. It was obviously her loss, not his.

"Well," she sighed, bunching the crocheted shawl beneath her fingers, "it's over." She looked up again. "Thank you for coming. I know how busy you must be."

In an apparent attempt to cheer her up, Blake proceeded to tell her exactly how busy he'd been in the nearly four weeks since he'd seen her last. He spoke of work and his stay in Washington. He elaborated on the excitement of the convention, of the jubilation of the victory parties afterward, of the Claveling campaign's strategy for the weeks ahead.

Danica listened quietly. Blake had to have said more to her in that hour than he'd said in the past thousand. Yet not a word had been of a personal nature, at least none that directly concerned Danica. She recalled similar monologues she'd heard on those rare occasions when her family had gathered together for dinner. Her father would ask her about school, then after hearing her initial response, would nod and launch into a dissertation on a subject not remotely related either to Danica or school. She wondered if Blake enjoyed hearing himself speak as much as her father did, and was appalled at how much more alike the two men were than ever.

She was more appalled, though, when out of the blue Blake announced that her mother would be arriving in Maine the next day.

"Mom's coming *here*?"

"You don't expect her to be going to a hotel when you could clearly use her help."

"Her...help." Danica carefully swallowed the bitter words that threatened to spill, but evidently she was less successful at concealing the cynical look in her eye.

"Look, Danica, I've got to get back to Boston tomorrow. Eleanor felt that you shouldn't be alone at this time, and I agree. She's concerned about you. She and your father were both very upset when I called."

Strange, Danica hadn't given a thought to notifying her parents of what had happened. She must have simply blocked out that particularly odious chore from her mind. Of course they'd be upset. They'd wanted a grandchild . . . as though it were their God-given right. Well, what about *her* rights? What about the child *she'd* wanted? What about the warm, close family life she dreamed about having for years and years?

"I wish you'd told her not to come," Danica murmured.

"Why ever not? She's your mother. It's her place to be here."

Danica's laugh held a touch of hysteria. "Her conscience must be coming to life after all these years. She never worried about 'her place' before. At least, she never worried about it with regard to me. She and Dad were always out doing something that was more important."

"You're being ungenerous, Danica. What she and your father did they had to do."

"That's a matter of opinion. Mine differs from theirs."

Blake's nostrils flared. His handsome features suddenly took on a harder cast, one she'd never seen before. She wondered if she was getting to him . . . finally.

"Your mother loves you." He spaced his words as though he were talking to a child. "She wants to be here. I had no idea you objected to her company."

"It's hard to object to something you've had so little exposure to. I wonder what's come over her all of a sudden. Belated maternal instincts. Maybe she's going through menopause and—"

"That's enough, Danica." He got to his feet, automatically smoothing the crease in his trousers. "I think you're just upset. You need some rest. I'll go get my bag from the car and change. Maybe you'll be in a better mood when I'm done."

He never saw the who-in-the-devil-do-you-think-*you*-are glance that hit his back as he headed for the door, and it crumbled as soon as he was gone. By the time he'd returned and changed his clothes, Danica's anger had given way to fatigue. She was tired. Tired of wanting and not having. Tired of needing and going without. Of course, things seemed worse right now, she told herself. The doctor had warned her that she might be depressed for a time but that it would pass. She could only take one day at a time. One day at a time. One day at a time.

FOUR DAYS LATER she breathed a sigh of relief when Eleanor Marshall kissed her goodbye and started back for Connecticut. Within minutes, she was out the glass slider, across the deck, down the stairs and running along the beach.

"Michael!" she bellowed from the sand beneath his house. "Michael!"

Mercifully, soon he was out on the deck, stunned at the sight of Danica standing with her bare feet planted firmly in the sand.

"I thought she'd never leave, Michael! I nearly went out of my mind!" Her call was fraught with pent-up frustration. The tension in her body was marked.

"Take it easy, Dani." He trotted down the stone steps. "Take it easy. We'll talk it out."

"Oh, God, Michael. I don't know what's gotten into me. For years I wanted her attention; then suddenly I had it and I felt stifled!"

He was beside her, taking in her look of wide-eyed exasperation. Unable to help himself, he grinned.

"What's so funny?"

"You. You look beautiful and independent and . . . and impulsive. Do you realize that I've never seen you quite this way?"

"Laugh, then, if you want. But I've got the worst case of cabin fever and if I don't *do* something, I think I'm going to scream."

"You already did. Twice. Wanna do it again?"

About to argue, she looked at him, then squeezed her eyes shut, balled her fists and let out the loudest, most satisfying scream in the world. When the sound rose beyond the rocks and the pines and died, she dropped her chin to her chest, took a deep breath, then let it out very, very slowly. "Ahhh." She raised her head. "That felt good."

Grinning still, Michael wrapped her in his arms and whirled her around. He'd missed her. Oh, he'd stopped by twice, as a neighbor and friend, to say hello and offer his services to her mother, but he hadn't had a chance to visit with Danica. He hadn't wanted to push his luck that far.

"You're looking better," he said when he set her back on the sand. "I take it you got lots of rest."

"She wouldn't let me do a thing. Not that she's great around the house, mind you. I should be grateful we had a cook all those years. Then again, maybe if we hadn't, she'd have learned to make something other than baked chicken and hamburg."

"That's all you ate?"

"We alternated. Chicken on Sunday, hamburg on Monday, chicken last night. She left a hamburg patty in the refrigerator for me to broil tonight."

"What about lunches?"

"Tuna salad. Egg salad."

Michael winced. "And breakfast?"

"Oatmeal . . . every . . . morning."

He threw back his head and laughed.

"It's not funny, Michael. Between meals she doted like a mother hen. I didn't know how to act. One thing's for sure, my mind was so occupied trying to figure her out that I didn't have time to dwell on the . . . on the baby."

Her expression sobered at the last. Draping an arm around her shoulder, Michael drew her into step beside him as he began to walk slowly along the beach. They talked of her mother and of her father, who'd called and spoken to her twice. She told him of the visit she'd had from a flower-bearing Sara, of the sweet, sweet call she'd gotten from Ginny McCabe and the more dutiful ones she'd received from city friends. He told her of the progress he'd made in his writing, of the discussion he'd had with his editor and the plans they had for publicizing his book.

And they talked about the baby she'd lost, Danica's feelings, her discouragement but resignation.

In the end, though, the one thought that played most heavily in Danica's mind was the realization that in another two weeks she'd be returning to Boston.

Chapter Eight

THE NEXT FEW MONTHS were difficult ones for Danica. By the time she returned to Boston she was still trying to acclimate herself to the fact that there'd be no baby come spring. She rationalized that her miscarriage was perhaps a blessing, that as the doctor had suggested, the baby hadn't been healthy from the start. She reminded herself of all she'd read, that having a child was the worst thing she could have done if, by doing so, she'd hoped to save a floundering marriage. But she hadn't been hoping that. Not really.

The fact was that though her marriage was far from ideal, there were iron bonds holding it together, albeit ones that had less to do with any true love between Blake and her than with external factors such as social convenience and appearance and, of course, expectation.

True, a baby might have added a more personal link to the marriage, but the major reason she'd wanted one had been to give some meaning to her own life. She'd wanted to be a mother. She'd wanted to be able to create a little world with her child, a world which would welcome the love she had to give.

Many, many times she imagined that her miscarriage had been a form of divine punishment. She was married to Blake, but she loved Michael, and that was wrong, so the theory went. But it wasn't, she inevitably argued. Could something that was so beautiful, something that felt so right, be wrong? Could something that made her feel whole, that made her feel treasured, be wrong? Could something that drew from her warmth and caring and concern for another human being be wrong?

There were no answers to her questions. And as if accepting the loss of her baby wasn't enough, the return to Boston, itself, was something akin to drug withdrawal. She missed Michael terribly. The contrast between her life in the city—the meetings and luncheons and cocktail receptions and charity benefits—and that she'd led all summer—biking the streets, walking the beach, reading, thinking, spending time with newfound friends—was harsh.

Blake was Blake, and if possible, more distant than ever. She told herself that he was simply up to his ears in commitments. But the fact remained that they made no use of what little time they did have together to discuss anything, much less their relationship. Blake never spoke of her miscarriage. He never spoke of Maine. She wondered for a time if he resented her love of the place, but as the weeks passed and she dutifully remained on Beacon Hill, she felt his resentment was unwarranted.

He arrived home at night talked out and tired. When he traveled, he rarely called. In desperation, Danica once again began to think of working. She took to reading the help-wanted ads in the paper each morning, but somehow seeing job demands in print made her acutely aware of both the scope of such a commitment and of her own very vague qualifications. She began to discreetly send out feelers among the people with whom she came into contact—the development director at the hospital, the curator of the museum, the university president with whom she often talked at dinner parties.

September yielded to October. The leaves turned, then fell. She was thoroughly discouraged and on the verge of escaping to Maine, which she knew would be wrong because she couldn't expect that Michael would have solutions that she couldn't find herself. Moreover, she told herself, she couldn't always run to him when things were rough. It wasn't fair to either of them. He would allow her to use him, she feared, but she had to learn to be independent. If she was dissatisfied with her life, she had to take it in her own two hands and remold it.

The opening came when she least expected it, while she was attending a benefit lecture given at the Women's City Club by a renowned economist. Blake was out of town, so Danica had gone alone, not because she was a fan of the speaker or because she was deeply involved in economics, but because she'd helped plan the affair, the proceeds of which were being put toward a scholarship fund at one of the smaller local colleges.

She knew many of the people there and spent much of her time at the subsequent reception talking with them. When the conversation waned or, rather, when her interest in the conversation waned, as it always did, she excused herself and graciously approached a group that included the young woman who had taken charge of publicity for the event.

"You did a wonderful job, Sharon. The crowd is more than we'd dared hope for."

Sharon Tyler smiled and sent her eyes in an encompassing sweep of the room. "It's more than I'd hoped for, either, and I couldn't be happier. Sometimes you can plug and plug an event and then have it fall through. It's gratifying when the reverse happens."

They talked for a bit about Sharon's other work; then Sharon introduced Danica to the three people with her. The Hancocks were a couple Danica had met in passing once before. The third member of the group was an older gentleman, a man in his late seventies, whom she'd never met but whose name rang an instant bell. James Hardmore Bryant. Former Governor of the Commonwealth.

"Governor Bryant, it's a pleasure to meet you." She'd had a moment's pause when an instinctive wariness reared its head, but the man before her was so gentle-looking that she was easily able to smile as she offered her hand. When he proceeded to speak, his voice echoed that gentleness.

"It's *my* pleasure, Mrs. Lindsay. I understand that you played a large role in organizing this affair, and I'd like to thank you. The cause is a good one." His smile was sweet in its wrinkled way, and it was genuine, as was the concern he went on to express. "It's hard for young people nowadays. At one time college was thought to be a luxury of the privileged.

If you had the money, you went, and you went wherever you wanted to go. Today, the competition for college admittance is frightening, and the financial commitment is even worse. Yet a college education is a necessity if one hopes to rise in the world. There, too, things were different in my day. Whether or not you had a degree tucked under your belt, you could go out there, and if you had a few brains and a little ambition, you could make something of yourself.

"Take the case of Frankie Cohn. He had nothing. Dirt poor, his family was, but he needed a job, so they borrowed the money to buy him a paper route." He lowered his voice. "In those days you didn't just volunteer for the job. You had to put down hard cash for the rights to the list of customers." He paused only for a breath. Danica sensed that he loved to talk, but she was enjoying listening, as were the others, so she smiled her encouragement when he went on.

"He took on that first route when he was twelve, and it was hard work. He was a skinny kid and he used to keep the papers together with a strap and hoist the whole load—sometimes it was nearly as big as he was—onto his shoulder. There weren't bicycles as you and I know them in those days, and a little red wagon wouldn't have gotten him far. In order to get the papers in the first place, he had to take the streetcar—he wore a badge on his left arm that allowed him to ride for free—and he'd pick the papers up at one station, ride back to the station nearest his route, then start to deliver. The route, by the way, was four miles from his own house. On Sundays he'd be up at four in the morning to take the streetcar to pick up the papers, come back to the basement of a nearby hotel, where he had to put them together, then deliver the lot. He'd walk the four miles home for breakfast, then the four miles back to collect money from each of his customers. In wet weather he'd wear big hip boots. On cold, snowy days his mother sometimes cried when he left. But he did it."

Danica was shaking her head. "That's amazing."

The Governor raised both brows. "You haven't heard the best. He kept that morning route for two years, then took on the afternoon and evening routes and hired seven kids to do it for him. He used to handle all the money, keeping track of everything in his little book. By the time he was seventeen he was in charge of delivering papers in all parts of the city.'' He made a gesture with his hand. ''Of course, the city was different in those days. Safer.'' He chuckled. ''Once he was accosted by a drunken prostitute. He pushed her away and ran like hell.'' The smile faded. ''But he could've found that anywhere. Frankie Cohn loved Boston, and he got to know it by heart. Also made a neat profit for himself. Five thousand in one year, and five thousand was a lot of money then. He's a millionaire today.''

''Cityside Distributors,'' Alan Hancock injected, supplying the key that had instant meaning for Danica, who'd seen the name dozens of times on bills that had come in the mail for Blake. Alan smiled. ''James is wonderful when it comes to stories like this. He's been on the scene for so many years that he's a treasure trove of information.'' He turned to the older man. ''James, you've got to write them down. You're missing your calling, keeping everything to yourself.''

The Governor's ruddy complexion grew all the more so. ''Ach, I haven't got the patience for that. Never did. Never will. Besides, no one wants to read about an old man's ramblings. No, I think I'll just save them up for times like these.'' He glanced at his watch. ''But it's past my bedtime, ladies and gentleman. I'd better be running. It's a long way home.''

Sharon chuckled and nudged Danica. ''Governor Bryant lives just a little ways down on Beacon Street.''

''At my age, young lady,'' James admonished with a grin, ''that's a long way.'' Nodding once, he made a graceful exit.

The talk within the group lingered for a bit on James Bryant's days in the State House, then turned to the college he supported, the same one that would offer the scholarship being established by the evening's proceeds, then to the Hancocks' daughter, who was a sophomore at a college out of state.

Danica's thoughts moved less quickly. An earlier part of the conversation stuck in her mind. It was there when she arrived home that night. It was still there two days later when, in a moment of impulsive bravery, she picked up the phone and called James Hardmore Bryant.

"Governor Bryant?" she began, sounding far more confident than she felt, "this is Danica Lindsay. Perhaps you remember. We met at the Women's City Club the other night?"

"Of course, I remember you, Mrs. Lindsay," came the gentle voice. "I'm not so old that I can't appreciate a pretty face when I see one. Did I tell you that you look very much like my late wife, DeeDee, God rest her soul? A wonderful woman she was. Oh, we fought like cats and dogs and she never did like me running around like I owned the city, but we did have forty-two good years together.... But there I go again. You didn't call to hear me reminisce about my marriage, now, did you?"

Danica smiled. "No, though it sounds like a lovely story. I'd like to hear it another time, which is in a way the reason I'm calling." She took a steadying breath. "I wonder if I could come see you. There's something I'd like to discuss."

"Something you'd like to discuss." He lowered his voice. "Sounds serious."

"It could be. Well, that is ... it's just something I've been thinking about. I don't live far from you. I could come over at your convenience."

The Governor cleared his throat. "Now, let me see. I've got my appointment book right in front of me. Ahhhh. Today's free. And tomorrow. And the next day." He chuckled. "I'm not in demand the way I used to be. You name a time. What's best for *you*?"

She was already feeling better. The research she'd done in the library the day before had told her that James Bryant had been a powerful chief executive. The image of the spirited Irishman had clashed with the more mellow impression she'd received the other night. Other things she'd read had, in part, explained the mellowing, and she assumed much of it had simply come with age. Still, she hadn't been sure how he'd react to her request.

"I could make it tomorrow morning at ten, if that's all right with you."

"Couldn't be better. It'll give me something to look forward to. I'll see you then, Mrs. Lindsay."

"Thank you, Governor."

She set down the phone with a sense of satisfaction, but by the time the morning rolled around she was feeling more anxious than anything. But, she reasoned, she had nothing to lose. So she set out on foot, heading down the hill to Charles Street, then over to Beacon. At ten sharp she was at James Bryant's door. Five minutes later she was seated in his high-ceilinged drawing room, pouring the tea that the Governor's maid had dutifully provided.

"I'd do that myself," the Governor explained, "but my hands have a nasty habit of shaking." He raised one in demonstration. "Some women today are offended by the thought of doing such menial work, so, my dear, please accept my apologies."

"No apology necessary, Governor—"

"James, please." He scratched the top of his head, which was bald except for the thin fringe of gray that ringed it. In Danica's mind, the gesture was an awkward one. When it was immediately followed by the slight lowering of his head, she realized that he felt self-conscious. Again, not quite the image of the elder statesman, but entirely endearing. "They insist on calling me Governor, when I haven't been that for some twenty-odd years. It's a form of respect, they say, but I've had plenty of respect in my day, and I no longer need to intimidate anyone. So, please, make it James. Now, what is it that's brought you to my humble abode?"

It wasn't quite humble, with its stately furniture, its tall windows, its original oils on the walls, but Danica wasn't about to argue. "I've been thinking about your stories and about Alan Hancock's suggestion that you write them down. I, uh, I agree with him."

"That's because you haven't heard but one. They'd bore you to tears. At least, that's what they always did to my son. He told me so. He'd yawn and fidget. Still does."

"That's because he's your son, and perhaps because he's too close to you to appreciate them." The insight had been a spontaneous one, though her own case was different. Early on she'd come to resent the life that kept her father at such a distance.

But James was holding firm. "He's just not interested. Can't stand politics. Many people are that way, you know." He reached for a tea cake and belatedly offered one to Danica, who shook her head. "Funny," he said, turning the cake around in his hand, "when you're in the middle of it all, it's like that's all there is in the world. It's addictive, politics is. It completely takes you over."

"There are many people who agree with you, many people who love it as much as you do," Danica reasoned, knowing well of what she spoke. "But Frank Cohn's story isn't a political one. It's a charming anecdote that carries the flavor of another era. I'll bet you have many more like that just waiting to be told. What I'm suggesting is that you put together... not exactly your memoirs, though your own story would make a wonderful frame for the others... but a collection of profiles, anecdotes, if you will, about the Boston of forty, fifty, sixty years ago."

He was frowning. "You're serious." She nodded. "It's always been something of a joke when people have mentioned it, but you are serious."

"Very much so," she said softly.

He closed one eye. "Why?"

She'd known he'd ask the question and was prepared for it. "Let me tell you a little about myself. I have a degree in English from Simmons, but I've never really done anything with it because I married early—actually the year before I graduated—and I've lived the role of the wife ever since. I have no children and therefore more time on my hands than I want. I've been looking for something constructive to fill that time. It occurred to me while you were talking the other night that we might be able to work together to get your stories into print."

There was a long silence, during which James Hardmore Bryant ate his tea cake start to finish. Only after he'd dusted the last of the crumbs from his tweed trousers did he speak.

"An interesting proposition. But what makes you think you'd be qualified for the position of my, er, my collaborator? You've said yourself that you have a degree and no experience."

For the first time she had a glimpse of the James Bryant who'd once been on top of the heap. Though he hadn't spoken harshly, there'd been a command to his words that must have stood him in good stead in his heyday.

Setting her teacup on the tray, Danica folded her hands in her lap as though to conceal the fluttering in her stomach, which, of course, she told herself, he couldn't see, but they'd reached the hard part and she wanted to project conviction.

"I believe I do have experience in things that might help if we should decide to work together. My husband and I are both active in the community. Over the years I've dealt with many prominent people. I'm comfortable with them. I'm attuned to their thoughts. I've interviewed them, if you will. In some cases I've helped put together brochures and fund-raising material incorporating personal material much as I might do for you. I think the key word is *organization*. I'm very good at that."

She paused. When James sat rubbing his lower lip and gave no indication that he wished to speak, she went on. "But my experience goes beyond that. I grew up in a household that revolved around politics. My father is William Marshall. He's been a member of the Senate since I was a child."

James dropped his hand and raised his head. "Well, why didn't you say that from the start?"

Something inside her snapped and impulse took over. "Because I wished I hadn't had to say it at all. I don't want anyone looking at me with greater interest because of who my father is. I'm my own person—" she dropped her voice "—or at least I'm trying to be."

As soon as the last words were out, she realized that they'd been unnecessary. She was trying to secure a job, not an analyst. Determined to repair whatever damage she might have done, she resumed speaking in a calm and confident tone.

"The fact is that being William Marshall's daughter, I'm not ignorant of the political milieu. My parents sheltered me where the limelight was concerned, but through osmosis, if nothing else, I've learned a lot. I've heard most of my father's stories at least once, not to mention those of the guests he's entertained." She smiled. "You're not the only one who likes to tell stories. You're just different in that you've got the time now to do something with them. Am I wrong?''

"I wish you were, but you're not. I've got more time than I know what to do with."

"Then, why not try what I'm suggesting? You've got nothing to lose. Neither do I, for that matter."

He thought about that for a minute, then gave her a side-long glance. ''What makes you think any publisher will buy my, er, our book?''

"You've had years of experience in circles of power. Yours is a well-known and respected name, and it carries clout. Given the dubious quality of some of the books out there, I think that a publisher, especially a local one, will jump at the opportunity to print something as interesting as this.'' It was a calculated guess, but it was all she had at the moment.

James knew it, too. But he was intrigued both by Danica's faith and her determination. ''Well, then. Exactly what is it you propose?''

She took a deep breath. ''I propose that we talk a bit, then that you let me approach several publishing houses. If and when we get a show of interest, better still an offer, we can begin the real work.''

"And how do you suggest we do that? I haven't got the patience to sit and write things down."

She'd remembered that from her first meeting with this man and had thought it all out. ''You can talk to me. I can ask you questions. We can tape our conversations and have them transcribed. From there on it's really be a matter of organizing and editing.''

He arched both brows. ''I think you may be simplifying things, but I'll be damned if you don't make it all sound tempting.... You'd want to be paid, of course.''

This, too, she'd thought out. She certainly didn't need the money, though there was a legitimacy to being paid. If James Bryant was to respect her, he'd have to see her in a professional light. ''When and if we hear something positive from a publisher, we can draw up an agreement with regard to advances and royalties. There wouldn't have to be any monetary output on your part. The overhead will be negligible.''

She moistened her upper lip. "From what I gather, neither of us needs this money to survive."

He gave her a crooked grin. "You gather correctly."

She held her breath. "Then... ?"

He tugged at one ear. "They really are boring stories after a while."

"That's because you've heard them so many times yourself. All we're asking is that people read them once."

"And you really think some publisher will go for the idea?"

At that moment Danica knew she'd won. "As I said before," she quipped excitedly, "we've got nothing to lose."

"YOU'VE GOT *nothing to lose?* Danica, do you have any idea how much *time* a project like this could take?" her father bellowed.

Danica held the phone away from her ear, then returned it to speak calmly. "I have time, Dad. So does Governor Bryant. There isn't any rush. Spread out over a year or two, it won't be bad. It's not as if the material is timely. If it's waited this long to see the light, it can wait another while longer."

"It can wait forever. I don't see the necessity of it."

She bit her lip in a bid for strength. She was determined not to be cowed by her father, had been steeling herself for his call since she'd told Blake about her plans the evening before. She knew Blake, knew that he'd call William. A tiny part of her had hoped that, given the nature of the work she proposed, her father would be sympathetic. After all, it could be he who was proposing a similar book based on his own experiences. Unfortunately, sympathy was too much too ask. What she was getting was pure dismay.

"There isn't a necessity," she replied quietly, "and there doesn't have to be. Few published books are necessary. They may be interesting or educational or entertaining, but they're not necessary."

"Then why are you doing this?"

She took a breath. "Because I want to."

"You've never thought of working before."

"You've never been aware of my thoughts. I've toyed with the idea for a while now. This is the first time something that

I felt was feasible has come up. My schedule will be flexible and I can work at home."

"I thought you said you'd be going to Bryant's place."

"Yes, but only for several hours at a stretch and at our mutual convenience. He lives five minutes from here. It'll be easy. It's not as if I'm taking a job in an office, working nine to five and commuting each way."

"I don't like the idea of your working at all. Neither does Blake."

"Blake didn't tell me he had any objections." In fact, beyond an initial surprise, he'd taken the news with relative calm, when she'd expected far worse. It still puzzled her that he hadn't put up a fight, particularly when he'd apparently expressed some hesitation to William. She wondered if he'd done so purely for William's benefit; he had to have known what the other's reaction would be.

"Then, Blake was being diplomatic," William stated gruffly. "I don't have to be. It was bad enough that you barricaded yourself in that house in Maine for the summer when you should have been with Blake. You're his wife, for God's sake. Blake Lindsay's wife doesn't have to work. William Marshall's daughter doesn't have to work."

"Of course I don't *have* to. I *want* to."

"I say you're making a big mistake. Why in the devil do you feel you have to jump into something you don't know the first thing about?"

Danica bristled. "Are you saying that you think I can't do it? That you think I might make a fool out of myself?"

"There's always that chance."

"I'm glad you've got so much faith in me."

"Sarcasm doesn't suit you, Danica. I'm only trying to think of what's best for you."

"Are you, Dad? Are you really? But what about me? Don't *I* have a say as to what's best for me? I'm not a little girl anymore. I've lived with myself for twenty-eight years and I think I have some idea of what I want."

"And what you want is to work with that old coot? How many copies of his book do you think will be bought? How many best-seller lists do you think it's going to make?"

"That's not the point," she gritted. "The point is that I want something to do and the prospect of doing *this* appeals to me."

William was silent for a moment. "Are you feeling all right, Danica?"

"Of course. What does that have to do with anything?"

"This work idea. Maybe you're still depressed about the baby. It's understandable. In time you'll come to your senses."

"I have come to my senses," she said under her breath.

"Speak up. You're mumbling."

"Nothing. It was nothing." She felt suddenly tired.

"Look. Why don't you put off making any decision for a while. Things are busy now. Just go on doing what you've always done. Be there for Blake. Relax. Who knows? Maybe you'll get pregnant again. You'll certainly have your work cut out for you then."

She'd had enough. "Uh, Dad, I've got to run. Blake will be home any minute and I'm not dressed. Give my love to Mom, will you?"

"But she wants to speak with you."

"Another time. Really. I've got to go. I'll talk with you soon. Bye-bye."

BLAKE WASN'T DUE HOME for another two hours, and though Danica had been fully dressed when her father had called, when Blake finally breezed in an hour after expected, she was in her robe and ready for bed. The only reason she'd waited up was to tell him that she was driving to Maine the next morning and that if she wasn't back by eight he should have dinner without her.

MICHAEL WAS ECSTATIC to open his door and find her there. He held her for a long, long time, enjoying the softness of her body, the sweet, fresh scent of her skin. "Ahhh, I've missed you," he growled against her hair.

"I've missed you, too." Neither had called the other on the phone. In unspoken agreement they'd realized that it would be difficult. Michael would have felt awkward if he'd called and Blake had answered. Danica would have felt awkward if Blake found a slew of calls to Maine on his monthly bill. More critically, each sensed that it would be too difficult to hear the other's voice and then have to say goodbye.

Fitting a firm arm to her shoulders, Michael led her into the house. She freed herself only to kneel and greet a fast-growing and exuberant Rusty, but she quickly returned to Michael's side, unwilling to stay away for long. They had one day. She needed all the sustenance she could get.

She also needed encouragement, and she got it. Michael burst into a smile the instant she told him about her decision to work with James Bryant.

"Danica Lindsay, that's fantastic news! Tell me everything."

She did just that, detailing her initial introduction to James and the germination of her idea, the reading she'd done on his life, the mental calculations she'd made concerning the possibility of the project and the subsequent meeting at which she'd put it all forward to James. She told of Blake's reaction and of her father's. And she told of her excitement...and fear.

"Maybe I'm crazy, Michael. I don't know the first thing about putting together a book. I've been operating on sheer guts up to now, but it's time to put words into action. Where do I go from here? What do I do? Whom do I see?"

"First you sit back, take a deep breath and relax." He spoke slowly, reassuringly. "Then you tell yourself that everything you've said to Bryant, and to Blake and your father, for that matter, was correct. Because it is, Dani. You've got the time and the desire. Regardless of how widespread the audience for a book like this will be, there is a market for it. And that's where you start. What you told Bryant was right on the button. The two of you have to talk; then you've got to write up a proposal to send to various houses."

He elaborated on the contents of such a proposal, making suggestions and giving hints that had worked for him. She asked him questions galore, jotting notes for herself as he made their lunch. Later he mentioned the names of several publishers whom he thought might be interested, and she noted those, too, but when he offered to make calls on her behalf, she gently refused. Likewise, she was resistant to his suggestion that he call his agent.

"I think I'd like to try it myself first. Do you...do you know what I mean?"

He smiled. "Of course I do. And you're right. It'll be that much more rewarding for you to do it on your own."

"It's not that I'm not grateful—"

His hand on her lips cut her off. "Say no more. I know what you need, and that's to be independent. It's hard for me, y' know. If I had my way I'd probably be smothering you just the way you've been smothered in the past."

"You'd never do that."

"I don't want to, but it's a temptation at times. I want to help you, to make things easier for you. I have to keep reminding myself that you need to do this yourself."

She took his hand and held it tight. "Thank you for understanding. Nobody else does. I think that's going to be the worst part of all this. It helps just knowing that you're here." She felt suddenly guilty. Their time together was passing, focusing entirely on her. "How's your book coming, Michael?"

"Nearly done. Another few weeks should do it."

"That's great! Are you pleased with it?"

"Very. So's my editor, from what he said after reading the first half. I don't think I'll have any major problems."

"You look tired." On impulse she brushed the hair from his forehead. It was a joy to touch him, to care for him. "Late nights?"

"Yeah. When things roll, they roll. And since I don't have anything else to do with my time . . ." The last was said on a note of gentle accusation which Danica felt to her core.

She looked down. "I wish I could be here more. It's lonesome in Boston."

"With all those people around?"

"It's lonesome."

He touched his finger to her chin and tipped it up. "I know. I bury myself in work so that I won't have to think about how quiet it is here."

"You're not raising Rusty right. He's supposed to be your best friend."

"*You*'re my best friend."

"Michael..." She wanted to scold him for tormenting her, but she realized that she'd been the one to start it all by materializing on his doorstep that morning. Instead, she leaned forward against him, sliding her arms around his waist, pressing her cheek to his chest.

"Dani?"

"Just hold me...just for a minute," she whispered.

He swallowed hard. "You're playing with fire."

"I know. But I...I need...just hold me, Michael."

He didn't argue further, because he needed so badly to do what she'd asked. His arms closed around her, strong and protecting. "Dear God, I love you," he whispered, unable to stem the words he'd been aching to say all day. She wouldn't return them, he knew, but the way she was holding him in return was enough.

Minutes passed and neither of them moved away. Danica rubbed her cheek over the wool of his turtleneck, imagining she felt the soft sprinkle of his chest hair, wanting desperately to touch it. Michael concentrated on the sleekness of her back beneath his hands, the press of her breasts against him, her soft curves just waiting to be explored.

When his body grew tight, he tried to think of baseball or basketball or hockey, but it didn't work. "I need you, Dani," he warned hoarsely, "and it's only getting worse. I thought once you'd gone back to Boston, I'd be able to regain control of myself, but I lie awake at night thinking about you and I get hard and sore and..." He drew her head back so he could see her face. She looked as stricken as he felt.

"Let me make love to you, sweetheart. Let me—"

"Oh, God. We can't."

"Why not? The feeling's there. It's inevitable."

"But I'm married. I can't be unfaithful—"

"You're already being unfaithful," he argued, then half wished he hadn't when her eyes filled with tears. But it needed to be said, he realized. At least he couldn't seem to keep himself from saying it. "Dani, you *already* feel things for me that you shouldn't feel.'' Taking her face in his hands, he brushed his thumbs back and forth along her cheekbones. "You don't have to say the words, but I know that you love me. If we were to make love, it'd only be an expression of what we both already feel."

"I can't," she pleaded, "I can't."

"I'm not quite sure what it is you have with Blake, but it can't come close to what we feel for each other."

"I'm bound to him."

"You're not in love with him, at least not the way you're in love with me. Do you have any idea how beautiful it would be for us?" He ignored the tiny sound of desperation that came from her throat. "I want to touch you, to kiss you all over. I want to see you, all of you. I want you to be naked, naked and warm and wet. You would be, Dani. I can feel you trembling right now."

"I'm frightened. You're scaring me, Michael!"

"No, I'm only putting into words what you've thought about yourself. Am I wrong?" When she didn't answer, he pressed. "Am I?"

"No! No! But I can't make love to you. I'm not free!"

"With me you're free." His low voice quivered. "You'd touch me, Dani. You'd undress me and kiss me and move over me—"

Jerking from his hold, she bolted up from the sofa. Her body was hot and cold and tingling and taut and felt utterly foreign to her. "Stop it, Michael. Please? I can't do what you want. I just can't."

Her crushed expression gave him the control over his body that neither baseball nor basketball nor hockey had been able to do. Closing his eyes for a minute, he took several deep breaths, then slowly pushed himself to his feet. "Okay, sweetheart. I'll stop. But I want you to think about something for me. I want you to think about what *you* want. You know what I want. You know what Blake wants. You know what your father wants." When she swayed, he drew her against him and she didn't resist. "I want you to think about what you could have." He pressed her hips lightly to his, just enough to alert her to his still aroused state. "I won't force anything. I couldn't do that. When you come to me, I want it to be because *you* want it. I want you to need me to be inside you as much as I need to be there.''

She moaned softly and began to shake. "Don't say things like that," she whispered. "I can't take it."

"But you're not moving away." If anything, she'd arched her hips closer.

"It feels...so good..."

He was the one to put inches between them. "Then, remember it. Remember how good it feels now, when you're back in Boston." His eyes fell to her breasts, then lower. "Think about how much better it'll feel without clothes and inhibitions and regrets. Think about it, Dani, because I'll be doing the same. Somehow we're going to have to come to terms with all this." He gave a tired sigh and rubbed the back of his neck. "Somehow. Someday."

There was a thick silence, then Danica's broken "And in the meantime?"

He took a breath. "In the meantime, I guess we'll have to go along as we have."

"I wasn't sure if...if you'd rather I didn't come..."

"That'd be the smartest thing. But it's not possible. We both know that. You don't come up much now, anyway."

She lowered her chin. "No. Blake can't...and well, now that I've got this project... What will you be doing once your book's done?"

"I thought I'd take a few weeks off. Maybe go to Vail and do some skiing."

She met his gaze. "That'd be fun."

"Do you ski?"

"No. My parents wouldn't let me...the risk and all...when I was playing tennis, and Blake never wanted to... Damn, I'd better be going. This isn't getting any easier."

There was another silence, then: "Will you let me know what's happening?"

She brushed at her tears. "I will."

"And you'll call me if there's anything I can do to help you with your work?"

"Uh-huh."

He cupped her chin in his hand and spoke more quietly. "Will you think about what I've said?"

He was looking at her with such love that it took Danica a minute to catch her breath. "I don't have much choice, do I?"

He smiled. "No. You don't."

"Then I guess I'll be thinking about what you've said." She forced a smile. "Wanna know what my tea bag said this morning?"

"Sure. What did your tea bag say this morning?"

"It said, 'Often it takes as much courage to resist as it does to go ahead.'"

"Smart tea bag. Who writes those things, anyway?"

"Smart men."

"Hmph. If they were really smart, they would have written something like 'True love awaits you by the sea in Maine.'"

"That'd be a fortune cookie."

"Cookie . . . tea . . . same difference." Before she could respond, he swept her up for a quick hug, then all but shoved her out the door. "Better leave now or I'm apt to throw you over my shoulder, shackle you to my bed and make love to you until you beg for mercy."

"Brute," she teased, but she was running down the path toward her car. She still had the house to check, then the drive back to Boston, and she knew she'd better keep moving because to one increasingly large part of her the thought of being shackled to Michael's bed was very, very sweet.

TWO AND A HALF WEEKS LATER, Michael threw caution to the winds and called her on the phone. He reasoned that as a friend he had every right to do so. As the man who loved her . . . well, no one but her had to know that.

"Lindsay residence."

"Mrs. Lindsay, please."

"Who may I say is calling?"

He grasped the phone tighter. "Michael Buchanan."

"One minute, please."

In less than that, Danica picked up the library extension. "Michael?"

"Hi, Dani."

"Michael," she breathed, feeling the abundance of tension with which she'd lived for the past few days begin to ease at last. "Oh, Michael..."

"How are you, Dani?"

"Better, now."

"It's been that bad?"

"Only in my mind.... You know he won."

"Yup."

"Blake's ecstatic. So's my dad. You'd think Jason Claveling's election was the Second Coming."

"After all their work, they've got a right to be pleased."

"Mmmm. Well, at least that's over. Somehow, though, I keep waiting for the other shoe to fall."

"Do you think Blake's expecting an appointment?"

"He joked about it a while back, but I'm beginning to wonder. God, Michael, can you imagine what would happen then? If Blake accepts a position in the Claveling administration, we'd have to move to Washington. That's the *last* place I want to be."

"I don't know. There are many people who'd find it exciting."

"Would you?"

"Not particularly, but then, I'm antisocial."

"You are not antisocial. You're anti-insanity. It's mad down there. Power and politics. Politics and power." She made a sound deep in her throat. "Madness. Sheer madness."

"There's no point in worrying about it now, Dani," he pointed out soothingly. "The election was just yesterday. Claveling will be taking time off to rest before he begins to think about any appointments."

"I suppose.... Did you finish your book?"

"Yup. It's off. I'm heading for the Rockies tomorrow. What's doing with you and Bryant?"

"The proposal's all done. I'm ready to mail it out. Maybe I'll have heard something by the time you get back. When will that be?"

"Sometime before Christmas.... Any chance you'll be up at the house?"

"Uh, I'm not sure. We always spend the holiday with my parents. Afterward, though, I might...I could, but...maybe it's not such a good idea."

"You mean, I'm scaring you away—" he began, then caught himself and lowered his voice. "There isn't any chance your phone is tapped, is there?"

The thought hadn't occurred to her, though it should have. "I, uh, I don't know," she replied, shaken.

"Mmmm. Well, if you can come up," Michael went on with deliberate nonchalance, "it'd be great. Sara races out to ask about you every time I pass the store. And Greta and Pat call all the time."

"How's Meghan?"

"Adorable."

"And Rusty?"

"Resisting my every attempt to house-train him. I think I'm going to confine him to the beach."

"You wouldn't do that. It's cold now, and he's just a puppy."

"He's getting huge, which makes it all the worse."

Danica laughed in spite of herself. "Poor baby."

"Him...or me?"

"Both.... Michael?" Her voice grew soft, but mindful of his warning, she guarded her words. "It's good to hear from you."

"Can I call again?"

"I'd like that."

"Well then, take care."

"You, too, Michael. Don't break a leg."

He chuckled. "I won't. Bye-bye."

"Bye."

A WEEK BEFORE CHRISTMAS Danica was upset enough not to care if Blake did see the call on the bill. She tried to call Michael, then tried again the next day, but he wasn't home. When he got through to her on the third day, she was instantly relieved.

"Thank God, you're back" were her first soft-breathed words upon hearing his voice.

"I'm not back. I took a detour in Phillie to spend time with Corey. I wasn't sure if I should call." He dropped his voice. "Are you okay?"

"No. I'm torn to bits inside. Blake is in seventh heaven. So are my parents and his parents and our friends, and they all expect me to be, too. Secretary of Commerce. Can you believe it? I swear he had this in mind from the start. Never once did he stop to consider what I might have wanted."

"Shhh. It's okay, Dani. It won't be that bad."

She spoke brokenly. "I can't make it to Maine, Michael. Blake wants to go to Washington to look at places to live."

"I understand. Maybe it's just as well. You and Blake have a new life ahead of you."

"Maybe Blake. Not me. At least, not *that* life."

"What do you mean?"

"I've already told him that I won't live in Washington. I'll commute for weekends if I have to, but I'm staying here."

"How did he take that?"

"Well. Actually, complacently."

"And you're hurt."

"You'd think he'd have been upset. You'd think he'd *want* me there. After all, I am his wife. It's strange..."

"What is?"

"I've begun to wonder...I mean, he accepted my going to Maine last summer with literally no fight. He didn't argue when I told him I'd be working with James Bryant. Now he seems perfectly agreeable to the idea of a long-distance marriage. It's almost as though he's glad to have me occupied and out of his hair.... I wonder if he has a mistress."

"Oh, Dani, I doubt—"

"It's not impossible. After all, we could easily be—"

He cut her off with an "Uuuuh! I don't think you should say things like that." It was a subtle reminder that something spoken might be irretrievable. "Besides, Blake has his image to consider. I doubt he'd do anything to jeopardize a position he's worked so hard to get."

"I suppose."

"Give him the benefit of the doubt."

Michael had no idea why he was standing up for Blake Lindsay when he wanted to scream at the man for way he treated his wife, but he had to do it. The alternative was to give encouragement to something that might be totally false, and given his own less than impartial involvement in the situation, that would be wrong. He never wanted to be accused of actively encouraging Danica's alienation from Blake; if there was to be alienation that would lead to a breakup, it had to be the sole doing of husband or wife.

Danica sighed. "I guess I *have* to give him the benefit of the doubt since the outcome suits me. It would have been worse if Blake had insisted I live full-time in Washington.... Michael, I haven't heard anything on the book yet."

"It's too soon. Don't be discouraged. Sometimes it takes two or three months for an editor to get a chance to read a proposal."

"Are you sure?"

"I'm sure."

They talked for a while longer, and when Danica hung up the phone, she felt better.

She felt even better when, in the first week of January, she received a summons from one of the most prestigious publishing houses in Boston.

Chapter Nine

THE DAY AFTER Jason Claveling was inaugurated Blake was sworn in as his Secretary of Commerce. Danica stayed through the festivities, feeling pride in her husband in spite of herself. A stunning complement to him, she received her share of praise. None, however, came directly from Blake, who was more emotionally wrapped up in himself than she'd ever seen him. When she returned to Boston several days later, he didn't blink an eye.

Having signed a contract with the publishing house that had been their first choice, Danica and James spent every afternoon together, talking, discussing, recording their words for transcription by one of Danica's ballet friends who she knew needed the money.

Danica enjoyed her time with James. He was interesting, sharp even in spite of his age, and lacked the arrogance that so turned her off to politics. Often he'd turn around and ask her a question about herself and one of her own experiences. He seemed to accept her as an equal in their enterprise, and that enhanced her enjoyment of it. At last she felt she was *doing* something. Between mornings spent at occasional meetings and ballet, afternoons spent at James's town house and evenings spent reading what had been transcribed, she was busy.

She commuted to Washington several times a month to attend receptions and parties with Blake, and though she found the air of social climbing, of ambition, of competition and power hunger to be oppressive, she was satisfied to discharge her responsibility to Blake—and to her father, whom she saw more often than she ever had.

William accepted her presence with a this-is-your-rightful-place attitude and proceeded to pay her not much more heed than Blake did. Neither man asked about the work she was doing in Boston, as though ignoring it would make it go away. Eleanor, strangely, was the one who expressed interest, and though Danica did talk with her, she felt wary. She couldn't understand her mother's interest now, any more than she'd been able to understand Eleanor's coddling the August before. As had been the case then, Danica didn't quite know how to react. More than once she wondered if Eleanor was doing William's bidding. *Snooping* was an unkind word, but given the woman's distance through Danica's childhood, Danica couldn't help but imagine that there might be some ulterior motive for her attentiveness.

Michael called Danica in Boston from time to time. He was traveling, doing research for a book on the roots of the environmental movement, spending time reading and interviewing in many of the nation's large cities. He purposely avoided the Northeast, fearing that the temptation to see Danica would be too great, particularly now that he knew how many of her nights were spent alone. He didn't want to take advantage of the situation. Moreover, he knew that she needed to be alone, to think. Her days were filled and she enjoyed her work; he gleaned that from the detailed phone conversations they held. And her tone of voice, sometimes growing exquisitely soft, sometimes broken, hinted that she missed him as she would never have expressed in words. He had to have faith that in time, when she felt comfortable with herself as an entity independent of both Blake and her father, she'd be more able to take a stand with regard to her future and to him.

BY LATE MAY, having finished most of what he needed to do on the road, Michael headed for a few days' R and R visiting friends and his sister in Washington.

"Hey, Mike!" Jeffrey Winston half rose from his seat in the crowded restaurant to catch his friend's attention.

Michael quickly made his way to the table, shaking hands, then embracing the man he'd been close to for years. They'd met in college and had served together in Vietnam. For a time they'd been brothers-in-law. The two were remarkably alike—both tall and rakishly good-looking, both intelligent, introspective and dedicated to their work.

"How's it going, Jeff? God, it's good to see you!"

"You, too, stranger. It's been too long," Jeff snagged a passing waitress around the waist and motioned for two more beers before turning back to Michael. "Cilla tells me you've been on the run."

Michael teasingly held up a hand. "Nothing clandestine. Just doing research for my next masterpiece."

"The last one was great, Mike. Religious and racial bigotry—whew! Remember the talks we used to have on that topic?"

Michael grinned. "Where do you think I got the idea for the book?"

"Yeah, but you carried it off, while I couldn't have written the first chapter. How's it doing?"

"Not bad. We're into a second printing, which isn't saying all that much given the size of the first one, but at least the book's sales have exceeded my publisher's expectations. It always helps to do well in their eyes.... But tell me about you, pal. What's this I hear about a promotion?"

"Cilla's been talking."

"Why shouldn't she? It's exciting. He-e-ey, I'm her brother and your friend. She knew I'd want to know. That doesn't mean she's printed it on page one. Besides, she's proud of you."

"She is? Funny, she always hated what I did when we were married."

"It wasn't what you did that she hated. It was what you *didn't* do, i.e. tell her all the little details."

"I couldn't, Mike. She's the press, for Christ's sake. I couldn't tell her what I was working on when it was confidential."

"You didn't trust her to keep it that way and she knew it. But, hey, I'm not blaming anything on you. It takes two to make a marriage work or not work. Cilla's constantly curious, about anything and everything. She can be pretty intense when she wants to be. She's like Dad in that way. I'm sure she was no joy to live with."

"I don't know," Jeffrey mused, "we had some good times. If it hadn't been for her occupation . . . okay, okay, *and* mine, we might have made it. I don't think she trusted me any more than I trusted her. She was constantly worried that I'd pry her sources out of her and then turn around and launch an investigation." He snorted. "As if I had the power . . ."

"Do you now? Come on, give. What's the story on the promotion?"

Jeffrey took a breath and sat back in his seat. Talk of Cilla always got to him. He had so many misgivings, so many lingering feelings for her. Lately, he seemed obsessed with the good times they'd had. In the six years since they'd divorced, he hadn't met another woman who came close to her in fun or challenge or sheer sexual abandon.

"The promotion. Uh, well, I'm in charge of DOD's investigative unit. It's not that I can go out looking for things to investigate, but when we get a referral, even a tip, I decide who's going to do the work and then keep tabs on things."

"So it's mainly administrative?"

"More so than before. I still do the nitty-gritty—you know I love that part—and I can assign myself to work on some of the plums, which is nice. It's a challenge."

"What are some of the things you're doing?"

Over roast beef sandwiches, Jeffrey talked. He kept his voice low and leaned forward from time to time, but he trusted Michael with his life, literally and figuratively. It occurred to him that if he'd trusted Cilla a fraction as much, they might not have split. When he asked himself why he *hadn't* trusted her, he didn't like the only reason he could find, so he stopped pondering it.

"Is that the current project?" Michael asked after Jeffrey had told of an investigation into leaks of classified information within the State Department.

"No. Something else has just come up." He frowned. "It's a tricky thing."

It was Michael's turn to lean forward, which he did with both brows raised in invitation.

Jeffrey wavered. "I don't know. It's still pretty vague."

"Come on, Jeff. It's me. Michael."

"This is a little different from the counterinsurgency work we did in Nam.... Ah, hell. You'll keep quiet. Besides, there's not really much that's classified yet." Putting both elbows on the table, he spoke quietly. "You've heard of Operation Exodus."

"U.S. Customs Service, isn't it?"

"Mmmm. It's a program that was set up a few years back to halt the illegal export of high-tech products to the Soviet bloc. From the beginning it had plenty of opposition, congressmen and exporters who felt that it hindered the flow of trade abroad. The government's theory is that since the Soviet Union is years behind us in research and technology that can vastly improve its military systems, it will beg, borrow or steal what it can. One vital acquisition can advance them ten years. The same semiconductors and integrated circuits that are used in video games also go into guided-missile systems. Small computers, which businesses here use every day of the week, also can be used by the military to efficiently plot and track movements of troops. Laser technology used by our doctors can be used to disable enemy communication satellites."

"Dual-use technologies."

"Right. Like I say, it's a sensitive issue. There are constant battles being waged on what items should or should not be on the restricted list. Any number of advanced technology items could possibly be used for defense by a hostile country. Whether they *would* be is another story. The Pentagon takes the hard line, wanting to clamp down on every possibility. The Commerce Department is obviously more attuned to the country's commercial interests. It maintains that by stringently controlling what Americans are allowed to export, we yield a lucrative market to European concerns."

"What about the Coordinating Committee for Export Controls? Doesn't it have a say as to what's sold to Eastern Europe?"

"To some extent. Any one of its delegates can veto an American company's request. Mmmm, CoCom makes it easier, that's for sure, especially now that Germany and Japan are members. But the organization is voluntary. Member countries may agree on what is and is not sensitive material, but they have no obligation to enforce CoCom's bans.''

"Which means that the Commerce Department could, by rights, go ahead and issue a license to a company for export of goods that CoCom has vetoed.''

"Right. Not that that's happened often. Our government is firmer than others. But there have been slips, situations where licenses have been granted to companies they shouldn't have been granted to—companies headed by shady characters, companies with suspicious business contacts in other countries. Over the past few years Operation Exodus has managed to thwart smuggling of some pretty important stuff to the East.''

"So I've read," Michael said pensively. "So where do you come in?''

"The Department of Defense has begun to suspect that certain super-minicomputers are finding their way to places they shouldn't be. Our intelligence agencies are seeing restricted items with very definite American stamps on them in use in countries which shouldn't have them. So . . . we're investigating.''

"Hey, exciting!''

"That's the spy in you speaking, Mike. Got a lot of mileage out of that book, didn't you?''

"It sold well. Hmph, it did more than that. Somebody saw it and liked it and because of it asked me to teach a course on intelligence work and counterespionage at Harvard next fall.''

"No kidding? The JFK School?''

Michael nodded. He'd just gotten word of his appointment. He was looking forward to being in Boston once a week . . . for more reasons than one.

"You've never taught before, have you?''

"Only onetime seminars. This'll be an experience. From what I hear, the students are sharp. By rights I should have a Ph.D. to teach at a place like that, but I guess they felt my

book—and the others I've written—were credential enough.''

''I'd think so. What are you working on now?''

They talked for a while about Michael's latest project, then
about mutual friends that one or another had seen, then,
inevitably, about the legs of their waitress.

''Why does it always come down to this?'' Michael asked,
laughing. ''You'd think we were still in college, sitting around the frat house rating the coeds on a score of one to ten.''

''Some of them were dogs, weren't they?''

''Hmph. The same dogs are probably gorgeous today.
Gorgeous…and successful…and married. And here we sit,
the two of us, with no one.''

''Is that a note of wistfulness I hear? A change of heart in
the confirmed bachelor?''

''We ain't gettin' younger, pal.''

''But wiser. Maybe we're getting wiser.''

''I sometimes wonder,'' Michael mused and happened to
glance at the opposite side of the restaurant. ''I don't believe
it. She's here.''

Jeffrey twisted to follow his gaze. ''Cilla! When did *she*
come in? I didn't see her before.''

''We weren't exactly looking around.'' Michael kept his
eyes glued to his sister. She looked up once, met his gaze but
quickly returned to her discussion with a well-dressed man of
the diplomat type. ''I spent yesterday with her. She knew I
was meeting you here, but she didn't say anything about her
own plans.''

''Maybe she wanted to surprise you.''

''Maybe she wanted to surprise *you*.''

Jeffrey gave a half-laugh. ''She's done that. Look at the
guy. He's not her type. No flair. No excitement.''

''She's probably interviewing him for a piece she's writing.''

''I hope so. Jeez, I'd hate to think she's gotten desperate.''
He paused, still staring at Cilla. ''She looks good, doesn't
she?''

''Uh-huh.''

''Wonder if she does date much.''

Michael was grateful that Jeffrey wasn't looking his way. It was hard to keep his lips from twitching. "No one special. I think she's pretty fed up with it all. Face it, pal. You spoiled her for other men."

"Y' think so?" Jeffrey asked, then jerked his gaze back to Michael. "Don't shit me. *You* guys spoiled her. Made her too independent for her own good. I couldn't tame her, that's for sure."

"You've both mellowed. Maybe you should give it another try."

Jeffrey was shaking his head a little too quickly. "We have a basic conflict of interest. Her work and mine."

"It's only a matter of trust.... Don't you ever wish you had a family?" Michael asked hesitantly, wondering if he was the only one with the sudden affliction.

"All the time. But Cilla's not the type to slow down. Can you imagine her nine months pregnant and racing around the city after one story or another?"

Michael chuckled. "I almost can. She'd give birth on a street corner, stick the kid in her purse and keep going."

"A kangaroo. Just like a kangaroo, hoppin' all over the place with a kid in her pouch."

"Or an Indian squaw with a papoose on her back. Still, they loved their babes, the Indians did."

Jeff cocked his head to the side. "Why do I hear a message in this?"

"Do you?" He glanced up. "Hey, look. Here she comes."

Sure enough, Cilla was approaching their table, having left her companion behind to pay the bill. "Look who's here." She leaned down to kiss Michael, then nonchalantly put a hand on Jeffrey's shoulder. "Hi, Jeff. How's it goin'?"

"Great, Cilla. Just great. Mike and I were having a fascinating talk."

"Oh? About what?"

"Kangaroos."

Cilla shot Michael a strange look before returning to Jeff. "Are you thinking of adopting one?"

"I had one once."

"You never told me that."

"It was strictly confidential. Classified information."

Cilla gave an exaggerated nod and diplomatically went along with the gag. "I hope you had more luck house-training it than Mike had with his pup."

"I had no luck at all. Finally had to let her go...for her sake *and* mine. I do miss her, though. She had her moments."

"We all do," Cilla said with a sad sigh. She rubbed her hand across Jeff's broad back. "Well, I'd better run." Leaning down, she pressed her cheek to his, waved to Michael and was off.

"Fool kangaroo," Jeffrey muttered.

Michael studied his friend but said nothing. He'd seen the light in Jeff's eyes when Cilla had been near, had seen the flush on his sister's cheeks when she'd been talking to Jeff. He was sure that strong feelings still existed between these two people who meant so much to him. Nothing would make him happier than to see them get back together, though it was out of his hands, as it should be. After all, he mused, who was he to be matchmaking when his own love life was at loose ends.

"Hi, Dani."

"Michael! Where are you?"

"Back home at last. Boy, does it feel good. It's beautiful up here now. Everything's blooming."

"I saw. I was up several weeks ago and it was pretty then. It wasn't the same though without you there.... Did you get everything done that you wanted to?"

"Yup. I'm all set to spend the summer writing."

"Me, too."

"You're kidding! You finished all the taping?"

"Uh-huh. James is heading to Newport for the summer, so it's just as well. Everything is transcribed. Now the fun part starts."

"You can do it, Dani. I've told you that before."

"I know. Still, it's a little awesome holding all this stuff in my lap and knowing that I've got to put it into some intelligible form."

"Jump in. That's what I do. The worst part is the anticipation. It's not so bad once you get going."

"I'm counting on that.... How's Rusty?"

"He's a monster. You won't believe it when you see him."

"He didn't give Greta and Pat any problems while you were away?"

"Are you kidding? Their house is full of crap anyway."

"Michael," Danica scolded, but she was laughing, "that's not fair. Greta and Pat's house is wonderful."

He smiled. It was so good to hear her voice, so much better to hear her laugh. "I know it and I know you know it, so it's okay for me to say what I did."

"How are they, anyway?"

"Terrific. They're wondering when you're coming up. *I'm* wondering when you're coming up."

She beamed. She didn't care how dangerous it was, but she'd gone more than eight months without seeing Michael and she was starved. "I'll be there in a few weeks."

"For...how long?"

It was her surprise and she savored it. "Till Labor Day."

"Till Labor Day?" He'd assumed, given Blake's new status, that she'd have to spend time in D.C. "Sweetheart, that's great!"

"I think so. I need the time there...very badly."

He hesitated for just a minute. "Things have been rough?"

Her voice grew more quiet. "I guess you'd say that. There's not much for me in Washington."

"Blake's busy?"

"Blake's busy. It's worse than it was here. He loves everything about the place—the glitz, the pomp, the power—everything I hate."

"Have you told him so?"

"Yes. He says that it's only for four years, but he's not kidding me. If Claveling's reelected it could easily be for eight, and even if it isn't, Blake's hooked. If it's not a Cabinet position, it'll be something else. Not very promising for the warm, close family I wanted."

There was nothing Michael could say to that. He wanted to say that *he'*d give her the warm, close family she wanted, but she already knew it. The ball was very definitely in her court.

"Well," he said with a sigh, "at least coming up here will be a break."

"Don't you know it," she said with feeling, and he laughed. "Unfortunately, my mother may be spending some time there with me."

"Uh-oh. She's still feeling maternal?"

"I don't understand it, Michael. I *still* don't understand it. All of a sudden she wants a close mother-daughter relationship. When I'm in Washington, we see each other. When I'm here, she calls at least twice a week. That's more than Blake does."

"Maybe she knows that and feels badly."

"No," Danica replied thoughtfully. "There's something more. I think she's feeling her own mortality."

"She's been sick again?"

"Oh, no. She's fine. It's just that, well, it's almost as if she's looking back on her life, looking for something now that she didn't have then."

"Have you discussed it with her?"

"We don't get into talks like that."

"You could..."

"I know. But I feel awkward."

"Maybe it'll be good if she comes up, then. Maybe you'll be able to work through that awkwardness."

"I don't know. I still feel so much resentment. You remember how awful it was when she was up last summer."

He remembered very well. "You weren't at your best then, Dani. This time you can do things with her, take her out, maybe introduce her to some of the people you've met here."

"She's already met you. You're the one who matters most. And if she's around... it's so hard to pretend..."

"Shhh. Let's face that when it comes. In the meantime, just concentrate on getting away."

"I will.... Michael? I'm glad you're back. It makes me feel better knowing you're there."

"I'll always be here for you. You know that, don't you?"

"Yes," she whispered. She did know it. Regardless of where he was, she knew he'd come running if she needed him, and she loved him all the more for it.

"Take care, sweetheart."

"You, too, Michael."

MICHAEL SAT BROODING for a long time after he hung up the phone. On the one hand, he was ecstatic. Danica would be his for the summer. On the other hand, he was stymied. Danica wasn't really his, not in the way he wanted.

He'd spent much time talking with Cilla on the subject of Danica and Blake, but it had taken him nowhere. Indeed, Cilla had seen Blake several times since he'd arrived in Washington. She'd watched him in action at various functions and could only report that he was the epitome of propriety. On none of the occasions when she'd seen him—and several were evening affairs—had Danica been present, yet he'd neither been with another woman nor shown the slightest interest in flirting with one. The only thing Michael could conclude was that the man was a stiff. Unfortunately, he was the stiff to whom Danica was tied, and for the life of him, Michael didn't know what to do about it.

SEVERAL DAYS BEFORE she was to leave for Maine, Danica received a surprise call from Reggie Nichols.

"Danica Lindsay, how would you like company for a day or two?"

"You can come? Reggie, I'd love it! I've been trying to get you here for months. Just tell me when and I'll pick you up at the airport."

Reggie affected a lazy drawl. "Oh, any time would be fine. I'll just browse through the newsstands until you get here."

"You're there *now*?" Danica asked excitedly.

"'Fraid so."

"I'll be right over. Give me . . . fifteen minutes?"

"Terrific! I'm at the Delta terminal. I'll be waiting outside."

"This is great! I can't wait to see you!"

Reggie laughed. "Hurry up then."

"Right! See you in a minute!" Slamming down the phone, Danica jumped up from Blake's desk and ran for her coat and keys. It'd been a year since she'd seen Reggie, and she was very definitely in the mood to talk. Reggie Nichols fit the bill as only one other person could, and *he'd* be there for her in another three days. It was her lucky week, she told herself, feeling absurdly lighthearted as she headed for the airport.

She'd barely pulled up at the terminal when she spotted Reggie. She honked and waved, then slid from behind the wheel to run around the car and hug her friend. "You've made my day, Reggie Nichols!"

"Shhhh. I'm traveling incognito. See the shades?"

The sunglasses were oversized and dark but did little to disguise the Reggie Danica knew so well. "You look great!"

"I don't know. Same bumpy nose." She scrunched it up, then ruffled her layered hair. "Same mousy mess."

"You look great," Danica repeated firmly. "Come on. Let's put your bag in and get going. I don't like sharing you with the airport."

During the drive back to Beacon Hill Reggie explained that she had the French Open behind her and the All England Championships ahead of her, that she'd come back for a rest in between and on pure impulse had flown to Boston. "I'm not coming at a terrible time, am I?" she asked. There was a quiet urgency in her voice that alerted Danica to something. Reggie looked tired. And older.

"You couldn't have picked a better time," Danica assured her friend gently. "Blake is in Washington, and I'm getting ready to go up to Maine. If you'd called a week later, I'd have been gone."

"How is Blake?"

"Fine."

"You're really jet-setting it now, I guess."

"Nah. You know how much I hate Washington. I only go there when I have to. But, wait, first tell me about you. How's the tour going?"

As they neared the town house, Reggie told Danica about the tournaments she'd played. An hour later, after they'd dropped off her suitcase and the car and had walked across the Common to Locke-Ober's for lunch, she was still talking.

"It's getting worse all the time," she moaned, refilling her wine from the bottle the steward had left chilling in a stand by their table. "I'm not getting younger, and everyone else is."

"But you're a fantastic player, Reggie. What you've got in experience makes up for what they've got in energy."

"That's what I've been telling myself for the past few years, but you know something? It's not true anymore. They're good, Danica. They've got good legs, good arms and good court sense. Me, well, my knee kicks up and my back aches and I'm just plain tired."

Danica studied her friend. "You had the big one this year, didn't you?"

"Thirty? Yup. And it shows."

"Not from where I'm sitting," Danica began in denial, then softened her words. "What I see is a woman who is tanned and healthy-looking and in remarkable shape. But neither of us are eighteen anymore, are we?"

"Noooope."

Danica nudged a piece of brook trout with her fork. "Are you thinking of stopping?" she asked softly.

"Yyyyyup."

She looked up. "Are you really?"

"I'm not sure I have any choice. I'm not winning the way I used to, and the effort is killing me." Reggie paused. "Do you remember when we first went to Armand's? We were on our way up then. Each year we won a few more tournaments. Each year we moved up in rank. It was slow, but it was steady and exciting."

"Steady for you, slightly shaky for me."

"That was something else, Danica. You had reasons for not wanting to play."

"Yeah. I wasn't winning the big ones."

"Okay. Well, that's where I am now." She took a healthy gulp of wine, then set the glass down. "Only it's harder on the backward slide. I was on top for a long time, maybe too long for my own good."

"Success can't be bad."

"When it gets into your blood and then you lose it, it can." She looked at Danica. "I ask myself where I am, *who* I am, and I don't have the answers. Sure, I can retire now and rest on my laurels, but they'll fade pretty fast when the new superstars take over. I really don't know where I'm going anymore, and it's mind-boggling.''

Danica didn't know what to say. Her heart went out to Reggie. "Have you discussed things with Monica?" Monica Crayton had been Reggie's coach for the past seven years, ever since she'd split with Armand in a technical squabble.

"Monica. Well," she sighed, "Monica is looking around. She won't admit it, but I've seen the way she sidles up to some of the younger players. Hell, she's not blind. She sees what's happening. She knows that it's only a matter of time before I retire, and she's looking out for her own future. I can't blame her, really. I suppose I'd do the same if I were in her shoes.''

"Do you ever talk to her about what you should do . . . after?''

"If I don't know, how would she? God, it's awful. I mean, I've had a tennis racket in my hands since I was six. For as long as I can remember I knew where I was headed. There was never any question. Tennis was my future. Suddenly now I don't know anymore.''

"Just because you won't be competing doesn't mean you have to leave the game. You could coach.''

Reggie took a deep breath. "I've thought of that. And I could. But it wouldn't be the same, sitting on the sidelines watching someone else make it.''

"There would be pride in it.''

"Maybe. Then again, maybe I'd be a lousy coach. It's like starting all over again. It's scary.''

"How about teaching at a tennis academy? You could easily do that. I'll bet Armand—''

"I couldn't ask Armand, not after the way we parted.''

"Then, what about another school? There are hundreds of them out there now. With your name alone you'd be able to get a position.''

"Maybe. Then again, maybe I'd be bored. It seems forever that I've been thinking of my year in terms of the pro tour. Without that tension, without that—'' she made a subtle jab with one fist ''—that adrenaline flow—''

"From what you say, that adrenaline flow isn't doing the trick anymore. Really, Reggie, you've got choices."

Reggie looked her in the eye. "I think *you* made the right one way back then. I'd give anything to be in your shoes. Look at you: you've got a husband in the President's Cabinet—the *President's* Cabinet—you've got *three* homes, and you're financially set for life."

Danica smiled sadly. "The grass is always greener, isn't it?"

"Uh-oh. Things with Blake are still rocky?"

Danica rolled her eyes and motioned for the check. As she and Reggie walked slowly back, arm in arm through the Common, she brought Reggie up to date on exactly how rocky things were.

"He doesn't see me at all, Reg. I'm there, but he doesn't see me. It's like I'm a piece of furniture."

"The bastard. What's wrong with him that he can't see something good when he's got it?"

"You're prejudiced, but that's beside the point. The point is that Blake sees a million good things he's got, only I'm not one of them. It's really an ego trip for him down there. Maybe it was here, too, but I never saw it."

"Maybe you didn't want to see it."

"No. I guess I didn't. I've always tried to rationalize—you know, he's busy and important and he appreciates me even if he doesn't say it. But I look at myself and my life and I know that something's got to give. I don't want to be an angry, bitter old lady forty years down the road. I don't want to look back and think of everything I've missed."

"Your work with James Bryant must help some." Danica had written her about it.

"It does. I really enjoy it. But . . ."

"But what?"

Danica looked at Reggie, then away. She motioned toward an empty bench and they sat down. June was in its glory, and its glory was epitomized in the vibrant canopy of trees, the sweet smell of grass, the sounds of emerging humanity that filled the Common.

"There's a man, Reg."

For a full minute Reggie didn't say a word. "A man. As in *other* man?"

"Uh-huh."

"You've never mentioned anyone in your letters."

"I'm sure I mentioned him...just not in the proper light."

Reggie frowned, trying to recall. Then her eyes widened. "The fellow from Maine?"

Danica nodded. "No one knows, Reggie. You're the first person I've breathed a word to. You won't say anything, will you?"

"Have I ever said anything?" Reggie retaliated in teasing reminder of the adolescent fantasies the two had shared when they'd been younger.

"No." Danica smiled, remembering those days. "No, you haven't."

"And I won't now. Michael...was that his name?"

"Yes. Michael. He is the most wonderful person you'd ever want to meet."

"Back up a bit. You first met him when you bought the house?"

Reliving it as she spoke, Danica told Reggie about those earliest days, about the slow development of her relationship with Michael, about biking and Rusty and her miscarriage. She told about the winter that had been, about the calls, about how Michael had been her touchstone when she'd had no other.

"You're in love with him. It's written all over your face."

"Now, yes. I usually keep it well hidden."

"Does Blake know anything?"

"Blake's met him. He knows that Michael and I are friends. He doesn't really seem to care, but that's the way everything's been between Blake and me lately."

"How far has it gone...with Michael? Have you slept with him?"

"God, you're blunt."

"Would you want me to be any other way?"

"No. No." Danica inhaled sharply and shook her head. "No, I haven't slept with him. I can't."

"Why not? If you love him—"

"I'm married, Reg, remember?"

"Hell, Danica, married people do it all the time. I know. Some of the best men I've dated have been married."

"You haven't."

"I have, and I did it with my eyes open. Not that I went out looking for them. They came to me, willing and ready. I suppose it's a little like popping pills. I've never done that, but I've needed a high from time to time. A good man, a nice, strong sexy one, can give you that, even if it's only for a night."

"But there's more to it with Michael and me. It's not just sex, and it wouldn't be a one-night stand if it started."

"Will it start? You're heading up there for the summer. Is Blake going to be there at all?"

"I doubt it. He gives me the same line that he'll make it whenever he can, but I doubt he will."

"Which means you'll be alone with Michael. What are you going to do?"

"I don't know," Danica said in a small voice.

"What do you *want* to do? Dream for a minute. If you had your way, what would you do?"

Danica didn't have to take a minute to dream because she'd been doing it for months and months. "I'd divorce Blake, move permanently to Maine, marry Michael and have six kids."

"Then *do* it!"

"I can't! It's just a dream. I can't divorce Blake. Do you have any idea how hurt he'd be? Do you have any idea how hurt my parents would be?"

"To hell with them. What about *you*?"

Danica gave a clipped laugh. "You sound like Michael."

"You've talked to him about divorcing Blake?"

"No. He knows that I feel an obligation to my family, though."

"What good are obligations if you're miserable?"

"But I'm not. Not really. I mean, I do have a lot to be grateful for. And now that I'm working with James, there's some satisfaction."

"But you're missing so much," Reggie said more gently, then thought. "Is there any way you can work things out with Blake?"

"Resurrect our marriage? I don't know, Reg. I was trying to do that when I bought the house in Maine and look what's happened. Blake and I are growing further apart. He's got his own life. He's always had his own life. Because of that, I've begun to build one for myself. We're heading in different directions. I'm not sure if either of us can turn around and find the other."

"Then you've got your answer."

"No, I don't. There's still that ugly little word, *divorce*. I don't want it. It scares me."

"It's just a word, hon, just a word with a little paper work involved. People do it all the time, precisely because they re-alize that their marriages have failed. And it's easier than it used to be. You could fly to Haiti—"

"Please, Reggie. I don't want to talk about it."

"Okay. We don't have to. Not now, at least. But at some point you may have to face it."

"Not now. Not now."

"Okay."

Reggie fondly squeezed her arm, then gaily informed her that she wanted to go shopping in the Marketplace. By the time they returned to the town house much later Danica had managed to shove that ugly little word to the back of her mind. Reggie kept her mind occupied with tales of off-court escapades, both her own and those of other players Danica knew. Mrs. Hannah made their dinner, then they settled on the bed in the guest room to reminisce about the days at Armand Arroah's house. Danica felt like a teenager again, and was grateful that Blake wasn't around to look down his nose at the snickering and laughter that echoed through the halls.

No more was said about either of their futures until much later, when they'd stolen down to the kitchen for tea and cake and Reggie raised her hand for attention. "Listen to this." She read from her tea bag. "'We often discover what will do by finding out what will not do.' Is that apt or is that apt?"

"Listen to mine. 'The best kind of wrinkles indicate where smiles have been.' Neither of us has wrinkles. Is that good . . . or bad?"

Neither one of them knew the answer. While Reggie distracted herself by marveling that the sun hadn't weather-beaten her face into a thorough mass of wrinkles, Danica pondered switching to another brand of tea.

Chapter Ten

SINCE SHE WAS TRANSPORTING a word processor and its bulky accessories, not to mention dictionaries and reference books, in addition to her personal things, Danica allowed Marcus to follow her to Maine in the Mercedes. While she opened the windows and aired out the house, he emptied both cars, then helped her set up the word processor in the den. He was anxious to please, offering to run into town for food, but she gently refused. She breathed a grand sigh of relief when he finally pulled the Mercedes from the drive and headed back to Boston.

Dashing into the bedroom, she threw off her skirt and blouse and was in the process of tugging on jeans when she heard Michael's voice.

"Dani? Dani, it's me!"

Heart pounding as she shimmied into a T-shirt, she raced back into the living room just as Michael was opening the screen.

"Michael!" She was in his arms then, being swung off her feet and around. "Michael, oh, Michael, it's good to see you!" Her arms were around his neck, his around her waist. "I thought Marcus would never leave."

"So did I," he growled. "I've been hiding behind the rocks, waiting."

"You haven't."

"I have."

He set her back then. "Let me look at you." He did, head to toe. "You look wonderful. Your hair's longer. I like it."

"So do I." She combed her fingers through his own clean hair. "Yours is shorter. I like it, too."

He colored. "The barber got carried away. It'll grow."

"No, I like it." What she liked was the way the front still fell over his brow but not low enough to hide the faint creases that made him look distinguished. She liked the way his side-burns were trimmed, making his jaw look all the stronger. She liked the way the back was layered, feeling feathery and soft to her touch. "It's so good to see you," she breathed, not caring if she repeated herself, because the words bore repeating.

He hugged her again, then kissed her softly, gently on her lips. "I thought you'd never get here," he murmured, reluctantly dragging his mouth from hers. "It's been so long."

"I know." She moved her hands over his chest, savoring his warmth, as though in proof of the living man before her. For so long he'd been in her dreams. It was hard to believe she was here with him at last.

Taking her hand in his, he led her to the deck, asking her about what she'd done since he'd spoken with her last, then, as she talked, guiding her toward the beach and their favorite rocks. She wanted to know more about his travels than he'd told her on the phone, and asked question after question, all of which he answered eagerly.

"I have some news," he said when they'd reached a comfortable breaking point. He'd debated waiting to tell her but had realized that she'd be hurt if she felt he hadn't been forthright. "I've got a teaching position for the fall."

Her eyes lit up. "Michael, that's great! Where?"

He hesitated for only a minute. "Harvard."

"Harvard?" Her eyes widened all the more. "That's . . . that's so close!"

"I know. I wasn't sure if it would upset you."

"Upset me? I think it's *wonderful*!"

"It'll only be one afternoon a week and just for the fall semester; I've never done anything like this before so I'll have to spend a lot of time this summer getting ready, but I think it's kind of exciting."

"'Kind of'?" she mocked, then wrapped an arm around his waist and squeezed. It amazed her that she'd come to be so physical, but then, Michael inspired no less. "You'll be in Boston one afternoon a week. Now, that's exciting."

He grinned, unable to take his eyes from her face. "I think so. I was hoping...I mean, I thought...well, maybe we could have dinner together every so often."

She knew what he was saying, or not saying, as the case truly was. If they saw each other in Boston, it would be on her turf. They'd be breaking an unspoken agreement, paving new ground, perhaps making things more difficult. But she had little choice. "I'd really like that."

"You would?"

Her smile had faded and she'd grown serious. "Yes, Michael, I would. This past winter was very long. I'm not particularly looking forward to a repeat of it." She tore her gaze from his and sought the solace of the sea. "But I keep asking myself the same questions, and I don't have any answers yet." She glanced back at him. "Maybe I'm being unfair to you."

"Am I complaining?"

"I can't promise anything," she warned softly.

"I know, sweetheart, I know. I also know how much I missed *you* all winter, and I'm not looking forward to a repeat of it, either." He took a breath. "Please take this in the right light, because I don't want you to feel guilty about anything. I didn't go looking for a position in Boston. It came to me, and the opportunity was too good to pass up. Being able to see you will be frosting on the cake. If it happens, it'll be wonderful. If not, then I'll just concentrate on the pleasure of teaching.... But this is crazy. Here we are with the whole summer to look forward to and we're worrying about the fall. I've got another surprise. Wanna see it?"

"Is it as nice as the last one?"

He wiggled his brows. "Depends on your preference...man or beast." Turning away, he set his lips and whistled loudly. He repeated it seconds later, then waited.

"Rusty?" Danica whispered, looking down the beach as Michael was doing. Moments later a large and handsome Labrador retriever loped into view. "Rusty! My Lord, look at him!"

With Michael right behind her, she scrambled down the rocks, falling to her knees to give Rusty a sound hug. "You're beautiful!'' she exclaimed, clutching his thick pelt while his entire rear end wagged.

"He's been waiting for you."

"He has not. He couldn't possibly remember me."

"Sure he does. And even if he didn't, he's got a good eye for women."

"You're training him."

"Yup."

She stood. "He's magnificent, Michael. I'm so glad you got him."

"So am I. We've had some good runs together on the beach. You'd be pleased watching."

"I can't wait. He's a special dog made for a special man." She couldn't hide the adoration in her eyes when she gazed up at Michael.

"God, I'm gonna be swellheaded pretty soon. Come on. I want to see your word processor."

He saw that, and the piles of papers and tapes she'd brought. When they returned to his house, he showed her the galleys for his book on sports and the reams of notes and outlines for his newest baby. They discussed it for a while, then drove into town together. Michael took great pride in showing her off there, not only to Sara but also to Sara's husband and the druggist and the librarian and the kitchen shop proprietor, all of whom Danica had come to know well the summer before.

They stopped at the market for food, then returned to Danica's house, where she cooked Michael what he swore was the best dinner he'd had in weeks. After an evening of quiet talk and smiles, though, he very wisely said good night.

IT WAS A PATTERN of closeness that was to repeat itself as the weeks passed. They biked together each morning before going their separate ways to work. As often as possible they had dinner together, sometimes at her house, sometimes at his, sometimes out. They shopped together, walked the beach together, talked about everything from Dutch elm disease to the plight of the miners in Appalachia. They spent a Sunday with the McCabes on their boat, which was perfectly wonderful since Danica and Michael had eyes only for each other and Greta and Pat indulged them their pleasure.

In mid-July, Eleanor Marshall came for a visit. Danica was indeed in better shape than she'd been the summer before, but she still found her mother's presence to be limiting, particularly when she wanted to be with Michael. At Danica's insistence, he joined them for dinner on several occasions. Not only was she desperate to see him, but she wanted her mother to get to know him.

Unfortunately, she underestimated her mother's perceptivity.

"DARLING?" Eleanor had been home for three days, waiting for a moment when she and William were alone. They were having cocktails in the den prior to a rare quiet dinner. "There's something I want to discuss with you. It's . . . about Danica."

William settled deeper into his high-backed chair. "I'm glad you went up there. I just can't get away."

"I'm sure she understands. But that's not what I wanted to discuss. I'm worried about Blake and her."

"What about them?"

"It's not right the way they never see each other."

"*I've* told her that. She doesn't listen to me."

"What does Blake say?"

"Blake can't do anything about it," William clipped gruffly. "He can't be traipsing north all the time when he's busy in Washington, and he can't force her to stay there. What in the hell does she have against the place, anyway?"

"She never did like it. You know that."

"But I don't know why. Okay, so she doesn't like going out every night. You'd think she could force herself for Blake's sake."

"She doesn't want to. That's what worries me."

Ice cubes clinked as William rapped his glass against the arm of his chair. "She's got more than most women could ever dream of having. I don't know what's wrong with her. She should be grateful. Instead, what does she do? She buries herself with that old fart Bryant—"

"She says he's nice."

"This whole working thing is ridiculous. She's no bra-burner; at least, *I* never brought her up to be one. What possessed her to want to work? I still can't figure *that* one out."

"She says she loves it."

"Stubborn fool, she probably wouldn't admit it even if she didn't." He brooded for a minute. "Someone's influencing her. That's the only explanation. You say she's met a lot of people up there?"

Eleanor smoothed her dress over her knee, pressing the silk with her palm. "She introduced me to quite a few. They seem nice enough. I'm worried though..."

When she didn't go on, William scowled. "What is it, Eleanor? Spit it out."

"Maybe I shouldn't..."

"Eleanor," he warned, lowering his brows in command.

"The one... her neighbor... Michael Buchanan..."

"He's trouble. I could have bet on it."

"No, no. He's very nice. *Very* nice."

William sighed. "What are you suggesting, Eleanor?"

Eleanor's expression was pained. She didn't know if she was doing the right thing. On the one hand, she felt she was betraying Danica. On the other, she knew her ultimate loyalty had to rest with William, who would surely be furious if something did happen after she'd kept mum.

"I'm wondering," she sighed, "if it's possible that Danica could be involved with another man."

William pulled in his chin. "With Buchanan?"

"They seem very fond of each other."

"Did they *do* anything?"

"In front of me, of course not. They were very proper. Danica went out of her way to be nonchalant when he was around, but I saw. A woman sees things like that."

"Things like *what*?" William demanded impatiently.

"Expression. Tone of voice. Little things. She's not that way with Blake."

"Blake is a man. Buchanan is... is..."

"A man, too," Eleanor provided softly. "A man who's just as good-looking in his way as Blake. A man who's just as successful in his way as Blake. A man who is *there*, while Blake isn't.''

But William was shaking his head. ''Danica wouldn't do something like that. She wouldn't dare.''

''Danica isn't a child anymore, dear. We both seem to have missed that somewhere along the line.''

''She wouldn't dare. That's all there is to it.''

Eleanor pressed her lips together, then nodded. ''Well, I just wanted to mention it to you.''

William finished his drink. ''Why?''

''I thought maybe you'd want to speak to her. Or to Blake. You know, not to make any accusations, just to suggest that they should try to be together more. I wouldn't want anything to happen, Bill. Blake's in a position of great visibility. If Danica does something foolish, you and Blake could both be embarrassed.''

''Hmm. Maybe.'' He inhaled deeply. ''By the way, Henry and Ruth were asking for you today. I saw them at the club.''

For the moment, the discussion of their daughter was over. Feeling that she'd discharged her duty, Eleanor gratefully seized on the subject of her friends. William, though, thought about the matter of Danica and Blake for a long time. He didn't want to confront Blake and risk being closed off by a man he considered to be an important friend and ally. He didn't want to confront Danica, who would surely deny everything.

No, he decided, there was a safer way to handle the matter. Determinedly, he put in a call the next morning to Morgan Emery.

ON A SATURDAY MORNING in late July, Michael suggested they drive north along the coast to Camden. Danica, who didn't care where they went as long as they were together, readily agreed. For comfort's sake, and because she was feeling particularly feminine, she wore a new blue sundress she'd bought in Boston that spring and strappy sandals.

Michael was more quiet than usual. From time to time, when she glanced at him, he smiled and squeezed her hand, but he said little.

"You seem preoccupied," she ventured softly. "Is something wrong?"

"No, no. Well, not really wrong. I, uh, there was a special reason I wanted to bring you up here." They were no more than ten minutes from their destination.

"Another surprise?" she teased.

"In a way. There's someone I want you to meet."

"Last time I heard that, I found Cilla on your deck. Who is it, Michael?"

"Her name's Gena. Gena Bradley."

Danica thought, then shook her head. "I don't recognize the name. Who is she?"

"Bradley is her maiden name. She reverted to it after her divorce. When I was a kid, it was Gena Bradley Buchanan. She's my mother."

"Your *mother*? But...but...I thought she lived in New York. I hadn't even realized your parents were divorced." Michael rarely talked of his father for reasons he'd already explained, and though he'd spoken fondly of his mother, Danica had just assumed their relationship had suffered some from the rift.

"It happened after we all left the roost. My memories are of the family together."

"What happened?" Danica breathed, stunned. "I thought ... I mean, the picture was always so pretty..."

"It was pretty, at least for us kids. We always knew that Gena had an independent streak. She was our greatest champion when Dad was trying to steamroller us. And I don't think she was all that unhappy then. She loved us, and she and Dad had struck what seemed to be fair compromise."

"Then ... why ... ?"

"When we'd all left and there was just Dad and her, she realized something was more wrong than she'd thought. She discovered that Dad was seeing someone else, a younger woman."

"Oh, Michael..."

"Gena was really hurt, mostly because she felt she'd been so loyal all those years. He didn't fight the divorce. And she moved up here."

"It must be a comfort having you so close."

"I don't see her as often as I'd like." He shook his head in admiration. "She's a remarkable woman. More independent than ever. She's not the type who expects her children to hold her hand. She's made a new life for herself and stays so busy that we all but have to make an appointment to see her."

Danica couldn't help but contrast Michael's mother and her own. The situations seem to have been reversed. She was glad, for Michael's sake, that he'd gotten the better end of the deal. "What does she do?"

"What *doesn't* she do. She owns a small real estate concern in Camden. She teaches Russian at an adult ed program. She pots."

"Pots?"

"Works with clay. She's really pretty good. Do you know that big slate-colored lamp in my bedroom?"

Danica cleared her throat. His bedroom had been off-limits. "No, uh, I don't happen to know that big slate-colored lamp in your bedroom."

Realizing too late, Michael shot her an embarrassed glance. "Right. Well, uh, anyway, she made the base and had it all wired up for me. She sells her things to some of the local shops." He paused. "You've got one of them."

"I do?"

"The ashtray in the den."

Danica heard the quiet pride in his voice. "Your mother made that? Why didn't you tell me?"

"It was pleasure enough for me to know."

"I love it!" She lowered her voice. "I keep paper clips in it, though. Do you think she'll mind?"

He laughed and shook his head. "I keep telling her that she should try to sell in New York, but she claims she doesn't have the time. She says she doesn't want the pressure and that if she enjoys what she's doing, that's all that matters. I wish I could be as content. It's not that I need adulation, but I'm not sure my work would mean much to me if people never read my books."

"The situations are different, Michael. Your mother—"

"Call her Gena. She'll want that."

"...Gena is at a different stage in life, and in a sense she already has public exposure. Her four greatest works are out on the streets of the world—Brice and Corey and Cilla and you."

Michael grinned. "You two will get along fine. Just fine."

But Danica was suffering momentary cold feet. "Does she...does she know about me?"

"I've spoken of you, but only as a friend." He grew solemn. "I haven't told her everything. Given her own experience in life, I'm not sure she'd appreciate the fact that I'm in love with a married woman."

If Gena suspected anything, she kept it to herself. To Danica, she was warm and welcoming, to Michael openly adoring. Danica easily understood where Michael's physicality came from. Gena, too, was a toucher.

She was slender, more petite than Cilla, and had an attractive crop of short silver hair. Michael had her brown eyes—or maybe it was the warmth in them which was familiar—but there the physical similarity ended.

As with Cilla, Danica found herself quickly drawn to this other woman in Michael's life. Gena was interesting and nonconforming in a way Danica found thoroughly refreshing. Though Michael claimed that Cilla was like their father in terms of agressiveness, Danica could see where she got her impulsiveness. In the course of the day Gena excitedly dragged them to see the house she'd just sold to a painter, corraled them on the spur of the moment into the local movie house to view a short foreign film she'd heard was superb, scrambled on Michael's shoulders to hang a bird feeder she thought was too low, and cooked the most delicious vegetarian dinner Danica had ever imagined could be made.

"Tired?" Michael asked as they drove back to Kennebunkport much later that night.

"Mmmm. But pleasantly so. She's wonderful. How lucky you are to have a mother like that."

Her tone held appreciation, perhaps a little envy, but no bitterness, and for that Michael was grateful. He hadn't wanted to underscore Danica's own problems by introducing her to Gena. Indeed he's spent hours worrying that that might happen. In the end, though, he'd simply wanted these two women to meet. Danica's reaction to the day had convinced him he'd been right. Moreover, he was thrilled with the genuine affection Gena had shown Danica. It pleased him to know that his mother saw the beauty in the woman he loved.

CILLA WAS SURPRISED to look up from the jumble of notes on her desk to see Jeffrey approaching. She wasn't sure what had alerted her to his arrival, certainly not his footsteps when the city room was filled with the steady click of computer keyboards. She broke into a smile, but waited for him to speak first.

"Hi," he said softly.

"Hi, yourself."

"I was passing by and just thought I'd drop in. I wasn't sure you'd be here. You're usually out running around."

There had been no censure in his voice to discourage her. "I don't get any writing done when I'm out running around. For that matter, I don't get much writing done here." She gestured toward her cluttered desktop. "Look at this mess. I'm not terribly organized."

"You manage to get the job done." As unobtrusively as he could, he slid into the chair adjacent to her desk. No one in the large room appeared to be paying him much heed. He was grateful to go unrecognized. "I read your piece on political corruption. It was good."

"It said nothing you didn't know before."

"But it was well researched and presented several new angles. Have you gotten any response?"

"You mean, from official-type people, as in we-want-to-look-into-this? Not exactly. But then, I didn't expect to. Official-type people work in strange ways. They keep things confidential until all of a sudden they're knocking down your door screaming for your sources."

"Come on, Cilla. I never did that."

"You didn't have to knock down my door. You were already inside," she argued, then promptly softened her tone and looked down. "But you're right, Jeff. You never did that. Even though I was afraid you would."

"You shouldn't have been. I was the first one to realize that you couldn't divulge a source."

"Still, you always asked."

"I was curious." He leaned closer for privacy's sake, as well as for the simple pleasure of being nearer Cilla. "*Personally* curious. Not professionally. Personally. One part of me wanted to know everything you were doing." He lowered his voice all the more. "I suppose it was a kind of possessiveness, a very male need."

"Possessiveness isn't limited to men. We feel it, too."

"That's the feminist in you talking, the woman who wants the upper hand."

"It is not! I don't need to have the upper hand all the time. Don't impose your insecurities on me, Jeffrey Winston. It's not fair."

He was about to soundly refute her claim when he caught his breath, then slowly let it out. "You . . . may be right."

"I . . . what?"

His lips thinned. "Don't make me say it again. It was hard enough the first time."

"You acknowledge that you have insecurities?"

"I always did acknowledge it. Just . . . not to you."

"Well," she sighed, "that's something. I guess we've both got them."

Jeffrey wanted to talk more, but he knew there was a better time and place. He'd come here to see if Cilla was truly as receptive as Michael suggested she might be. "So," he began more casually, "anything juicy on the fire?" He'd been trying to lighten things up but realized instantly that he'd only opened another old wound. To his amazement, Cilla didn't see it that way. She was frowning, studying the telephone that sat on the desk.

"I don't know. I got the weirdest call this morning."

"From whom?" He winced. "Chalk that. Is it anything you can talk about?"

She shot him a helpless glance, one he'd never seen before. "Sure. There's nothing to it, really. Except that . . . instinct tells me . . . I can feel there's something there, but he wouldn't say much."

Jeffrey waited patiently, telling himself that he'd have to trust Cilla to speak if she wished. He was rewarded when she met his gaze. "It was a man. He wouldn't identify himself. He mumbled something about sexual favors and power and lust. I don't know. He may have been drunk, or stoned. But it was like he had second thoughts the minute he called. I can't help but feel that he had something legitimate to say." She paused, then threw a hand in the air. "He hung up before I could get anything concrete from him."

"He'll call back if he wants. He knows where to reach you."

"Still, it's frustrating. I keep thinking that he's somewhere out there and that I can't begin to imagine who or where he is."

Jeffrey admired her dedication, which was as wholehearted as ever. But there was something else, something that took the edge off. She seemed less confident, more vulnerable. He wondered if she was indeed mellowing as Michael had said.

"Uh, listen, Cilla. The reason I came by...well, I thought maybe we could have dinner together. I know you're often out with the gang—" he tossed his head toward the others in the room "—and I realize that it's important for you—"

"When?"

"Excuse me?"

Cilla had never been a shrinking pansy. She smiled. "When would you like to have dinner? I could make it Thursday night if you're free."

"Thursday night?" He somehow managed to master his surprise. He'd fully expected she'd make things challenging at the least. But he was too old to play games; maybe she'd outgrown them, too. Thursday was just two days off. He grinned, leaned forward and quickly kissed her cheek before he stood. "Thursday's great. Should I pick you up?"

"You know where I'll be," she said in that same soft tone that had emerged from time to time.

Again he was surprised. He'd half expected her to suggest they meet at a restaurant. Mellowing? Very definitely, and becomingly. With an unsteady breath, he grinned. "Right. See you around eight?"

"That'd be great."

He nodded, then was off. Cilla stared after him, thinking that he had to be most handsome man in the room. She felt very satisfied, and excited. It occurred to her that she hadn't felt that way in a long, long time.

MORGAN EMERY SHIFTED to a more comfortable position in his place of concealment just beneath the deck of the elegant cruiser he'd rented. It had been four weeks since William Marshall had hired him, and he was beginning to wonder whether the money was worth it after all. He'd hidden behind boulders, skulked in rural doorways, walked in and out of restaurants, seen more of the southern Maine coast than he'd ever wanted, and he was getting nothing, at least nothing worth anything.

Oh, he had pictures, but not a one was truly compromising. He had shots of the two on the beach, shots of them in the car, shots of them riding bicycles, shots of them coming out of the local library, shots of them at one or the other's front door. There'd be a hand on a shoulder and he'd hold his breath waiting to photograph a kiss, then nothing. There'd be an arm around a waist, so close to a caress, then it would fall away. There'd be a face before a face, a smile, then a backing off. Even now, as he trained the telescopic lens of his camera on Michael Buchanan's deck, all he could see was two people, sitting in separate chairs, eating the steaks they'd just grilled.

Emery's mouth watered, but when he groped for the last ham and cheese sandwich he'd brought, his appetite waned.

Surveillance. He hated it. Long hours sitting, waiting. What he loved was the action of the big city, where a private investigator could sink his teeth into something meaty. This? Hell, this was baby-sitting. High-paying, sure, but with little challenge.

Unfortunately, when a member of the United States Senate offered you a job, you didn't turn it down. Personal pull was worth a mint, and William Marshall had pull. A good word from him might, just might, get Emery another stint working undercover with the Feds. Now, *that* had been a challenge, playing the part of a fence in a sting. He'd had a good time. Maybe he should have been an actor. Hell, he had the looks...

At movement on the distant deck Emery grew alert, but it was another false alarm. They were carrying plates into the house. And there was the damned dog again. Oh, he had fantastic pictures of the dog. It was a beautiful beast, he had to admit. But Marshall didn't want to see the dog.

What in the hell was the matter with them? Was Buchanan a eunuch? A beautiful woman...hours with her each day...and zilch.

With a snap, Morgan Emery tugged his equipment into the boat, then swiveled around and hoisted himself into the pilot's seat. It was a magnificent craft, he mused, sliding his hands around the gleaming brass steering wheel. Marshall had given him carte blanche on expenses, and he'd reasoned that he'd wanted to look properly posh on the water. Someday, someday maybe he'd own a boat like this himself. He deserved it. Hell, what he deserved was a pretty young thing from town and a night of hot sex. He'd be impressive. And since he had the boat till morning...

With due care he resisted the urge to push the throttle all the way forward and take off in a wild spray of sea water. But the automatic pilot had kept him cruising slowly, and he couldn't accelerate without risk of drawing attention to himself.

One thing was for sure. He'd be damned if he was going to sit around any longer. Marshall wanted pictures. He'd give him pictures. If they were innocent, that was Marshall's problem. His own job was done. Over. Fini.

DANICA HAD JUST RETURNED to the deck and was looking out to sea when Michael came from behind to slip his arms around her waist. She leaned back against him and covered his hands with her own.

"Pretty, isn't it?" she breathed.

"The sunset or the boat?"

"Both. So very peaceful." She tipped her head against his chest. "It must be even more so out there."

"On the boat?"

"Mmmm. The waves aren't too high. The breeze is light." She took a slow breath. "It'd be nice to have a boat like that. I wonder whose it is."

Michael squinted at the sleek cabin cruiser that was moving steadily away. "I can't see the name. It may be out of Bar Harbor or Newport, or somewhere on Long Island."

"Mmmm, dream material. I didn't see anyone on deck. What do you think they're doing? Maybe drinking champagne below or eating by candlelight?"

"Maybe bailing bilge water."

She elbowed him and he chuckled. "You're awful, Michael. Here I was, creating a beautifully romantic picture and you shatter it in one fell swoop."

"I'm sorry. Go ahead. Create."

She couldn't resist the temptation, though her thoughts turned inward. "If I had a boat like that, I'd be free. Oh, not in the most real sense, but then, being on a boat like that would be a fantasy anyway. I'd just . . . take off. Cruise away. Separate myself from the land and its restraints." She lowered her chin and gave a self-conscious laugh. "You must think I'm crazy."

"No. Not at all." He realized that Blake could buy her a boat like that in a minute. She could probably buy it for herself. *He* could buy it for her. So it wasn't the dream of having the boat that was beyond reach, but rather the dream of freedom. Freedom. What he'd give for her to have it! "I hear what you're saying. One summer, when I was in college, I crewed on a windjammer up here. It was hard work, but was it ever fun. We had passengers on for a week at a time, but the joy came on the days we were alone, when we could put up the sails, catch the wind and fly. We'd just lie out on the deck and relax. I felt like I owned the world then. All my worries were back on shore. I was free . . . for a little while at least."

"Sounds heavenly." Turning, she slid her arms around his neck. Darkness was quickly falling, cloaking the real world, though not enough. "But too short. I can't believe where the summer's gone. It's been wonderful."

"It has, hasn't it?" he asked. His fingers moved along the base of her spine, itching to climb higher. "When do you have to be back?"

"I told Blake I'd be in Boston a week after Labor Day." Religiously she'd talked to him on the phone every Sunday, but they'd had little to say of import. She wasn't interested in his doings in Washington any more than he was interested in what she'd been doing in Maine. He made no mention of flying up, and she was actually grateful. She felt estranged from him, physically and emotionally, and if he felt it, too, he didn't seem to care. "Thirteen days and counting. Reluctantly. When do you start in Cambridge?"

"The middle of the month. I'll be going down for orientation before classes actually start."

"You'll be staying overnight?"

"Only at the start. I've taken a room at the Hyatt. It's on—"

"Memorial Drive. I know where it is. It's not . . . far from me." Hearing her own words, she was stunned. He was going to be so close, so *close*. She tried to picture the room he'd have overlooking the Charles, but all she could see was a large, empty bed. When her knees grew weak, she wrapped her arms tighter around his neck and pressed her face to his throat. She felt so torn, so torn.

Michael crushed her even closer. His arms crisscrossed her back, fingers reaching the soft side swells of her breasts. "I don't know if I should tell you to think it or not to think it," he moaned. "We've got to do something, Dani. We've got to do *something*." The torment had been getting worse, the agony of wanting her, needing her, and not having her in every sense.

"I know," she murmured brokenly. "I just wish I knew what to do."

"Just kiss me, then," he rasped, lowering his head and taking her mouth with the hunger that boiled from inside. Her hunger matched it, and she held nothing back, offering her lips, her tongue, her breath in the fevered exchange. Her body arched toward him, and when he unwrapped his arms and inched his hands to her breasts, a small, catlike purr slipped from her throat.

He'd never touched her there, but she'd imagined it many, many times. His hands caressed her and she grew fuller beneath his nurturing.

"So beautiful," he murmured hoarsely, his forehead against hers. When he brushed his thumbs over her nipples, they grew even more taut. She whimpered softly, unable to draw away because she loved what he was doing, but knowing that he'd have to stop.

"Thirteen days, Dani. That's all we've got."

"I know, I know."

"I want you, sweetheart."

"I know." *I want you, too,* she thought. But she also thought of Boston and Blake and all else she'd be returning to when those thirteen short days were done.

Michael spread his palms over her breasts, memorizing their very feminine shape for a final moment before slowly lowering his hands to her waist. He was breathing heavily. He knew that his shorts did little to hide his hardness, knew that she had to feel him with their hips pressed together that way. He could feel her warmth, could imagine her moistness. He also knew that she still wasn't ready in the emotional sense that would make it all okay the morning after.

"I'd better get you home," he whispered. She nodded, though she was loath to move. "I don't know how much control I'll have if we stay here much longer. I've ached to touch you this way, but it only makes me want more."

Again she nodded, but this time she moved back. Chin tucked to her chest, hands clasped tightly before her, she was the image of misery. "I don't know what to do," she breathed so softly that he wouldn't have heard it had he not been so close.

He felt her misery, her confusion, tenfold because he wanted answers but had none. "We've got time, sweetheart," he said at last.

Her head flew up, eyes wide. "Thirteen days. That's all. Thirteen days."

But he was shaking his head even as he struggled to contain his own urgency. "We've got more. We've got weeks, months. The situation isn't simple. We can't put a time limit on it."

"But . . . it could go on forever!" she cried, hugging herself in place of him.

Again he was shaking his head. "It won't. When the time's right, something will give. You'll know it when it happens. Either way."

Later, long after Michael had walked Danica home, he was thinking of what he'd said. The summer had brought them even closer. She was so totally a part of his life that he couldn't bear the thought of it otherwise. Yet, she could, indeed, go either way. She could go back to Boston and realize what he already had, that they were made for each other, that their life together would be unimaginably sweet. She could also go back to Boston and, for reasons beyond his control, decide that she had to stay with Blake.

He couldn't force the issue mainly because he was afraid of the outcome. He knew that she loved him, knew that she had little left with Blake. He also knew that though the bonds tying her to Blake were fraying, they remained strong.

In the final analysis, he wanted her to be happy. If that meant a reconciliation between Blake and her, he'd have to accept it. In the meanwhile, all he could do was to wait and hope and do everything he could to make the time they had together very special.

Wandering out onto the deck late that night, he thought about the last. His eye caught on the horizon, which was dark and without the lights that would mark the passing of a boat. He recalled the handsome cruiser they'd seen earlier, recalled her dreams, her wistfulness.

It was then that inspiration hit.

Chapter Eleven

EARLY THE NEXT MORNING Michael raced into town, where he found that the fates were very definitely on his side. Not only could he rent a cabin cruiser like the one Danica had dreamed on the night before, but the very *one* was a rental, being returned that same morning. Paying the full price in advance, he made the arrangements, then dashed back to Danica's house.

"Guess what!" he exclaimed, beaming proudly as he presented himself at her door.

She smiled, adoring the boyish way he looked when he couldn't contain his excitement. There was always something new with him. She knew he'd make life exhilarating to say the least. "What?"

"It's ours."

"What is?"

"The boat."

"*What* boat?"

"The one we saw last night."

Her eyes grew round. "*That* boat? What do you mean, 'it's ours'?"

"I've just rented it for the weekend."

"You're kidding. No, you're not. Michael, I don't believe it!"

"Are you pleased?"

"You know I am! For the weekend? It's *ours*?"

He shrugged, but he was grinning. "Unless you'd rather just go to a movie or something."

"No way!" She pressed her hands together before her lips. "Oh, Lord, this is wild. I'll have to . . . have I got . . . what do I wear on a boat?"

"You've never *been* on one before?"

"Different. Very different. High heels and cocktail dress type thing." She glowed. "This will be so much better!"

Her excitement alone made it all worthwhile. "You can wear whatever you want, Dani. The more comfortable, the better." He paused. "I could have taken it for today and tomorrow, but it was just coming in this morning and the owner wanted to clean it up. Besides, these being weekdays and all, I figured you'd want to work."

Danica shook her head in continued amazement, both that he'd actually rented the boat and that he'd respected her work enough to plan around it. Not that she wouldn't have dropped everything to go on that boat with Michael. . . .

"I can't wait," she breathed, then threw herself into his arms. "Thank you."

Not trusting himself, he quickly set her back. "My pleasure. Now . . . work."

"No bike ride?"

He shook his head. "I've got to take Rusty to the vet, then spend the morning on the phone. Some notes I took in San Francisco aren't right. I have to straighten them out before I make a mess of this whole book. After that I'd better get to finishing the plan for my class." He teased her with a glower. "You're not the only one around here who has to work, y' know."

She smiled and took the hand he offered, squeezed it, then watched him head back down the drive. Quickly, though, her thoughts turned to the weekend, and she sensed that working her way through the next two days was going to be easier said than done.

By SEVEN O'CLOCK Saturday morning she was up and dressed and packed and waiting. After much deliberation she'd chosen to wear jeans and a shirt, putting varied changes of clothing in the small overnight bag that now sat by the door.

Michael had rented the boat from ten that morning to the same time on Monday. He'd said he'd be by at nine so that they might stop for food before heading for the Yacht Club.

He would have been furious had he known she'd spent the entire afternoon before in the kitchen, but she hadn't been able to concentrate on her work, and she rather fancied the idea of sitting on deck with wine and homemade pâté, stuffed mushrooms and pea pods, and ramaki. She'd baked a Black Forest cake, too, dashing out to the store for the freshest of heavy cream, the finest of semisweet chocolate, the richest of kirsch. All of her goodies were packaged and waiting in the refrigerator.

She wandered from room to room, looking out a window here, straightening a throw pillow there. She glanced at her watch, then began to wander again. She was on the deck with her face turned to the late August sun when a thought struck.

Blake would be calling on Sunday and she wouldn't be here. If he was worried—and she wasn't sure he would be, though she couldn't take that chance—he might call Mrs. Hannah, or worse, her father. She didn't want that.

Running back into the den, she picked up the phone, then hesitated. She had no idea where he'd be. She had no idea what his Saturday schedule was in Washington. In Boston, he'd have been up early and headed for the office, then the club. Deciding to take the course that would prove least embarrassing should she be wrong, she dialed his condominium.

The phone rang five times and she was about to hang up when he answered. Groggily. He'd been sleeping. Unusual.

"Blake? Hi."

"Danica?"

She could see him peering at the clock that sat so prominently on his nightstand. "I'm sorry. Did I wake you?"

"No. Uh, yes. I overslept. I should have been up an hour ago."

"I . . . I thought I'd call you now because I'm going out on a boat with some friends and I won't be here tomorrow." It was only a tiny half-lie, she reasoned, and if Rusty was coming, no lie at all. She prayed Blake wouldn't ask more.

He didn't. "That should be nice for you. How long will you be gone?" His tone was strictly conversational, as if it didn't really matter how long she'd be gone but he felt some show of interest was called for.

"Just for the weekend. I'll be back on Monday."

"Well, have a good time."

"Blake? How are things there?"

"Very well, thank you."

"Is anything new?"

"Uh, no. Not that I can think of."

"All's well at the Department?"

"Very well."

She didn't know what else to say. "Okay. I guess I'll be going then. Talk with you next week?"

"That sounds fine. Bye-bye."

Only after she'd hung up the receiver did Danica realize she was gritting her teeth, but then, it wasn't the first time. Lately, when she talked to Blake, she'd been tense. He was always perfectly calm, properly composed—even today, after she'd woken him up. She pictured him lying in bed, with his hair barely mussed and his pajamas just so. For the life of her, she couldn't picture herself beside him. The thought held no appeal whatsoever.

It was a travesty, the stale ritual they were living. She wondered if it bothered him, wondered if he was even aware of anything amiss. He always seemed so complacent. She knew that they couldn't keep on this way, yet . . . yet . . . the alternative . . .

Unable, no, un*willing* to start her weekend by brooding, she left the den in a rush. For lack of anything better to do, she carried her overnight bag to the driveway, then returned to the kitchen to transfer things from the refrigerator to a large box.

Michael was early, and she couldn't have been happier. "What in the devil have you done?" he exclaimed when she lifted the box from the kitchen table.

"Just made a few things to eat."

He quickly took the box from her. "You didn't have to do that, Dani. I didn't mean for this weekend to cause you work."

The contrast struck her again. Blake would have objected on principle to his wife cooking, while Michael was simply and genuinely concerned that she'd put herself out.

"It was fun, Michael. And don't tell me you won't be hungry all weekend."

He lowered his chin. "Now, I didn't say that. But we could have easily made do with store-bought things."

"We'll still need plenty. Are we all set?" She glanced toward the Blazer. "Rusty's coming!"

"We're dropping him at the Greta and Pat's. They miss him."

Danica made a face that said she wondered, but she didn't argue. She didn't want to share Michael with anyone, not even man's best friend.

After making the appropriate stops, they arrived at the Yacht Club shortly before ten, loaded the boat, and were off. Michael knew exactly how to handle the craft, and he patiently pointed out levers and buttons and switches for Danica's benefit. She was content to stay close by his elbow, watching, listening, enjoying his nearness and the sense of release that increased with each nautical mile they put behind them.

Heading north, they cruised slowly and comfortably. At midday, Danica brought sandwiches up and they ate side by side, enjoying the food nearly as much as they did the tangy air and the salty sea. By midafternoon, they'd passed seaward of Biddeford and Saco and were well into Bigelow Bight, approaching Casco Bay.

Changing into shorts, Danica stretched out on the forward deck, spreading her arms wide, delighting in the way the wind whipped across her skin.

"Like it?" Michael asked, sliding up beside her. He, too, had changed from his shirt and jeans into a close-fitting tank top and shorts.

"Ahhh, yes." Aside from an initial peek, she kept her eyes closed. "It's won-der-ful."

He slipped his hand between the open tails of her shirt and rubbed the warm flesh of her middle. "You'd better be careful. The wind is deceptive. You can get sunburned."

"Nah. It's too late in the season for much of anything to happen. Besides, my skin's conditioned to the sun. I'll be fine." Her heart was pounding. She chose to attribute it to the exhilaration of the ride, but it slowed as soon as Michael withdrew his hand and stretched out nearby. "Michael? Who's steering?"

"My good friend, Auto. I must have forgotten to point him out. He's a gem."

With a smile, she flipped over onto her stomach and looked across at the shoreline. "Those poor people stuck on land. If they only knew what they were missing."

"Many of them do. They're just not as lucky as we are."

"We are lucky, you know that?" It occurred to her then that even if her relationship with Michael went no further than it had already, she'd be forever grateful that he was her friend. He'd made her life so much easier to take. He'd inspired her to do so much.

"Why the sad face?"

She glanced down to find him squinting at her, shading his eyes with his hand. "Sad? I hadn't realized."

"What were you thinking about?"

She hesitated for just a minute. "You."

"Good thoughts or bad ones?"

"Good ones, of course."

"Why 'of course'?"

"Why not?"

He didn't falter. He'd been thinking about it too much. "Because I may be complicating your life a helluva lot."

"Complicating?" She shimmied closer and propped her chin on her arms on his chest. "You're the best thing that's ever happened to me."

"You shouldn't say things like that. They'll go right to my head." They were going right to other parts as well, but he forced those to the back of his mind.

"But I mean it, Michael. Since I met you, my life has had so much more meaning. I keep thinking what it would have been like—things between me and Blake, his appointment— if I hadn't had you. Even when I'm in Boston, I feel better just knowing . . . I've said all this before, I think."

"I like to hear it," he responded quietly. "It helps me cope with everything *I*'m feeling." When her expression grew pained and she opened her mouth to apologize for causing him what had to be terrible frustration, he put his hand against her lips. "Don't say it. I don't mind what I feel. In some ways my life wasn't much better than yours was before we met. I always tried to tell myself that it was full, that I was doing everything I wanted to be doing, but deep down inside I knew something was missing. Maybe if you'd never come along, I'd never had put a finger on it. Maybe I'd have settled for second best without realizing it." He moved his fingers only to lift his head and kiss her softly. "I have to be grateful for what we've had, for what we have right now. It means more to me than you can imagine."

"You're getting maudlin in your old age, Michael Buchanan," she whispered, but there were tears in her eyes and her heart was dangerously full.

With a low growl, he rolled over until she was pinned to the deck beneath him. "No worse than you, pretty lady." With a final smack to her lips, he was up and headed back toward the steering wheel. "I need a swim," he muttered under his breath.

"What?" she called.

"Nothing, sweetheart. Nothing." He didn't want to swim, because the water was like ice, but he had to do something or he'd be attacking Danica before long. She was so beautiful. He cursed softly.

"Michael, what are you saying?" She began to get up.

"You stay there," he growled, pointing to the deck, then he held his open hand up and spoke more gently. "I'm just talking to myself. An old habit. I forget sometimes."

Though Danica stayed put, she wrapped her arms around her knees and sat looking back at Michael. He was so beautiful. Tanned just enough. Muscled just enough. Windblown just enough. And he was beautiful inside, too. She hadn't imagined that a man could be so sensitive to a woman's thoughts and wishes and needs, but he was. He put Blake and her father to shame, because he had success and so much more.

Looking at him, catching his gaze when he looked at her from time to time, she felt a familiar tingling deep inside. She knew what it was, where it was headed. *Don't think it. It's forbidden.* Could anything that promised to be so beautiful be wrong? she asked herself. *There's Blake to consider. He's your husband.* Blake doesn't want me, and I don't want him. *You're married to Blake. You're legally bound.* Can a piece of paper mean more than the feeling two people hold for each other? *What about your parents? They raised you to abide by commitments.* I'm a grown woman now. I have to make my own commitments. *But there's no future in it. You aren't free.* I'm . . . no, I'm not free, am I . . .

She swiveled on her bottom and faced the front of the boat so Michael wouldn't see the agony she felt. She concentrated on the waves, the shore, the horizon, anything to distract her. After a while, when she felt under control, she returned to sit by his side. From time to time they talked about what they saw—a distant sailboat, the gulls that soared overhead, points of land they passed. Often they simply shared the silence, though it wasn't really silent with the steady hum of the motor and the intermittent slap of waves against the hull, but those were hypnotic in their way and very peaceful.

Unfortunately, Danica couldn't settle the war within herself. It was like indigestion of the mind, she mused, and it gnawed relentlessly. Her thorough awareness of Michael's nearness made things simultaneously better and worse. She saw the way his shoulders flexed as he handled the steering wheel, saw the play of bronzed skin over muscle, sensed the strength, which was virility at its best. She saw the fine mat of tawny hair that edged above his tank top, the finer sprinkling on his forearms, even finer on the backs of his hands. She remembered the way his lips had felt earlier, the way his long, hard body had felt when he'd pinned her down for that too brief moment.

She felt she was toying with the fires in hell, but she was freezing and she needed the warmth to survive.

"There." Michael pointed. "That's the island I want."

She tore her gaze from his body and followed the line of his finger. "How do you know? We've passed so many."

"That's the one. I know. These are my old stomping grounds, remember? The big island to the left is Vinalhaven Island. Several of the other smaller ones are privately owned. So is this one, I think, but it's uninhabited. We'll drop anchor near its shore."

The island, a broad hump in the sea speckled with low-growing pines, was indeed uninhabited. They circled it once and saw sign of neither house nor humanity. Choosing the east side of the island for its relative calm, Michael killed the engine and, with Danica scrambling to assist him, dropped anchor.

"Now—" he turned to her and spoke with the satisfaction of the skipper who'd done his day's work "—I would like some wine." With comical suddenness he grimaced. "Oh, shit, do we have a corkscrew?"

She laughed. "I saw one down below. Don't ask me to use it, though. It doesn't have ears, so it'll take brute strength."

"Brute strength I've got, but I may need replenishment pretty quick. Can any of the stuff you made be eaten cold? I'm famished."

Smiling, she nodded. "I think I can find something." She climbed down the few steps into the cabin, which looked golden in the late afternoon sunlight that was filtering through the windows. Michael followed, taking the corkscrew she handed him and deftly opening the wine. In turn, she set out pâté and crackers for him to start on while she cooked the ra-maki on the small butane stove.

"Mmmm, is this good!" he managed to garble through a mouthful of pâté. "You really made it yourself?"

"Yup," she answered without turning around. Something about the smallness of the cabin, the fact that they'd dropped anchor, the knowledge that they'd be spending the night here, was making her edgy. It wasn't that she was afraid Michael might force her into something she didn't want; she knew that he'd simply spend the night beside her if need be. What frightened her was the "something she didn't want" part be-cause she didn't know if it was true. Her insides were a taut rope, with Michael at one end and Blake at the other. Mi-

chael was stronger and looked to be winning one moment; the
next Blake gave a persevering tug.

When the ramaki was done, she joined Michael, but she
merely nibbled on a cracker, the most her stomach could take.
Even the wine, which might have settled her, held little appeal.

"Did I ever tell you about my friends who have a houseboat on the Mississippi?" Michael sat back against the di-
nette cushion, his wineglass in his hand.

She forced a smile, knowing he was trying to relax her.
"No. Tell me about your friends who have a houseboat on the
Mississippi."

"It's this big box of a thing. Ugly as sin. But fun? It's fantastic. A little home, really. I was down in Natchez once and
they picked me up..."

Danica struggled to concentrate on what he was saying, but
she barely heard a word through the bedlam in her mind.
Michael was so close, so dear, so willing. *There are other factors
to be considered.* Those factors aren't here! *They should be.* But
they're not and if they were, really were, I wouldn't be agonizing like this now. *You're making a mistake.* Maybe I'm only
correcting mistakes of the past. *The past isn't over.* It is! There's
nothing there! *But you can't divorce Blake, can you?* Oh, God, I
can't think. *Are you being fair to Blake? Are you being fair to Michael?* What about me? What about what I want?

She squeezed her eyes shut and covered her face with her
hands.

"Dani?" Michael had his arm around her shoulder. "What
is it, sweetheart?"

Bolting from her seat, she pressed her trembling hands,
then forehead to the cool paneled door of the forward cabin.

He was behind her in an instant, turning her to see the tears
that streaked down her cheeks. "Don't cry, sweetheart," he
begged. "Please, don't cry."

"I'm so tired, Michael."

He was breathing as hard as she was. "Maybe you—"

"I'm so tired of fighting it," she sobbed and sagged against
him. "My mind goes i-in circles and my insides churn and the
only thing that m-makes any sense is that I love you."

He was very still for a full second, then fiercely closed his arms about her. "You've never said the words before," he breathed unevenly. "You've looked them and acted them, but you've never said them before."

"I've thought them for such a l-long time and I've fought it because one part of me says that I shouldn't, but I c-can't help the way I feel! It's draining...the war is...and it makes me weak." She lifted her tear-streaked face to his and whispered, "Make me whole, Michael. I need you so badly."

He swallowed hard. "Do you know what you're asking?"

She nodded slowly. "I'm tired of fighting ghosts that shouldn't be there. I'm tired of letting something meaningless take away from me the one thing that has the most meaning in my life. I'm tired of feeling stifled, of feeling that there's so much love inside that if I don't do something with it I'm going to burst. I love you so much."

"Oh, God," he murmured, smoothing her hair back with hands that shook. "Are you sure? I want you to be sure. I don't think I can bear it if you're sorry afterward."

Lifting her hands to his face, she gently traced the features she so adored. "I won't be sorry. This has to be the best thing I've ever done."

Michael's body was already alive and when he saw the love in her eyes his control snapped. His mouth captured hers and ravaged it, but the ravaging was two-sided because Danica's control was gone as well. Having made the decision, she felt an urgency she'd never known.

The door to the forward cabin was open then and, barely severing their kiss, they stumbled in and fell onto the V-berth. She was tugging at his tank top, greedily running her hands over his chest, his back, his chest again, while he tore at the buttons of her shirt. When they were both bare from the waist up, he hugged her to him. Her breasts flared against his chest and he wanted to touch them, to kiss them, but she was already tugging at his shorts and he knew that he had as little patience as she did. They'd lived over a year of foreplay; there wouldn't be any teasing now.

Their hands tangled as each fought with the other's fastenings. Zippers were tugged, fabric was pulled, and then they were naked and straining for the final fulfillment, which would attest to their love.

"I love you, Dani. I love you," Michael gasped as he reached down to spread her thighs. With a deep groan he entered her, and she cried out at the beauty of the union. But there was no time for more than repeated murmurings of their love as they thrust violently toward each other, away, then back again, deeper, harder. And then there was no breath even for that because everything they felt for each other was gathering toward an explosive climax that went on and on in seemingly endless spasms until, at last, they fell back on the bed in a state of utter exhaustion. The sound of harsh panting filled the small cabin, slowing gradually as the minutes passed.

Danica couldn't move, but it wasn't that Michael's weight was too much, because she loved that, too. She loved the way his chest, his belly, his thighs pressed hers. She loved the way his entire being filled her senses. She was spent but exhilarated, tired but happy. When, with a moan, he slowly slid to her side, she turned with him, reluctant to let him go far.

"I love you, Dani," he whispered, folding her in his arms and pressing his face to her hair. "I love you so much."

She ran her hand along his damp skin to his hip. Her pulse was still racing, but at a breathable pace now. "You're so wonderful. And I love you, too."

"I never imagined it'd be that way. I mean, I knew it would be fantastic. Everything else between us always has been. But in my dreams I imagined undressing you slowly, looking at you, touching and kissing every part until you couldn't take it anymore."

"I couldn't. I thought I'd die there for a while when I couldn't get your shorts off."

He chuckled and shifted position so that he could see her face. It was flushed and damp. He gently kissed dots of moisture from her nose. "Are you happy?"

"I've never been more so."

"No second thoughts?"

"None. How could what we did be wrong? You said it once yourself, that it was only a deeper expression of what we already felt."

"That it was, but there was nothing 'only' about it. It was...un-be-lievable!"

She smiled, knowing she felt more feminine and better loved at that moment than in all of the moments of her life combined. She smoothed her hand up from his hip to his chest, delighting in the firmness of his skin, in the rock-hard strength beneath. She closed her eyes and took a deep breath, imprinting the manly scent of his love-warmed body on her senses.

They lay like that, enjoying the quiet closeness as their bodies fully recovered from what had hit each with such force. Then Michael was gently pressing her back to the bed.

"I want to look at you now," he explained in a voice that shook with emotion. The light in the cabin was waning, but it was enough to cast a glow on her skin, and propped on an elbow, he took in every inch. His eyes touched her breasts, first one, then the other, slid down to her navel, then lower.

Had it been anyone but Michael looking so openly at her naked body, Danica might have tried to cover herself. She wasn't used to such exposure, but the pure adoration in his eyes made mockery of her modesty. Tiny ripples of excitement surged through her as his gaze explored one spot, then another. When his hand slid around and over her breast, she bit her lip. Her nipple responded with an instant tightening, which its mate mirrored when his fingers spread the joy. She was trying not to arch off the bed when his hand fell to caress her hips, then her stomach, then the fair curls at the apex of her thighs.

She lost the battle. A small whimper slipped through her lips. She closed her eyes and turned her head to the side even as she strained closer to the fingers that were opening her, stroking her. "Michael!" she gasped.

Without removing his hand, he leaned forward to lick the corner of her mouth. "You're lovely." His voice was thick.

"I'm awful. I mean, after that...I was so...I should be weak and tired...this couldn't be..."

"It feels good?"

"Oh . . . yes . . ."

"That's how it should be."

She turned her head and looked up to find that he was grinning. "Not again. I couldn't be . . . I shouldn't . . . it's too soon . . ."

"You're not the only one who feels it." His voice was hoarse but held a definite satisfaction. Reaching for her hand, he drew it down his body. She resisted at first, but he was firm in the gentle way that was Michael, so she let him curl her fingers around his renewed tumescence. When her eyes widened in surprise, he laughed. "When it's good, it's good."

"But I didn't think men could . . ."

"I believe," he teased gruffly, "that you've got proof to the contrary in your hand." He was showing her the motion that most pleased him, and when she'd begun, timidly at first, to mimic the caress on her own, he returned his fingers to the warm, hidden spot that cried so silently for them.

Michael marveled at her innocence. From the very first he'd known that she'd been sheltered from many of the greatest joys of life, but he'd never allowed himself to think of her innocence in sexual terms. She'd been married for nine years. He'd assumed that she was thoroughly aware of a man's body . . . and her own. It seemed he'd assumed wrong. And in more ways than one he was pleased. He'd be the one to teach her the fine art of love, to teach her the glory of her own body and the ways she could glory in his. She might not have come to him a virgin, but in many ways she was as pure, which made her every response that much more sweet, that much more stimulating. She wasn't acting on habit or foreknowledge or training. She was acting on love.

This time he entered her only after he'd done the kissing and touching he'd so long dreamed of doing. He tasted every inch of her skin, nipping and sucking until she whimpered and cried out his name, which only encouraged him all the more. She was writhing and clutching his back by the time he'd reached his own limit, and he watched her face as he slowly eased into her, delighting in the wonder she couldn't possibly hide because it was too strong, too real, too heart-felt.

As much as his body would endure he prolonged the mating. He buried himself deep in her, then withdrew, slowly, nearly completely, before surging forward again. She sighed and moaned and sought his lips in a frenzy, but only when she caught her breath, held it, then burst into ragged gasps did he permit his own powerful release.

Arms and legs entwined, they slept then. When Danica awoke, the cabin was totally dark. Disoriented, it took her a minute to remember where she was and what was causing the weight that curved around her waist and over her legs.

"Hi, sleepyhead," came a familiar voice in the darkness.

"Michael! My God, for a minute I didn't know..."

"Was it strange?"

"Yes. No. I mean, I've slept like this so often...no, that's not what I mean...I mean, I've dreamed of being with you so much that there's nothing strange about it, but it's so dark and at first I wasn't sure if I was still dreaming but your leg is very real and...and I'm...babbling..."

He was laughing. "Don't stop on my account, sweetheart. I love it."

"I love you," she breathed, snuggling closer to his warmth as her heart resumed its normal beat. "What time is it?"

"Nearly ten."

"Have you been awake for long?"

"Long enough to get *my* bearings and to realize that I wasn't dreaming, either."

"Are you hungry?"

"Very."

"I can't move."

"I could always munch on cold ramaki."

"Yuk. Throw it overboard. Let the sharks have it."

"There are no sharks in this water, Dani."

"Oh." She took a breath. "Something else will eat it, then. As for me, I could go for one of those nice big juicy steaks we bought."

"That's supposed to be my line."

"Then, we'll reverse roles all the way. You cook."

"Wh-whoa, wait a minute. I always cook. At least, whenever we're at my house I do. *You* cook. I can't move."

She pressed a kiss to his chest. "That was my line. I think we're going in circles. How 'bout if we both cook?"

"Hmmm, I guess I can live with that. Of course, there's still the problem of getting off this damned bed."

"I don't know. This bed is pretty nice."

"I am *not* going to serve you dinner here."

"You're serving dinner?" she asked sweetly.

With a growl, he scrambled to his knees and picked her up, crawled to the edge of the bed, then promptly stumbled across the minuscule floor space and into the door. Danica yelped. Michael turned to brace his back against the wood.

"Shit, this place is too small."

"That's what you get for playing macho. Put me down. My funny bone kills."

He lowered her slowly, deliberately letting her body slide down his. "Good thinking. We'd never have gotten through the door that way." His hands were crossed over her bottom. "Wanna shower together."

"No way." She was arching back from him, rubbing her elbow. "I saw the shower. It was definitely not made for two."

"I think you're shy." He began to rotate his hips against hers.

"Mostly practical. And at the rate *you*'re going, bud, you won't be able to fit in that shower even alone."

"Are you complaining?" he asked in a husky tone.

"Me? Complain about you?" Elbow forgotten, she put her arms around his neck as he hoisted her up and spread her legs to circle his hips. "I'd never complain."

"You don't sound sure," he murmured against her lips.

"It's not that I'm not sure, it's just that...I think the steak can...wait a little...longer..." Her voice had grown steadily softer and the last of the sound disappeared into his mouth as it closed over hers. Drawn into his kiss, she waited for him to lay her back on the bed, but instead he simply raised her hips and lowered her onto his waiting hardness. She gasped and clung more tightly to his neck, then muffled another cry against him when he began to do something with his finger that made the rhythmic thrust of his hips all the more electric. She was sizzling, then burning, then exploding into a million scattered pieces, and she wouldn't have cared if she'd died just then because she knew she'd have died happy.

THE STEAKS, when they were finally cooked, sometime around midnight, were delicious, as was their lovemaking when they returned to bed soon after, then again when they awoke at dawn. Danica had never known the physical pleasure Michael showed her, though she knew it would have been nothing without the love that surged uncontrollably between them. If she was stunned by her own abandon, which only increased each time, she was no less stunned by Michael's gentle skill, his patience, his fiercely tender passion. As she grew freer in touching his body, he grew bolder in touching hers. At one point, when he slid her to the edge of the bed and knelt between her knees, she demurred, only to be gentled by soft words, then sent to heaven by a velvet tongue, and that inhibition fell with the rest.

By the next morning she doubted she'd ever walk again. "I feel about eighty years old," she told Michael over a breakfast of bacon and eggs.

"You don't look it. You look positively glowing."

She grinned. "Now that's a line if I've ever heard one. You're just making excuses for what your beard did."

He stared at her cheeks, then rubbed his jaw. "I think you're right. I should have shaved before . . . before . . ."

But she quickly reached out to stroke the light stubble. "No, no. I was just teasing. I didn't mind it. You look handsome with a shadow. Did anyone ever tell you that?" When he shook his head but still seemed unsure, she went on. "I remember it from the day I met you for the very first time. You looked so roguish then, but you were gentle, always gentle. I don't think you could be any other way."

"With you, no. You inspire it." He leaned forward to kiss her, sweetly and at length, before dragging himself off to shave.

Danica insisted on watching, which was not the easiest thing given the size of the head, but it was a small intimacy to go with the others and was a precursor of the day to come. They were beside each other constantly, holding hands, kissing, touching, making up for lost time and enjoying every minute.

They cruised leisurely through Penobscot Bay, then made their way slowly south, back down the coast, before dropping anchor for the night by an island just east of Port Clyde. They ate in style, by candlelight, with wine, and spent hours lying on the V-berth just talking, being close. Their lovemaking was different then, slower, more savoring, richer for the knowledge each had gained of the other, fuller for the confidence they shared.

Sated and content, they fell asleep. When Danica awoke the next morning, it was to the sound of the engine and the forward motion of the boat. Throwing on her clothes, she ran to the helm.

"Why didn't you wake me? I should have gotten up with you!"

Michael quickly drew her close to his side. "It's only seven, and you were exhausted." He kissed her temple. "This thing's due back at ten, though. I figured I'd better get a move on."

The thought of returning to land put a damper on what was already a cloudy day. Danica tried to push it from her mind. "Have you eaten anything?"

"Nope."

"Would you like something?"

"Yup."

With a gentle smile and a promising pat to his stomach, she returned to the cabin and made breakfast. After they'd eaten, she cleaned up as best she could, then returned to his side. But the closer they came to Kennebunkport, the more uneasy she felt. Occasional glances at Michael told her that he too sensed the encroachment of reality. Though he maintained a constant physical contact with her—an arm around her waist or her shoulder, or her hand held tightly in his—he seemed somehow distant. They were thirty minutes from home when he abruptly killed the engine and turned to her.

"Divorce Blake, Dani. Divorce Blake and marry me."

For a minute she couldn't breathe. She wondered if she'd known it was coming, if it was precisely this that she'd feared might happen if their fantasy was given full reign.

"I know how you feel about divorce," he went on, his features tense, "and I know how you feel about your family. But we've got something that most people spend a lifetime looking for and never find. We can't just let it go."

Danica stared up at him, wishing more than anything he hadn't raised the issue but knowing that he wouldn't have been Michael if he hadn't, particularly given the weekend they'd just spent. She was almost surprised he'd waited this long. Looking down, she took an unsteady breath, then moved to the far side of the boat and tucked her hands deep in her pockets.

"Talk to me, Dani. Say something."

She hesitated, and when she finally spoke, her voice was soft and filled with a feminine version of the pain she'd heard in his deeper voice. "What can I say?"

"Say 'yes.' Say 'no.' Say *something*."

She shook her head and hung it lower. "There's not much I *can* say. I've been through this so many times myself. I've asked the questions and made the arguments and gone back and forth with my mind saying one thing and my heart saying another, and I just don't know what the answer is. I . . . don't think I can do anything . . . at least not yet."

Michael clenched a fist in frustration. "But what have you got with Blake that I can't give you?" When she simply shook her head and refused to look at him, he went on. "You hate Washington, which Blake loves. He hates Maine, which you love. Boston is the only ground you really share and do you really share it at that? From what you've said, the time you spend together is purely for the sake of social obligation. It's a marriage without feeling. . . . Am I wrong?" She didn't answer. "*Am* I? When was the last time you laughed with him? When was the last time you enjoyed yourself, really enjoyed yourself, with him? When was the last time you made love with him the way you did this weekend with me?"

Her head flew up. "Never!" Then she lowered her voice to a near whisper. "We haven't made love in over a year."

He'd suspected as much, though he'd felt guilty hoping it. "Have you missed it?"

She answered in the same small voice. "No. It's a mutual aversion at this point."

"Then what have you got with him?"

"Sex isn't everything."

"But it's something, one thing, and it's supposed to be a vital part of any marriage. The fact that it doesn't exist in yours, that neither of you seems to care, should tell you something."

She looked up then, her expression one of defeat. "Of course it tells me something. It tells me a whole lot. But there are so many other things to consider."

"Other things . . . or other people?"

"Whatever. Oh, Michael, don't you see? I know what you want, and in so many ways that it hurts, it's what I want, too. It's just that I've lived with certain other things for so long that I can't just turn around and ignore them as if they don't exist."

"Didn't this weekend mean anything to you?"

"God, yes! It's meant the world! In some ways I feel like a totally different person. I was never . . . I was never this way with Blake."

He had to hear her say the words. "What way?"

She faltered, feeling self-conscious but knowing that what she said was the truth. "Free with my body. Free to let go. Free to enjoy my partner's . . . your body."

"And why do you think that is?" he asked quietly.

"I *know* why, and so do you! It's because we love each other, because you're that kind of person and maybe because I always was but never knew it before. But it doesn't change things, Michael, at least not everything. I still have other responsibilities." She took a shaky breath. "This weekend puts a new light on things. When I said I had no second thoughts about our making love, I meant it, but that doesn't mean I can forget about everything else. I need time, Michael. I know that's asking a lot, but I need time." She looked away. "I have to consider what all of this will do to Blake. I have to consider what it will do to my father."

"To hell with your father! What about what it'll do to *you* if you stick with Blake? Have you stopped to consider that?"

"I don't have to. I'm the one who's been unhappy for years."

"So . . . ?"

She pressed her palm to the deck by her hip. "I'm also the one who has always wanted to do the right thing."

"The right thing as your father defines it, Dani."

"He is my father. I can't write that off."

Sensing he was pushing too hard, Michael softened. "I know. I know. It's just that I wish I could make you see that you've spent your life trying to please him and it hasn't worked. Because of his ambition, what should have been wonderfully carefree years for you were years of sweating and struggling on one tennis court or another, and for what? Something you once enjoyed lost all meaning. Same thing with your marriage. You had dreams of what you wanted, and where have they gone? You've tried to please your father, and that's noble and good and it shows that despite everything you love him. But maybe you *can't* please him. Maybe it's not worth it, if the price you have to pay is too high. It was with tennis; you realized that yourself. Isn't it time you analyze your marriage to Blake the same way?"

"It is, and I have. It's just that things are complicated."

"They don't have to be, Dani. You've got a life of your own now. You're not dependent on Blake. You've got your own interests, your own friends, even the means to support yourself."

"It's not a matter of money."

"I know that. But at some point you've got to stand back and see yourself as the strong, independent woman you are. You don't need your father's approval. And besides, your father won't be around forever—"

"Michael!"

He held up a hand and spoke very softly as he approached her. "He's mortal, Dani. Just like the rest of us. Someday something's going to happen, and when it does, are you going to find yourself looking back resenting all you didn't have, all you didn't do?"

"Michael, please..."

He had his hands on her shoulders and was gently kneading the tension he found. "You don't need *anyone*'s approval if you decide to do what you truly believe is right, sweetheart. I wish you could see that."

"I'm trying... but it takes... time..." Unable to help herself, she crumbled against him. "Don't make me make promises now, Michael. I can't. I just can't."

Feeling her agony because it was his own as well, he folded her in his arms and held her tightly. "God, Dani, I love you so much. I want us to be together, but if I can't have that, at least I want to know that you're happy. I think that's what bothers me most. I hate the idea of your suffering through this charade with Blake, because that's all it is, a charade."

Danica had no argument. So much of what Michael said was right, but when she thought of going back to Boston or Washington and announcing she was going to divorce Blake, she felt something akin to terror prickle her skin. Blake would be hurt, her mother would be disappointed, her father would be livid and the press would be in seventh heaven.

And then there was Michael, whom she loved more than she'd ever loved another soul. For a long time she didn't speak, but simply drank in his nearness and the strength that was always there. When she looked up, his tender expression touched her. With a melancholy smile, she whispered her fingers across the crow's feet at the corners of his eyes, then the grooves by his mouth. "You've got creases."

"I've earned them."

"But they're the best kind." She thought of the tea tag she'd read to Reggie that night in Boston. "You've been happy. Regardless of what you say about feeling something was missing, you've been happy."

"Happiness is relative. I'm happier now."

"But your life has been good. I hope I don't do anything to spoil that," she said more quietly.

"How could you? You bring me joy."

"I also bring you pain, and I wish it didn't have to be. You love me and want to marry me, and I love you but I can't marry you. At least, not now. Not yet. There's too much I have to work out. Will you give me time, Michael? Will you wait?''

He took a deep breath and released it slowly, willing the knot in his throat to ease. "I haven't got any choice, do I?''

''You do,'' she said fearfully.

''No, Dani. I haven't got any choice at all. I'll wait because you're worth it. I want you to remember that. You're worth it.''

Chapter Twelve

THE WEEKEND AFTER DANICA RETURNED to Boston, she flew to Washington to see Blake. He'd requested that she accompany him to a dinner party on Saturday night given in honor of a visiting dignitary, but even if he hadn't asked her down, she would have gone. She had to talk with him. *One* of them had to broach the topic of their deteriorating relationship, and it appeared that he wasn't going to be the one.

As it happened, he was at the office when she arrived on Saturday morning, and he returned only in time to change into a tuxedo and take her out. When she awoke on Sunday morning, he was playing squash. The first opportunity she had to talk with him was that afternoon, a short time before she was due to fly back to Boston.

His houseboy had fixed them an early dinner, then had left, and they were alone. Blake was about to vanish into his den when she stopped him.

"Blake? Have you got a few minutes?"

He glanced at his watch. "I need to make several calls before we leave for the airport."

"Can't it wait? There's something I'd like to talk to you about."

Though he seemed vaguely discomfited, he returned to his seat. "Yes?"

"I think . . . I think that we ought to discuss what's happening."

He hesitated for only an instant. "All right. What's happening?"

She resented his deliberate blandness, and that gave her the courage to blurt, "Our relationship. It's going nowhere." She saw a flicker of something in his eyes, but it was gone before she could identify it.

"Where did you expect it to go?" he asked in a pleasant tone, flashing her a patronizing smile.

"I'm not sure, but I didn't expect it would stagnate."

"Is that what you think it's doing? Danica, we've been married for nine years."

"And by rights we should be closer than ever. But we're not. We lead very separate lives."

"Whose fault is that?" he asked calmly.

"I won't take the full blame. Marriage is a two-way street. Each partner has to give."

"Danica, what do you want of me? I've got a critical job with the government. I give as much as I can."

"To the government, yes."

"And not to you?" His laugh was short, his handsome features hard and belying humor. "What would you have me do?"

"You make no attempt to come see me in Boston. You didn't make it up to Maine once this summer." She wasn't sorry about either fact, but she felt they had to be said.

"My life is here now, and I'm very busy. I'm grateful that you're willing to make the trip down from time to time."

She felt she was dealing with a piece of wood. "Don't you want anything more, though? Don't you think that a marriage should be something more than an occasional weekend together?"

Blake pondered that for only a minute. "There are many kinds of marriages. In some the partners are inseparable. In others, such as ours, they lead independent lives. Commuting marriages are common nowadays. And as I recall, it was originally your idea. You were the one who didn't care to live here."

"You know why, but you don't seem to want to accept it."

"I accept it perfectly well, which is why I don't know what's upsetting you. As I see it, we've reached a satisfactory compromise. What's the problem?"

In a bid for patience, Danica took a deep breath. "Blake, do you see other women here?"

"Of course I do. There are women everywhere I go."

"Do you *date* other women?"

He lowered his brows in his first show of impatience. "Of course not. I'm married to you. I wouldn't date other women."

"But don't you want to *be* with a woman?"

"What are you getting at?" he growled.

She couldn't believe he was so thick. "You're a man, Blake. I'd think you'd want female companionship far more than you're getting it."

"I'm busy. I don't have time to think about female companionship, much less seek it out." He gentled his voice. "Seeing you when you come down is enough."

She sighed. If he'd intended his words to be flattering, they weren't. He was thinking solely of himself, as though by rights the parameters of their marriage should be defined by his needs. "Well, maybe it's not enough for me," she said quietly. "Maybe *I* need something more."

For an instant he was stunned and she actually felt sorry for him. "I hadn't realized," he murmured at last. "I guess I've been so busy that I haven't thought about that."

"I have. A whole lot. There are times when I wonder... when I wonder if it wouldn't be better for both of us if we were free. You could find someone to satisfy your needs here. I could find someone to satisfy my needs in Boston."

"What are you suggesting?" he asked, his body deadly still.

"Maybe we should think about a divorce, Blake."

"A divorce? I don't want a divorce! That's the craziest thing I've ever heard!"

Studying the utter horror on his face, she was humbled. But she'd come too far to stop just yet. "Maybe it's the most practical," she offered softly. "You don't seem to take great joy in my company. I don't think you're particularly interested in what I'm doing."

"Of course I am! I ask you about your work, don't I?"

"Mostly I tell you about it. There are times when I feel you're hardly listening."

"I'm listening. I always listen. But it's your job. I would no more tell you how to go about doing it than I would expect you to tell me how to do mine."

She was shaking her head. "That's only a small point among many. We share so little in life, Blake. We have different interests, different friends.... Do you remember when the last time we made love was?" He should have. She certainly did. It had been sixteen months ago, in Maine, when she'd all but seduced him, when she'd become pregnant.

He shrugged and frowned. "I don't keep a scorecard."

"Doesn't it occur to you that it's been a while?"

"Danica, I don't define my life in terms of sex. I'm forty-six years old. I think of other things now."

"Well, I'm twenty-nine, and I do think about the non-existent love life I have with my husband."

Jumping from his chair, Blake paced to the far side of the dining room. He stood with his back to her, his hands on his lean hips. "Is that what you're missing most? Sex?"

"Of course it isn't. It's just one other thing that makes me wonder whether we've got anything left at all."

"Christ, I don't believe this," he muttered. "I'm the one who should be going through a mid-life crisis, not you." He whirled around. "What is it you want?"

She crushed her linen napkin into a ball in her lap and spoke very quietly. "I want a family, Blake. I want a husband who's around, and children—"

"We tried for children and you lost it!"

Stung, she lashed back. "*We* weren't trying. *I* was."

He made a dismissing gesture with his hand. "The end result was the same. I thought I was being considerate giving your body a chance to recover."

"For sixteen months?"

He totally ignored that. "And as for a husband who's around, I *am* around. Around *here*. If you wanted, you could be with me more. It's been your choice to stay in Boston."

"But things weren't any different in Boston. You were always busy there, too."

"Damn it, I have a career. A very important one. I never promised you I'd sit around at home holding your hand, did I? *Did* I?"

He was angry and Danica felt her own rebellion wane. "No."

"I never gave you cause to believe that we'd have anything other than what we have now."

"When we were first married—"

"We were both a lot younger then. We had fewer responsibilities, and being married was a novelty. But the honeymoon's over, Danica. It has been for a long time. We've moved on, and I think you're being very shortsighted if you feel no pride in the direction we've gone. It's not every women whose husband is named to the Cabinet."

"But what about me?" she asked in a small voice. "What about the direction I've gone?"

"It seems to me you've done pretty well," he retorted, gaining force as she lost it. "I give you the kind of freedom that some men would never give their wives because I'm self-confident enough to allow it. You've got your work with Governor Bryant. You've got your friends. You've got your house in Maine. You even have that Buchanan fellow. Let me tell you, some husbands would never stand for *that*. Some husbands would be jealous. But I'm not. I realize you've got to have your own friends, and I'm happy you do." His eyes grew steely, boring into her. "But what I won't stand for is talk of divorce. I don't want one. You're my wife, and I like it that way. The arrangement we have is very comfortable for me. So I'd suggest you grow up a little and accept what's best for you."

Incensed, she opened her mouth to protest when Blake stalked from the room, calling over his shoulder, "Now I'm going to make those calls you've kept me from, and after that I'll drive you to the airport. You can leave the things on the table. John will clean up when he gets back."

In a state of utter speechlessness, Danica stared after his retreating figure. Only when she heard the den door shut did she blink, then swallow. She hadn't known what she'd expected, but it was certainly a little more tenderness than he'd shown. Either that or that he'd have agreed to a divorce. But he hadn't. He'd rejected it in no uncertain terms. He'd opted for the playing out of their prescribed roles...just as her father would have done in the same situation. She wondered if her mother had ever put her foot down, then decided not, because her mother was an accommodator. And Danica? What was she? She couldn't bear the thought of continuing with Blake, particularly after what she'd found with Michael. But the battle lines were drawn. Blake would fight her. She knew her parents would fight her, too.

Thoroughly discouraged, she allowed Blake to drive her to the airport. He made no reference to their talk, indeed said little during the drive. She made no attempt to break the silence because her thoughts were too raw. Their parting was as dispassionate as was everything else about Blake. When he leaned down to give her a dutiful kiss, it was on her cheek and she was grateful. Her lips ached for another man, and having known his kiss so thoroughly, one from her husband was a sacrilege.

DANICA TRIED to settle back into routine, but her thoughts were never far from Michael. She worked diligently with James, going over what she'd written during the summer, discussing the direction of the last few chapters of their book, but her concentration when she was home alone was often broken by brooding. She resumed her ballet classes, delighting in seeing all her friends again, but they didn't come home with her, either. On those mornings when she had board meetings at the Art Institute or the hospital, she found herself looking at the other women around the table, wondering if they were happy in their marriages, if they were loyal to their spouses and their spouses to them. She knew that several of them were on second, even third marriages, and she wished she were close enough to any of them to talk about it. But there was a formality among these people that she could never quite breach, so her questions went unanswered.

On the day that Michael was due to arrive in Boston, she stayed home, waiting. His call came at three in the afternoon.

"God, I'm sorry, Dani. I wanted to call you sooner, but they've had damned meetings scheduled since ten. How are you, sweetheart?"

"Missing you. When will you be done?"

"I should be free by six. Can you make it for dinner?"

She answered quickly and without pride. "I can make it for anything. You name the time and place."

He smiled at her urgency, which fed his own. "I love you."

"I love you, too.... Time and place?"

He named them, having decided that a small Greek restaurant on the outskirts of the Square would give them the privacy they sought. "Dani, maybe I should pick you up. I'm not sure I like the idea of your driving around at night."

"No, this is better. I'll lock all the doors. It'll be fine."

"You're sure?" He knew that what she said made sense. Though neither of them had spoken of proprieties, both knew that the more unnoticed their meeting went, the better.

"I'm sure... I can't wait, Michael," she whispered.

"Me, neither. I'm not sure how I'm going to make it through these meetings. It was bad...morning..." The connection broke momentarily.

"Ooops. There's your dime."

"That wasn't any three minutes," he yelled to an operator who wasn't listening.

"You'd better go, Michael. We'll have plenty of time to talk later. Okay?"

"Okay. Love you."

"Love you, too."

Danica hung up the phone feeling warmed as she hadn't since she'd returned from Maine ten days before. She basked in the feeling for the rest of the afternoon, then dressed with special care. With just a momentary touch of guilt, she told Mrs. Hannah that she'd be having dinner with a friend and that she wouldn't be back until late, but she was firm when the housekeeper suggested that Marcus could drive her wherever it was she was going.

"Thank Marcus for me, but I really feel like driving myself," she said, taking the keys to the Audi and heading out to the courtyard. She hadn't lied. She felt strong, full of energy, very much on top of the world.

Her headiness didn't diminish even when it took her ten minutes and three trips around the block to find a parking space. She was running when she reached the restaurant, but it was a wise expenditure of energy in light of the self-control she had to then exercise to keep from flying into Michael's arms and telling the whole world she was in love.

With Michael in much the same state, they babbled steadily through dinner, not seeing what they ate and caring less. They skipped dessert. He couldn't get the check fast enough. Then they were out of the restaurant and he was walking her to her car, leaning low to kiss her in the opportune darkness of the quiet side street. Drawing back at last, he reached into his pocket and pressed his hotel key into her hand. "I'll follow you until we get there. Then you go on up. I'll join you in a minute."

She nodded, which was all she could do because she was shaking all over and it wasn't from fear of discovery. Being so near Michael yet unable to touch him, to say those things her heart needed to say, had been sheer torture. Only with the greatest of control did she manage to start her car, then wait until Michael had pulled up beside her. The ten-minute drive seemed endless. Her excitement grew such that her body was high-pitched and taut by the time she finally pulled into the parking lot. Michael pulled in beside her, then sat.

Taking a deep breath to steady her movements, she slid from the car and entered the lobby of the hotel, took the elevator to the eighth floor, found the room and let herself in. Once there, she leaned back against the door and waited, heart thudding, body trembling, juices flowing in anticipation of Michael, his manly body, his love.

His knock came so softly that she mightn't have heard it, given the hammering of her pulse, had she not been braced against the door. She peered out. He slid in. Then they were in each other's arms, hugging, kissing, laughing and sighing until even that wasn't enough.

"You look beautiful," Michael rasped, sliding her thin wool sheath up over her hips. "I love your dress." The item

in question was over her head and discarded in a heap that
would have made lie of his praise had Danica not understood, and shared, his impatience. She was tugging at his tie.

"You look gorgeous all dressed up," she said in hurried
breaths. She left his tie draped loosely around his neck while
she attacked the buttons of his shirt. "I've never seen you this
way. You'll drive your female students wild."

"I won't even see them," he managed, sending her slip the
way of her dress. He fumbled with his belt, jerked down his
zipper and shucked his pants while she threw her stockings
aside.

Within minutes they were naked and falling on the bed,
each touching the other with a greed born of a deprivation
that seemed to have stretched for longer than ten days.

"I love you. Oh, baby, I love you," he panted, making a
place for himself between her legs and thrusting upward.

Danica cried out and held him tightly, wrapping her legs
around his waist, rising from the bed to meet his deep thrusts.
It was only minutes before they climaxed, then an eternity of
bliss and a slower, more reluctant return to earth.

"I've missed you," she breathed against his damp chest.
"It's seemed like forever."

He held her snugly against him, an arm around her shoulders, a thigh over hers anchoring her to his hip. As physically
sated as they were at that moment, neither would allow sleep
to steal even a second of the time they had together. When
they'd recovered enough to talk, they did. When talking gave
way to revived physical needs, they made love again. Then
there was more to say, more to share. All too soon, and with
great reluctance, Danica pushed herself from the bed and
reached for her clothes.

"I wish you didn't have to leave," he said.

She stepped into her panties, then sat to pull on her stockings. "So do I. But I've got to get home or Mrs. Hannah will
wonder." Even as she spoke, she hated the words. She didn't
want to have to hide when what she was hiding was so right,
so wonderful. She knew that Michael felt the same because his
jaw was tight, his expression grim.

She fastened her bra and pulled on her slip. Then, unable to resist, she looked back at Michael's sprawled form. "You have a beautiful body," she murmured, running her hand through the hair on his chest. It was warm and looked more golden than tawny in the dim light that flowed from the nightstand, and she felt she was touching a treasure. But the treasure didn't end at his chest. It descended over the lean plane of his stomach, over narrow hips and the limp but nonetheless impressive parts that made him man, over the sinewed strength of legs that stretched forever. She met his gaze and smiled. "A bronzed god with a heart of gold. I love you, Michael."

Grasping her elbows, he hauled her over him and kissed her in eloquent return of the vow. By the time he was done, he was no longer limp, and she had to force herself from the bed to keep from responding to his desire.

"You'll be here for another day?" she asked.

He pushed himself up against the headboard and dragged a sheet over himself in the hope that what was out of sight would be out of mind. "I finish up tomorrow afternoon. I could drive back tomorrow night—" when she gasped, he grinned "—but I won't. I'll stay over if you can think of good reason why I should."

Throwing caution to the winds, she returned to the bed. As she kissed him, she stroked him through the sheet, stopping only when he'd begun to arch upward in greater need.

"Good reason," he rasped. "That's it. Of course, I'll be in agony until then. Dani, you're not playing fair."

Because she loved him so much and because what she'd started had affected her nearly as much as it had him, she kissed him again, this time sliding her hand under the sheet.

"Take off your panties," he whispered into her mouth. "Just your panties. I'll be quick."

"No. Let me."

"Dani . . ." But he moaned and said nothing more, because she knew what she was doing and he couldn't think with the pleasure she gave him. When she eased the sheet back and leaned lower, he tried again. "Dani . . . no . . . ahhhh, my God . . . I want . . . Dani . . ."

She was using her tongue and lips as he'd done on her, and the love she felt for him bridged whatever gaps had remained in her education. Eyes closed tightly, head pressed to the side, he strained upward. The tendons of his arms stood out vividly. His outspread fingers dug into the sheet. He gasped her name once more, caught his breath, then felt his body explode.

She was kissing him sweetly on the mouth when he finally regained awareness. "That was wonderful," she said with a feline smile, and, though still dazed, he sensed the full extent of her love.

"That was wonderful," he echoed, but weakly, because every inch of his body felt drained and limp. He took a long, shuddering breath. "And you've won because there's no way I can touch you any more tonight. I don't think . . . I'm going to move . . . till morning."

"No need," she said softly. "When do you have to get up?"

"Seven," he mumbled without opening his eyes.

Without another word, she picked up the phone and requested a wake-up call, then quietly finished dressing and kissed him softly. He was already asleep. For a final moment she gazed at him from the door, then, smiling, carefully shut it and headed home.

THE NEXT NIGHT was every bit as heavenly. They ate at a different restaurant this time but returned to his hotel in much the same manner and spent the next hours in bliss. Unfortunately, the bliss faded when Danica dressed to leave.

"I don't like this, Dani. I don't like having to sneak around with you as though what we're doing is wrong. I don't like having to starve for a week between feedings."

She laughed and gently stroked his cheek. "You've been with Rusty too much. He always did make a fuss about mealtimes."

"I'm not talking about food," he growled.

"I know." She grew more serious. "I know. But I don't know what to say."

"Say you'll divorce Blake. This is getting ridiculous."

"I need more time, Michael. I'm trying. I've put the bug in his ear and all I can do is twist it around until he gets the message."

"What if he never does? Maybe the guy needs a good swift kick in the ass."

"I'm trying, but we knew it wouldn't be easy."

"If you're waiting for *him* to suggest the divorce, maybe you're going about it the wrong way. Maybe you should tell him about us. Maybe you should tell Mrs. Hannah you'll be out all night."

"I can't. I can't do that. Please? I need you to be supportive. I'm doing what I can in the only way I know how."

Seeing, hearing her agony, Michael pulled her head to his chest and moaned. "Okay, sweetheart. And I'm sorry if I push you, but there are times when I get so impatient."

"I get that way, too, and it's so much worse because I feel an awful responsibility on my shoulders."

He stroked her hair. "I wish I could take some of it for you. Maybe I should go to Washington. Maybe *I* should have a talk with Blake."

She brought her head up fast. "No! Don't do that. You'll only end up taking the blame for something that isn't your doing at all."

"Isn't my doing? Hell, I'm screwing the man's wife—" At Danica's stricken expression, he quickly amended the thought. "I'm in love with his wife, with every last intimate inch of her." He lowered his voice. "Better?"

She nodded. "There's nothing sordid about what we do."

"I know, sweetheart, and I apologize for using that word. It's just that I get frustrated and angry and I wish something would happen."

"It will. In time. It will."

It happened sooner than either of them thought. That night, when Danica returned to Beacon Hill, Mrs. Hannah was up waiting with the urgent message that Danica's mother had had a stroke.

THE HARTFORD HOSPITAL was no different from any other, with its long halls, its antiseptic smell and the ever-present

sounds of bleeps, rustling uniforms and muted conversation.
Danica came to know it all well over the next two weeks as she
sat at her mother's bedside.

Eleanor had been fortunate. Only her right side had been
paralyzed, and even then she was slowly beginning to regain
a measure of movement. Danica helped her eat, pushed her
wheelchair around the halls, waited patiently while she was in
physical therapy, and, more than anything, filled the void left
by William Marshall's absence.

Oh, he had come. He'd come immediately after Eleanor
had been admitted. He'd shown up on each successive weekend. But he always had to return to Washington, where
pressing business waited. Danica was reminded of when her
mother had had her hysterectomy, when William had been
about as doting. She was reminded of when she'd had her own
miscarriage, when Blake had popped up for twenty-four
hours, then had left. And she was reminded of Michael,
who'd been there, who'd cared for her, who'd told her without words that she was far more important than any work he
might be doing.

Indeed, Michael had driven to Hartford several days before to see Eleanor. Though Danica hadn't had much time
with him alone, she'd been deeply touched by his thoughtful-
ness. As for Blake, his lavish floral bouquet sat wilting now on
the windowsill; he hadn't made it north at all.

Ironically, the freest times for Danica were during visiting
hours, when a steady stream of the Marshalls' friends fil-
tered in and out of the room. Danica would excuse herself
then, promising her mother she'd be back soon, and would
wander around the hospital or the nearby downtown area
wondering why she was being so attentive. In the end, she
only knew that she couldn't be any other way. What had happened in the past didn't seem as important as that what she
was doing now gave her satisfaction. Eleanor, for all her
faults, was her mother, and it was obvious from the frightened glances she sent toward Danica when Danica was leaving, from the way she held Danica's hand with her own strong
left one, from the way she seemed more relaxed when Danica was around, that Eleanor needed her.

More than once Danica wondered whether Eleanor's recent attentiveness hadn't been a forewarning that something
wasn't right. The doctors had said she'd had high blood pressure for years, though Danica had never known it. Her father, on the other hand, had his own thoughts on Eleanor's
stroke.

"She's been worried about you lately, Danica."

They were sitting in the coffee shop on the third Sunday.
Eleanor was to be released from the hospital the following
week.

"There's been nothing for her to worry about," Danica
commented as casually as she could, given the sudden pre-
monition she felt.

"She doesn't think so. She came back from Maine last
summer quite concerned about you and Blake."

"About me and Blake? I'm not sure I follow." She certainly did, but she wanted to know exactly what her father had
to say.

"You're never together anymore. You live in different cities and you leave him to go about his business on his own.
That's no way to run a marriage."

"I don't know. It doesn't seem to be much different from
the way you and Mom ran yours."

William grew stern. "It certainly *is* different. Your mother
has always been with me, whether in Washington or Hartford. It's only lately that she's been here more, and that's because she's been tired."

"Then I guess Mom's a better person than I am. She's
undemanding and self-sacrificing."

"She's been a good wife. I'd have expected you to follow
her example."

"Times have changed. Commuting is much simpler now."

"That's a lot of hogwash. Commuting was always simple
if you wanted to do it. You, obviously, don't want to do it.
What's the matter with you?"

Danica felt her anger rising, but she forced herself to speak
in an even tone. "I have interests that Mom never had."

William Marshall had never been one to beat around the
bush when he had something on his mind. "You've got this

Buchanan fellow. What in the hell are you doing with him? That's what got your mother so upset. She's been worried sick that something's going on that you're going to regret one day."

"Now just a minute, Dad," Danica warned. "If you're trying to blame Mom's stroke on me, that's unfair. According to the doctor, she's had high blood pressure for years, and that could as easily be from trying to keep up with the life you want to lead as from worrying about me. Let's not throw accusations around because we'll never know what caused the stroke."

"You haven't answered my question, young lady. I asked what was going on between you and that fellow in Maine."

Danica stared at her father for a full minute. "He's a good friend, probably the best I've ever had. You should be grateful he gives me his time. God only knows, no one else does."

"What in the hell is that supposed to mean?"

She sighed. "Ach, this isn't the time or place."

In deference to her reminder, he lowered his voice, but that was the extent of his surrender. "No, girl, spit it out."

"It's not important. What *is* is that we try to get Mother out of here and back on her feet."

"That will happen anyway. She's got the best of doctors and therapists, and I've already hired a full-time nurse to take care of her when she gets home."

"I'll stay on for a while. She needs someone who loves her."

If Danica was trying to get a message across, she failed. William was still thinking about the stack of photographs Morgan Emery had handed him. "You're avoiding me, Danica. I asked you what you were doing with Michael Buchanan."

"And I answered." It was all she could do not to wilt beneath William's cutting stare, but she managed. She loved him because he was her father, and she'd always tried to please him, but short of outright lying, she'd be damned now by whatever answer she gave.

"Then listen to me, and listen good. I want you to stay away from him. He and his family are trouble from the word *go*. He'd like nothing more than to embarrass us, and if you do something to compromise Blake, you'll be doing just that. Honestly, Danica, I never thought I'd have to have a discussion like this with you.'' When her mouth remained set, he went on. ''Stay away from Buchanan. Your running all over Maine with him is indecent. Blake Lindsay is a good man, and he's your husband. For your mother's sake, if nothing else, behave yourself.''

Danica felt like a chastised child and her resentment nearly overpowered her recollection of where she was and why. She would have liked nothing more than to tell her father to mind his own business, to tell him to clean his own house before he worried about cleaning hers, but she said nothing, at least on that score. One part of her feared the repercussions of such an outburst, and for her mother's sake, if nothing else, she controlled herself.

Gathering her purse, she stood. ''I think I'll go back up and see how Mom is doing.''

William stood and took her elbow. ''Do we have an understanding, Danica?''

''You've said what you wanted to say. Trust me to do what I feel is right.''

''That's a nonanswer if I ever heard one,'' her father grumbled. ''Maybe I steered you wrong after all. You should have been a politician.''

''God forbid,'' Danica replied with a deliberate touch of humor.

Unfortunately, William wasn't deceived, or rather, he didn't particularly trust his daughter. He felt that he barely knew her, that any number of things could be going on in her life that he didn't know about. For the most part, he didn't care what she did. He certainly wasn't interested in getting a rundown on her charity work or even the work she was doing with James Bryant. The matter of Michael Buchanan, though, was something else. He was damned if he'd have a scandal rock his family.

He'd seen those pictures, had studied them time and again. Though there had been no evidence that Danica was having an affair, there was plenty of evidence that she might well do so in the future. He'd warned Danica, but he couldn't be sure she'd listen. What he needed was solid evidence one way or another, and the only way to get that would be to keep Emery on the case. It was only a matter of money, a small price to pay if by doing so he could prevent Danica from making fools of them all. With evidence, something compromising, he could confront her. Better still, he could confront Buchanan, even the senior Buchanan if need be.

But…that was a ways off. First, he had to get Emery on the stick. Once he'd done that and once he knew that Eleanor was safely installed at home, he'd be able to return his full concentration to more important business in Washington.

NOVEMBER IN THE CAPITAL tended toward the chilly, yet Cilla had always preferred it to spring, when hoards of sightseers flocked to see the cherry blossoms and the myriad of historical sights the city offered. But then, she'd always been a rebellious sort. She liked to root for the underdog in a baseball game, eat spinach instead of peas, wear her skirts long when designers said hemlines were rising. She thrived on doing the unexpected, so it was no surprise to her when she found herself very happily in bed with her ex-husband.

"Ahhh, Cilla, we always were good together," Jeffrey breathed when his pulse had finally begun to slow.

She tipped her head on the pillow to look at him. "In bed, yes. Why is it, do you think?"

"Chemistry?"

"I think there's something more. We're both committed, intense. Making love with you is always fierce. It's a challenge because there's always some new little part of you that comes out."

"Like a puzzle. We're both puzzle freaks."

"Mmmm. Ironic, isn't it? The same thing that makes us dynamite in bed keeps us apart out of it."

Jeffrey took a deep breath and drew her head to the crook of his shoulder. "Let's not talk about that."

"We have to at some point. This has been going on for two months now. We've been together several nights a week, but there's still a barrier there."

"Just like the old days."

"Right. Doesn't it bother you?"

"Of course it bothers me. Why couldn't you have made your millions producing homemade chocolate chip cookies?"

"Why couldn't you have made yours inventing Trivial Pursuit?"

He tucked in his chin to look at her. "Have you played?"

She stuck hers out. "Sure. I'm unbeatable."

"That's because you've never played against me."

"And what makes you think you'd win?"

"I never miss a question on history or geography or science or sports."

"That still leaves entertainment and art. You forget, I've got the memory of an elephant."

"Mmmm. I bet we could team up and win championships all over the place. Hey, that's an idea. Why don't we both resign from our jobs and go on the road as trivia experts?"

She snorted. "We'd probably fight over who was going to roll the die."

"No, we never fought over petty things." He'd grown pensive. "Just over the big things, like cases we're working on."

She rolled over and propped herself on his chest. "Okay. Let's see how far we've come. Tell me about what you're doing."

"Cilla..."

"See. You still don't trust me. You trust me to do all kinds of wicked things to your body, but you don't trust me with your thoughts."

"God, we've been over this so many times before."

"And we'll go over it many times more. Unless—" she made to rise from the bed "—you'd just as soon call it quits now."

He snagged her back. "I don't want that. You know how I feel about you."

"No. Tell me."

"You know."

"I...want...to...hear...the...words."

He gave her a crooked smile. "You like it when I'm vulnerable, don't you? It gives you the upper edge."

"There you're wrong. There's nothing 'upper edge' about it. We're talking equality. I know that I'm at my most vulnerable when I'm with you. I just need to know that I'm not the only one."

"You're not, Cilla." He hesitated a minute longer. "I loved you when we were married, and I love you still…. Hell, I feel so naked when I say that."

"You are naked."

He arched a brow and looked down the creamy length of her back. "So are you."

She caught her breath at his near tangible caress. "Guess so. I do love you, Jeff. So help me, I've tried not to. I've dated plenty since the divorce, but I keep coming back. In my mind, at least."

"Not only your mind."

"Well …"

"Come on. Give a kiss."

Her eyes grew sly. "Where?"

"Here, for starters." He pointed to his mouth and opened it when she came. But it was only for starters because the combination of chemistry and challenge and love was a potent one with a will of its own, and before long they were sprawling over and around each other in a mutual search for satisfaction.

Some time later, when they were once again at rest in each other's arms, Jeff sighed. "And we're right back where we started, aren't we, with a roadblock smack in front of us."

Cilla rubbed her cheek against the matted hair on his chest. She closed her eyes and took a deep breath. "I'm doing a story on toxic waste seepage into the Chesapeake Bay. The problem is that the source of the seepage is a chemical plant, which is owned by a very prominent and politically active taxpayer."

Jeff went still for a minute, not so much because of what she'd said but because of the fact that she'd said it. Without prompting from him, she'd offered him a part of her work that she would at one time have guarded religiously. He felt very good.

"Have there been reports of the seepage before?"

"Oh, yes. For years officials have known the Chesapeake had problems. It was once thought to be the nation's most productive body of water, but that's changing. Industrial wastes from Pennsylvania flow in through the Susquehanna. Toxic kepone spills in through the James from Richmond and Norfolk. Even treated sewage adds chlorine toxicity to the bay." She took another breath and forced herself on. "The particular chemical plant I'm looking at is in Baltimore harbor. It's owner has passed around enough money to keep its spills under raps."

"Have you got evidence?"

"Of the seepage? The Army Corps of Engineers has documented it."

"What about the money? Any evidence?"

Cilla looked up at him because his questions were coming strong and fast and she felt a habitual wariness rear its head. Jeffrey read her instantly.

"I'm sorry. That's the interrogator in me at work. And I'm not this way because of my job. The reverse is more accurate. I'm good at my job because I am this way. But it's just me now, Cilla. Just me. It won't go any further. Please. Trust me."

She saw the sincerity in his expression and knew that if they were to have any hope for a future together, she had to do as he asked. She nodded. "We're getting evidence of the money, but it's slow. Things have been well hidden. We've got to be careful because if word gets around that we're on to something, that many more doors will suddenly close on us."

"Sounds familiar.... I'm having the same problem." In general terms—and with an ingrained caution—he outlined the investigation he was undertaking into high-tech espionage. "We know that Bulgaria received the goods. We know that they came from Austria. We even identified the Austrian firm that did the shipping, then...nothing. There's got to be an originating American firm, but we can't find it. Records have been destroyed; storefronts have been physically demolished. It's frustrating as hell when you *know* what's been done is illegal but you can't clinch it with hard evidence.''

Cilla pondered his frustration, then spoke with reference to her own. "That's the worst part, I think. Time passes and you know that the public good is in danger, but you have a responsibility to do and say nothing until you can back your words up."

"But you can't give up because you *know*. You *know*. And there's a responsibility in that, too. Maybe it's a good guy complex and corny as hell, but damn it, it gets into your blood."

She slanted him an understanding smile. "I know . . . And it's nice to know you know."

He returned the smile, surprised that the sharing had been relatively painless. "Hey, any more word from your sex maniac?"

"Which one?"

He punished her teasing by pinching her bottom. "The one who called you that day wanting to talk about power and lust?"

"Oh. That one." She sighed. "No. No more calls. I did meet this guy, though. It was at a diplomatic reception. He was kind of standing by the wall looking disgruntled, like he wasn't terribly happy to be there but he just couldn't stay away. When he started talking to me, I could have sworn the voice was the same."

"As the one on the phone?"

"Mmmm." She shrugged. "I'm probably wrong. I mean, the telephone usually manages to mangle tones."

"Not that much. What did he have to say at the reception?"

"Oh, he railed on about the power of the wealthy and how you had to play their game if you wanted to survive in this town."

"He's right."

"But he sure was angry."

"People who have to play by others' rules usually are. What was his position?"

deeply into both his teaching and his writing. It worked, though the end result was self-defeating. He finished the book and sent it off to New York shortly before Christmas. At the same time, his classes ended. Since his appointment had been only for the half-year seminar, he had nothing left but to grade the term papers he's assigned in lieu of exams.

Exhausted by the pace he'd kept, discouraged by the fact that his love for Danica was growing even as his hopes that she'd divorce Blake were fading, he decided that he needed to get away. Not to do research for another book. Simply to get away.

He was in the process of studying travel literature one Monday morning in mid-January when his doorbell rang. Rusty reached the door before he did. "It's okay, boy." He scratched the dog's ears as he opened the door. Then, in a flash, he knew it wasn't okay. He'd never formally met the man standing before him, but the face was familiar enough to even the most impartial of observers, of which group he was definitely not one.

"Michael Buchanan?"

"Yes. Senator Marshall."

"You've been expecting me?"

"No. I recognize your face from newspapers and television." He could see no resemblance to Danica, but perhaps he simply chose not to. "I think I assumed that one day we'd meet."

William Marshall stood sternly, with a small portfolio beneath his arm. "That day is here. May I come in?"

Nodding, Michael stepped aside. A glance toward the drive revealed a rental car—it was too small and common a model to have actually belonged to this United States senator—and no other driver. He deduced that William had flown into Portland and driven down himself. It was not terribly promising if he'd hoped for an amicable chitchat, but then, he hadn't. There could be only one reason for William Marshall's seeking him out, and William, it appeared, had no intention of mincing words.

"I have with me," he began, "some photographs I believe you would like to see." He had already unclasped the portfolio and was pulling out a handful of prints.

Michael took them, looked first at one, then the next and the next, all the while struggling to contain the nausea that had begun to churn in his stomach.

"Where did you get these?" he asked, though his voice was hoarse and clearly revealed his shock.

"They were taken by a private investigator."

Michael's words came slowly and were laden with disbelief and disdain. "You hired an investigator to follow your own daughter?"

"And you," William added remorselessly. "Aren't you going to ask why?"

"I don't think I need to do that," Michael answered. "The pictures speak for themselves. The fact that you had them taken says the rest."

"Then you're smarter than I thought. Not that I'd have expected less from John Buchanan's son—" he pointed to the pictures, which hung limply in Michael's hand "—though you really were pretty stupid pulling this stunt."

"My father has no place in this. You're talking to me."

"That's exactly right, and I want you to listen. You're to stay away from my daughter. You're not to see her ever again."

"I'm not a young boy, Senator, and your daughter isn't a child. Do you really think you can lay down laws and have people obey them just like that?"

"I'm not the one laying down the laws you've violated. You've been having an affair with another man's wife. That's adultery."

There was no point trying to deny it. The photos in his hand showed him kissing Danica in her car, showed him holding her hand under what he'd thought was cover of a dimly lit restaurant booth, showed Danica entering a hotel room, then himself passing through the same door. Short of capturing the two of them in bed, the photos were condemning.

"I know exactly what it is. I also know that your daughter is stuck in a miserable marriage and that I've been able to give her a love she's never had."

"You're talking out of turn, boy. You don't *know* what she's had and what she hasn't."

"We've talked about many, many things, Senator Marshall. And regardless of what you think to be the case, Danica's perception of it is what matters."

"This is all beside the point," William stated boldly. "The point is that I'm prepared to use those pictures. I'll show them to Danica's husband, who can easily use them in an alienation-of-affection suit. I'll show them to the press right at the time your newest book is being reviewed. I'll show them to your father, if need be. The point is that you're going to get out of my daughter's life and stay out."

A slow fury rose in Michael. "You're threatening me."

"Damned right I am!"

Michael's nostrils flared when he inhaled. The strain of not hauling back and punching the man in the nose was tremendous. His fingers clenched the photographs, bending them, though he didn't notice. "It won't work," he said in a deadly quiet tone. "I won't be intimidated like one of your underlings in Washington. You may have power there, Senator, but you're off your turf here. The fact is that you'll hurt yourself and your family far more by making these photographs public than you'll hurt me. I've got little to lose. My readers will buy my books regardless of any dirt you sling, and my publishers will keep on buying them because they're good. As for my father, he relinquished control over me years ago. In fact, the one person, the *only* person, who will suffer badly from these things is Danica. If you love her at all, I'd think you'd want to spare her that."

William was shrewd. "I could say the same to you. If *you* love her at all, I think you'd want to spare her that."

He'd hit home, and for a minute Michael had no answer. Only for a minute, though. Then sheer disgust for the man before him took over. "I love Danica more than you could ever imagine. She's warm and intelligent. She's loving and giving. The only thing I don't understand is how someone as beautiful as that could have been spawned by someone as ruthless as you. Go ahead, Senator Marshall. Do what you want with your pictures." He shoved them forward. "I can promise you that when both Danica's marriage and her relationship with her parents fall apart, I'll be there to pick up the pieces. In fact, that's not such a bad idea. I've been wanting to take care of her for a very, very long time. Go ahead, Senator. Sling your mud. But don't be surprised when it lands right back on your own face."

Not quite prepared for such a show of force, William stared silently at the cold-eyed man before him. He wasn't bullheaded enough to deny that part of what Michael had said was true, but he *was* bullheaded enough not to give up.

"You say she'll come running to you," he ventured confidently. "I say she'll go in the opposite direction. So where does that leave us?"

"It leaves us with Danica right in the middle." Michael paused, then went on in what he hoped would be a conciliatory tone. "Look, Senator, I really don't wish any harm or unpleasantness on your family. I've never had any part in the differences you and our papers have had. When I first fell in love with your daughter, I didn't know who she was, and by the time I found out, it was too late. For both of us. We were already involved, if only in an innocent sense."

He took a weary breath. "If you think it's fun, or easy, being in love with a married woman, you're nuts. I'd give everything I own to have it any other way. As it is, I've decided to go abroad for a few months. Danica needs time. So do I ... Does that make you feel any better?"

"What will make me feel better is your word that you won't try to see her when you come back."

"I can't give it. I'm sorry."

William pulled himself up to his full, stiff height. "Then, you're going to have to remember that I've got these pictures. Think about them when you call her on the phone, when you plan your little trysts, when you sneak in and out of hotels with her. If you thought it was hard before, it'll be that much harder in the future. Because I know what's going on now. These prints will be hanging over your head, and you never will know when I'm going to use them." He turned to leave, then gestured over his shoulder. "You can keep those copies. I've got others and the negatives locked safely away."

Michael clamped his lips together. He had nothing further to say, other than *Bastard! No good son of a bitch! Filthy, lousy blackmailer!* With eyes hard as stone, he watched the man who called himself Danica's father climb into his car and back from the drive. Only when the car had disappeared from sight did Michael close the door. Then, with the force of disgust and anger and frustration, he slammed his fist against the wood, welcoming the pain as a diversion from the deeper, more searing pain within.

"HI, SWEETHEART."

Danica settled into his arms, uncaring who saw. "Michael, I'm so glad you came in." Then she drew back. "You look so tired." She slid her hands from his shoulders down his arms, only then encumbering what he'd kept hidden. "My God, what did you do to your hand?"

He glanced sheepishly at the bandages. "I just...had a little accident. It's nothing."

"Michael, it's a cast. It couldn't be nothing. And it's your right hand. How are you able to do anything?"

"I manage. A little slowly, perhaps. But I manage."

Cradling his injured hand against her breast, she met his gaze. "Something's wrong, isn't it? I can hear it in your voice. Something's wrong."

"Dani, I can't stay tonight. I've got to get back."

"But I thought..."

"I just had to turn in the last of my grades, but I wanted to see you." He'd been taking a risk, he knew. Marshall had been right; the threats he'd made weighed heavily in Michael's mind. Not that they would have kept him from her. He'd meant his part of it. But he was uneasy and had kept a form of surveillance outside the restaurant before Danica had arrived. More than once he'd thought of the photographer who'd stalked them, and he'd castigated himself for not seeing anyone. If this had happened in Nam, he would have been reprimanded, if not removed from his assignment. But it wasn't Nam, and he hadn't been prepared. He hadn't been looking. He hadn't wanted to look. To look would have been paranoid and would have cast something ugly over what he and Danica had done.

"Michael, what is it?" Danica knew there was something he wasn't saying and she was frightened.

"Dani," he began, cupping her shoulder with his left hand, "Dani, I'm going away for a while."

For a minute she couldn't speak. She swallowed, then took a breath. "What do you mean . . . away?"

"I'm flying to Lisbon. I'm going to visit friends and explore the continent for a while."

"A while?"

"A few months."

Her breath was unsteady. "But why?"

Even as his eyes voiced his apology and begged her forgiveness, he began to speak the words he'd so painstakingly prepared. "I need to get away, sweetheart. You need me to get away."

"I don't—"

He put a finger against her lips. "You need to be alone for a while. You've got your book to finish and lots of other things to do."

"But I want to be with you. Those things don't matter."

"Between your mother and me, you've lost a lot of good time. But it's more than that. You need to think about Blake . . . and about us. *I* need to think about how much longer I can wait."

"No . . . Michael . . . no ultimatums . . ."

"It's not that, sweetheart. It's just a chance to breathe, to reassess, to plan. All fall I've been pulled in different directions. I'm tired. That's all. I need time to recoup."

"We could take the time. I'd come up to Maine and—"

"Would you take off and go to Europe with me?"

"I . . . I can't," she whispered. "You know that."

"I do. And that's my point. We have to find some other way, Dani. It's just no good, sneaking around like this. Maybe, by the time I get back, something will have changed. Maybe Blake will agree to a divorce. Maybe you'll decide to go ahead anyway and fight him. Maybe I'll feel renewed enough to pick up where we left off. But, God, I'm so tired.... Aren't you?''

"Yes, but I can live with it because the alternative is worse. Seeing you, being with you, is the focal point in my life." Slowly, dazedly, she shook her head. "A few months. I don't know what I'll do if I can't see you in all that time."

"You'll do just fine. In fact, you'll do even better than that. You'll be forced to see what a strong, independent woman you are. It's one thing when I say the words, another when you see them for yourself. And you need that. You need it if you're ever going to be able to fight the odds that are still against us."

In defeat, she dropped her forehead to his chest. "I'll miss you, Michael."

"And I'll miss you. More than you can imagine."

When she raised her face, her eyes were filled with tears. "Will you be careful?" she whispered.

He nodded. "Take care of yourself, love." He lowered his head and gave her a soft, sweet, lingering kiss. His eyes too were moist when he drew back. He swallowed once, then turned to her. "Go on, now. It'll be too difficult if you stay."

Knowing he was right, she began to walk back in the direction of her car. She looked back once, but Michael's figure was a blur through her tears. Tucking her head lower, she began to run. Only when she reached the Audi and had locked herself inside did she give way to the gulping sobs that welled up. Still crying, she started the car and headed home. When her tears didn't abate after several turns around the block, she finally parked and went in. It was long hours into the night before her tears gave way to sheer exhaustion and she fell asleep.

FOR A WEEK Danica was unable to do much of anything but idle through the motions of life. At times when she least expected it she'd start to cry again. The sense of desolation that filled her was worse than anything she'd ever known— worse than the loneliness she'd felt as a child, worse than the unhappiness she'd felt before she'd met Michael, worse than the continuing frustration she felt with regard to Blake.

She told herself that Michael would be back, that several months wasn't all that long a time. She reminded herself of the women who, in times of war, sent their husbands off for indefinite periods and even then without knowing whether they'd return alive. She told herself that Michael did need the trip, that he'd been working too hard, that he deserved a vacation. No amount of rationalizing seemed to help, though. She felt cut off from him, and hence from a part of her own soul. She missed him terribly.

At long last she threw herself into her work, realizing that it held her only salvation. She visited James several times a week and wrote furiously when she was at home. She poured her physical energies into ballet until the teacher had to remind her that the point of the exercise was grace and control, after which she took her frustrations out on the pavement, walking for a furious hour through the Common each afternoon.

Once a month she flew to Washington to satisfy her obligation to Blake. He said nothing on the matter of divorce, indeed acted as if it had ever come up. Though he made some attempt to be more solicitous to her, she knew it was a strain on them both, and she was always relieved to return to Boston.

For the most part, the people she saw from day to day were unaware of her torment. She managed to keep it in control when she was out. Eleanor, once again, was more perceptive.

"Something's bothering you, darling. Would you like to talk about it?"

Eleanor had recovered remarkably. Though her walk held a slight limp, there were no other visible signs of her stroke. Indeed, she'd traveled to Washington the week before, though she'd felt more comfortable returning to the quieter Connecticut countryside.

At Danica's suggestion, they'd driven to a small restaurant in Avon, where they were dawdling over the last of their lunch. Hearing her mother's question, and sensing that she simply had to talk about it and that the time had come to trust Eleanor as a friend, Danica began in a quiet voice.

"It's about . . . Blake and me . . . and Michael.''

Eleanor pressed her lips together. "I think I suspected that.''

"How much do you know?''

"I know that you and Blake are growing apart, and that what you feel for Michael is very strong.''

"I love him.''

Eleanor was still for a long moment. Danica could see her disappointment and wondered if she should have said anything after all. But she'd needed to. She'd come to respect her mother over the past few months. On the sheer chance that Eleanor might have comforting words to say, the risk was worth it.

"And Blake?'' Eleanor asked quietly.

"I . . . no, what I feel for him isn't love.''

"What happened? How did it die?''

"I'm not sure it did. I'm not sure it was ever really there. Oh, I wanted to marry him and I thought I was in love. Looking back, though, I think that what I saw in Blake was the perpetuation of the life-style we all wanted for me. When I compare what I feel for Michael with what I feel, or felt, for Blake . . . well, there's no comparison. They're both men, but so very, very different.''

"I see.'' Eleanor looked down, frowning. "What do you propose to do?''

"I don't . . . know. I talked to Blake about the possibility of divorce.'' When her mother winced, she reached out and took her hand. "I don't like it either, Mom. The thought of it ties me in knots. But then I look at what Blake and I have left, and it's so little. I can't believe he's any happier with the arrangement than I am, though he says he is.''

"Does he know about what you feel for Michael?''

Danica drew her hand back and averted her gaze. "No. I haven't been able to tell him.''

"Why not?''

"He'll be hurt. He'll feel betrayed, and he'd be justified in doing so.''

"So you do still feel *something* for him.''

"I respect him, and I do feel compassion.''

"Two very basic requisites for a marriage."

"But I don't feel love! I love Michael! And it's tearing me apart, leading a dual life this way."

Again, Eleanor was silent for a time. "How long has this been going on?"

"It'll be two years this spring since I met Michael. But things have been deteriorating between Blake and me for much longer."

"Why are they coming to a head now?"

Danica studied the silver spoon by her plate. "Because Michael's away now. Because I realize that he's not going to wait forever and that if I don't do something I might lose him."

"Then the divorce is what you want?"

She looked at her mother. "What I want is to be happy. I'm not happy with Blake. With Michael I feel as though every dream I've ever had can come true. He loves me as much as I love him. He encourages me to grow, to do things with my life. He's always there when I need him."

"He's not there now," Eleanor said softly. "Darling, maybe you haven't been fair to Blake. Maybe you haven't given your marriage a chance."

"It'll be ten years this June. If that isn't giving it a chance, I don't know what is."

"But Blake has grown, too. Maybe you haven't made enough of an effort to grow alongside him rather than away from him. He is your husband. You owe him a certain responsibility."

"What about *his* responsibility? He's given me very little encouragement."

"Men are that way sometimes, particularly men like your father and Blake. They get wrapped up in themselves. They need prodding from time to time."

Danica was shaking her head. "I've prodded, but I get nowhere. I tried even harder with Blake after I met Michael, because I was afraid of what I was feeling. I didn't want to feel it. You have to believe that, Mom. I didn't want to fall in love with Michael. It just . . . happened. And regardless of what anyone says, it's the most wonderful thing that's *ever* happened to me." She paused. "I was hoping that you'd feel a little of what I do, but maybe that's asking too much."

"I'm trying to understand, darling. It's just that I see things from a different angle. Do you remember the day we talked about how I view my role in your father's life?" Danica nodded. "I am happy, but that's not to say that there haven't been times when I've wished for some things to be different. There was the guilt I felt in leaving you so much. There's the guilt I feel now in leaving William in Washington and the selfish desire to have him here with me. We all have our crosses to bear in life. It's simply a question of accepting them."

"And when the cross gets too heavy? When bearing it exhausts you, when it becomes self-defeating?"

"It's all a matter of the mind. You can do anything you want in life . . . if you set your mind to it."

DANICA SET HER MIND to finishing James Bryant's book. By the end of February it was in her publisher's hands. Then she set her mind to thinking of another project she might tackle. As it happened, James gave her the contact, and the recommendation, she needed. At his bidding, though he was uncharacteristically smug about it, she called a man named Arthur Brooke, who proceeded to express great pleasure that she'd called and asked if they might meet to discuss a proposal he wanted to make.

Over lunch several days later at the Bay Tower Room, Arthur Brooke offered her the role of hostess for a weekly current affairs talk show that his radio station wanted to produce.

"I realize that you've never done anything like this before," he explained while she sat in a state of shock, "but James has raved about how well versed you are in current affairs, and I can see, myself, after talking with you for an hour, that you're both poised and articulate. We want a fresh voice for our programs. I believe yours is it."

Pressing a hand to her thudding heart, she forced herself to speak. "I'm so . . . surprised. I never expected anything like this when James suggested I call you."

"James is a rascal for not prewarning you. He's probably sitting at home right now chuckling to himself."

"He's a wonderful man."

"I agree. . . . Well, what do you think?"

She sucked in a breath and let it out through her teeth. "I think that your proposal is . . . very exciting. I'm not as sure as you seem to be, though, that I can do the job."

"There's really nothing to it. For an hour every week, you'll sit in the studio and talk with one or another of the local public figures. At the beginning we'll set everything up. After a while, if you want, you can make your own decisions as to whom you'd like to interview. You'll need to prepare some beforehand, bone up on a particular issue. We'd like to stick to timely issues, which means that some of the preparation may be last-minute. On occasion, if there's nothing pressing in the news, we might invite an author to be on the show, in which case you'd have to read his book. But with the awareness you've already got of what's happening in the world, I think you'll do just fine."

Danica still had some doubts, but she was smiling. "When did you hope to begin?"

"In another month. We have a Wednesday evening slot that will be perfect. . . . Is it a go?"

While one small part of her wanted to beg time to think, the other, larger part was driven by sheer impulse. She nodded quickly. "It's a go."

She felt better that night than she had in weeks, and spent hours wandering around the town house with a smile on her face. She called her mother to tell her the news. She sat down and wrote a long letter to Reggie. But when she thought of calling Blake, her smile faded. It wasn't Blake she wanted to call. It was Michael. Only she didn't know where he was or when he'd be back.

That weekend as prearranged she flew down to Washington. Blake was pleased for her in that same detached way he'd reacted to her work with James Bryant. She waited for her father's call, but it didn't come. Only that part of her which had hoped he might be proud was let down. The other part, the larger part, was relieved that he hadn't put a damper on what was to her a challenging prospect.

After her return to Boston she set about pouring through the local papers with a thoroughness that managed to fill her time somewhat. Still, she couldn't help but think of Michael, wondering where he was and what he was doing, whether he was well, whether he was missing her as much as she missed him. She wanted desperately to tell him about the radio show, to share the excitement, to express her uncertainties and savor his encouragement.

The following weekend, feeling that she'd burst if she didn't find an emotional outlet, she drove to Maine. But it wasn't the seaside house in Kennebunkport at which she stopped. Rather, she drove on to Camden.

Gena, who was thrilled to see her, proceeded to chastise her properly for not having come sooner.

"But you're so busy. I wasn't even sure if I should come today."

"Busy? Nonsense. I always have time for those I love."

At the words, which were so freely and sincerely offered, something inside Danica broke. She bit her lip, but her eyes filled with tears, and before she knew it, she was being held by a cooing Gena.

"Hush, Dani. Hush. It'll be all right," Gena whispered, stroking her hair.

"I miss him . . . so much," Danica breathed brokenly. "I thought it . . . would get better in time, but it hasn't. And now, with . . . this new thing, I miss him all the more."

"Whoa." Gena eased her back and gently brushed at the tears on her cheeks. "What new thing?"

Slowly, regaining her composure as she went, Danica explained about the radio show. Gena's excitement was every bit as genuine as her expression of love had been, but it was the last which stuck in Danica's mind most.

"Gena?"

"What is it, pet?"

Danica struggled for the words, but she didn't know which ones were right, so she simply started to talk. "We've only met once before and neither Michael nor I said anything . . . but you seemed to know.''

Gena smiled. "I know my son. I could see very quickly that he loved you. He's never come right out and said anything, maybe because he was afraid of my reaction. He told you about my own marriage, didn't he?" Danica nodded. "Well, what he may not know is that his father is happy with his second wife. More aptly, Michael may not want to see it. He feels a loyalty to me, which is fine, except that he doesn't realize that I've come to terms with what happened." She reached for Danica's hand. "The only thing that saddens me is that the two of you have such hurdles to cross. I know you love him. I felt that affinity with you from the first." She smiled. "The sight of the two of you talking together, your heads so close, your hair so similar in color, your eyes smiling into one another's . . . it was beautiful. I couldn't have wished for a better woman for my son than you. You'll make his life very full and rich."

"You sound so optimistic, as though we really will be together some day."

"I know it, Danica. I said that there were hurdles to cross, but I didn't say they were uncrossable. If you set your mind to it, you'll see yourself clear and happy."

Danica remembered what her mother had said about matters of the mind, and she thought of the irony that these two women should express such similar thoughts with such different meanings. Eleanor implied that Danica should set her mind to making her marriage work, Gena that she should focus on extricating herself from a marriage, which was obviously a source of pain.

"Have you heard from him?" Danica asked hesitantly.

Gena grinned. "I certainly have." She patted Danica's knee. "Wait here." Within minutes she was handing over a series of letters.

"But these are for you," Danica argued. "I . . . I shouldn't be seeing them."

"Nonsense. You love him as much as I do. I think he intended them for you as much as for me."

"He hasn't written to me."

"I'm sure it wasn't for not wanting to. Go ahead. Read the letters. You'll see." When Danica still hesitated, Gena coaxed her with a short nod. "Read them."

Carefully, Danica unfolded the first letter and read about Michael's adventures in Portugal, then Spain. Though his script was uneven, she presumed because of his injured hand, his style was familiar and flowing, and she took pleasure in his description of the people, the cities, the countryside he'd seen. What caught her breath, though, were occasional breaks in the compelling narrative. "I wish Dani could see this with me," he wrote of Barcelona. "The port is so different from the ones we've seen together." Then, again, in a second letter, when he'd crossed up into the Loire Valley in France: "I've been biking from place to place. Dani would absolutely love it here. There are long stretches of level road with views to the far horizon. On the other hand, she'd probably think I'm crazy. It's cold as hell some days."

All told, there were five letters. After leaving France, he'd traveled through Belgium and Holland, in both of which places he had friends, before moving on to Denmark. She lingered over the last letter, rereading its final lines many times. "I miss you, Mom. I was never one to be homesick, but it's different this time. Either I'm getting old or simply sentimental, but I keep comparing things I see to what I have at home. I wonder how Dani's doing. Have you heard from her? . . . See? My mind must really be going. You've got no way of answering my question since you don't know where I'll be next. I'm reminded about something I read once, actually, on one of Danica's tea bags. 'If you don't know where you're going, any road will get you there,' it said. When I started out on this trip, I think I *wasn't* sure where I was going. But I sure as hell am now. I'll be home by the middle of April. Can't wait to see you. All my love, Michael."

Lowering the letter at last, Danica blotted tears from her lower lids. "He's a very wise and wonderful man," she whispered.

"I think so. Has he been any help?"

Danica knew Gena was referring to the messages that might, indeed, have been meant for her in the letters. She nodded. "He's always a help. Even when he's gone. I can see that now. He was right to go. I needed time to analyze my priorities."

"And have you?" Gena asked gently.

With growing confidence, Danica smiled. "Yes. Yes, I believe I have."

TWO DAYS LATER she flew back to Washington and flat out asked Blake for a divorce.

Chapter Fourteen

"HE WON'T DO IT, Michael. I asked him point-blank, and he said no."

They were in Kennebunkport, at Michael's house, where Danica had flown the instant he'd called her to say he was back. It had been a happy reunion on both sides, with Danica's tears flowing freely and Michael's contained only with great effort. They'd talked about his trip with the excitement of two children, though both of them knew the excitement was primarily in being together again. He told her that his book on sports would be hitting the shelves any day, and she informed him that it already had, that she'd read it and loved it. When she told him about her radio show, the first installment of which had come off with high praise the week before, he was beside himself with pride, hugging her, telling her that he'd known all along she could handle anything she wanted, demanding to hear the tape she'd brought with her. But Danica was anxious to tell him that she'd definitely decided to divorce Blake.

"He refused, even when you bluntly said you didn't love him?" Above and beyond his own slightly biased feelings on the matter, Michael couldn't comprehend a man clinging to a dead cause.

"He refused. Absolutely refused. It was a repeat of last winter, when I mentioned divorce as a possible mutual option."

"Did he say why he was so against it?"

"At first he just stomped out of the room like he did last time. When I followed him and pressed, he informed me that he needed a wife and that I'd signed the papers nearly ten years ago and that that was the end of it. I kept arguing, but he didn't want to listen. It was really heated, I mean, not like me at all. I'm usually more docile, and I think he was shocked. He kept asking what was wrong with me. When I told him about you, he didn't bat an eyelash.''

''You . . . told him about me?''

''I had nothing to lose. I said that I loved you. Strange, he wasn't even surprised. Or maybe he just covered it up. Do you want to know what he said?''

''You bet I do.''

''He said that he didn't mind if I had a dozen lovers, as long as I was discreet about it and kept up the front of our marriage.''

''He said *that*?''

''More. He said that he was glad I'd found someone and that if it made things easier for me, he was happy. What *kind* of a husband would say something like that?'' There was no hurt in her voice, only confusion.

''Beats me,'' Michael breathed. ''So where does that leave us?''

''Not much further than we were before. When I threatened to call a lawyer myself and file for divorce, he assured me that he'd fight it. He harped on how cruel I was to even think of hurting my parents this way, but I'm telling you, Michael, it's getting to a point where I really don't care.''

''You're angry, sweetheart.''

''Aren't you? It's not fair that he can manipulate us this way. What does he hope to gain? What could possibly be in it for him?''

Michael thought for a minute. ''If he had a mistress he liked but didn't particularly want to marry, staying married to you would be a convenient excuse.''

''I asked him about that once, and he said that there wasn't another woman. He seemed so repulsed by the idea that I believed him.''

''Do you think that his refusal to consider divorce may have something to do with his ties to your father?''

''I don't see how. They were friends long before Blake met me. I'm sure my father pulled his weight when it came to getting Blake his appointment, but that's a fait accompli. Blake has plenty of power on his own now.''

Michael blew out an exasperated breath. ''So we *are* back to square one.''

''No,'' she said thoughtfully. ''Not really, because I've made up my mind.'' She smiled gently at Michael. ''Being without you these past months helped in the perverse way I'm sure you intended.''

''Now, Dani—''

''Shhh. I'm not criticizing. I'm admiring. You were right. I did function on my own. The publishing house is thrilled with James's and my book. The radio station is pleased with my show. I know now that I can manage on my own, but the point is that I don't want to simply 'manage.' There's so much more . . . am I making any sense?''

He slid his fingers into her hair and stroked her cheeks with his thumbs. ''You're making lots of sense, sweetheart. I think I realized many of the same things when I was abroad. It wasn't the same without you.'' His eyes explored her features. ''Being away made me bolder, or perhaps just more desperate. I don't care who in the hell fights us; we'll somehow find a way.'' He kissed her once, then a second time when their lips didn't want to part. At last, they sat back holding hands.

''Blake might come to his senses when he's had time to think about what I said,'' she ventured hopefully.

''Maybe, but I doubt it. This wasn't the first time you mentioned divorce as a possibility, so he couldn't have been totally stunned.''

''I just don't understand the man. You'd think he'd have more pride than to want me now.''

''It can work the other way round, though. He may be too proud to admit that his marriage has failed.''

''But if that were true, you'd think that he would have been furious when I told him about you. God, I can't figure him out! He's making this all so difficult.''

''No one ever said life was easy.''

''I suppose. . . . Michael?''

''What, sweetheart?''

"Will you wait it out with me? If nothing happens by the end of the summer, I'll go ahead and see a lawyer, but I'd rather Blake could see his way to an amicable agreement."

"So would I. And of course I'll wait. That's what my coming back was all about."

She raised his hands to her lips. "You're so special, Michael. You know how much I love you, don't you?"

Michael eyed the ceiling. "Well, now that I think of it, I could use a reminder from time to time."

"Now's the time."

"Where's the place?"

She looked around. "That sofa looks about right."

"Okay. How?"

She grinned and slid to his lap. "I think you'll figure that out soon enough."

He did.

CILLA JOINED JEFFREY at the restaurant in Georgetown where they'd been meeting for dinner every Friday. They settled at a table in a quiet corner and ordered drinks. She smiled at him; he smiled back.

"So," he breathed, "what's doin'?"

She shrugged. "Not much.... How about with you?"

"The same."

"Nothing new at the Pentagon?"

"Nope.... The city room's still humming?"

"Uh-huh." She took a long sip of her drink.

Jeffrey did the same, then set his glass down. "I bumped into Stefan Bryncek yesterday."

"Oh? How's he doing?"

"Great. Sheila had another baby. Their third. A boy this time."

"Stefan must be pleased by that."

"He sounded it. He's been waiting for a boy."

Cilla nodded. She spread some cheese on a cracker and handed it to Jeffrey, then made one for herself. "Did you read that Norman was promoted?"

"Mmmm. Managing editor to associate editor, isn't it?"

"Uh-huh. Jason Wile left to be editor-in-chief of a magazine in Minneapolis, so the space opened up. I'm pleased for Norman. He deserved it."

"Do you ever think of editing?"

"Me? I'd make an awful editor. I get too involved. Besides, I like the action of chasing stories down. I can't see myself in an editorial position." Her eyes narrowed. "And if you're thinking that I could have whatever position I want just because my father owns the paper, you're wrong. He's a chauvinist. In his mind, women are far too emotional.... Many people think that."

"Aw, come on."

"No, Jeff. Think about it for a minute. Don't you feel the same?"

"I never said that."

"No, but it's come across subtly at times. You feel women lack that certain ... professionalism to be on top."

"You're putting words in my mouth."

"But aren't they true? Think back to when we were married. Wasn't so much of the hesitation you had about confiding in me due to the fact that I'm a woman."

"You're a *newspaper*woman."

"But if I was a newspaper*man*, wouldn't it have been different?"

"Sure. I wouldn't have been married to you."

"Jeffrey," she warned, "you're skirting the issue."

He lifted his glass and took a drink, thinking that Cilla was right on the money. "Okay. Okay. It is possible that your gender had something to do with it. But I'm trying to change. It's been six years since the divorce, and in that time women have popped up in some pretty responsible positions. I'd have to be blind not to see it, dumb not to try to accept it. But attitudes don't change overnight. I grew up in a male-dominated household. It may have been wrong, but that's the way it was. When I was in college, women were still looking first and foremost for that M.R.S. degree."

"That's because they were told that was where they'd have the best chance of advancement. It doesn't mean that they weren't intelligent or responsible."

"I *know*," Jeffrey stated quietly. "I *know*."

He opened his menu and studied it. Cilla followed suit. When each had made a choice, the menus were closed and set back on the table.

"What are you having?" Jeffrey asked.

"I thought I'd have the lemon veal. It was good last time.... How about you?"

"The steak."

She nodded, observing that he'd chosen the most macho offering. She wondered what he'd say next, whether he planned to share his work with her tonight.

Jeffrey took another drink, then pressed his moistened lips together. He had no intention of saying something if she didn't. If she wanted to be the liberated woman, he vowed, *she* could take the first step.

Cilla stared at Jeffrey, seeing that same closed expression he'd worn so often during their marriage. It was unfortunate. For both of them, their work was nine-tenths of their lives. When they couldn't share that, there was little left. But... if he was disinclined to discuss things of substance, why should she?

Jeffrey stared at Cilla, willing her to open up. She was stubborn sometimes. Wonderfully so. Maddeningly so. He supposed he was no different, but, damn it, she should be more flexible. They were at an impasse again, sharing nothing but the same silence that had plagued their married life. He wanted more, though. He'd already told her that. He wanted another try. There was so much to love in Cilla. Maybe if he bent a little . . .

Cilla began to waver when she realized what was happening. The same rut. The same brick wall. Neither of them giving in, therefore neither of them benefiting. One of them had to take the first step. One of them had to make a show of faith.

She opened her mouth and took a breath at the very same instant he did. They both smiled. He dipped his head in deference. "Ladies before gentlemen," he said, then rushed on when she scowled. "Okay, I'll tell you mine first, if you'd rather."

Determined not to appear the weaker, she held up a hand. "No, no. I'll go first." She set her chin. "I heard from him again, the power-and-lust guy."

Jeffrey's eyes widened. "Good deal!"

"Uh-huh. He called two days ago."

"What did he say?"

She hesitated for only as long as it took to remind herself that Jeffrey was interested, not prying. "It wasn't what he said so much as how he said it. He wasn't mumbling, and his speech wasn't slurred. He sounded sober as a stone and very angry."

Jeffrey reworded his question to sound less pointed. "He was coherent in what he said then?"

"Very. He said that he knew I was a responsible reporter and that he was sure I'd be interested in his story. Front page material, he said."

"... That's all?"

She shook her head. "He said that there were compromises being made in high places. That sexual favors were being traded among some very powerful factions."

"So what else is new?"

"That's what *I* said, only not in so many words. But when I tried to push him for details, he got nervous. When I suggested we meet somewhere to talk, he didn't respond. Unfortunately, I let my eagerness get the best of me and I asked for his name. I told him that his call lacked credibility if he wouldn't identify himself."

"What did he say to that?"

She sighed. "He hung up."

"Oh.... Y' know, Cilla, it really isn't a new story. Everyone's heard about Elizabeth Ray. Wheeling and dealing with sex isn't unusual."

"No." She grew defensive. "But what if... what if we're talking about something like... like a spy plot? What if there is *real* compromising going on? You know, secrets being passed around that threaten this country's security?"

He arched a brow. "Did this fellow give you any hint that that was what was happening?"

"No...no, but he didn't say it wasn't. I'm telling you, Jeff, I feel something. Call it instinct or intuition, but there's something behind this. You're right, everyone does know about the Elizabeth Rays of the world, and I'm sure this fellow must too, but he still felt that what he had to offer was front page copy."

"He may just be a crackpot."

Cilla knew Jeff was playing devil's advocate, and she wasn't offended. He was saying nothing more than her editor had said. Of course, she didn't necessarily agree. "That's possible. But I do have this feeling. More than that, I still think the voice was the same as that of the man I spoke with at that reception a while back. I've been pouring through stacks of file photos, trying to recognize a face, trying to think about who might have been at that reception."

"Did you call the embassy where it was held?"

"The attaché I spoke with wasn't much help. He had the list of official guests, but he wasn't eager to hand it out, and even then he said that each of the invited guests had been given *several* passes, so the possibilities were that much broader. I explained that I desperately needed to locate a man I'd seen there, but this particular attaché wasn't terribly sympathetic. I think he thought I was on the make, trying to track down this gorgeous, nameless, would-be lover."

Jeffrey grinned. "I think I'd think that, too, if I'd gotten a call from you like that. You've got a damned sexy voice, Cilla."

Feeling light-headed and strong now that she'd taken the first step in communicating with Jeff, she cocked her head to the side. "Oh? I think you've got a one-track mind."

"Not really. I can appreciate your sexy voice even while I'm thinking about your call . . . and my lead."

"Your lead?" she asked, arching a brow. "In the Maris case?" When he shook his head and donned a smug grin, she sat straighter. "Okay. Your turn. What lead?"

"Do you remember I told you about the high-tech theft that's been going on?"

"Sure."

"Well, I think we're finally onto something. A shipment of sensitive microchips—a restricted commodity—was stopped at the Swedish border before it made it into the Soviet Union. We've traced it through several mediating companies to one in South Africa that actually exists."

"Ahhh, no dummy storefront this time?"

"Nope. That's what's so promising. We've got a team in Capetown working on it now. It may take a while because our guys are working undercover, but we suspect that this particular company may be the source for a whole batch of similar shipments."

"And you want it all."

"You bet. It's possible that only one American company has been repeatedly involved, though I can't believe any one company would be so stupid. More likely, the South African firm has multiple contacts here—scientists, business people, diplomats, students—each of whom has a shopping list of what the East wants. It's mind-boggling when you think of it."

"Frightening."

"Very. The problem is that if we rush and close in on the South African firm based simply on this one shipment we've stopped, the contacts will only sell to someone else. Money talks, and there's a whole load of money in illegal export."

"So the motives aren't political?"

"In some cases they are. In many, though, they're financial. Of course, a true patriot wouldn't be tempted regardless of the amount of money offered, but we're not dealing with true patriots here."

Cilla nodded her agreement. "It's disgusting when you think of it. There are so many legitimate ways to earn a living. I was talking with a fellow last week who used to be one of the biggest bookies around. He earned a bundle, then one day wiped his hands clean and got out. He's in real estate development now, and while I detest what he did, and the fact that he founded his business on dirty money, I have to respect him more than someone who would knowingly jeopardize the country's security. Bookmaking may be illegal, but at least its victims are willing ones. In the case of something like what you're talking about, *all* of us stand to lose."

Jeffrey sighed. "Well, that's what I'm hoping to prevent, at least to prevent from happening again. I wish Commerce was on top of this, but, damn it, I'm not sure it is. Lindsay may be effective, but his interests clearly lie with big business."

"That might explain it, then," Cilla observed wryly.

"Explain what?"

"The fact that he seems so narrow. I've been watching the guy, and he's always straight and proper. I don't think there's a flexible bone in his body, much less a warm or sensitive one."

"There has to be. He's married, and to a stunner, I'm told."

Cilla eyed him cautiously. She started to speak, stopped, then forced herself on. "You don't know anything about her?"

"Only that I hear she's beautiful and that she's Bill Marshall's daughter."

"... Nothing else?"

It was Jeffrey's turn to grow cautious. "You know something that I don't."

"When was the last time you saw Mike?"

"Your brother? Last summer."

"But you've spoken to him since."

"A couple of times."

"And he didn't say anything about the woman he was seeing?"

Jeffrey frowned. "Come to think of it, I've asked him several times if there was anything new in the legs department and he . . . very deftly avoided the issue each time. . . . Is there someone?"

For the first time in a long time, Cilla wondered if she'd put her foot in her mouth. But . . . she really did trust Jeffrey . . . and she knew that Jeffrey trusted Michael and vice versa. "Maybe he was trying to protect her," she murmured.

"Protect *who*?"

Cilla puffed out her cheeks, then let the air seep through her lips. "He's in love, Jeff. My brother Michael is very thoroughly and sadly in love."

"Why 'sadly'?"

"Because the woman he loves is Danica Lindsay."

"The *wife*? You've got to be kidding!"

She was shaking her head. "I wish I was. Not that Danica isn't every bit as wonderful as he thinks. I spent some time with her up at Mike's place last summer. She's a fantastic person, just perfect for him. But..."

"She is married."

"Umm-hmmmmm, though not happily, from what Michael says. That's why I've been watching the husband. He seems totally, and I mean totally, devoted to his job. I keep trying to figure out if he's got another woman, but he seems removed from anything like that. Unless he's being very, very sly about it."

"I'd think he would, given his position.... Geez, Mike's in love with *his* wife? That takes a little getting used to. I never thought of Mike as the type who'd go for a married woman."

"Because of Dad, you mean."

"Partly. Also because he's exquisitely straitlaced. Hell, when we were in college, he wouldn't even look at another guy's girl."

"Jeffrey..."

"Okay, so he'd look. We'd both look. But if I liked what I saw, I'd go up and talk with her. Mike wouldn't."

"Well, I think this situation is a little different. He fell for her before he knew she was married. She loves him, too."

"Jeeeeez. Will she divorce Lindsay?"

"Your guess is as good as mine. Blake Lindsay was a successful businessman before he came down here. He supports Danica in the style to which she's accustomed, and he happens to be in but good with her father."

Jeffrey's thoughts were running further. "Lindsay was in microelectronics, wasn't he?"

"Mmmm. I'd think you'd want to talk with him about your own work."

"Ve-ry carefully. Commerce and Defense have had their differences. But if I could strike up a casual conversation with the man in some nonofficial contest, maybe I could pick up something."

"For Michael . . . or you?"

"Both," Jeffrey mused, liking the idea more and more. Then he grinned. "I'd also like to meet this woman someday. She must be something to have snagged Mike."

Cilla returned his grin. "I think I can arrange a meeting once summer comes. That's when she spends most of her time in Maine. Her house just happens to be down the beach from Michael's. Of course, you'd have to drive up with me for several days . . ."

Jeffrey found he liked that idea nearly as much as the idea of slyly seeking Blake Lindsay out. But while he left the former for Cilla to arrange, he was on his own regarding the latter. For several weeks he looked for an opening, then finally found it when one of his superiors mentioned in passing that the Secretaries of Agriculture, Transportation and Commerce were going to be at a large dinner party and that it wouldn't hurt to have a representative from Defense present. Jeffrey promptly volunteered.

THERE WERE nearly three hundred people at the party, which was held on the lawn of a sprawling home in Virginia, but Jeffrey had no trouble locating the face he sought.

"Handsome bugger, isn't he?"

Cilla, who'd come along for the ride partly because Jeff had invited her and partly because she was dying with curiosity to see what he'd learn, nodded. "He does stand out in a crowd. Dark hair, classic features, a smile that dazzles, a tuxedo that—"

"I get the point, Cilla. You don't have to rub it in."

Her arm was already through his elbow, partly because she was having trouble standing on the lawn in high heels, but she held it tighter. "I didn't say I preferred his looks to yours. There's something untouchable about him. I like to touch."

Jeffrey grinned down at her. "So I've noticed. By the way, you look gorgeous."

She was wearing a strapless gown whose hem was ragged by design and vaguely wanton. "I was going to wear red, but pale pink seemed more sedate."

"Sedate?" he echoed hoarsely, then cleared his throat. "Oh. Okay. If you say so." He couldn't take his eyes from a taunting hint of cleavage.

Cilla leaned even closer, putting her mouth to his ear. "Do you remember that time we were at the Dittrichs', when we slipped into the gardener's shed and—"

"Christ, Cilla," he cut her off with a growl. "What are you trying to do to me? I've got a mission here, or have you forgotten?"

"Not me. I just wanted to make sure *you* hadn't."

"I hadn't. I hadn't." He cleared his throat again and looked across the lawn through the shade of his brows. "Come on. Let's ease over this way." He saw Blake Lindsay in the distance; that was where he headed. Then, abruptly, he halted.

"What's wrong?"

"Damn it," he swore through his teeth.

"What is it, Jeff?"

"*You*. My God, I must really be out of it. Either that or you've well and truly got me wrapped around your little finger."

Cilla screwed up her face. "What are you talking about? I haven't done a thing."

He patted the slender hand that clutched his arm. "No, hon. It's not your fault. *I'm* the one who should have realized." He lowered his voice even more. "It wasn't very bright, my bringing you here."

"Why ever not? Nearly all the men have dates."

"That's not the point. In my own mind I think of you as Cilla Winston. But you're not, are you? You're Cilla *Buchanan*. All we need is for Lindsay to hear that name, and if he knows anything about what his wife is doing, he'll be suspect."

Cilla looked stricken. "I hadn't thought of that. Damn it, I should have!"

"We *both* should have. But look, there's nothing we can do now except steer clear of each other for a while. There may be one or two people here who know we've been married, but if we put a little distance between us, others may not make the connection."

"Much as I hate the thought, I think you're right."

"Good girl." He gave her bottom a light pat, then moved off, confident that Cilla could fend for herself. She was a strong woman, he mused, and while there were times when he wished she was a bit less so, at the moment he was grateful.

He continued on at an ambling pace, stopping from time to time to acknowledge a familiar face, but maintaining a steady direction. Luck was on his side. The man with Lindsay was someone he knew, giving him the perfect excuse to approach.

"Thomas, how are you?"

Thomas Fenton turned his head, then grinned. "Jeff Winston!" He offered one hand and slapped Jeffrey's shoulder with the other. "Good to see you. Where have you been?"

"Not playing tennis, unfortunately." The two men were members of the same tennis club. Occasionally, when they found themselves without other partners, they played each other. "Gotta get back to it." He patted his stomach. "Everything's going to pot." He cast a glance at Blake, prompting Thomas to make the introductions.

"Blake, this is Jeff Winston. A good man. Mean serve. Jeff, Secretary Lindsay."

Jeff offered his hand to Blake's cool, practiced shake. "I've been following your work, Mr. Secretary. It's impressive."

Blake thanked him, and for several minutes the two men talked of relatively general, harmless matters dealing with life in Washington and the Claveling presidency. When Thomas Fenton excused himself and moved away, Jeffrey began to close in. He was hoping to learn whatever he could about the decision-making hierarchy of a corporation such as the one Blake had headed before his appointment. "I understand you had experience as an administrator back in Boston."

"That's right. My firm grew to be larger than I'd originally expected. It took a lot of watching over."

Jeffrey gave him a quizzical smile. "I've always been fascinated by bureaucratic hierarchies. I assume you had underlings to help."

"I had to. There were four different divisions, each with a chief. I held regular briefings with them, though they handled the details of day-to-day production themselves."

"You set policy, of course."

Blake shrugged with one brow, nearly imperceptibly, duly modest. "It was my company."

"Were you the contact for sales, or did you have a special sales force?"

"There was a sales force, but the contacts were mine."

Jeffrey sighed in appreciation. "Not bad. Plenty of responsibility on your shoulders, though. You must have had the final word on what of your products went where."

Blake only had time to nod before two other couples joined them, and Jeffrey knew his chance was gone. He'd wanted to ask if there was ever occasion when something happened that Blake didn't know about, such as one of his division chiefs channeling a sale on his own. Jeffrey would have been interested in knowing whether, in his own investigation, he had to look further into the bureaucracy than simply the top. But it was lost . . . for now. He was bemoaning his fate when his ear perked up. One of the women was asking about Blake's wife.

"I haven't seen Mrs. Lindsay here. Couldn't she make it?"

Blake smiled with just the right amount of regret and shook his head. "She's back in Boston. She does a radio show there now."

"How exciting!"

"Yes. It's a current affairs talk show. Unfortunately, she has to spend hours each week preparing for it, so she can't spend as much time here as she'd like."

"You must miss her," the second woman observed.

"I do. But she's a modern woman and she's doing her thing. I'm very proud of her."

One of the men slapped him on the back. "You should be. She's a feather in any man's cap. . . . And speaking of feathers in one's cap, you must be very pleased with the import restrictions the White House announced this week . . ."

When the conversation took off along more political lines, Jeffrey stood by, observing Blake. After several minutes, when others approached, he excused himself from the group as unobtrusively as possible. He mingled, talking with whoever happened to be close, scanning the crowd to keep track of Cilla, all the while trying to crystallize in his mind the impression he'd gotten of Blake Lindsay based on those few short minutes with him. Much later, on the way home with Cilla, he discussed his feelings.

"It's strange, Cilla. He eludes me. You were right in that he's straight and proper. He says all the right things, makes all the right gestures. When he was asked about his wife, he gave a perfectly plausible explanation for her absence, even set the scene for her continuing absence. He claimed to miss her, but he seemed happiest when he was talking shop."

"Did you pick up anything on that score?"

"Not as much as I'd hoped. But look, maybe it was a half-assed idea anyway. I'd probably do better consulting with some less conspicuous corporate head. I had to be careful with Lindsay; I didn't want to sound too inquisitive."

"You can do that, Mr. Winston."

"Mmmm, but I have been better, haven't I?"

"You have." She snuggled closer to his side. "I think we both have."

"I HAVE A PROPOSITION, DANI."

"Uh-oh. Another one."

"This one's really exciting."

"Okay. Shoot."

It was early June. Danica was spending several days in Maine before returning to Boston to wrap things up before the summer. She no longer talked with Blake every week, but rather only on those occasions when he called to say that he wanted her with him on a particular date. She'd refused him several times, yielding only when he pointedly mentioned that her father would be at a particular affair.

It wasn't that her father still intimidated her; she'd meant what she'd told Michael, that she'd reached a point where she was beyond that. Rather, her deference was well planned, her mind set. The matter of divorce was between her and Blake. When they came to an arrangement—and she was sure it would eventually happen, because she didn't believe that Blake would take her animosity forever—she'd simply inform William of their decision. She didn't want to give him cause for involvement any earlier, and at that late point his arguments would be moot.

"Well," Michael began, "it's about a treasure hunt."

"Sounds interesting."

"There's this fellow I know—actually, he's an army buddy—who's into salvaging."

"Treasure hunting sounds more romantic."

Michael grinned. "You are a romantic, d' you know that?"

"I guess I am. Funny, when I was first married, I thought the most romantic things were the cards and flowers and gifts Blake would give me."

"And now?"

"They seem drab. Programmed. He never forgets a formal occasion, but the gifts are a travesty, given the ill will between us. I don't know why he even bothers. The feeling isn't there. Actually, I think his secretary does the dirty work. She must have all the proper occasions marked on her calendar."

"So what *does* turn you on?"

"Romantically? The quiet times we have together, like now. The talking and sharing." She leaned forward and gave him a gentle kiss. "Now *that*'s a treasure."

"Speaking of which, let me finish with my proposal."

She straightened with mock discipline. "Your proposal. Right. I'm listening."

"My friend—his name's Joe Camarillo—is convinced that he's located the wreckage of a small liner that sank in 1906 off the coast of Nantucket. He believes there could be up to a million in gold coins aboard."

"You're kidding!"

Michael shook his head. "He spent months studying government reports and underwater surveys in the National Archives, and he's convinced that what he's found is the *SS Domini* buried in twenty feet of sand. He and a crew will be diving this summer. We're welcome to join them if we want."

"*Join* them? What would we do?"

"Observe, more than anything. I think I can get an interesting piece out of it. We'll be following the everyday activity of the crew, interviewing them and, of course, reading anything and everything we can find on the *Domini*."

"'We'?"

"You can be my assistant. That is, if you're interested."

"You *know* I'm interested, Michael! I've never done anything like that!"

"Then you'll come?"

"I'd love to! But...but what about my show? I suppose we could tape it beforehand, but it's got to be current. I don't think I can hibernate on a boat *all* summer."

"No sweat. We'll be free every weekend. I can drive you back to Boston. You can tape your show. If we're late getting back, we can take a small cruiser out to rendezvous with Joe's boat."

Danica found herself growing more and more excited. "It might just work at that. If I'm working, I'll have a legitimate reason for avoiding Washington. Not that Blake expects I'll come during the summer. But my father might ask questions. If I'm *working*, he can't raise too much of a fuss."

At Danica's mention of her father, Michael, who'd been fully pleased with the prospect of both working and living with Danica, grew sober. "Has he, Dani? Has he been making things difficult for you?" All too well Michael recalled the visit he'd had from William Marshall. It had been months ago, and even after he'd returned from abroad and resumed seeing Danica, he'd heard nothing. He often wondered what the senator had up his sleeve and had more than once opened his door expecting to find a pair of thugs waiting to break his legs, but it hadn't happened. It was possible that the senator had backed off and thrown in the towel. Somehow, he doubted it, and that made him nervous—precisely as William Marshall had intended.

"He hasn't been overly warm," Danica said, "but then, he and I were never on the closest of terms. He abides my presence. I'm sure in his eyes, I'm a great disappointment."

Michael knew that William hadn't dragged out his photographs for Danica's benefit, and that was some relief. Still, perhaps more subtly, William was making his point. "How do *you* feel about that?"

"About disappointing him? Not the way I once did, that's for sure. You were right, Michael. I don't think I *can* please him. He and I function on totally different levels. I like to think that mine reaches higher, to things like personal satisfaction and happiness and love, but who knows. His is just so . . . different."

"It always has been. What do you think he'll say when you finally do leave Blake?"

"I already have left Blake, at least for all practical purposes. When the formal break comes, I'm sure my father will be livid. That's why I'm waiting. When Blake comes to his senses . . ."

Her words trailed off as, simultaneously, she and Michael thought the word *if*. But neither of them wanted to consider that possibility, at least not yet. Which was one of the reasons a summer working with a salvage crew sounded so good. For Danica, it would be another step away from Blake. For Michael, it would be another tie with Danica.

"Should I tell Joe we're on?"

"Yes."

"Are you sure?"

"Very."

Michael hugged her then, appreciating both the commitment she'd made and the risk involved. He wouldn't have thought it possible, but his love for her was still growing.

Chapter Fifteen

"HE CALLS HIMSELF RED ROBIN and we have a meeting set for tomorrow!" Cilla exclaimed, beside herself with glee as she opened the door to Jeff. Any reservations she might have had about so freely blurting her news were swept away by her excitement.

Jeffrey stepped inside and closed the door behind him. "Red Robin?"

"As in power-and-lust?"

"Ahhhh, *Red Robin*. Very dramatic. Sees himself as another Deep Throat, does he?"

"I don't know, but I'm sure not going to dismiss that possibility. I keep thinking of what he has to say, and my mind starts to whirl. Can you imagine my getting an exclusive on something really big?"

"You've done it before. Maybe that's why he chose you."

She frowned. "I've wondered about that. From the start he's asked for me directly. There must be some specific reason."

"You're responsible, like he said. Where are you meeting him?" When Cilla hesitated, he scowled. "I'm not looking for a piece of the action, Cilla. It's just that I have images of Deep Throat and a shadowy garage late at night, and the idea doesn't thrill me too much. Give me a little credit for feeling protective, and *don't* tell me I'm being chauvinistic."

"All right," she said quietly, realizing that one part of her, the softer, feminine part, liked feeling protected. "I won't.... I'm meeting him at nine o'clock in a parking lot in Bethesda."

Jeff easily recognized the address she gave him. "It's open enough, but it'll probably be deserted at that hour."

"I'll be okay. He couldn't possibly want to hurt me."

"What if he's a sex maniac who's been leading you on all this time?"

"Oh, Jeff, I doubt it. And anyway, I can't not go. I can't risk losing an opportunity like this."

"You could if it meant you'd be hurt. No story is worth that."

"I won't be hurt. If it'll make you feel any better, I'll bring along a can of mace."

Jeffrey snorted. "That'll do a lot of good. He could grab it out of your hand and turn it on you, then rape you and do any number of other ugly things."

"He *won't*. Damn it, Jeff. I thought you'd be excited for me. Maybe I shouldn't have told you after all."

"No, no, hon. I'm sorry. It's just that I'm worried. Maybe I should go along with you."

"Yeah. One look at you and he'll run off without a word. You're big, Jeff, and you can be intimidating."

"That's the point."

"No, the point is that I want this story."

"What if I hide in the back seat of the car. You could leave the windows open and yell if there's trouble."

She folded her arms over her breasts. "I think you do want in. This is *my* case, Jeff. You've got plenty of your own."

He sensed they were reaching an impasse and he didn't want that. He liked to think they'd come further. Pushing his fingers through his hair, he sighed. "I do, which is precisely why I don't 'want in,' as you so bluntly put it. I simply want to make sure you're safe."

"I will be. Trust me."

"I trust you," he snarled. "It's the other guy I'm not so sure about."

Cilla turned and took several steps away. On the one hand, she was determined to go. On the other, she respected Jeffrey's fears because, indeed, the same ones lurked in a distant corner of her mind. She also—contrary to what she'd said—respected Jeffrey's motives, and she wanted to meet him halfway. "What if you were to follow me and park several blocks away. If I had a beeper in my pocket, I could press it if there's any real danger.''

Jeffrey didn't have to think about it. "That would make me feel better.''

"Good." She turned. "Can you get the beepers?''

"Easily.... Cilla? Thanks.''

She suddenly felt totally comfortable with her decision. They'd reached a compromise. It was another step in the right direction. Smiling, she nodded. "You're welcome.''

THE PARKING LOT WAS DARK when Cilla pulled into it at eight-fifty-five the following evening. Seeing no other car, she parked, then sat and waited. And waited. Nine o'clock came and went, then nine-fifteen and nine-thirty. By ten o'clock she had the distinct impression she'd been stood up. She waited until ten-thirty, then started her car and sat with it idling for another five minutes before finally leaving.

Jeffrey was sympathetic, though not surprised. He knew better than to remind her of the crackpot theory, though, and suggested that as a consolation prize she lead him back to her place and take her frustrations out on his body. She liked the idea, and not only because of the guilt she felt in having dragged him along on what had proved to be a washout. He was a wonderful diversion, for a time at least. The following morning, though, she was back at her desk in the city room, staring broodingly at her word processing screen. When Red Robin called her shortly before noon, she had to work at sounding pleasant.

"I waited for you last night,'' she said.

"I . . . couldn't make it.''

"You said your story was urgent.''

"It is. I just . . . I just couldn't make it.''

He sounded very nervous, and she wasn't sure how much of it related to his having to call her after he'd stood her up. "It's okay,'' she lied. "I spent the time working through other stories in my mind.... Listen, if you got cold feet, you shouldn't have. I respect my sources. I don't reveal their names. I don't even know yours.''

"Red Robin is enough, and my story is better than your others."

"I want to believe you, which is why I was there last night."

His voice grew muffled, as though he was covering the phone. "Tonight. Same time. Same place."

"How do I know you'll—"

The line clicked, then went dead, and she knew he'd hung up. She quickly called Jeffrey and arranged to meet him at her apartment at seven. But four hours after that, they were back.

"Damn it! That man is incredible!" She savagely threw her purse on the sofa. "Twice in a row—who does he think he is?"

"He thinks he's a man who's got a story no one else has and that you'll come running when he calls."

"Well, he's right. But maybe you were, too. Maybe he doesn't have anything after all. I was so *sure*. My instincts haven't failed me like this since . . . since . . . since I agreed to divorce you."

Jeffrey put a comforting arm around her shoulder. "We both blew it that time. It was an emotional issue. This, on the other hand, is an intellectual one. I wouldn't do any different than you've done."

"You wouldn't?"

He shook his head. "Sure, there's a chance that it's a hoax all the way. But if it isn't, if the guy really does have something big to tell you, he may just be very, very nervous."

"He's a coward, is what he is. Why is he coming to me, anyway? He could go to the authorities."

"He may feel they won't believe him, that they're corrupt themselves. He may be afraid that if he goes to the cops he'll lose his anonymity. He may believe that the people he's out to expose have enough power to have him silenced."

"He may just want headlines," she sneered.

"Don't you? I mean, isn't it *your* byline you want on this thing?"

"Low blow, Jeff. You know I want the byline, but there's the story, too. Give me credit for a little civic responsibility."

"I do, hon. I do." He took her shoulders gently. "Look, let's just relax. If he calls back, you can put him on the spot.

Tell him that you think he's full of crap and that if he makes another date and stands you up, you won't accept his calls. Call his bluff. That might scare him more than anything."

"It might just drive him to a rival paper."

"No. He wants you. He's specifically asked for you. If he's got something to tell, you're the one he'll tell it to.... So cheer up. He'll call back. And if he doesn't, well, then you won't have to spend any more nights sitting in a dark parking lot."

As it happened, there was another night, early the following week, though she didn't have to sit for long. She barely had time to park her car, turn out the lights and grit her teeth when a dark form materialized on the pavement. Not a car, but a man. She stared, refusing to believe at first that he'd actually come. Disbelief quickly changed to excitement when he headed right for her, then was promptly quelled when the professional in her took over. She noted that he was clever to have come on foot, thereby preventing her from catching his license plate, which of course she'd had every intention of doing.

He approached slowly, cautiously. She opened her door and stepped out, reassured by the slight weight of Jeffrey's beeper in the pocket of her skirt. She remained silent, waiting for Red Robin to speak first, *if* this man was in fact Red Robin.

He came to a halt several feet from her and ventured a hesitant "Miss Buchanan?"

She wanted to say that she didn't know of any *other* fool who would come here for the third time, but instead she simply said, "Yes?"

"You're right on time. Early, in fact."

The night couldn't hide Red Robin's wiry slimness, or his glasses, or the head of dark, curly hair, which contrasted sharply with his pallor. Nor could it diffuse his features enough to prevent her realizing that he was, indeed, the man she'd seen at the reception so many weeks ago.

"I have been each night. I didn't want to miss you."

"Look. I'm sorry about that. It's just that . . . that this is difficult."

"I'm sure it is, Mr. . . . ?"

"Red Robin's fine."

She'd had to try, but she wasn't surprised that she'd failed. At least the man didn't look dangerous, she decided. She could probably put up a good fight if he turned on her... unless he had a gun... or a knife... but she had her beeper... it was so dark...

She cleared her throat and forced her thoughts ahead. "You have something you want to tell me?"

"I think I've given you the vague outlines."

"'Vague' is no good. My paper won't print it."

"Try diplomatic corps."

"Still too vague."

"Try the United States Senate or... or the Cabinet."

She shook her head. "I need specifics."

"Try differential hiring and firing."

Again she shook her head.

"Try sexual harrassment."

"Nothing new. Try again."

He took a deep breath, frowned, then breathed, "Try *homo*sexual harrassment."

Cilla grew very still. The data bank of her mind flipped through cases she knew of. They were few and far between and had only involved one, maybe two, recognizable names. But he'd mentioned three very powerful groups, and his implication was that he had many names to offer. Homosexuality was a new twist to an age-old scam.

"You have my attention," she said. "Go on."

He fiddled with the lapel of his jacket, then nervously thrust his hands in his pockets. "There are powerful men in this town who have certain other men on their payrolls for doing nothing."

"Every bureacracy has its deadweight," Cilla pointed out.

"Well, it shouldn't! There are others of us who are more than willing to work, yet we're shunted around to make room for the favorites."

Cilla noted his anger and wondered if he was hurling accusations purely out of revenge. "You feel you've been wronged?"

He started to answer, then stopped. When he did speak, his tone was carefully modulated. "The fact is that many people have been wronged. Not only are the taxpayers footing the bill for the sexual antics of some of its most prominent leaders, but these same leaders are being influenced by people who are using their . . . their sexual prowess for precisely that purpose.''

''We're being compromised.''

''Exactly.''

''Can you give me an example?''

He looked away and pressed his hands to his sides.

Cilla prodded. ''I'll need specifics, Red Robin. I've already told you that.''

''I've given you specifics.''

''You've given me the general nature of the offense.'' She paused. ''What is it you want of me?''

''I want you to expose these people.''

''You're the one who knows who they are. I can't conduct blind witch-hunts, particularly not if we're dealing with as important people as you suggest. I need specifics . . . names, dates, places, files.'' She studied his profile. His brows were lowered, his lips tight. ''Look, this is done all the time. A source comes to us, tells us all he knows; we verify it, then print it. I can assure you that you'll remain anonymous.'' She was beginning to wonder where he fit into the scheme. If he'd lost his job or been demoted, her theory of revenge might fit. But if there was something more, a personal vendetta, she had to know. ''Why have you come to me? Why do you want all this exposed?''

He brought his head around. ''Because it's wrong.''

''But why do you feel so strongly about it? Have you lost your job?''

''No. I have one.''

''Where?'' She didn't want to mention that she remembered meeting him before lest he get all the more nervous.

''It's not important.''

''It is if I'm supposed to get a fix on what you're saying.''

''It's not important.''

''Then I have to assume you're gay and that you've been jilted and are out for revenge.'' It was a variation on her earlier thought and came spontaneously, spawned in part by the frustration of having to pull teeth.

He drew more agitated. "Assume what you will. My personal situation is beside the point."

"It's not if it's the reason you've dragged me here." She knew she was goading him, but she remembered what Jeffrey had said about calling his bluff. She did need specifics, damn it, and if she had to badger Red Robin for them, she'd do it.

He took a step back. "Don't you want the story?"

"Of course I want it, but you haven't *given* me anything yet. Come on, Red Robin. Tell me something solid."

He shook his head, turned to walk off, then stopped. He looked down at his feet unsurely, then whirled to face her. "Did you know that much of the inside information we get on the Middle East comes from gays who infiltrate the upper echelons of those embassies?"

"Which embassies?"

"Did you know that one of the deputy secretaries of Labor is having an affair with a man who is a union lobbyist?"

"Which secretary?"

But Red Robin only shook his head and started off. He didn't turn this time, and when Cilla called out to him, he ran faster. Within minutes she was standing alone in the parking lot, her hands hanging limply by her sides.

"I need more!" she yelled to the night. "I need evidence!"

But the night didn't have it and all she could do was to hope that Red Robin heard and would think about what she'd said.

WILLIAM MARSHALL WALKED BOLDLY through the offices of the Department of Commerce and announced himself to Blake's secretary. "He's expecting me," he added curtly, then stood straight while Blake was buzzed. Given his choice, William would not have requested this meeting. He'd spent weeks debating it, had seen Blake socially any number of times during that period but had been unable to speak frankly with others about.

"Bill!" Blake appeared at his door and gestured. "Come on in." The two shook hands, then sealed themselves in Blake's office. "I was surprised when you called. Is everything all right?"

William settled into an upholstered armchair and propped his briefcase against the desk. "I'm not sure. That's why I wanted to talk with you."

Sinking into a matching chair, Blake frowned. "About what?"

"Danica. When was the last time you saw her?"

Blake's features tensed, though he maintained an even smile. "She was down last month. You saw her with me at the Weigner reception."

"You haven't seen her since?"

"She's busy now that she's got this radio show of hers. It's a wonderful opportunity for her, don't you think?"

William ignored the question. "Will you be seeing her much this summer?"

Blake hesitated, growing more wary. "I doubt it. She spends her summers in Maine."

"It might be a good idea if you tried to get up there."

That was the last thing Blake wanted to do. "Why?"

William pressed his lips together, wondering if he was making a mistake by confronting Blake but not sure where else to turn. He'd threatened Michael, but Michael had threatened him back and even now continued to see Danica. As for Danica, she was totally guarded when William was around, and he hadn't even *shown* her his pictures. Somehow he doubted she'd pay him any more heed than Michael had done. William didn't like feeling impotent, and that was precisely how he'd begun to feel on this matter.

"Because," he began angrily, "I think that she's far too involved with this Buchanan fellow, and if you don't do something to stop it, she's apt to embarrass us all. You do know that she sees him, don't you?"

Blake kept his expression bland while he chose his words with care. He had no idea how much his father-in-law knew, but was sure that Danica wouldn't have told William what she'd told him. "I know that they're good friends. They like each other. It's only natural that they spend time together, particularly as his house is so close in Maine.''

''They're more than good friends. They're lovers.''

For a minute Blake was taken aback, not because he was hearing something he didn't know but because William had said it. ''How do you know that?'' he said coldly.

''I have pictures!''

This did stun Blake. ''Of their *making love*?''

''Not, uh, not exactly. But only an imbecile would fail to read between the lines.''

Blake sat back stiffly. ''Have you got them here?''

William drew the packet from his briefcase and handed it to Blake, then waited while the other man studied the prints inside. ''I'm sorry to have to be the one—''

''How did you get these?'' Blake growled.

''I hired a private investigator.''

''On what authority?''

William realized that Blake was angry at *him* and decided that it was a defense mechanism. Accordingly, he softened his tone. ''I'm her father. I've been looking at her from a greater distance than you have, so it's understandable that I'd have suspected things sooner. I wanted to know if there was any cause for alarm, so I hired someone to follow her around for a while.''

''You shouldn't have done that, Bill.'' He tossed the photos on the corner of his desk. ''It's not your business.''

''I think it is. She's my daughter. What she does reflects back on me. As far as I'm concerned, she's betrayed us both.''

''She's an adult and I'm her husband. This is a matter between Danica and me.''

''You don't see her often. You have no idea what she's been up to.''

''I know more than you give me credit for.''

The conversation was not going as William had expected. He'd assumed he'd be bringing Blake shocking news, even more, shocking evidence, yet Blake seemed barely surprised. And he was more angry at William than at his own wife! ''Do you mean to say that you've known about this all along?''

''I've known about it. Danica told me.''

"She...*told* you?" For someone who had always been able to gauge and regulate others, William wondered if he was slipping.

"She told me."

"So what are you going to do about it?" William roared.

Blake grew all the more composed. "Nothing."

"*Nothing?* Blake, what kind of insanity is *that*? Your wife's carrying on with another man, *with* your knowledge, and you're just going to sit back and let it go on?"

Blake found a certain satisfaction in seeing William so ruffled. It made him look all the more in control by comparison. "Danica is discreet. You would never have known about this yourself if you hadn't hired an investigator. She's with Buchanan mostly in Maine, where no one's going to see or care."

"Don't *you*?" William gasped, unable to believe what he was hearing.

Blake took a deep, even breath and let it out slowly. "Of course I care. Danica's my wife. But I try to understand her. She's going through a crisis of some sort, perhaps sowing the wild oats she never sowed before we were married. I have faith in her, though. She knows which side her bread is buttered on. She'll get tired of Buchanan soon enough. You'll see."

William scowled. "You sound so damned confident. If it was me, I'd be screaming down the walls, making her toe the line."

"And she'd only rebel more. Don't you see, Bill? The more upset I get, the longer she'll carry on. Danica knows what her responsibilities are. When I need her here, she comes."

"Do you know what she's doing this summer?" William peered at him through narrowed eyes.

"She's on a boat hunting for gold." He chuckled. "Pretty amusing, actually."

"I don't see any humor in it. You know who she's with, don't you?"

"Buchanan. He's hoping to get a book out of it. She's working as his research assistant."

William snorted. "Fat chance."

"I believe her. She did a good job for Bryant. I'm sure she'll do no less for Buchanan."

"My God, man, but you're innocent. Do you honestly believe she's working? Doesn't it strike you that a boat is a perfect place for an ongoing affair?"

"There are four other men on that boat. I doubt she'll have the privacy to do much of anything. In fact, my guess is that she'll come back from the summer never wanting to step foot on a boat again. It can't be luxurious living, and we both know Danica's used to that."

William sat forward. "If you were smart, you'd hit Buchanan with an alienation-of-affection suit."

"Why would I want to do that? There'd be publicity, for one thing. For another, if I brought suit, it would only serve to alienate Danica." He held up a hand, pleased with his show of self-assurance. "Trust me, Bill. I know what I'm doing."

"Could've fooled me," William mumbled as he rose from his seat. "Well, I've said what I came to say. It's in your hands now."

"That's right." Blake stood to see the other man out. "And Bill? No more investigators, please. Let me handle this my own way. We've been friends for a long time. Danica's antics I can take; your interference I can't. I appreciate everything you've done, but it's mine now. Okay?" It was the closest he'd ever come to telling William Marshall off, and he rather enjoyed it. He was a force in his own right now, and it was time Bill accepted that.

William held up both hands palm out. "You can have it. Just don't come crying to me when she makes fools of us all, because I'll remind you of what you've said today. If she hurts her mother, it won't be because I didn't try to stop her." Lowering his hands, he flung open the door and stalked out, determined to have the final word.

Blake let him go because he knew he'd made his own point. The last thing he needed was for Bill to be sticking his nose in, trying to change a situation that suited Blake just fine.

Closing his door, he leaned back against it and raised two fingers to massage the tension from the bridge of his nose. Lord only knew, he had enough to worry about without having Danica on his neck, he mused, then pushed himself wearily from the door and headed back to his desk.

DANICA WAS HAPPIER than she'd ever been. Michael had rented a small cabin cruiser for the summer—one not quite as fancy as that they'd been on the summer before, but they hadn't wanted to look pretentious mooring a luxury craft alongside Joe Camarillo's modest salvage vessel.

Actually, the smaller cruiser suited them just fine, since most of their hours were spent with the crew abroad the salvage vessel. Though Michael dived with the men from time to time, Danica opted to remain on deck. Salvage vessel or not, it still gave her the same sense of freedom she craved. Away from land she didn't think of Blake or her father, but concentrated on helping Michael in whatever way she could.

Once a week they cruised back to shore and drove into Boston, where Michael waited proudly while she taped her program. She was always happy to return to the sea, though, loving the small cabin where she and Michael talked for hours at night, made love more often than not, and were nearly inseparable.

Late in July they returned to Kennebunkport to entertain Cilla and Jeffrey for the weekend. Gena, who'd been keeping Rusty, joined them, and the five had many hours of lively discussion. It was a warm, lovely time for Danica, the glimpse of a dream come true. She felt she was one of the family, and she basked in the love and closeness enveloping her so snugly. To her delight, Cilla and Jeffrey relaxed totally with her, drawing her into discussions of their cases in a way that stimulated her mind as well as her heart.

"Red Robin." She grinned. "I love it!"

"He's a doozy," Cilla remarked, lips thinned. "I think I'd like to wring his neck, though. He's the worst kind of tease."

"You haven't seen him in a month?" Michael asked.

She shook her head. "We've met twice, and he calls from time to time wondering why I haven't printed his story. I keep telling him that I need more, but I can almost hear him shaking in his boots."

"What will you do if you can't get more?" Danica asked. "Can you go ahead with anything you've got?"

"I'm working to verify the few things he's told me, but it's hard. The kind of liaisons we're talking about are very well hidden. I've gone to several gay bars, but someone high in government isn't about to frequent those places, and anyway, when I start asking questions, everyone clams up. I have to be so careful, so vague. I can't ask if so-and-so has ever been seen there because, given the power level involved, I'll be in real trouble if I start pointing fingers. Anyway, gays protect each other."

"Not Red Robin," Michael reminded her.

"Mmmm. He finally did admit that he was gay, which was some victory. I assume he's been spurned. He's angry, but he's also frightened. I'm hoping that at some point his anger will overcome his fear and he'll give me what I need. It's one thing if I have evidence to work with, but can you imagine how awful it'd be to accuse an innocent man?"

"It always is," Gena remarked.

"Well, in this case, it'd be even worse. Homosexuality isn't something you can necessarily prove, and innuendo alone can wreck a marriage. I like to think I'm a responsible enough journalist to avoid that kind of thing."

"So where do you go from here?" Danica asked.

"I try to follow up any leads Red Robin gives me. If I'm lucky, I'll find other witnesses, people who will corroborate Red Robin's claim. If I wait long enough, I may come across other jilted lovers; I'm told that gay men have a higher turn-around in relationships than gay women. As far as Red Robin's allegations of policy-setting favors go, I need dates of hirings and firings, evidence of suspicious decision-making, perhaps even a third party who will state that a questionable compromise was made."

"It's going to be tough," Jeffrey warned. "The capital is a strange place. On the surface it's a wonderfully exciting, fun-loving place. Subcutaneously, though, it's a hotbed of jealousy and mistrust."

"Good phrase, Jeff," Michael quipped, grinning. "'Hotbed of jealousy and mistrust'... good phrase." He dodged the paper cup Jeff threw his way. "The question is whether you can use it in your own work. How's it going, by the way?"

Jeffrey frowned. "Not bad. We're getting there."

Michael sensed that he'd reached a point in the high-tech theft case where he couldn't discuss it openly, so rather than prodding he steered the conversation along another vein. He was surprised when Jeff raised the issue himself later.

Having left the women to talk at the house, the two were walking the beach, at Jeff's suggestion. Rusty, one of the men, was trotting along beside them.

"I think we may have a problem, Mike."

"What kind of problem?"

"The investigation I've been working on. We've been able to trace illegal shipments of restricted goods back to several American companies. We're waiting for more so we don't blow the whole thing by cashing in the chips too early."

"Sounds solid."

"It is. The only thing is..." He looked clearly pained.

"Go on, Jeff. Don't keep me in suspense."

Jeffrey sent him an apologetic look, which held far more meaning than Michael could appreciate at that moment. "We've traced one of the shipments back to Eastbridge Electronics."

Michael stopped in his tracks and stared at his friend. "Eastbridge?" he echoed weakly.

Jeffrey nodded. "This particular shipment was made nearly two years ago. It contained computer equipment with high-speed integrated circuits that are heavily restricted for export by our government and, needless to say, highly coveted by Moscow."

Michael was trying to assimilate the information. He could only mutter a soft, "Shhhhit..."

Jeffrey went on quietly. "Lindsay approved the shipment, but the main contact was one of his henchmen, a guy named Harlan Magnusson, who headed his computer division. The stuff was sold to a firm in Capetown, then went on through two dummy firms until it finally reached the Soviet Union. We have solid evidence all the way."

"Shhhhit!" Michael propped his hands on his hips, then altered his stance and raised a hand to the back of his neck. "Lindsay! Christ! Why would he *do* something like that? The guy didn't need the money.... You say the shipment was made two years ago?"

"Several months before Claveling's election. There was only one shipment, but it's condemning as hell."

"At least the crime isn't compounded. If he'd let his company get something through after he'd been named to the Cabinet, he'd be in double trouble. How did he get a license, anyway? He didn't have anything to do with Commerce at that point."

"No. The license application said nothing about high-speed integrated circuits."

"And Customs didn't catch it on its way out?"

"They can't catch everything. In this case, the computer housing was older and suggested a different kind of matter than what was actually inside. Operation Exodus notwithstanding, this was one that slipped through." He sighed. "As far as Lindsay's motive goes, your guess is as good as mine."

Michael swore a third time and raised his eyes to the clouds. "I don't believe it." He met Jeffrey's gaze. "What do you do now? How much time until . . . ?"

"The Justice Department already has it and should be going before a grand jury any day. It'll take a while—maybe a couple of weeks—before indictments are returned. Like I said, Eastbridge is only one of what may total eight or nine. We're going after them all at the same time."

With a moan, Michael turned toward the sea. "Poor Danica. She may not have loved the guy, but she did respect him."

They walked on for a time in silence while Michael struggled to ingest what he'd learned. Finally Jeffrey stopped and faced him. "I'd think you stand to benefit from all this."

"Yeah. I'd have chosen any other way, though." He shook his head. "I still don't believe it."

"Well, I wanted to warn you. When things break, they won't be pretty. Danica's going to need *someone's* support."

"She's got mine. She's always had mine. I only wish I could somehow spare her..."

"There's no way you can, Mike. I only wish I wasn't the one who headed the investigation. I really like Danica. She's apt to hate me after all this."

"No. She's not that way. She'll understand that you've done what you had to do."

"I hope so, for many reasons. Things have been really good between Cilla and me. If she'll consider it, I want to talk re-marriage."

"Hey, Jeff, that's great!" Michael said, meaning it even if he had to push to sound enthusiastic.

"I think so. And . . . if you and Danica can ever get to-gether, well, I wouldn't want anything to come between us."

"It won't. I'm telling you."

"I've thought it all out. There's no way anyone can accuse her of helping me." When Michael sent him a quizzical look, he explained. "You know the press better than anyone. I'm sure one of the scandal sheets will have a field day suggesting that Danica may be thrilled with her estranged husband's fate."

Michael couldn't even begin to ponder the scandal sheets when his mind was racing. "What do you think he'll get?"

"He could get up to twenty years, plus half a million in fines. He could also be acquitted. I don't know the exact na-ture of his relationship with Magnusson. I'm sure a defense attorney can make a case for Lindsay being unknowingly conned."

"That's a way off. There's so much we'll have to get through first. Will you . . . will you give me warning before things break? I don't want to say anything to Dani now. She'll only be upset and there's nothing she can do."

"Lindsay may be called to testify before the grand jury. He's sure to have some forewarning."

"He may not say anything to her. From what she's said of the guy's confidence, he may assume that he'll escape indict-ment, in which case he won't tell that he was even ques-tioned. She hasn't spoken with him since June. . . . Will you let me know, Jeff? As a friend?"

Jeffrey put his hand on Michael's shoulder. "Of course I will. I'll give you a call as soon as I know anything definite."

Michael let out a breath. "Thanks. I'd appreciate that."

"I still feel like the villain."

"Lindsay's the villain, damn his soul. I hope he gets what he deserves!"

"Now *that* is the 'other man' in you speaking. Personally, I agree with you. In the end, though, it'll be up to the courts to decide."

MICHAEL KEPT REMINDING HIMSELF that it was a matter for the courts when, over the next few weeks, he found himself time and again seething inside that Blake should have betrayed Danica, not the other way around. He knew he was being unfair, that the man was innocent until proven guilty, that perhaps he had indeed been duped by his henchmen. But Michael was emotionally involved, and even *without* this latest twist of fate, he had enough cause to resent Blake Lindsay.

Michael's greatest challenge was in maintaining an easygoing front for Danica. Oh, he was happy when he was working with her, eating with her, making love to her. During those times he readily surrendered to her charm, letting the love they shared blot out all else. In the quiet times, though, when he'd stare unseen at her across the boat, when he'd hold her sleeping form in his arms in the wee hours of the night, he couldn't help but worry, but feel the pain she was sure to experience when that fateful call from Jeffrey came.

Two weeks passed, then a third. Michael and Danica had driven to Boston every Monday, then had returned. He kept Jeffrey informed of how to reach them at any given time, but there was no word and Michael was growing tense. In his mind, time was running out. He wanted to stop it, to turn it around, to give Danica and him just that little bit more time, but he couldn't.

Inevitably, Danica sensed his preoccupation.

"Something's been bothering you," she said softly one night, coming to sit by his side in the kitchenette of their boat. She brushed the sandy hair from his brow. "I know you're trying to hide it from me, but it won't work. What is it, Michael?"

He looked at her, debating, debating, finally opting to preserve the happiness of the last few days they'd have together on the boat. "Nothing, sweetheart. I'm just thinking how wonderful it's been this summer and I'm not looking forward to returning this tub on Friday."

She smiled and kissed the tip of his nose. "But Joe's giving up for now. He wants to clean up the things he's found, then get back to the Archives." The crew hadn't found a thing by way of gold on the bottom of the sea. True, the ship they'd found had proved to be the *SS Domini*, and it had yielded some very beautiful nautical artifacts, but . . . no gold.

Michael put an arm around her shoulder and anchored her close. "Are you disappointed that we didn't hit the jackpot?"

"But we did." She grinned. "You and I, at least."

Closing his eyes, he brought her fully against him. "You're so wonderful. God, I love you." The words had been whispered with a desperation that Danica might have caught had she not been so enthralled with their quiet force.

"I love it when you say that." She raised her mouth to his and met his hungry kiss. When it ended, she drew her head back. "I'm going to see a lawyer right after Labor Day. I have the name of the best divorce attorney in Boston. I think it's time Blake and I stopped playing games."

"Shhh. Let's not think about that now," Michael said. Cradling her face in his hands, he kissed her again, deep and long. His tongue swept through the inside of her mouth, parrying erotically with hers until breathlessness tore them apart. "Make love to me, Dani," he gasped, needing to know the strength of her love because he was frightened, so frightened.

She needed no coaxing. While her lips continued to play with his, her hands went to the buttons of his shirt, releasing them all, spreading the shirt open. Then she lowered her head and moved her mouth over the firm flesh she'd unclothed. She dampened his light hair with her tongue and laved his nipple until he moaned. Releasing him only long enough to lead him to the V-berth, she sat on its edge and went to work on his belt and fly. Slowly she pushed his jeans over his hips, leaning forward to kiss each new inch of skin as it was unsheathed.

By now she knew his body as well, no, more intimately, than her own. She knew what pleased him, what was sure to propel him to heights of pleasure. Using that knowledge, she pushed him back to the blanket and drove him to height upon height of near fulfillment. When she felt he had reached a limit of control, she stood and slowly removed each piece of her own clothing.

"You're tormenting me," Michael accused in a rasping voice.

"No." She sank down over his body, brushing her bare breasts against his chest. "I'm loving you, Michael, very, very much."

There was no part of him she didn't love then, both in thought and act, and Michael wasn't so disciplined that he could lie back and idly endure the ecstasy. He twisted around to love her as well, worshiping all the tiny, private spots on her body, which she'd always saved for him.

When at last she straddled his body and impaled herself, the fire they shared leaped out of control to engulf them both. Though Danica held the position of dominance, Michael took her, again and again. They'd never loved with such abandon, with such fury. And later, when their sweat-slick bodies lay languorously entwined, Michael vowed that whatever happened in the days to come, Danica would be his.

Chapter Sixteen

AFTER BIDDING an affectionate farewell to Joe Camarillo and his crew on Friday morning, Michael and Danica turned in their boat and drove back to Kennebunkport. It was the third week in August. Since most of the local celebrities were away and the producers of her show had suggested she take two weeks off, she'd decided to stay in Maine until after Labor Day, when she'd return to Boston and file for a divorce from Blake.

Having given up all pretense of living apart, she and Michael had agreed that she'd stay at his house. They slept late on Saturday morning, savoring the comfort of his bed after weeks on the smaller, harder V-berth. After awakening, they showered and dressed, then worked together in the kitchen, cooking brunch. They had just about finished eating when the doorbell rang.

Michael eyed Danica. "Were you expecting someone?"

She shrugged. "Not me. It's your house. Were *you* expecting someone?"

"And share you for a minute? No way."

The bell rang again. Popping a parting kiss on her cheek, Michael headed for the door. Even before he opened it, he felt a chill run through him. The chill became ice when he saw Cilla and Jeffrey, the latter carrying an ominous-looking folder under his arm. He looked from one to the other, seeing the strained looks on their faces.

"Hi, Mike," Jeff, said quietly. "Can we come in?"

Danica came from behind Michael and burst into a smile. "Cilla and Jeff! Perfect timing. We just got back."

Jeffrey looked from Michael to Danica, then back. "I know. I tried to contact you on the boat and found out you'd returned it."

"We did. Yesterday."

Danica was startled by Michael's hard tone. "Michael . . ."

He put a protective arm around her shoulder. "What are you doing here, Jeff?" His voice was low and filled with anger. "I thought I said I'd handle it."

"Handle what?" Danica asked, but again she was ignored.

Cilla and Jeffrey were both concentrating on Michael, with Jeff the logical spokesman. "I wanted to be here. It's part my doing and I wanted to be the one to take the blame."

"Michael, what's going on?" Danica's tone was no longer calm but had escalated to one of utter confusion.

"It's all right, sweetheart," he said, holding her closer. "Cilla, couldn't you have stopped him? All I needed was a phone call."

"I agree with him, Mike. His argument makes sense."

Knowing that he was outnumbered and that it was too late to remedy the situation anyway, Michael stepped back to let Cilla and Jeff come in.

"What's this about, Michael?" Danica asked fearfully.

"Come on." He was leading her to the sofa. "Let's sit down."

She let herself be led, then seated, because she didn't know what else to do. Cilla looked pale, Jeffrey pained. And Michael, who was evidently more informed than she, looked more tense than she'd ever seen him.

Jeffrey began very quietly, directing himself to her. "I want to tell you about the case I've been working on." He outlined it briefly, then faltered when he came to the hard part. From the moment he'd decided that he had to break the news to Danica himself, he'd been trying to think of an easy way to say what had to be said, but there was none. "Danica, Eastbridge Electronics is one of the firms we've traced illegal shipments to. Indictments will be returned on Monday. Your husband is going to be named on several counts."

Danica eyed him blankly. "Excuse me?"

Michael put a light arm around her waist. "Blake is in serious trouble, Dani. It may be that he's done nothing wrong, but Jeff—and I—felt you should be prepared."

"For what?" she asked, still unable to assimilate what Jeffrey had told her.

"He's going to be charged with selling restricted items to the Soviet Union," Jeffrey explained as gently, as calmly, as he could. He was also simplifying the charges, but he felt she didn't need to know the details. "Once the indictments are handed down, he'll be arraigned, then released on bail until the trial."

Her body was completely still, save the visible thumping of her heart. "You must be wrong," she whispered. "Blake would never do anything like that."

"We've been studying this problem for a long time," Jeffrey countered softly. "We have solid evidence. The question isn't whether Eastbridge made the shipment, because we know it did. We have papers from several sources to prove it. Rather, the question is whether your husband knew what the shipment contained and, if so, why he approved it."

She was shaking her head, her eyes moist. "He wouldn't..."

"Believe me, the Justice Department would never take on a man as prominent as your husband if it didn't have a good cause."

Danica turned her head. "Michael, there's got to be some mistake," she pleaded.

"I wish there were, sweetheart. Blake may be exonerated, but he will have to stand trial."

For the first time in this group, Danica felt on the outside. She inched away from Michael. "You knew about this before."

"Jeff told me last time he was up."

"And you didn't tell me," she accused, needing a scapegoat for the horror she felt. When Michael tried to take her hand, she pulled it away.

"I didn't see the point. There was nothing you could have done but be miserable."

"Danica," Jeff broke in, "Blake appeared before the grand jury more than a week ago. He didn't see fit to tell you, either."

But Danica was still staring at Michael. "You should have told me! I had a right to know!" She jumped up from the sofa and headed for the bedroom.

"Dani, wait!" He started after her, but Cilla caught his hand.

"Let her go, Mike. She needs a minute alone."

He knew that it was true. Despite everything they'd shared, there was still the past, which was what Danica had to come to terms with now. Sagging back into the sofa, he hung his head. "I wish you'd let me tell her, Jeff. It might have been easier without an audience."

"Come on," Cilla chided softly. "We care for her and she knows it. She'll be back in a minute. You'll see. And besides, there's *no* easy way to tell a woman something like this. Better Jeff should take the flack than you."

"Obviously, I'm taking it anyway."

"She's upset. She's looking for a heavy, and you're here. She won't hold anything against you, not when she can think clearly. She knows how much you love her and that what you did was out of that love."

Michael took a deep, unsteady breath, then raised his gaze to Jeff's. "It'll hit the papers Monday?"

Jeff nodded.

"I won't be touching it, if that's any consolation," Cilla offered. "I'm far too emotionally involved with this one. Damn, how could he do this to her!"

"I doubt he was thinking of her," Michael gritted. "I doubt he's *ever* thought of her. That was one of the big problems with their marriage. He put his career before everything else. Unfortunately, Dani's going to suffer the fallout."

Jeff screwed up his face. "I still can't figure a motive. Several of the other companies we've caught did it for the money; we've got records to show they were floundering financially. A third company has had known leanings toward the East; in hindsight, Commerce should have been wary of issuing it any license. But Eastbridge—damn, I can't figure it out."

"Who will be named in the indictments?" Michael asked. "Lindsay and Magnusson?"

Jeffrey grew still. "Plus the corporation itself. At least, that was what we thought. Unfortunately, Magnusson showed up in an alley two days ago with a bullet in his head."

"He was *murdered*?" Michael asked, stunned.

"Looks that way." He dug through his folder and tossed a set of photographs on the coffee table. Cilla and Mike both leaned forward to study them. "Someone wanted him silenced. The cops haven't got a lead yet."

One of the pictures showed the body at the scene of the crime, a second the scene with the traditional white chalk markers, a third the body as it lay in the morgue. When Cilla leaned closer, Jeffrey took her arm.

"Maybe you shouldn't, hon. They're pretty gruesome."

But she was staring at the morgue shot and was ash white for reasons other than the gruesomeness of the print. "My God!" she breathed, "that's him!"

Jeffrey nodded. "Harlan Magnusson. The former head of Blake Lindsay's computer division. He came to Washington with his boss, but he's been shuffled from one position to another in Commerce."

"No, Jeff." She was clutching his arm. "That's *him*. That's *Red Robin*!"

The air in the room went very still, only to be broken by a weak "Red Robin?"

Three heads swiveled around to see Danica approaching. Michael quickly gathered the photographs together and turned them over, but the harm was done.

Danica was staring at Cilla. "Harlan Magnusson is Red Robin?" she asked in a distant voice. "But Red Robin is..." Her eyes lowered to the photographs and grew glassy. "He was Blake's right-hand man," she murmured. "They went everywhere together...to meetings, on business trips..." She swallowed convulsively and seemed to gasp for air. Michael was by her side in an instant and she clung to his arm. "I never liked him. He was too nervous, too aggressive, and he used to glare at me. I was jealous of the time Blake spent with him..." She swayed on her feet and Michael tightened his hold, but she was looking at Cilla again. "You said that Red Robin was . . . was . . ." She pressed a trembling hand to her throat and whispered, "I think . . . Michael, I think I'm going to be sick . . ."

Trembling nearly as badly as she, Michael picked her up and ran for the bathroom, where he supported her while she lost the contents of her stomach. When there was nothing left to lose, he bathed her forehead with a cool cloth and helped her rinse her mouth. Then he carried her to his bed and gently laid her down. Though she kept her eyes shut tight, she clutched his hand.

"It's all right, sweetheart," he soothed. "Everything's going to be all right."

For a time she said nothing. Then: "I feel so sick. So . . . dirty and used."

"Shhh. That's not true."

"No wonder he never came near me." Michael knew she was talking of Blake. "It wasn't *me* after all. It was the fact that I'm a woman. He must have suffered through the few times we were together, when all along he wanted to be with . . . with . . ." She heaved again, but there was nothing left to vomit. Michael ran back to the bathroom for the cloth and placed it gently on her throat.

"Take it easy, Dani. It'll be all right."

The stillness with which she lay belied the roiling torment in her mind. After several long minutes, she opened her eyes. "It all makes sense now—why he wasn't upset when I started coming up here, why he hated the place, why he seemed almost . . . relieved when I told him about you."

"He may not have shown it, but he was probably under a great deal of stress."

"You're more compassionate than I am."

"I wasn't married to him. It's natural that you feel hurt, and I'm not trying to condone what he did." To the contrary. He felt a slow anger boiling within. "He did use you. You were his key to acceptance. No wonder he was so vehement against getting a divorce. You were his cover. As long as he had you, he didn't have to worry about anyone suspecting the truth."

Danica rolled onto her side and tucked her knees up tight. Her insides were trembling in the aftermath of shock. "I can't believe it," she whispered, squeezing her eyes shut as if doing so would erase the ugly images that dominated her thoughts. Then she laughed, but it was a harsh sound. "Wait until my father finds out. It's poetic justice."

"He'll be as shocked as you are. He had no way of knowing, Dani. No one did."

"*Will* he find out? Will it come out in court?"

"That depends on Blake's defense attorney. The formal charges won't mention it. There's nothing illegal about a homosexual relationship between two consenting adults. As far as I know, the four of us here may be the only ones who know of the relationship between Red Robin and Blake. Cilla certainly won't mention it, and she's the only one who can identify Red Robin. Now that he's dead, so is her lead.... It does make sense now. Cilla's always wondered why Red Robin went to her rather than another paper. He must have thought our papers would be that much more interested, given the relationship between Blake and your father and the history of animosity between your father and our papers."

But Danica wasn't thinking of either her father or the Buchanans at that moment. "Do you think Harlan specifically wanted to expose Blake?"

"If Blake had shunted him aside when they came to Washington, it's possible. But Red Robin never did give Cilla Blake's name. And . . . there's always the chance that the relationship between the two men was innocent."

Danica's mind was working clearly enough to realize the odds against that. "No. There were too many signs . . ."

Michael agreed, but he had to be realistic. "We'll never really know, now that Harlan's gone. As far as the trial goes, I doubt the issue of homosexuality will come up . . . unless the defense attorney feels that it's Blake's best chance for proving that he was unknowingly duped."

"God, I hope it doesn't come out." This time her laugh held a touch of hysteria. "I can't believe the irony of all this. When my father warned me about being involved with you, he kept saying that he didn't want the family embarrassed.

He's going to *die* if Blake's…Blake's…comes out." Her voice broke and she curled into an even tighter ball, covering her head with her hands as though she was embarrassed even with Michael.

He wouldn't have it. Easily overpowering her resistance, he cradled her in his arms and spoke softly. "What Blake did has no reflection on you, sweetheart. He may not have realized what he was when he first married you. Gays have come out of the closet in the past ten years. He may have suppressed those instincts for a very long time." When she burrowed deeper against him, he went on, needing to have everything out in the open. "There are many men who lead dual lives for years, who are happily married even while they have lovers on the side."

"We didn't have a happy marriage. He used me."

"In the end, yes. But he may have truly loved you once. He may still love you in his way."

"His way makes me sick."

"I know, sweetheart."

"I feel…soiled."

"I don't see you that way. Knowing what we do now, I respect you all the more. Over the years you've given him every benefit of the doubt. You have to be credited with sticking by him so long."

"I didn't know!" she cried, berating herself.

"How could you?"

"I should have seen, but it never occurred to me. I kept asking him about other *women*. No *wonder* he was repulsed by the idea." She moaned softly. "I was so stupid. I actually forced myself on him that last time."

"You what?"

She raised her head. "The last time we made love was two years ago last May. He hadn't come near me in months, and I'd met you and was frightened by the attraction I felt for you, so I went home to Blake and seduced him." Her eyes teared. "I was fantasizing about you the whole time, Michael. Who do you think *he* was fantasizing about?"

"Shhhh." Michael pressed her head to his chest, unable to bear the pain in her eyes. "Don't torment yourself, sweetheart. It's not worth it."

Her voice came muffled from his chest. "It's not that I wanted him then any more than I do now. We never had much of a sex life. Sex was always...perfunctory with us. Now I can see why. It's just that...I feel so angry! He should have been honest. When I told him about you, he should have let me go. He had no right to do that to me...to us."

"I feel angry, too. Believe me. But anger won't get us anywhere. We have to think of the future. *You* have to think of the future."

"I don't want to...and you know why."

He did. He knew Danica. She'd foresee the ordeal that Blake was facing and would feel it her duty to stand by his side, at least until the trial was done. Michael didn't like the idea; in his book, Danica had suffered enough at Blake Lindsay's hand. But he knew that she'd view deserting Blake now as callous, and he had to admire her for it.

They remained in the bedroom until Danica felt stronger, then rejoined Cilla and Jeff, who'd cleaned up the remains of Michael and Danica's brunch and had perked a fresh pot of coffee. Cilla insisted on making Danica a cup of tea, then took her out to the deck while the men talked inside.

"What do you think?" Michael asked softly.

"I think we may have our motive. If Lindsay and Magnusson were sexually involved, Magnusson could easily have swung his weight to get that shipment out. We know that he was the contact. Lindsay may never have even known about it if, because of their relationship, he gave Magnusson an inordinate amount of freedom." He paused, thinking. "But I talked with Lindsay briefly at a party several months back. He said that the responsibility of the company had been his, that he knew of everything that happened. Of course, that may have been arrogance speaking."

"So you do think he was conned by Magnusson?"

Jeffrey shook his head. "I think the guy knew exactly what was going on. His signature's right there on incriminating documents. But I do think that'll be his defense. And we'll never know otherwise, will we?''

Michael had said similar words to Danica. The fact was that Harlan Magnusson, a key element in the case, was dead. Michael wasn't sure he liked the implication. "Do you think Lindsay could have had something to do with Magnusson's murder?''

"Nah. It doesn't fit. As far as I know, Lindsay's been strictly on the up and up as Secretary of Commerce. Sure, he already knew of the investigation when Magnusson was murdered, but I can't believe he'd be so stupid. He's in a powerful position. He's well respected. Even if he was worried that indictments would be returned, he had to have known that he'd easily have the upper hand if it came down to Magnusson's word against his. Murder is something else entirely. There's no logical reason he'd risk it.''

"Who do you think did?''

"Probably someone representing the guy in Capetown, who just happens to be a paid operative of the KGB. I'm sure it was a professional job, which is another reason to rule Lindsay out. For something that professional, he'd have had to hire a hit man, which would have only given him someone *else* to worry about. No, Lindsay wouldn't buy into that.''

"Do you think the cops will?''

"I'm sure they'll consider it once the shit hits the fan on Monday, but I doubt it'll go far.''

Michael sighed and sat back in his seat. "Christ, I hope not. That's all Dani needs." He glanced toward the deck. The two women stood at the railing, Cilla with her arm around Danica's shoulder, talking softly to her. "Will the trial be held in Washington?''

"Uh-huh. That's where Lindsay personally filed for the export license. Falsifying the information on that application will be one of the charges." His voice grew even quieter. "You're not still angry at me, are you, pal?''

"No. It's done. Maybe it was for the best. I think Dani's going to need all the support she can get over the next few days.''

HER EMOTIONS RAGED in a perpetual circle. She was angry, then hurt, then frightened, then self-abasing, then angry, again and again. Cilla and Jeff stayed until Sunday night. They bolstered her as best they could, talking openly, if gently, about every aspect of what had happened, agreeing with Michael that the more Danica got off her chest, the better. They talked about what she could expect when she joined Blake in Washington, as they all knew she would, and tried to prepare her for any ugliness she might find.

Cilla saw the ordeal through Danica's eyes, and as a reporter whose stories had more than once prompted other ordeals, she found it a humbling experience. Jeffrey, an investigator who'd seen many of his targets go to jail, had a similar view of the other side and was enlightened. Michael, who loved Danica, felt her pain as his own and wondered if things would ever be the same again.

When Monday morning rolled around, Danica clung to Michael for a long, long time.

"Are you sure you want to do this?" he asked softly, smoothing her hair from her cheeks.

"I have to. It's the only way."

"You could stay here."

"If I was a different sort of person, yes. But I'm not."

"Are you sorry we told you?"

"No! It's helped. If Blake were a man, he'd have told me himself. But you all were wonderful this weekend. I can think clearly now. I'm going to need a level head if I hope to make it through all this."

Michael felt utterly helpless. "What can I do, sweetheart?"

She put her arms around his neck and pressed her face to his throat. "I'll call you. Knowing that you're here . . . well, that's the biggest help."

"Will you call? Will you let me know what's happening?"

She nodded, unable to speak.

"I love you, sweetheart."

She drew back her head, studied the features she knew and adored, kissed him very lightly, then disengaged herself and ran toward the car. Michael was reminded of the winter before, when she'd done much the same after he'd told her he was going away. He hadn't wanted a repeat of that. Damn it, he wanted her with him!

But the car was disappearing from the drive, its sound a low purr, then a growl, which faded and faded, then . . . nothing. He walked slowly around her house and down to the beach, knowing that all he could do was to wait and watch and hope that Danica's strength would see her through.

MRS. HANNAH SAID NOTHING about Danica's early return from Maine. The house, as always, was in order, but Danica could only look around and wonder at the farce she and Blake had lived there. One part of her didn't want to touch a table, a lamp, a stick of furniture. The other part very carefully took a seat in the den and waited for the inevitable call to come.

It was nearly two in the afternoon when the phone rang. Clenching her fists over her fluttering stomach, Danica willed herself to be calm. When Mrs. Hannah came to the door to announce that Mr. Lindsay was on the phone, she nodded politely, waited for the housekeeper to depart, then slowly, coolly lifted the receiver.

"Hello?"

"Danica, thank God, I found you. I tried the house in Maine, then Buchanan's house. He told me where you were. Danica, something's happened. I need you here with me."

Where she'd thought herself emotionally played out, an anger flared. She diligently curbed it, aided by the perverse satisfaction she felt at hearing Blake's ruffled tone. "This is sudden, Blake. What's happened?"

"I'd rather not talk about it now. There's been a terrible misunderstanding. Look, I've been in touch with Hal Fremont. He's going to pick you up and fly here with you."

Danica tensely twisted a button on the soft leather sofa. "Hal? Your lawyer? Is there a legal problem?"

"Later, Danica. Can you be packed and ready in an hour?"

"Yes."

"Good. I'll see you later."

He was about to hang up when Danica blurted out, "Don't you think you should tell me now?" She was thinking about the press, which, if it knew of the indictments, would be sure to meet her plane. It wasn't every day that a member of the Cabinet was indicted on charges not far afield from treason.

"I can't. Hal will fill you in on the plane. I'll see you soon."

He hung up then, and Danica could only seethe at the idea that he was leaving his dirty work to others. With great effort, she composed herself and marched upstairs to pack the suitcase that Mrs. Hannah had just finished unpacking. Of course, she mused cynically, the clothes she'd need in Washington were a world away from those she'd taken to Maine. *Washington* was a world away from Maine, where more than anything at that moment she wanted to be. But she had a mission, a final mission with regard to her husband, and that conviction gave her the strength to put her own wishes on hold.

Within the hour, Hal Fremont was at her door, looking as pale and somber as Cilla and Jeff had looked two days before. The only difference was that this time she knew its cause and she was able to maintain her poise through the short drive to the airport, then the flight aboard the Lear jet Hal had chartered.

Danica had no quarrel with Hal, who, as gently as he could, broke the news of Blake's indictment while the jet winged southward. "I don't know all the details myself," he explained, "but I think you should be prepared for the worst. Of course, Blake is innocent, but he will have to face the charges."

She'd listened to his monologue in utter silence, but her initial concern about having to act stunned proved to be groundless because, despite how fully Cilla and Jeff and Michael had prepared her, the whole business was shocking and that much more real coming from Blake's personal lawyer.

A car was waiting for them at National, and Danica had actually begun to hope that she'd beaten out the press, when the car rounded the corner near Blake's town house and she saw a large media contingent on his front steps.

"Oh, God," she murmured. "What do we do?"

"I'll get you in. Just keep calm and don't say a word."

The car had barely come to a halt when the hoard moved in. Hal stepped out first, shielding Danica with his back.

"Does Mrs. Lindsay have any comment about the charges being brought against her husband?"

Hal gave a curt "No," reached in for Danica and, when she'd climbed from the car, put a firm arm around her shoulders. He wasn't a large man, but he knew what he was doing. She willingly followed his lead toward the steps.

"Did you know of your husband's dealings in Boston, Mrs. Lindsay?"

"How did you feel to learn of the indictments?"

"Will your husband be resigning from the Cabinet?"

Hal raised his hand as he pushed his way through the crowd. "Mrs. Lindsay has no comment at this time."

They half ran up the steps, but the questions followed.

"How close was the Secretary to Harlan Magnusson?"

"Do you feel that there's a connection between Mr. Magnusson's death and the charges brought today?"

"Has there been any communication with Senator Marshall?"

The front door was opened, and Danica and Hal fled through. In the abrupt silence that followed its closing, Danica sank trembling into a nearby chair. "I don't believe them," she murmured shakily. "'How did I feel to learn of the indictments?' How do they *think* I feel!"

Hal patted her on the shoulder, then stepped aside. When she raised her eyes, she saw Blake standing on the stairs.

"I'm sorry you had to go through that, Danica," he said evenly.

She hesitated for a minute, though her gaze didn't waver. "So am I."

"Thank you for coming."

Aware that she was being watched not only by Hal but by Blake's houseboy and two other men who'd come to stand at the top of the stairs, she simply nodded.

Blake's voice seemed to lose some of its force then. "Why don't you and Hal come up to the den. You'd better hear what we've been discussing."

Given little choice, she followed Blake to the top of the stairs, where she was introduced to Jason Fitzgerald and Ray Pickering, the local lawyers Blake had chosen to lead his defense. Once in the den, she refused invitation of a seat and propped herself on the back windowsill in an effort to remove herself from the talk. When an hour later Blake's houseboy, John, told Danica that she was wanted on the phone, she was grateful for an excuse to leave the room.

More than anyone she wanted it to be Michael because she felt chilled to the bone and in need of his encouragement, but she knew that he wouldn't call her here, even though she'd given him Blake's unlisted number.

"Hello?"

"...Darling?"

Danica felt sudden tears in her eyes. "Mom," she sighed, "oh, Mom, thank you for calling." It hadn't even occurred to her to call Eleanor because she'd been conditioned for so long not to depend on her help, but she suddenly realized that, in lieu of Michael, Eleanor might be a comfort. "Where are you?"

"I flew down as soon as your father called me. Darling, I'm so sorry about all this."

"It's not your fault, Mom. But things are pretty awful."

"When did you get there?"

"About an hour ago. I flew down with Hal Fremont. Reporters are swarming all over the place. We had to fight our way through."

"Oh, darling, I'm so, so sorry. How are you...holding up?"

"Barely." She was about to say that it had been a draining three days when she caught herself. "I'll do it, though. I'll be good. You don't have to worry about that."

"I wasn't. I have faith in you—uh, darling, your father wants to talk."

"Mom?" Danica asked urgently. "Mom, I...I don't want to stay here tonight...with the press outside and all." It was as good an excuse as any, and the only one she felt she could offer Eleanor. "Can I...can I stay with you?"

"Of course, darling. I'm sure Blake will be with his lawyers for hours anyway. Why don't you call me when you want to come and I'll send the car."

"I will, and...thanks, Mom."

"Don't thank me. I'm glad I can finally do something to help you." She issued a muffled, if surprisingly impatient "Just a minute, William," then returned to Danica. "You'll call when you're ready?"

"Yes." She managed a weak smile. "Why don't you put Daddy on before he throws a tantrum."

"I think I'd better—"

"Danica?" Her father's voice held near belligerence. "Thank God, you're there, girl. I was worried you'd sit on your can up in Maine."

Forcing herself to adapt to the sudden shift of fears, she gritted her teeth. "I was in Boston. I came as soon as Blake called."

"Maybe you're finally coming to your senses." His tone grew even more authoritative. "Now, I want you to know that there's nothing to worry about. We've got trumped-up charges here."

"Daddy, the government has evidence that Eastbridge made those shipments."

"Well, Blake didn't. Someone's out to get him, and I don't know who in the hell it is, but he won't get far. Blake's lawyers will make sure of that. He's with Fitzgerald and Pickering, isn't he?"

"He's with them now."

"What are they saying? He's not resigning, is he?"

"No. He spoke with the President earlier and they agreed that he'd take a leave of absence. Blake will give a press conference tomorrow explaining that he feels that he can't give his all to the Department while he's preparing for the trial and that the Deputy Secretary will be acting in his stead until the trial's over."

"Good. Sounds strong. No suggestion of guilt. What line of defense are Fitzgerald and Pickering planning?"

"I don't know. They're discussing that now. I think it will be a while before they can get the information they need from the Justice Department."

"Maybe I can speed that up."

"You'll have to discuss it with Blake. Should I get him on the phone?"

"No, no. Don't disturb him. He doesn't like my interfering."

"I'm sure he wouldn't mind your help."

"Well, he knows where I am if he wants me."

Danica detected a subtle anger underlying her father's words, and she wondered if he, too, was irked that Blake had put them all in this mess. "Have you been hounded by reporters?"

"A few. I handled them."

She nodded. "Well then, I guess I'd better get back to the den. I'll see you later."

"Be supportive, Danica. He needs you now."

"Don't worry, I know my place." She certainly did, and it wasn't here. Hanging up the phone, she stood for several minutes. She debated calling her mother to send the car right then. After all, she'd made her appearance. Blake had seen her. The press had seen her. Her father, though, expected her to stay for a time, at least. And since this entire ordeal was going to be her swan song, she mused, she could easily swallow her pride and acquiesce.

Rather than return immediately to the den, she wandered to the kitchen to make herself some tea. When John offered to do it, she suggested he see if the others wanted drinks or food. The few minutes alone that she bought were what she needed. When, teacup in hand, she rejoined the brainstorming session, she felt stronger.

Unfortunately, being closed in a room with three lawyers and Blake was enervating. She tried to concentrate on the discussion, which jockeyed between handling the press and anticipating the government's case, but after a time she tuned out, mentally exhausted. When the group relocated to the dining room, she could do nothing more than pick at the Oriental chicken John had prepared. Her thoughts centered on Blake, on the disgust she felt for him, the anger, the resentment. She kept thinking that if he'd been a good man he'd have given her a divorce months ago and she would have been spared all this. She kept asking herself why he'd done it, *if* he'd knowingly okayed that shipment and, if so, whether he'd truly expected to avoid punishment.

When, having finished dinner, the men prepared to return to the den, she called Blake aside. "Do you need me here now?" she asked quietly.

He seemed taken aback. "Where were you planning on going?"

"I'll be sleeping at my parents' place."

He stared at her; then his lips twisted as he turned his head aside. "It won't look very good if you march out of here for all the world to see. They'll grab on anything, including the fact that my wife isn't sleeping with me."

"We haven't slept together for months, Blake, but that's neither here nor there. You can inform the press that precisely *because* of them I don't feel I can stay here. Say they make me nervous, which is the truth. Say that I'm distraught over what's happened, which is also the truth. Say that my *mother*'s distraught and that I'm going to comfort her while you work with your lawyers."

"That might work for a day. At some point, though, we're going to have to present a unified front."

"I'm in Washington. Isn't that enough?"

"No. I want you with me when I appear in court for the arraignment tomorrow morning. I want you by my side at the press conference after that. And of course I'll want you sitting in court during the trial."

She wanted to lash out in anger, but she bit her tongue and willed herself to be calm. Her day would come, she told herself. What was she doing now was putting a down payment on her freedom.

"All right, Blake," she said slowly. "I will be there on those occasions you mention. But I won't live with you in this small town house for the next four months. If you want me to stay in Washington, we'll have to find some alternative setup."

He rubbed his forehead. "Danica, I don't need this. I've got enough on my mind right now without having to deal with your whims."

"Call them what you will," she countered, keeping her voice low and steady, a miracle given the fury she felt, "but you'll have to deal with them." She headed for the stairs. "I'm going to call for mother's car now. I'm exhausted. Needless to say, it's been a difficult day. You can pick me up tomorrow morning on your way to court. You know where I'll be." She was halfway down the stairs when Blake called after her.

"Danica?" She looked back. "I . . . can count on your support through this, can't I?"

She almost felt sorry for him because at that moment he seemed so unsure. She felt no sense of victory, though, only a great sadness that he'd brought all of this on himself. "Yes, Blake. You can count on me. I assure you I'll do nothing to hurt your case."

He came several steps closer and dropped his voice. "What about Buchanan?"

She was surprised. "Michael? He'd never do anything—"

"Are you still seeing him?"

"Yes. I love him. I told you that last spring."

"But while you're here, you won't . . ."

He didn't have to finish. She knew that once again he was thinking of himself. "No. I won't see him while I'm here. He agrees with what I'm doing. He's a good man, Blake, a decent, honest, compassionate man. And he believes in me much more than you ever did."

"I always believed in you."

"Not the way he does. He wouldn't have to ask if he could count on my support. But then, he wouldn't ever need it, at least not in the way you do now."

Blake stood for a minute staring at her and she realized that he looked every one of his forty-six years. "Well, at any rate, I'm glad to know you'll be standing with me. I'll pick you up at nine."

She nodded once, then continued down the stairs to call her mother from the lower living room. A glance out the window told her that the press throng had thinned, though even then she wasn't looking forward to making her way through, and there was no other feasible exit. She'd spotted her father's driver pulling around the corner when Blake came down the stairs.

"I'll walk you to the car," he said.

She saw that he had his suit jacket on again and that he looked perfectly composed, and she wondered if one of the lawyers had suggested that a show of husbandly care might impress the media. She would have objected had she not desperately feared the thought of warding off the microphones alone.

Glancing back out the window, she saw that the car was waiting. Taking a deep breath, she let Blake open the door, then lead her quickly down the steps.

"Mr. Secretary, what can you tell us about the charges made against you?"

"Mr. Secretary, have you spoken with the President?"

"Mr. Secretary, is there a resignation in the offing?"

Blake opened the car door for Danica and saw her inside before he turned, still with the car door open, and faced his inquisitors. "I'll be holding a press conference tomorrow. Your questions will be answered then. Now, if you'll excuse me, my wife is going to see her parents and I'd like to say goodbye." Before Danica could anticipate his move, he leaned into the car and kissed her. But the words he murmured against her lips weren't directed at her. "Thank you, George. I appreciate your coming for Mrs. Lindsay. Drive carefully."

Danica didn't look back when the car began to move. She simply pressed the back of her hand to her mouth and wondered if she'd ever make it through this last charade.

Chapter Seventeen

BLAKE WAS ARRAIGNED the following morning in the United States District Courthouse. Dressed in a sedate but stylish gray suit, Danica sat in the courtroom and listened while he pleaded innocent to each of the four counts against him. As had been the case when they'd entered the building, he took her hand in his when they left, and she didn't resist. She'd been up long hours the night before talking with Eleanor, who'd been wonderfully warm and infinitely proud of her, and she'd realized that if she was going to go through with the show, she'd have to do it right. Public appearances were all that mattered here; when she and Blake were alone and in private, well, that was something else.

From the courthouse they drove to the Department of Commerce, where Blake held the press conference he'd promised. Danica sat immediately to his right, his lawyers immediately to his left. She smiled at Blake when he smiled at her, looked poised if appropriately somber the rest of the time; in short, she handled herself as would the devoted wife of a man who was facing a grave challenge.

Later that afternoon, when she and Blake were alone in his condominium for the first time since she'd flown in from Boston, she raised the issues that were foremost in her mind.

"What happened, Blake?"

They were having drinks in the living room and had barely said two words to each other since they'd returned from a long lunch with Fitzgerald and Pickering.

He stared at her. "What do you mean?"

"How did it happen? How did that shipment containing high-speed circuits make it to the Soviet Union?"

"You heard what I told Jason and Ray," he said indignantly. "I had no more idea that those computers contained restricted circuits than I had that they were headed for Russia.''

"But you were the one who filed the application for an export license.''

"I thought I was shipping a decontrolled commodity.''

"You were always on top of the things like that.''

"I thought I was. Evidently I was wrong.''

His statement was thoroughly arrogant, containing no hint of the humility that his words should have suggested. Danica pressed. "Then Harlan was the one responsible?''

"Exactly.''

"How did he manage it?''

Blake took a healthy drink, then set his glass down on the arm of his chair. "Go ask him.''

"I can't. He's dead.''

"Exactly.''

"That must make your case easier. A dead man can't fight back.''

He stared at her. "What are you getting at, Danica?''

"He was murdered. Very neatly eliminated. You didn't have any part in that, did you?''

Blake bolted from his seat and stalked across the room. She could see the fists at his sides, the tension radiating through his shoulders. When he turned at last, his features were rigid. "I'm going to pretend you didn't ask that.''

"I had to ask it. Someone else is bound to, and I want to know the answer.''

"The answer is no. Finally and unequivocally, *no*. Look, Danica—'' he held out a hand and she saw that it shook "—I know that we've had our differences and I know that this trial business can't be pleasant for you, and even if you can't find it in you to believe me on the matter of the shipment, this you *have* to believe. I didn't kill Harlan! I could *never* do something like that. Believe I'm a crook if you will, but not a murderer!''

She hesitated for only a minute. "I do believe you,'' she said quietly. "I just wanted to hear you say it. In the ten years we've been married, I've never thought you capable of violence.'' She'd come to realize he was capable of other things she hadn't imagined, but she had to believe violence wasn't one of them.

"Thank God for that!" He slowly simmered down and returned to his drink.

"I think we ought to discuss where we're going to live until the trial is over."

"There's nothing wrong with this place," he growled over the lip of his glass.

"It's too small. There's only one bedroom and the den for sleeping." Her implication was clear; she had no intention of sharing his bed. She knew she'd get no argument there, and she didn't.

"I'll take the den, if that will make you happier."

That would leave her in his bed, where for all she knew he'd had lovers more than once. The thought made her flesh creep. "I think we should rent a house in one of the suburbs. That would give us both plenty of room. Look at it realistically. It's going to be a long few months before the trial starts, and since you won't be working, you'll be around more than you ever were. You'll go stir-crazy here, and I, well, I just don't want to be here."

He eyed her cautiously. "Then, you agree that you can't stay with Bill and Eleanor?"

"I *can*, but you were right. Mom helped me see that last night. It wouldn't look very good if we live apart."

"Bless Eleanor."

She bristled. "It was *my* decision, Blake. Now, will you go along with the idea of renting a house?"

He shrugged. "If you want to do the looking, be my guest. I'm sure you understand that I'm not of a mind to do it myself."

"I'll do the looking." She sighed. "I'm going to need *something* to fill my time." Setting down her drink, she reached for her purse. "I'll take a cab back to my parents' for now."

"I can drive you."

"No. You stay here.... Come to think of it, it might be a good idea for Marcus to drive the Audi down. I'd like some mobility."

"You can drive the Mercedes."

"You'll need it. Once we're out of the city, it'll be harder getting cabs."

"Another reason to stay here," he growled.

But that was out of the question. "I'll call Marcus later," she said on her way out of the room. In truth her mind was on another call, one she proceeded to make from a pay phone on a street corner several blocks from Blake's condo.

"Michael?"

"Dani! Oh, sweetheart, it's good to hear from you!"

"Same here," she said softly. The sound of his voice was like a balm. "I wanted to call sooner but I was worried about the phones being tapped and I wanted privacy."

"How're you doin'?"

"I'm . . . surviving."

"I saw it all on television at noon—the arraignment and the press conference. You looked beautiful."

"I was dying."

"It didn't show. . . . Blake handled himself well, I thought. Very dignified, very professional."

"That's his way. He's furious inside, but no one would ever know it."

"How's he . . . behaving toward you?"

"Not much differently than he always did. He did thank me for coming, but we had an audience at that particular point. He's big on appearances. Not that I mind if he ignores me most of the time. I don't want him *touching* me."

"Did he try?"

"Only for the sake of the press. He held my hand whenever there were cameras around. He kissed me once, for the cameras, but I doubt he'll try that often."

"Have you said anything to him about . . . about . . .?"

Her stomach twisted, then settled. "No. I confronted him about everything but that. It's my ace in the hole, Michael. When I use it, it'll carry weight."

"What did he say about the rest?"

"He denied that he knew what was really in the shipment. He's blaming the whole thing on Harlan. He also denied that he had anything to do with Harlan's murder."

"You asked him about *that*?"

She smiled sadly. "I've gotten bold, I guess. I wanted him to know that even though I'm here, I'm far from a blind supporter. I do believe him as far as Harlan's murder goes, though. I'm sure he had no part in that."

"I agree, but I still don't like the idea of your living with him in that condominium."

"I told him I wouldn't. I'm going to look for a house in the suburbs for us to rent. I want a yard with some trees and fresh air, plenty of bedrooms and a live-in housekeeper as a chaperone. Until then, I'm staying at my parents' place. That was where I slept last night.... My mother was wonderful. We talked for a long time. I mean, she was there, really *there*."

"Oh, sweetheart, I'm glad about that. If you get nothing else out of this ordeal, at least you'll cement your relationship with her. It's long overdue."

"I think you're right.... Michael?" She grew misty-eyed and her voice wavered. "I miss you so much. I think about you all the time."

"Me, too, Dani. I haven't known what to do with myself."

"Have you done anything with the stuff we gathered this summer?"

"No. Every time I look at it, I think of you and my mind starts to wander. I managed to go over the galleys for my book, though. They've been sitting here a while. My editor was getting pissed."

"What about your class?" He'd been appointed to teach another fall semester course at the School of Government. "Do you have much to prepare differently from last year?"

"I'll have to update things, but there's nothing major now that I've got the basic curriculum set.... How about you? Will you go up to Boston to do your radio show, or will you be staying in Washington the whole time?"

"I have to call Arthur. I'd like to continue to do the show. Being here the rest of the time is going to be bad enough. During the trial I'll have to skip the show anyway. It wouldn't be...seemly." She drawled the word with blatant sarcasm and rolled her eyes, but in so doing she caught sight of the cab. "Michael, I'd better go. My cabbie looks like he's getting impatient."

"Your cabbie?"

"I'm at a pay phone on the way to my parents'. I didn't want Blake to drive me . . . for obvious reasons. I'll give you a call in a few days?"

"I'll be waiting. I love you, sweetheart."

She smiled, but her voice was shaking again. "I love you, too. You're my strength, do you know that? Hold the fort for me, Michael."

"I will."

He threw her a kiss, which she answered with two, then she quietly replaced the receiver on its hook and ran back to her cab.

SEVERAL DAYS LATER Danica found the house she wanted. It was in Chevy Chase and was far enough from the capital to provide the respite she needed yet close enough so that Blake would have no trouble driving in to see his lawyers. Not that time was of the essence, since both she and Blake had more of it on their hands than they'd ever had before, but she'd wanted to be considerate, since she'd been the one to demand the house.

It was furnished and in move-in condition, with five bedrooms plus a suite for the help, and its yard was large, well guarded from the public by thick stands of trees. If the cost of the rental was exorbitant, Danica reasoned that it was money well spent. She chose for herself the bedroom farthest from Blake's, hired the woman she wanted, and made arrangements for Marcus to deliver the Audi.

Two weeks after Blake's arraignment, she flew back to Boston to pick up more things from the town house. While she was there, she made several calls, the last one of which was to Michael.

"I lost the radio show."

"*What?*"

"I met with Arthur today and he explained that my presence would detract from that of a guest."

"That's *absurd!*"

"I think so. I'm furious. Arthur claimed that the live call-ins we'd get would be asking questions of *me* and that he wanted to protect me from that. I argued with him, but his mind was made up.''

''Screw him, then. There'll be other opportunities for you, and when this is all over, you'll be able to laugh in his face.''

She smiled in appreciation of his championing. ''I also talked with James. He was angry, too, which made me feel a little better. You wouldn't believe it, Michael. I've called several friends to see how things were going—you know, at the Institute and the hospital—and they were cool to say the least. Some friends.''

Michael gritted his teeth. ''A little experience often upsets a lot of theory.''

''Excuse me?''

''I read that the other morning on one of your tea bags.''

She grinned. ''You're drinking tea now?''

''It settles my stomach.''

She wasn't instantly alarmed. ''Aren't you feeling well?''

''Only when I think of you down there, which is most of the time.''

''Oh, Michael...''

''I wish I were in Boston right now.'' A bulb lit. ''Hey, I could be there in an hour.''

''You'd kill yourself on I-95 making time like that, and anyway,'' she mused ruefully, ''I've got to get to the airport, and...''

He anticipated her next words and spoke with feigned mockery. ''And it will only be harder if we see each other. I know, I know. But it's so hard right now I sometimes think I'll die.''

''Don't you dare. I need to know you're there.''

''I think that's what keeps me going.... Will you call again soon?''

''As soon as I can. Take care, Michael.''

''You, too, sweetheart.''

TALKING WITH MICHAEL was her salvation. She called him every few days—Blake, for reasons of his own, had the phones checked regularly for bugs, which eased her worry—and she lived the times between with the memory of Michael's words, his gentle tone, and the knowledge of his love. They were the only things that kept *her* going when her days settled into a routine of doing little more than marking time.

The press no longer badgered; more immediate news had taken precedence. Danica wasn't a fool to think that the media wouldn't be out in force come time of the trial, but she was grateful for the temporary break.

She spent most of her time at the house in the first-floor garden room whose floor-to-ceiling windows let in whatever sunlight September had to offer. Blake had come to accept that this was *her* room, and he left her alone there to read, to knit—which she'd never done before, but which desperation now inspired—and to think.

She spent several days a week with her mother lunching, shopping, sometimes just talking. Eleanor made herself totally accessible, realizing that Danica had few friends in Washington and that those she might have had would possibly avoid her now.

"You look tired, darling," she commented one afternoon as they strolled slowly through the Smithsonian. "Maybe I shouldn't have suggested we come here. There's so much to see that it can be overwhelming."

Danica laughed softly. "I'm the one who should be worrying about you, but you seem to be holding up fine."

"I am fine, knock on wood. My leg gives me trouble from time to time, but it's nothing.... Aren't you sleeping well?"

"Oh, I sleep, but I still feel tired. I think its the tedium of the waiting. Sitting around with nothing to do but to think about where I am and why, where I *want* to be and why, where I'll be *six months* from now and why. I look down and find my knuckles white, and I realize that I've been clenching my fists without knowing it. Between tension and boredom, I sometimes think I'll lose my mind."

Eleanor hooked her elbow through her daughter's. "You won't, darling. You're strong. And what you're doing is the right thing. I know that it's difficult for you, missing Michael the way you do."

Danica smiled and offered a soft "Thank you for understanding. It's a help to know that I can tell you about things."

"Just don't tell me *too* much." Eleanor was only half joking. "Keeping things from your father is something new for me, and I'm not sure I like it."

"I'm sorry you're smack in the middle, Mom. I didn't want that."

"You didn't want to be facing a criminal trial with Blake, either, darling. Life doesn't always work out the way we want."

Danica gave a soft grunt of agreement. "Life is what happens when you're making other plans." When her mother sent her a quizzical look, she explained, "The tea sage," and Eleanor nodded.

"How's Blake taking all this?"

"He's unbelievably tense. I think he's really worried. Now that the hullabaloo has died down, he's focusing on the trial and what might, just might, happen to him if something goes wrong and he's convicted. The thought of prison, even of a minimum security one, doesn't thrill him."

"Can you blame him?"

"No. I wouldn't want to be in his shoes. He's a proud man. I think what he fears most is the humiliation."

"Does he discuss it with you?"

"We rarely talk. But then, we never did."

"He's not . . . rude to you, is he?"

"Oh, no. I don't think he'd dare because he knows that I do have an alternative to staying here in Washington with him."

Eleanor nodded. The one thing she and Danica hadn't talked about was the future. She assumed Danica would be leaving Blake once the trial was over, but she didn't want to think of that eventuality. "How is Thelma working out?"

"Just fine. She's a wonderful cook."

"I wasn't sure. You look like you've lost weight."

"I haven't been very hungry. My stomach is in knots most of the time. Blake's sitting like a stone across the table doesn't help."

"It's a trying time, darling. For both of you."

"Mmmm. You can say that again." She sighed. "Well, I am getting a beautiful sweater out of the deal. Do you remember that pretty cotton yarn I bought last week?"

"The nubby pink stuff? It was delicious."

Danica smiled at her mother's choice of words. "It's working up deliciously, too, and God knows, I've got enough time to work on it. For all I know, by the time this trial arrives, I'll have an entire wardrobe worth of sweaters."

"Is the trial still set for November?"

"The lawyers have requested that it be put off to December, ostensibly to give them more preparation time. Personally, I think it's more of a tactical move. I think they're hoping to cash in on the feeling of seasonal goodwill. It might just soften the jury."

"How long do they think the trial will last?"

Danica shrugged. "It could be a week. It could be a month." As she figured it, even allowing for the worst, she'd be back in Maine sometime in January.

"Will you do one for me?"

"Do what?"

"Knit me a sweater. I'd like to wear something you've made."

Danica squeezed her arm. "Sure. I'll do yours next." And after that she'd do the one she'd begun to picture, one designed for warmth against the cold, Down East sea air. She fantasized knitting a matching one for Michael, but knew that she couldn't be so crude as to do that in front of Blake. Maybe for Gena . . . or Cilla . . . or even Rusty . . .

BY THE FIRST WEEK IN OCTOBER Danica began to suspect that something was wrong. Well, not *wrong*, but different. And hopeful. Very hopeful.

With the knowledge that Michael's class met on Wednesdays in the back of her mind, she flew into Boston for an early afternoon doctor's appointment, then, nearly bursting with pride and pleasure and excitement, took a cab into Cambridge.

Michael was wrapping up the day's discussion with his class when she slipped into the back of the room. He paused midsentence to stare. She wore oversized dark glasses and had pulled her sandy hair into a knot under a chic fedora, but she hadn't fooled him. Not for a minute.

He cleared his throat and began to speak again, only to stammer dumbly and end up asking the class what he'd been saying. Several of his students glanced toward the back of the room and were grinning when they faced forward again. Michael failed to see their humor.

The woman he'd dreamed about for the past six weeks was thirty feet away and he still had to finish the session. Pushing away from the chair he'd been straddling, he fumbled through the notes he'd left lying on the table behind him, but his eyes couldn't seem to focus any more than his mind could. In the end, he simply deferred to the syllabus he'd given the students at their first meeting and dismissed the class.

He stood still for several minutes until the room had cleared, then stalked to the back of the room, pinned Danica to the wall and gave her the hardest, longest, most melting kiss she'd ever received. Then, having summarily dispensed with her hat, he buried his face against her hair, wrapped her in his arms and squeezed until she squealed for mercy.

"Why didn't you tell me you were coming, sweetheart? I would have called in sick, canceled my class, done anything if I'd known you were in town."

"I just came in this morning." She was beaming, eyes aglow. "Michael, it's so exciting... I tried to wait, really I did... I walked around the Square for what had to be hours... but I couldn't get here fast enough... and the man downstairs must think I'm deranged because I couldn't concentrate on the directions he gave me to find this room and I made him repeat himself three times... I'm so excited!" She clapped her hands to her lips, but her smile was as wide as ever.

Her effervescence was contagious. "What is it, Dani? My God, you're bubbling. Tell me!"

She put her hands on his shoulders. "I'm pregnant, Michael! I'm pregnant and it's *our* baby! Really *ours*, this time!"

It was the last thing Michael had expected. His eyes grew very round and his gaze dropped to her stomach while his voice jumped an octave. "Pregnant? Our baby?"

She nodded vigorously, wanting to scream and jump but controlling herself.

"Our baby?" There was wonder in his tone as he placed his palm where his gaze had been. "You're going to have our baby." This time it was a statement, and it was followed by a bone-crushing hug that lifted Danica clear off her feet. "Oh, sweetheart, that's *wonderful* news!" He set her down again. "You're sure?" When she nodded, he swept her up again.

Just then the nearby door opened and a young man entered. He stopped when he saw Michael and Danica, and grew red. "Uh, excuse me." He was about to retreat when Michael held him there.

"No, no. You've got your class. We're just leaving." Dragging Danica by the hand, he raced through the door, down the hall and into the office that had been loaned him for his afternoons at the school. When the door was firmly shut, he ushered her to a chair, then knelt by her knees. "When did you find out?"

She was clutching his hand and couldn't stop grinning. "This afternoon. I've been feeling lousy for a while and I assumed it was because of everything down there—" she gestured vaguely "—but when I missed my second period I knew. I flew in this morning to see my doctor here, and he confirmed it. I'm just so excited! You have no idea!"

"I think I do. You'd be bouncing off the walls if I hadn't pushed you into this chair. Hell, I'd be bouncing off them myself if I didn't have to hold you here!"

She took his face in her hands and kissed him softly. "I love you so much, Michael. Our baby is going to be so precious and bright and fantastic."

He closed his eyes and wondered if he was dreaming. "I know it will. Oh, Dani, I've missed you so much!" His voice cracked and he pressed his forehead to hers. "This means you'll come back to me."

"I'd have come back to you, baby or no baby."

He looked at her and his expression was urgent. "But you can do it now. Blake can't expect you to suffer down there when you're carrying another man's child."

"But I'm going to," she said with no less urgency. "Don't you see, Michael? The fact that I'm pregnant will help his case all the more."

"You want to help *him*?"

"I want to be free of him! That's what this whole farce is about. By sticking with him through the trial, I'll be discharging the last of my responsibilities as his wife."

"You don't owe him anything."

"But you know me, Michael. You know how I feel and what I've been raised to believe. This is the perfect solution for me. When the trial's over and I leave Blake, no one can say that I didn't do right by him."

"Your father will."

"Not when he hears what I have to say. And if he still insists that my place is with Blake, well, that's his problem. I won't feel any guilt."

Michael sat back on his heels. "That's what this is all about, isn't it? Guilt."

She reached out to touch his cheek. "I don't want anything to mar our marriage or the happiness we'll have together and with our baby. If we do it my way, nothing will."

He stood then and walked slowly across the room. "I still don't like it, Dani. Maybe I don't trust Blake. Who *knows* how he'll react when you tell him about the baby."

"He'll be thrilled, particularly knowing that he is the way *he* is. He'll love the idea of my sitting in the courtroom wearing maternity clothes. His lawyers will love it, too. The jury will be sympathetic. So will the press."

"Hell, I don't want you going through all that! The strain could do any number of things to you . . . or to our child."

Danica wasn't about to be deterred from her goal. "You're thinking about my miscarriage, but I asked the doctor about that and he doesn't see any problem. In the first place, I'll be sitting at home doing practically nothing for the next two months, and by the time the trial comes, I'll be past the critical stage. In the second place, the doctor saw nothing to suggest that there was anything wrong."

"He didn't foresee any problems last time."

Danica left her chair and went to him. "Last time it wasn't meant to be. Look at what's happened since, and you'll know I'm right." Taking his hand, she placed it on her stomach. "This time's different. I know it. I can feel it. And the fact that I've been feeling so awful is a good sign."

"It is?"

She nodded. "The doctor said so. It's when a baby takes well that a woman more often has things like morning sickness."

"You've had that?"

"It was what tipped me off. But it's nothing, not when I know its cause." She smiled, her heart overflowing with love for both the man before her and the baby inside her. "I feel so good now. I feel so happy. You can't be with me through that trial, but at least I'll have your baby. Do you know what that means to me?"

He looked from one to another of her features, then traced each with fingers that trembled. "I know that you have to be the most wonderful woman in the world," he murmured hoarsely. "I also know that the next few months are going to be absolute torment for me. Now I've got two of you to worry about."

Wide-eyed, she grinned. "Isn't it wonderful?"

He held his breath for a minute, then chuckled and shook his head. "You're amazing."

"Another variation on 'the most wonderful woman in the world.' Kiss me, bud. I've got to get back to the airport."

He kissed her then, and again more than once as he drove her to Logan. She was high on happiness, and it pleased him to see her that way. The knowledge that he was both biologically and emotionally responsible for that happiness was some comfort, given the many misgivings he had about allowing her to return to Washington.

AFTER LANDING AT NATIONAL, she drove directly to see her mother. She was still bubbling and knew she'd have to settle down before she faced Blake.

The housekeeper answered the door. "Ruth, where's my mother?" she asked, sweeping past.

"Upstairs, Mrs. Lindsay. She and Senator Marshall were about to sit down for dinner."

"Dinner!"

Just then Eleanor appeared at the top of the stairs. "Darling! I didn't expect you!"

"And I didn't realize how late it was! But I had to see you."
Danica paused, and for the first time in hours her smile wavered. "Where's Daddy?"

Eleanor started down the stairs. "On the phone in the den.
What's happened? You look..." She gestured eloquently with
her hands.

"I am." Taking her arm, Danica led her into the living
room. "I'm pregnant, Mom. It was confirmed today."

Eleanor turned to face her, her eyes wide with the very excitement Danica needed. "Pregnant? Darling, that's wonderful!" She hugged her, then set her back. "What does
Blake say?"

It hadn't occurred to Danica that her mother wouldn't immediately sense the truth. "Blake doesn't know yet. I'm going
to tell him in a little while." The chill in her tone was a hint.

"Darling..." Eleanor stared at her daughter for a long
minute, then let out a soft breath. "It's Michael's, isn't it?"

Danica nodded, smiling again. "You have no idea how
happy he's made me. First loving me, then giving me his
child. It's exactly what I need to see me through everything
here."

"Have you told him?"

Again Danica nodded. "I flew up to Boston this morning
to see my doctor there."

"You said you were driving to Virginia for the day."

"I didn't want to say anything. Not until I knew for sure.
And Michael teaches in Cambridge on Wednesdays, so I took
a cab over after my appointment. We didn't have long to
spend together, but I wanted him to be the first to know."

"How did he take the news?"

"He was thrilled but worried. He's concerned that the trial
will be too much of a strain. He wanted me to go back to
Maine with him, but I told him I wouldn't."

"You wouldn't?"

"No. I owe Blake this much, Mom. You and Daddy didn't
raise me to be a stoic for nothing." She squeezed Eleanor's
hand. "I'm so excited. Be happy for me."

Eleanor hugged her. "I am, darling. Truly."

"Is that Danica?" William's roar came from the upper floor. Moments later, he was trotting down the stairs and joining them in the living room.

"William, Danica has the best news we've heard in months. She's pregnant!"

"Well, it's about time...again." He leaned forward to kiss Danica's cheek. "Congratulations, honey. At least Blake will have something to keep him going now."

"Thanks, Daddy," Danica said quietly, sending her mother a warning glance. "I've got to run."

"Blake doesn't know yet, William," Eleanor explained, realizing that her husband might well pick up the phone and unwittingly spill the beans. "Danica's going to tell him to-night."

"Special dinner, eh? Well, then, run along. He'll be wait-ing."

Danica kissed her mother, waved to her father, then was out the door feeling like a little girl going off to school. Of course, there had been only a handful of days when her parents had seen her off as a child. For the first time she realized that her resentment had passed, and she guessed that it had some-thing to do with her improved relationship with her mother and the understanding that had come forthwith. At least El-eanor now saw her as an adult. She wondered when her fa-ther would, *if* he would.

But that, too, didn't seem to matter anymore. Her father would always be her father, but, come trial's end, she in-tended to live her own life.

BLAKE WAS AT THE DOOR when she arrived home. "Where have you been? I was worried."

She stepped past him and set her purse on the table in the hall. "I told you I'd be gone for the day."

"You could have seen a doctor here. There was no need for you to traipse all the way to Boston."

"I wanted to see the doctor I know. This town is strange enough for me as it is." Looking in the mirror, she removed her hat and smoothed her hair.

"Well, what's the verdict? Will you be well enough to stand by me through the trial as you promised?"

"I don't see why not." She turned to face him. "I'm pregnant."

"You're *what*?"

She laughed aloud, partly because his expression held such disbelief, partly because she was feeling so very, very good. "I'm pregnant, Blake. The baby's due in May." When he continued to stare, she couldn't resist a barb. "Aren't you pleased? If I'm lucky, I'll be into maternity clothes by the time of the trial. Think of how good that'll look on your behalf."

"I don't need your sarcasm, Danica."

She felt duly chastised. Regardless of the disdain she felt for Blake, he was going through a difficult time. "I'm sorry," she said and meant it. "It's just that this is the best thing that's happened to me in the last seven weeks and I'm very happy about it."

He was scowling. "Is it Buchanan's?"

She tempered a sudden burst of anger. "I haven't been with anyone else."

"And you didn't bother to think about birth control?"

"Honestly? No. You and I were married for eight years before I conceived. I've never had to think about birth control."

"Maybe you wanted it. Maybe you wanted his baby."

"Subconsciously I assume I did. I certainly do now."

"Does he know about it?"

"Yes." She was prepared to tell him how delighted Michael was, but he didn't ask.

"Who else knows?"

"That I'm pregnant? Just my parents."

"That it's Buchanan's child," Blake specified in a growl.

"Only my mother."

"Are you planning to keep it that way?"

She couldn't believe what he was asking. "Do you mean, am I planning on telling the world that this child isn't yours? What kind of fool do you take me for, Blake? Why in the hell do you think I'm doing all this?"

He looked at her strangely. "I don't think I've ever heard you swear before."

"There are *lots* of things you've never heard me say or seen me do, because I spent the first twenty-eight years of my life

in a padded cell and the past two working my way out of it.
I'm growing up, Blake. You—and my father—had better realize that. I've got thoughts and feelings, and I get angry
when someone insults my intelligence, which is what you did
a second ago. The fact is that I'd *never* be here with you if it
weren't for the trouble you've gotten yourself into.''

"I didn't *get myself* into trouble."

"All right. The trouble *Harlan* got you into.... Did you
think I came down here for the sake of some great love we
share?''

His surprisingly meek "no" was more powerful than the
most loudly shouted curse, because it reminded her once
again that he was facing hard times, and she felt instantly
contrite.

"Blake," she sighed, speaking softly, "I'm here because I
felt that my presence would help your case. Call it 'for old
times' sake' or whatever else you will, but I wanted to do it.
For you, and for my father." She smiled sadly. "Old habits die
hard, but they do eventually die. While this one still has a
breath of life, I'm using it to help you. A public announce-
ment that this child is Michael's is *not* going to help you." The
discussion had drained her and she spoke slowly. "Please.
Trust me to do what's right."

His words, too, came slowly and held an undercurrent of
defeat. "I guess I have no other choice, do I?"

"No." She straightened her shoulders and moved toward
the stairs. "I feel tired. I think I'll lie down for a while."

She was halfway up the stairs when he called after her. "Is
everything well ... with the baby and all?"

She smiled then, offered a confident "Yes. Yes, I think
everything's just fine," and continued up the stairs.

Chapter Eighteen

"WHAT HAPPENED?"

"I told him last night."

"Was he angry?"

"A little, at first. He came around though."

"On his own?"

Danica sighed. "Actually, with a little help. I lost my temper. I reminded him in no uncertain terms exactly what I was doing in Washington. I think my bluntness helped. He couldn't argue with anything I said, and my saying it got it out in the open. I also think that he's finally accepted defeat where I'm concerned."

"It's about time."

"Mmmm. He even asked me if everything was all right with the baby."

Michael tightened his grip on the phone. "Is it? How are you feeling today?"

"Not bad. The nausea comes and goes. It's always worse on an empty stomach, so I try to eat a little something as often as I can. I slept late this morning, too, and that helped."

"Good. How did Blake act today? Is he getting used to the idea?"

"I think so. He's been surprisingly cordial. He came in to me in the middle of the morning to ask if there was anything I needed."

"What did you say to that?"

"I wanted to say that I needed *you*, but I restrained myself. No sense rubbing salt on the wound. Blake knows he's lost."

"Just make sure he remembers it," Michael growled.

A SIMILAR THEME emerged in their conversation several days later. "It's like there's a truce in effect, Michael. I think it's much better for both of us. We talk more than we did before, and he's been solicitous when I've been sick."

"Not *too* solicitous, I hope."

She chuckled. "It could never be that, not with Blake. A leopard doesn't change its spots. They may fade in one season or another, but—"

"Is that true?"

"I don't know, but it sounds good for the purposes of my analogy, don't you think?"

"You're impossible, Dani," he said with affection.

"Well, I just don't want you to worry, but you do, don't you?"

"That Blake's going to try to win you back? Of course I do. I'm only human, and I feel particularly so, sitting up here all alone."

"You're not alone. You've got Rusty."

"Umm, the Labrador philosopher. Let me tell you, he may be great for helping me run my aggression out on the beach, but as a confidant, he leaves something to be desired."

Danica laughed, then paused. "You shouldn't worry, at least not about that, Michael. There's no way Blake could possibly win me back. I'm yours. The time I spend here is...is obligatory. Blake doesn't do anything in the least suggestive. He certainly doesn't touch me. I think that his verbal show of concern is as close as he can come to an apology for all he's put me through."

"There's more to come. That's what really worries me. Did his lawyers get the December date they wanted?"

"Uh-huh."

"Does Blake talk about it?"

"He's starting to, but I sometimes think that he's oblivious to my presence when he does. It's almost as if he's talking to himself, as if what's going on in his mind simply needs airing. He could as well be in an empty room, though. He doesn't expect any response from me. Maybe he's too embarrassed to look me in the eye."

"Has he told anyone of your pregnancy?"

"His lawyers. They were pleased."

"Do they know the truth?"

"No. Blake and I agreed on that. For all practical purposes, at least until the trial's over, this baby is his."

"I don't like that."

"It's all part of the scheme, though, and if I don't follow my game plan, *all* of this will have been a waste."

"I suppose. I still don't like it."

She smiled softly. "That's because you love me."

"Smart lady."

THE FOLLOWING WEEK Danica called Michael with an interesting piece of news. "You will *never* guess what happened this morning."

"You felt the baby kick?"

She laughed. "Not yet. It's much too soon. It's still a teeny, teeny thing, Michael."

"Oh ... You caught Blake talking to the wall?"

"Maybe in time that, too, but not yet."

Michael was enjoying the banter. He always did with Danica. But then, hearing her voice was what he enjoyed most, because only at those times when they talked did he feel truly secure. "Okay. I give up. What happened this morning?"

"I got a call from *Boston* magazine. They want me to keep a journal of what I'm experiencing waiting for the trial, then of the trial itself. They think it would make a dynamite article."

Michael stiffened. "Will you do it?"

"Certainly not! I told the fellow that it was too personal, that I couldn't possibly think of writing my private feelings for a magazine. When he offered me good money, I told him that it would be immoral for me to even think of cashing in on my husband's ordeal. That didn't sink in; he had the gall to ask if he could send a reporter down at intervals to interview me. Can you believe that?"

"Oh, I can believe it all right. I *know* how reporters work."

"Not all of them are like that. By the way, I had lunch with Cilla yesterday."

"I know. She called me last night. She knew I was worried about you and wanted to tell me that you look wonderful."

"We had a nice time together. She said she and Jeff are looking for a place."

Cilla had told Michael that, too. "But she's fighting the idea of remarriage."

"I know. And I feel badly. I guess Jeff wants it very much. But Cilla feels that they've got a good thing going now and that they ought to give it more time before they get 'tangled' in legal papers again. I think she'll give in after they've lived together for a while."

". . . Dani? How do you feel about Jeff?"

"I think he's great!"

"You don't hold anything against him, then?"

"Because his investigation exposed Eastbridge? Of course not. He was doing his job. But it was just as well that he wasn't there yesterday. I'm not sure Blake would have appreciated it. He's not quite as understanding."

"Then he doesn't know the connection between Cilla and Jeff?"

"Not yet."

"Did he give you any flack about seeing Cilla?"

"He was nervous at first. He knew Cilla was a reporter and he was worried she'd sink her claws into me and that I'd inadvertently say something I shouldn't. I told him that our meeting was personal, not professional, and I reminded him that Cilla was my friend and *your* sister."

"He must have loved that," Michael quipped.

"It did shut him up. But I have to give him some credit. He's been remarkably understanding of my need to get out. I have the freedom to come and go as I please."

"Do you? Do you get out much?"

She sighed and shifted the phone on her shoulder. "Actually, no. Where would I go? It's not as if I have friends here. I see Mom, and now Cilla, but that's really the extent of it."

Michael remembered how, when she'd been with him, they'd gone out each day, how she'd enjoyed meeting new friends and seeing old ones. "It must be lonely for you. What do you do with yourself?"

"I sleep." She smirked. "I've been doing that a lot. I've been knitting, too. You should see the baby blanket I'm making, Michael. It's almost done and it's adorable. I think I'll make several—I've felt so good working on it because I think about the baby and about you and how wonderful things will be next spring.''

"I like it when you say that. Sometimes I get discouraged.''

"Oh, Michael, you shouldn't. You know that it's only a matter of time.''

"It's always been a matter of time. I guess I'm just getting more impatient. I keep thinking about how much I want to be with you. I want to see every change in your body as the baby grows.''

"There's nothing much to see yet. My breasts are bigger. That's all.''

"That's *all*,'' Michael croaked, squeezing his eyes shut against the images that filled them. "Oh, sweetheart, this is doing nothing for my peace of mind, much less my, uh, my bodily state.''

Her voice came very softly. "Then, we're even. I lie in bed at night remembering all the ways you've touched me and wanting you to do it again. I love you so much, Michael.''

He sucked in an unsteady breath. "I love you even more, sweetheart. And I will do all those things again. I promise.''

"GUESS WHAT! Greta's pregnant too!''

Danica burst into a grin. "That's fantastic! Does she know about ours?''

"I told her. I told them both. I had to, Dani. We've been so close for so long and I was so excited when Greta told me their news that I just couldn't keep it in. She and Pat are pretty isolated, at least from the other people you know. They won't say a word—''

"It's okay! I'm glad you told them. It's not fair that you have to hide so much. I feel awful about that, Michael. I may be committed to letting the world think this is Blake's baby for now, but believe me when I say that I don't like it any more than you do.''

"I understand why you're doing what you are.''

"But I'm proud that my baby's yours, and it makes me sick to think of Blake taking the credit.... His lawyers did leak it to the press, by the way. There was a small notice on the society page two days ago.''

''Any reaction from that?''

''Not that I know of.'' Danica hesitated for a minute, thinking about the argument she'd had with Blake concerning concealing the true parentage of the baby. But there were times to bend, times when it was safe to bend, as in the case of Greta and Pat and the person she now considered. ''Michael? I'd like you to tell Gena. She'll be so excited, and I think she'll understand what I'm doing.''

Michael smiled and let out a breath. ''I know she will. Thanks, sweetheart. I've been wanting to tell her, but I didn't dare. Maybe I'll take a drive up there tomorrow.''

''She'd like that.''

''*I*'d like that.''

''How is . . . everyone in town?''

''Very well. They ask about you all the time.''

''Do you sense any hostility?''

''Because of the case, you mean? None. These people are different, Dani. They were never snowed because of who you were. They never particularly made the connection between you and Blake.''

''I was always with you. They probably know more of the truth than anyone.''

''If they do, they're not gossiping. They adore you. In fact, to a person, they've been totally sympathetic. Their main concern is that you're stuck in Washington having to face Blake's trial. They want you back up here.''

''So do I.''

''And I . . . How are you feeling?''

''About the same.''

''No cramps?''

''No, thank God. Just a constant queasiness. The doctor says it'll pass. I see him again at the beginning of the month.'' She gave him the exact day and time. It was, of course, on a Wednesday.

''Can I come with you?''

''Oh . . . I don't know . . . that might be pretty risky.''

''But what if I was just a friend, meeting you at the airport and chauffeuring you around.''

"You're not just a friend. I don't think we can carry the charade that far. Don't tell me you'd be satisfied sitting meekly in the waiting room while I see the doctor. Knowing you, you'll want to be in there with me asking a million questions. It'd never work, Michael. The doctor, the nurse, the receptionist—they'd all be sure to know."

"Well, then, at least meet me for lunch before my class."

She grinned. "Now *that* I think I can arrange."

"Good. I found this terrific Indonesian place. It's dark and you can wear your disguise—you know, a hat and dark glasses—and no one will ever know it's you. Hell, I might even forget it myself and think that I'm with a glamorous movie star. . . ."

DANICA WAS FEELING LOWER when she called Michael next. She'd hesitated for a long time but had finally dialed his number in pure selfishness.

"I'm warning you ahead of time, Michael," she began instantly. "I know that you expect a sweet, intelligent being, but you're about to witness something very different."

"What's wrong?" he asked in alarm.

"I'm going out of my *mind*! Some days are worse than others, but today was the pits! I started by throwing up, but that's nothing new, so I won't even comment on it." She spoke slowly then, clearly struggling to contain her frustration. "I have been walking around this house all day bored to tears. I don't feel like knitting. I don't feel like reading. I don't feel like going out because there's nowhere to go and no one to go with. Blake's been sitting in the living room staring at the walls and I don't want to talk to him anyway. His tension is contagious. He's coiled like a spring, and I get that way being with him for more than a minute. I don't have anything to do, Michael, at least not something that will take my mind off all this." She let out a loud breath. "So I'm calling you . . . and feeling guilty about whining."

He was so relieved that there wasn't a physical problem that he actually smiled. "Whine all you want, sweetheart. That's what I'm here for."

"It's not. You don't deserve it. You weren't the one who asked for this. *I* was."

"You didn't ask for it, Dani."

"But I was the one who chose to play the martyr."

"True," he drawled in an attempt to humor her. He knew that pregnant women leaned toward pickles and tears, but he hadn't thought to consider mood swings until now. On the other hand, he reasoned, even beyond pregnancy she had plenty of justification for testiness. The best he could do was to try to talk it out of her. "Why was Blake so bad today? Has something happened with his case?"

"Not necessarily today, but the tension's mounting. His lawyers are beginning to get a look at the documents the government has. Blake's signature is right there on the license application filed with the Commerce Department, then again on a paper okaying the shipment, but then, he knew it was. He still claims that he didn't know the integrated circuits were in the machines *or* that the machines were headed for Russia."

"Can he prove it?"

"No. But the lawyers feel there's a solid case for reasonable doubt. The prosecution has to prove his guilt beyond that if they want a conviction, but most of what they have is circumstantial evidence. It may be strong circumstantial evidence, but it is only circumstantial.... Still, there are so many ifs. I think that's what's getting Blake down. I don't know, maybe it's just boredom for him, too. And he doesn't have *you* to talk to."

"Does he talk to anyone?"

"Oh, yes. He plays squash at the health club several times a week and he sees old friends. But he's been warned not to say anything relating to the case and since that's what's preoccupying his mind these days, he really has no outlet other than Jason and Ray." She growled. "I'm getting tired of them, too. They say the same things over and over again."

Michael chuckled. "That's because you tune out and you don't hear the fine differences." He paused and grew more hesitant. "Dani, what if the jury finds Blake guilty? How will you feel?"

"I've thought about that a lot. I'll be sorry, I guess. I'd hate to see Blake go to prison. But it won't make any difference in my own plans. My job is to see him through the trial, to help him present the best image possible. If it doesn't work, well, it's out of my hands.''

"I was wondering.''

"Worrying, you mean. Don't, Michael. Is this or is this not the voice of a woman of conviction?''

"It certainly is, but that woman's also got a hell of a lot of compassion.''

"Which is why I'm praying that Blake will be acquitted. For *his* sake, not mine. My own course is set.''

"Does he know what it is?''

"He has to have guessed. We don't ever talk about it, about what's going to be after the trial, but he knows how I feel about you and the baby, and he's not dumb.''

"Does he know that we talk?''

"The phone bill came in last week.''

"Y' know, Dani, I've asked you more than once to call collect.''

"It's not a matter of money, and I don't want to call collect. I'm beyond caring if Blake knows we talk, and he hasn't said a word. Maybe he knows I'd be off the walls if I didn't have you to talk with.''

"You know you do. I'm always here.''

"Except on Wednesdays.''

"Except on Wednesdays. Are you all set for next week?''

"You bet, and I can't wait. It's been so long.... Michael?''

"What, love?''

"Thank you.''

"For what?''

"For letting me spout off like that.''

"Do you feel better?''

She smiled. "Yes.''

"Then it was worth every minute.''

EARLY THE FOLLOWING WEDNESDAY Danica flew into Boston. She'd made her doctor's appointment for midmorning so that she and Michael would have that much longer together. Though she'd expected to take a cab to the restaurant Michael had named, she was thrilled to walk out of the medical building and find the Blazer parked in front.

Quickening her step in time with her pulse, she climbed through the door Michael leaned to open, and slid onto the front seat and into his arms. He held her tightly for several moments, neither of them able to speak through the flood of emotions. Only when the driver of a slightly battered, if vintage, Mustang passed, honked and offered a thumb up did Michael set her back.

"Smart aleck kid," he murmured, but his eyes quickly returned to Danica's features. His fingers followed, then his lips, and by the time he drew back again she was floating on a cloud.

"Ahhh, Michael, that felt so good."

"You can open your eyes now."

"But will you be here?" she murmured, cinching her arms around his neck. "I can feel you, but I'm still afraid it's a dream."

"No dream, love. Open up."

She raised her lids slowly, and to her chagrin her eyes were filled with tears. Burying her face against his neck, she let him soothe her until she was more composed.

"Nothing's wrong, is it?" he asked in concern.

She brushed at the tears that lingered on her lower lids and shook her head. "I'm just so happy to see you."

He let out a breath. "Everything went well with the doctor then?"

"Wonderfully. I'm back to my normal weight."

"Back to?"

"I'd lost a few pounds at the beginning when I couldn't eat."

"But you can now?"

"Oh, yes. And I'm not anemic or anything. I have a prescription for vitamins, and he offered to give me something for the nausea, but I really don't want to take a thing. I don't trust drugs. Ten years down the road there's apt to be some horrible revelation that they cause mental block or something."

Michael chuckled. "I'm just as glad you're not taking them . . . as long as you're not too sick."

"Only when I'm hungry, and I'm hungry now. Let's go get some lunch, uh, brunch, before I barf all over your car. I didn't have much more than a piece of toast before I left Washington. I was too excited to eat.''

Tucking her close beside him, Michael headed off. When they'd been seated in the restaurant—he'd changed his mind and opted for simple American food rather than Indonesian in deference to the sensitivity of Danica's stomach—he wrapped her arm through his.

"I've eaten here once before, but the company wasn't half as nice.''

"Was she pretty?''

"Actually, there were three of them.''

"Three *women*?''

"Three professors. One was fat and bald, the second was thin and bald, and the third was so myopic that he kept his face close to his plate the whole time and didn't say a word.''

"Poor man.''

"Don't waste your sympathy. I understand he comes to life in the classroom. His course is one of the most popular at the school.'' Michael glanced around at the other patrons of the restaurant, then reached down and tugged Danica's chair even closer.

"We're taking chances sitting like this,'' she teased, leaning into him.

"Nah. No one will recognize either of us. With that wedding band of yours, they'll assume we're a happily married couple. Hell, Blake's borrowing my kid; the least he can do is to loan me his ring for a little while.'' His eyes were glued to her smiling face. "Cilla was right. You do look wonderful. Still a little tired, maybe, but you've got good color.''

"You look wonderful, too, Michael. Tell me what you've been doing.''

First he snagged a waitress to bring bread sticks for Danica. While she was munching, he explained that he'd finally begun to organize the notes they'd made the summer before. "There's still a load of research to be done, and I want to interview several other men who've been salvaging. They're all on the northeast coast, though, so it won't be a hassle. If I can get that out of the way before spring, everything else can be done at home.''

She knew he was thinking of when she'd be joining him, and she squeezed his arm in silent appreciation. "Does your editor like the idea?"

"Very much. The book won't be terribly philosophical, but it'll be a good read. Hey, have the publishers set a date for *your* book?"

She nodded and there was a wry twist to her lips. "January."

"That soon? I thought they were talking of March or April."

"They were. They've pushed it up."

"Did they say why?"

"Oh, yes. They were honest enough, I have to give them that." She paused. "They feel that the publicity surrounding the trial in December will familiarize the public with my name. They want to take advantage of that."

"Just what you didn't want."

"Mmmm. They may have a point in terms of sales, but I was a little disappointed. Especially for James. This is his book. I hate to have it tainted—"

"'Tainted' is *not* the case, Dani. There's nothing 'tainted' about you. You'll shine through that trial like the special lady you are. People will admire you. Wait and see. *Boston* won't be the only magazine after you."

She rolled her eyes. "Heaven help me then. I don't want to see *any* of them. When that trial's over, I'm leaving Washington, leaving Boston and taking up permanent residence in Maine. When I think of that, of being with you every day for the rest of our lives—well, I realize that I'm very, very lucky." She stopped talking and a pensive expression crossed her face.

"What is it?"

"Reggie came to see me yesterday."

"Did she!" Though Michael had never met Reggie Nichols, he felt that he knew her, what with all Danica had told him. "How's she doing?"

"Not great. It's amazing, the twists and turns life can take. At one point I thought my future hinged on being the best female tennis player in the world. When I quit, I was relieved but I also felt that I'd lost my claim to immortality. Now I look at Reggie. She's been at the top, she's had it all, and she's miserable. She's decided to retire when the current tour ends next March, and she's going through a real career crisis.''

''Still doesn't know what to do?''

''She says she'll probably coach, but she's not looking forward to it. When you've been in the limelight as long as she has, it's hard to step out. It'd be one thing if she had a family, a man or children to fulfill her, but she doesn't.''

''Many women today don't need that.''

''I know. But I don't think Reggie's one of them. I know I'm not.'' She leaned forward and kissed him softly on the mouth. ''That's why I'm so lucky. I look at Reggie and then at myself and I realize that I'd rather have my life any day. My future looks so bright . . . well, after December at least.''

They talked then about what was happening in Washington, and once their food had arrived, they talked between bites about all the other little things they hadn't spoken of on the phone. Michael suggested several good books she should read. Danica suggested a good movie he should see.

''When did you see it?'' he asked.

''Blake took me last week.''

''He's taking you out now?''

''Not often, and only in desperation. He doesn't know what to do with himself any more than I do.''

''Does he worry about bumping into people?''

''He did at first, I think. But depression does wonders. When things get so that you know you'll go mad if you don't get out, the risk of seeing people becomes secondary.'' She looked down at her sweater and frowned. ''Have I spilled something?''

''No. Why?''

''You keep looking at my, uh, breasts.''

He colored. ''I guess I want to see if . . . if they're really getting bigger.''

She laughed. ''Michael Buchanan!''

''Don't 'Michael Buchanan' me!'' He put his mouth to her ear. ''If it's my baby that's doing it, I want to see.''

She reached for the hem of the sweater. ''If you'd like, I can take this off.''

He stopped her hand with his, then moved lower to feel her belly. ''I can't wait until this grows. I dream of you lying in the living room several months from now, wearing nothing but the firelight. It'll cast a beautiful glow over your skin and I'll warm my hands on your big, fat, beautiful belly.''

She sucked in a breath, then moaned softly. "I knew this was going to be hard."

"It sure is." Before she realized what he was doing, he'd slid her hand to his fly and was pressing it close. Closing his eyes, he inhaled deeply; his exhalation was a throaty groan.

"Michael!" she whispered hoarsely, looking furtively around. "We're in a restaurant!"

"I'd do it anywhere, I'm that horny."

"You are a sex fiend."

He opened one eye. "But it is good with us, isn't it?"

She was grinning. "It is."

When he felt her fingers actively cupping him, he threw back her barb. "Danica! We're in a restaurant!"

"Mmmm..."

MICHAEL HAD TROUBLE teaching his class that afternoon, not so much because of his state of physical frustration as that of mental. He kept thinking about Danica returning to Washington, languishing in the house with nothing to do, and he realized that he'd been very thick. He couldn't drive back to Maine fast enough to get to work.

The next night, when Danica called, he was full of mystery. "I'm sending something down for you."

"Something? What is it?"

"You'll see. Can you be at the Lincoln Memorial at noon tomorrow?"

"Will you be there?" she asked excitedly.

"Not me. A messenger."

"What kind of messenger?"

"One bearing my surprise."

"*What* surprise?"

"You'll see then. Can you be there?"

"Of course I can, but the suspense may kill me. Can't you even give me a hint?"

"Nope."

"How will I know who your messenger is?"

"You'll know."

"Michael..." she warned, but he wasn't about to be coaxed.

"Indulge me. Noon tomorrow. The Lincoln Memorial."

DANICA WAS THERE EARLY. She looked all around her, but the faces she saw were both unfamiliar and in self-contained groups focused on the large statue of a seated Lincoln. Taking their lead, she studied the statue. Its gentleness, the look of wisdom about it, had always appealed to her. Michael knew that of all the memorials in Washington this was her favorite. She sensed he'd purposely chosen it as a rendezvous point.

Tucking her hands in the pockets of her coat, she surveyed the sightseers again, then slowly turned in time to see a cab pull up to the nearby curb. She glanced at her watch. It was still five minutes before the hour. She was about to turn back to the statue when a small, silver-haired woman emerged from the cab. After only a moment's pause, she started excitedly down the steps.

"Gena!" she called, then waved when the other woman looked up and grinned. Running the rest of the way, Danica hugged her soundly. "Oh, Gena, it is *so good* to see you!"

Gena was beaming when Danica finally held her back. "I'll have you know that this is the first time I've left Maine in three years."

"And you came just to deliver Michael's surprise?"

Nodding, Gena gestured back toward the cab. "It's inside. Come on. We'll find somewhere to eat and then we can talk."

Danica followed her back into the cab, then at Gena's suggestion gave the cabbie the name of a restaurant where she knew they'd be able to sit quietly and visit. Only when she settled back on the seat did Gena pass her the parcel Michael had sent. It was a large, thickly stuffed mailing envelope with Danica's name written in his bold script on the front.

"What's *in* here?"

"Papers and notes and assignments."

"Assignments?"

"Michael felt you could use something to help pass the time. The papers and notes are some of those the two of you made last summer. The assignments are suggestions of things you can research at the National Archives. He reasoned that since you were here, you could really help him out. He also said something about the Archives being a very peaceful, inspiring place to work.''

Danica laughed in utter delight and hugged the bundle to her chest. ''He is fantastic! I've been complaining about how bored I am. It'll be wonderful to have something to do!''

Gena gently touched her cheek. ''That may be part of why he sent it, but I'm sure that you'll be helping him, too. The work needs to be done and he's been so distracted.''

''I know. This all must be nearly as hard on him as it is on me.''

''It's just that he feels helpless. He was furious that he didn't think of this sooner. You only have a month before the trial begins, but if this helps pass the time, then you'll be doing *both* of you a favor.... You do look beautiful, Danica. How are you feeling?''

''Great! Well, better, at least.'' She glanced toward the thick plastic separating them from the cabbie and lowered her voice instinctively. ''I'll be through the third month in another two weeks. I think things are settling down.''

''I feel for you. I was so sick carrying Michael and Cilla.'' She paused. ''Any chance it might be two?''

''I asked the doctor that, but he doubts it. Twins usually skip a generation. Our children may be the lucky ones. It's still too early to tell with me, but I'll be happy with a single healthy baby.''

Gena squeezed her arm. ''We *all* will.'' She shivered and grinned. ''I think I'm nearly as excited as Michael and you. It won't be my first grandchild, but, well, Michael and I have always been like souls. And you'll be so *close*!''

Danica felt gratified, then grew hesitant. ''Gena? You do understand why I'm doing what I am now?''

''I love you all the more for it. Loyalty is a very fine quality, Dani. I know that there are times when you've felt it was a thorn in your side—''

''Michael told you about that?''

''He's told me most everything now and I'm glad he has. The way I see it, the only problem in your life is that your allegiances have been thrust on you. Now that you've chosen the direction of your own future, loyalty and responsibility will be positive forces. I know I've said this before, but it stands repeating. I couldn't have wished for a better woman for my son.''

Choking up, Danica hugged Gena again. ''I'll be very lucky having a mother-in-law like you,'' she whispered. ''Thank you—for coming today, for being Michael's mother, for making him the kind of person he is.''

''Don't thank me,'' Gena chided softly. ''Loving is what makes life worthwhile.''

Much later, after they'd eaten, Danica thought of Gena's words again. Smiling, she pulled the tag from the tea bag which lay damp and drained on her saucer. ''True love is the renaissance of life,' '' she read. Then she slipped the tag into her purse while Gena smiled knowingly.

THE WORK MICHAEL HAD ASSIGNED HER was a godsend and Danica told him that. ''I don't know what I'd *do* if I didn't have something to divert my mind. It's been really bad here. Jason and Ray are over every night working with Blake. They want him to take the stand.''

''It makes sense. He gives an impressive appearance and he's articulate. He'll come across looking and sounding like an honest, respectable businessman who was conned by one of his employees.''

''That's what they're hoping, but they want to make sure he's prepared. They go over and over his testimony, coaching him on exactly what words to use. Then they turn around and play the prosecution, trying to put him on the spot or get him to contradict himself or somehow punch a hole in his credibility. I'm usually asleep by the time they leave, but Blake is always a zombie in the morning. I try to cheer him up, but there's really nothing I can say.''

''He's still not thinking about the future?''

''Not about mine. He referred once to returning to the Department when all this is done, but he grew stony after that and I assume he was thinking about the alternative. Even if he *is* acquitted, the President may ask him to resign.''

"That would be illegal. Given our system of justice, a man is innocent until proven guilty, and if Blake's acquitted by a jury..."

"But we both know that little phrase 'beyond a reasonable doubt,' and we both know that, realistically, Blake is probably washed up here. Even if he *is* acquitted, he'll always carry a certain stigma. It's not right, but I think it's one of the things that worries him."

"And politics is politics," Michael mused. "Suing the President of the United States would be tantamount to political suicide. Blake may seethe inside, but he'll have to step down graciously and pray that his expertise will be called on at some time in the future."

"You've got it." Her thoughts moved on. "Whether Blake will want to return to Eastbridge is questionable. He founded it and built it from scratch into a large corporation, but he pretty much divorced himself from it when he got his appointment. Even if Blake is acquitted, the company will probably be hit with a stiff penalty for making that shipment. I doubt they'd want him back, even if he *did* want to go. It's strange, Michael. Eastbridge was his heart and soul for so long, yet he was able to turn completely off when he left for Washington—just as he turned completely off his own family when he went away to college."

Michael already knew the bare outlines of that relationship. "Has he talked with any of them since all this happened?"

"The night the indictments were returned, he called to tell them that he was completely innocent and that they shouldn't pay any attention to what they hear on television. To my knowledge, he hasn't spoken with them since."

"Nice guy."

"Maybe it's mutual. I just don't know them well enough to say. Things will be so different with us." Then she stopped. "Michael, have you talked to your father at all?"

"Yes, but not about us. Once the trial's over and we're together again, I thought we could both go to see him. He's been surprisingly open-minded when it comes to Blake. Maybe because he heads a large corporation himself, he can see how easily things go amiss."

"Has he ever had a . . . a similar problem?"

"None that involved the law, at least not in a criminal sense. There have been libel suits when he's had to answer for something one of his newspapers said. He may just identify with Blake."

"And, of course, you do nothing to encourage that," she teased, knowing that in spite of everything Michael would never malign Blake in front of John Buchanan.

"I've put in a good word here and there. When Dad finally learns the truth, I don't want him to think that I knowingly kicked Blake when he was down."

"I'm surprised that he's not more hostile, given Blake's relationship to my father."

"Nah. Dad may be a tyrant at times, but only concerning things he believes in. The differences he's had with your father have been ideological. Well, maybe there is a little jealousy there. I think he resents the power your father wields, particularly when it's wielded on the side Dad opposes. He's never had much of a quarrel with Blake. And I'm *sure* that he'd never hold anything against you."

"I'm glad. I wouldn't want to think I'd be coming between you and your father."

"Sweetheart, *life* came between him and me. As long as we go our own ways, we're fine."

She sighed. "With a little luck, maybe my father and I can reach a similar understanding."

"And that's another thing for you to worry about. Don't, Dani. Please? There's nothing you can do about it now, and you've got enough to handle. Everything will work out. You'll see. Everything will work out."

DANICA WASN'T SO SURE about whether her father would ever graciously accede, but Michael was right. She had enough to handle, coping with the day to day anticipation of the trial, without worrying about that.

Every morning she worked at the Archives studying old records and maps, homing in on ships that had sunk with suspected bonanzas on board. Some afternoons she stopped on her way home at the local branch of the public library to pour through books and newspapers and microfilms, reading everything she could about shipwrecks and recovery operations. The thrust of his book was going to be the romance of it all. This Danica could identify with. When she worked, she was for all practical purposes back on Joe Camarillo's boat in Maine, back on Michael's and hers in the nights. It was a blessed escape.

The trial drew nearer with each day, though, and she couldn't help but suffer from the anxiety that was palpable in the house in Chevy Chase. Her own fretfulness was mixed with a growing impatience. Phone calls to Michael were no substitute for the real thing.

On the second of December she flew to Boston for her scheduled doctor's appointment. Having entered her fourth month of pregnancy, she'd found that all sickness, even the pervasive fatigue that had plagued her so at first, had vanished. Her doctor declared her in excellent physical shape aside from a slight elevation in her blood pressure, but when he suggested she might take a mild sedative to help her through the trial, she refused. The worst was the waiting, she reasoned, and the trial itself couldn't possibly be as bad.

As he had the month before, Michael met her outside the medical building. This time, though, he brought lunch with him and they ate in his borrowed office at Harvard.

"I wanted privacy," Michael explained when he'd finished his sandwich and set the papers aside. He drew her from her chair and propped her against the desk. "Real privacy."

She didn't need to hear his hoarseness to know what he was thinking because he'd been looking at her for the past hour with the very same longing she felt. She slid her arms around his neck as he lowered his head, and ghosted her parted lips against his open mouth. Their sighs blended with the exchange of breath, as though one was giving life to the other and it was all they'd ever need . . . but it wasn't.

When Michael began to quickly undo the buttons of her light wool dress, she grew cautious. "Michael . . . here?"

"The door's locked. No one will bother us." He had the dress opened to the waist and was reaching inside to release the front catch of her bra. "I want to see you and touch you."

While she held her breath, he did both of those things, peeling the bra aside first to stare at the creamy fullness of her breasts, then to reverently trace his fingers over the pale blue veins that had newly appeared. She bit her lip and moaned softly, closing her eyes, delighting in the gentleness of his touch and its awe.

When he lowered his head and put his mouth against her, she threaded her fingers through his hair. She moaned again when he took her nipple in his mouth and began to suckle. His thumb rolled its mate, then he reversed the attention. She was instinctively arching her hips to his when he drew back. The moistness he left on her breasts felt cold to the air, making them pucker all the more.

He reached for his belt then, and she clutched his arms. "No, Michael. We can't..."

"We can and we will," he said forcefully, then softened his tone. But his fingers had the belt undone and were negotiating his fly, which took some doing because he was fully erect. "We've got a month's worth of hell ahead, sweetheart. This will be good."

He seized her mouth then and thrust his tongue deeply in prelude while he began to bunch up her dress. "Just slip your panties down," he rasped against her lips. "I need you so."

All thought of protest was gone because she needed him as badly. Her body was thrumming, her blood surging through heated veins. She stood only long enough to do as he'd asked. Then he had her dress to her hips and was pressing her back to the desk. Releasing himself from his pants, he spread her knees, raised them, then pressed forward.

She sighed as his hard length entered her deeply. "I've been so empty..." Then she couldn't say anything more because he'd begun to move slowly in and out and she could hardly breathe, much less return his kiss. Her fingers dug into his shirtfront while his held her bottom, manipulating her hips. Time and place fell by the wayside, the only thing of import being the supremacy of their union, its heat and its glory. It was no time before she cried aloud and burst into a sharp series of gasps. His own cry was deeper and louder, and he held himself close as he pulsed into her.

Then they were panting on each other's shoulders, laughing and wondering what a passerby in the hall would think of the sound effects.

Within Reach 367

"This has been . . . decadent, Michael, but so . . . so wonderful!"

He agreed completely. Holding her there, staying inside her as long as he could, he felt that there was a rightness in the world after all. It wasn't the sex in itself, but the love it expressed, that made what they did so precious. Separated as they'd been by so many miles for so long, he'd had to assert his love in this most basic way. Lord knew, there was little else he could do under the circumstances.

But slowly, reluctantly, his thoughts turned toward the future, as did hers. They dressed more somberly and both faces were grim by the time Michael dropped her at the airport.

"Take care, sweetheart, and remember that I love you," he said, memorizing her features with soft, sad eyes.

"I will," she said through gathering tears. She knew that the joy of the afternoon would linger with her, but she was already missing him. She also knew that there was no escape from what lay ahead. Turning, head down, she walked stoically toward her plane.

Chapter Nineteen

TWO DAYS LATER the trial began. Michael closely followed the proceedings on television and in the papers, but the calls Danica made to him every night were what he waited for.

"How do you feel?" he asked on that first night.

"Tired. I hadn't realized jury selection would be so slow. Two jurors picked out of eighteen interviewed. It could take as much as a week to get the full jury." Which would make it one week longer before she was free.

"But it's critical, sweetheart. You don't want a juror who's already made up his mind as to Blake's guilt or innocence. More subtle biases, well, I'm sure Blake's lawyers are looking for those. They'll want to stack the jury with professionals, for one thing, people who'll be able to identify with him."

"Mmmm. The foreman of a factory would identify with Harlan. A person from a lower socioeconomic bracket may resent Blake's wealth. On the other hand, the same person may be more awed by Blake's status, so it could go either way. I don't envy Jason and Ray. It's hard."

"How about the press? Does it bother you?"

"It was bad when we got to the courthouse this morning. They were all waiting," she lowered her voice, "like vultures hovering, ready to dive in for the kill."

"This is the first trial of the lot," Michael reasoned, "and since Blake is in such a prominent position..."

"Jason says that it'll get better as time goes on, that they'll lose interest." She sighed. "God, I hope so. It's bad enough going through the trial itself, but to have to deal with media questions and those microphones being stuck in our faces..."

"Were they questioning *you*?"

"They tried. They didn't get any more from me than they got from Blake, though."

"I saw the television clip and there you were," Michael quipped on a lighter vein. "Your dress was perfect—just enough of a hint of your pregnancy." As for himself, he had simply to close his eyes to see the added weight of her breasts, the thickening of her waist and the faint, faint rounding of her stomach. "You were the prettiest thing on the screen all night."

She moaned. "I would have rather stayed in the background, but Blake insisted that I be right there by his side when we met the press.... You can't believe how difficult it was to sit in court all day looking calm and composed, and this was only the *first* day of the trial."

"It'll be better once the actual trial begins. There'll be plenty to think about then."

"Mmmm. I'm not sure if that's good or bad."

IT WAS BAD. After five working days the jury was complete. Immediately after that the prosecution opened its case.

"Tell me you're discouraged," Michael offered.

"How did you know?"

"I heard reports on two of the networks, and I know enough about trials to imagine what you're feeling right about now."

"It's so...so nerve-racking having to sit there quietly while the other guy stands up and says all kinds of condemning things. For whatever differences Blake and I have had, I've never known him to be a 'ruthless hustler.' Did you hear that opening statement?"

"Just excerpts of it."

"It was powerful, Michael."

"I'm sure it was. But that doesn't mean Fitzgerald's won't be as good. Things only sound bad now because you can't rebut them."

"I hope that's true. Blake is really down. He barely ate dinner."

"Did you?"

"Some. For the baby's sake, if not my own. I'll be damned if I'll let this child suffer for things it has no part in."

"Shhh. You're a good mother already, Dani. That baby's a lucky kid."

LUCK HAD LITTLE TO DO with the events of the succeeding days. Everything Danica did was carefully planned and as carefully executed. She maintained her poise in the courtroom, never once wavering while document after document was introduced into evidence and witness after witness took the stand.

The Assistant United States Attorney prosecuting the case painstakingly detailed Blake's involvement with Eastbridge Electronics, then the licensing procedure that preceded the shipment in question and the fact that the items being shipped were restricted by the government. He brought in witnesses to testify that the high-speed integrated circuits had indeed been packed at and shipped from Eastbridge, then other witnesses—mercifully not Jeffrey—to outline the investigation that had traced the shipments back from the Soviet Union to Eastbridge.

Listening each day, Danica grew more and more discouraged. But back at the house she forced the healthiest of foods into herself and made sure she got the proper amount of sleep—well, rest, at least, because there were nights when, even after talking with Michael, she remained tense and sleep eluded her. The only thing that seemed to help during those late night hours when she'd lie awake in bed was when she'd put her hand on her belly and project her thoughts to the future. She'd picture her baby, newly born, perfectly formed, and Michael would be by her side, smiling, holding her hand, telling her how much he loved her, how much he loved their child. She'd wonder if it was a boy and tried to think of masculine names, then would switch and consider the feminine possibilities. She and Michael discussed it from time to time, but for the most part their conversations revolved around the trial.

With Christmas fast approaching, Danica grew more restless. "It'll be several more days before the prosecution rests," she told Michael on the twentieth of the month.

"It's taking longer than we thought." In the back of his mind, as in Danica's, there'd been the vague possibility that they'd be reunited for Christmas. That possibility was now dashed.

"Since the burden of proof rests with the prosecution, every little thing has to be spelled out. At least that's what Jason and Ray say. It seems to me that only a moron wouldn't be able to move faster, and as far as I know there are no morons on the jury."

"It's the system of justice, sweetheart. One step at a time."

"One quarter-step at a time."

"You're impatient. So am I. We'll get there, though. Maybe slowly, but surely."

The final witness the prosecution brought in was a surprise, and a shock. He was a man who'd been employed at Eastbridge at the time of the shipment, a man who claimed he'd been present during a conversation in which Blake had specifically referred to the high-speed integrated circuits, hence proving that he knew of their existence. On cross-examination Jason was able to tarnish the man's credibility, pointing out that the witness may have confused the point of the conversation in question and, more importantly, that he'd been dismissed from employment at Eastbridge for reasons of alleged incompetency, shortly before Blake had left.

Still, the testimony hurt.

THAT CHRISTMAS was one Danica wanted to quickly forget. Though she and Blake had agreed not to exchange gifts, he presented her with a gold watch—a "thank you," he called it, for her support. She felt cheap, and it wasn't because she hadn't bought anything for him.

They had dinner with her parents, but there was little to talk about that wasn't depressing, and because talk of the baby was downright embarrassing, given that William didn't know the truth, Danica avoided it. More than anything, she'd wanted to be with Michael, who, along with Cilla and Jeff and Corey, whom Danica hadn't yet met, had gone to Gena's for the day. Her only solace was in talking with him later that night.

"Michael?"

"Merry Christmas, sweetheart."

"You, too." She knew she was about to cry and she didn't want to do that, so she savagely bit on her lower lip.

"How did it go?"

"Okay," she managed, but sniffled. "Cheer me up. Tell me about yours."

He did, in great detail, and she loved every minute of it because she was imagining how things would be the following year when she and the baby would be there.

"Gena sends her love. So do Cilla and Jeff, *and* Corey, even though he said that you'll probably think him that much more of a lecher than you already do."

She laughed. Corey was the publisher of his own magazine, which was about as far to conforming with the other Buchanans as he went, since the magazine was a sophisticated version of *Penthouse.* Danica had seen it at Michael's house and had thought it . . . inspiring.

"I don't think he's a lecher. I can't wait to meet him."

"I don't know," Michael teased. "He's still a bachelor. Maybe I should put off this meeting till we're married.... By the way, he swore that our secret was safe with him."

Thoughts of the present tumbled in on her. "I wasn't worried," she said softly. "It won't be long now anyway."

"Another two weeks?"

"At most. Then we'll be . . . together . . ." Her voice broke and the tears she'd tried so hard to stem defied her.

"Shhhh. Don't cry, sweetheart." But he wanted to cry himself. As lovely as Christmas day had been with his family, a vital part of him was missing. "Soon, very soon, it'll all be over."

"It's just th-that I wanted to be with you t-today."

"Shhhh. There'll be other Christmases for us, Dani. The future is ours. Keep telling yourself that. I do."

"The future i-is ours. I know. The future is ours." It was to become a litany that she would repeat many times each day.

THE TRIAL RESUMED immediately after Christmas with the defense's opening statement, then the presentation of its case. Indeed, it was easier for Danica to listen because, as had been the reverse before, things now sounded good for Blake.

Jason went into a history of Eastbridge, tracing a record, which had been spotless for twenty years. He produced an independent accountant to state that, by his study, Eastbridge was neither in financial trouble nor had it benefited monetarily from the alleged sale. To the contrary, he claimed, the computers had been sold at a price in keeping with the older units in which the circuits had been housed, and East-bridge had actually taken a loss on the deal—all suggesting that Blake had not known of the presence of the higher priced circuits in the computers as the prosecution contended.

Numerous witnesses testified to Blake's good character. Others testified that a corporate head such as Blake might well not be in immediate touch with what was happening at the production and shipping levels.

Then, on the third of January, Blake took the witness stand on his own behalf.

"He was excellent, Michael. I have to hand it to him. Even after three days on the stand he spoke well and wasn't ruffled under cross-examination."

"So I heard in the news. Are his lawyers optimistic?"

"Yes, but guardedly so. It's hard to judge the jury's reaction. They looked sympathetic when Blake was being questioned, but then, they looked sympathetic during parts of the prosecution's presentation."

"Closing arguments begin tomorrow?"

"Mmmm. I'm not looking forward to that. The prosecution goes last. *That*'s what's apt to stick in the jurors' minds."

"No. The judge's charge goes last. If he's worth his salt, and I think you lucked out with Bergeron, he'll give a fair charge. And once the jury is locked up, they'll be looking at the evidence. That's what they have to base their verdict on— the evidence, not the theatrics of the lawyers." He knew he was taking the simplistic approach, knew that jurors were indeed often swayed by the antics of one lawyer or the other, but he sensed that Danica needed all the bolstering she could get. "And from where I sit, the media coverage has been relatively unbiased."

"But they're gathering round again. They can smell the moment of truth coming."

"It's news, sweetheart. You can't blame them for it. . . . By the way, you called the doctor, didn't you?"

"Uh-huh. He was wonderful. He said he'd fit me in as soon as I could make it to Boston. I made a tentative appointment for next week. With luck, the trial will be over by then . . .''

Michael's voice deepened. "How are you feeling, deep down inside?"

"Scared. I really want him to be acquitted, Michael. From a purely selfish standpoint, it'll make things so much easier for me."

"Less guilt?"

"Less guilt."

"Well, for what it's worth, though I don't think I'll ever forgive the bastard for what he's done to you, I'm rooting for an acquittal too. . . . You'll call me as soon as it's over, won't you?"

"Right from the courthouse. I promise."

"Collect?" he teased.

She gave a soft laugh of surrender and nodded. "Collect."

THE CLOSING ARGUMENTS were dramatic and heated on both sides. The prosecution portrayed Blake as an opportunist, a man so driven by power and greed that he felt himself outside the law. The defense portrayed him as a man who was human, a man whose authority had been circumvented by an employee whose overriding ambition had led to his involvement with the KGB and his subsequent murder by foreign factions.

As for the judge's charge, Danica wasn't sure what to make of it. Blake's lawyers felt that it leaned toward their side, but all she heard was the oft-repeated "beyond a reasonable doubt."

THE JURY WAS OUT for three full days. If Danica thought the earlier part of the trial had been difficult, it was nothing compared to the hell of waiting. Each morning, as they'd done now for over a month, she and Blake drove to the courthouse, where they were met by their lawyers and then ushered into the courtroom to hear the judge send the jury off to deliberate. Late each afternoon they returned to the courthouse to hear the judge dismiss the jury for the night when no decision had been reached. In the hours between, Danica and Blake sat in the offices of Fitzgerald and Pickering, saying little to each other. From time to time either Jason or Ray joined them to offer encouragement, but as the days passed, their words were more of a rationalizing nature.

Ideally, the jury would have been so convinced of Blake's innocence that it would have returned a verdict to that extent within hours. Realistically, as Jason pointed out, there was no way the jury could have reviewed the mountain of evidence offered in four weeks of testimony so quickly. Yet, as the days passed, minute by minute, hour by hour, Danica and Blake both began to wonder about the serious doubts the jury apparently had.

It was late on the third day when the call finally came. Jason, his features tense, came into the conference room where Danica and Blake had been sitting alone.

"The jury's reached a verdict," he announced quietly. "They're waiting for us."

Danica's heart thudded. Her gaze flew to Blake, who was pale and hollow-eyed.

"Do you know anything, Jason?" he asked, his voice a shadow of its former confident self.

Jason smiled sadly and shook his head. "No more than you do. We'll have to hear it together in court."

Blake nodded and stood. He straightened his suit, but the rest of him was as immaculately groomed as ever.

For a split second Danica swayed when she rose from her seat. Her knees felt rubbery, her arms and legs weak. But she steadied herself, and when she clutched Blake's arm, it wasn't for her own sake. Rather she was remembering the Blake she'd first married and the better days they'd had together, and her facial expression said that in spite of all that had come later she didn't wish him ill.

Blake met her gaze, studied it for a moment and gave her a rueful smile of thanks. Then, taking her hand in his, he led her after Jason.

They entered the courthouse through the back door, having to work their way through the media crowd only for the short distance from the elevator to the courtroom. Once inside, they took their familiar places, Blake at the defense table flanked by Jason and Ray, Danica directly behind Blake in the first row of seats.

The courtroom was packed, its air rife with expectancy. Danica took slow, deep breaths to steady herself, but it seemed futile because she began to shake all the more when the jury slowly filed into the room. As a group they looked grim, which could very well have been from fatigue, Danica reasoned, though she'd hoped for a smile or two in the direction of the defense table.

On command, everyone in the courtroom rose for the judge's entrance. When he'd been seated, he nodded to the clerk, who then faced the jury.

"Madam Forelady, has the jury reached a verdict?"

The woman who'd served as forelady of the jury since the start of the trial stood. "We have." She handed him a piece of paper. He then carried it to the judge, who read it, nodded and handed it back.

Clutching her hands in her lap, Danica wondered how such a small piece of paper could hold such weight. Years of work by Blake at Eastbridge, months of investigation by the government, weeks and weeks of trial preparation, then the trial itself, not to mention Blake's future—all hung in the balance of the words written on that paper.

The clerk's flat voice filled the courtroom. "Will the defendant please rise."

Blake stood, as did both Jason and Ray. Danica could do nothing more than press her fingers into the wool of her dress and hold her breath as the clerk slowly went on.

"On indictment number 85-2343, is the defendant guilty or not guilty?"

The forelady spoke clearly. "Not guilty."

A murmur went through the courtroom and Danica swallowed.

The clerk continued. "On indictment number 85-2344, is the defendant guilty or not guilty?"

"Not guilty."

Danica didn't hear the murmur this time because her pulse was pounding.

"On indictment number 85-2345, is the defendant guilty or not guilty?"

"Not guilty."

Danica's eyes were round when the clerk spoke a final time. "On indictment number 85-2346, is the defendant guilty or not guilty?"

The forelady raised her chin and took a last breath. "Not guilty."

For a moment there was total silence. Then the courtroom erupted into a cacophony of excitement. Blake, smiling broadly, vigorously shook hands with, then hugged, each of his lawyers. Then he turned to Danica and she was in his arms, holding him tightly.

"I'm so glad for you!" she cried, her voice broken as tears of relief and genuine happiness welled in her eyes.

"We did it, Pook. We really did it." There was something akin to wonder in his tone, but she was too emotionally keyed up to analyze its cause, and he was separating himself from her, at his lawyers' request, so that he might nod his thanks to the jurors as they filed out of the courtroom, then shake hands with the prosecutorial team.

Moments later Danica, Blake, Jason and Ray were facing the press outside the courtroom.

"How do you feel, Mr. Secretary?"

"Delighted," Blake answered. "Our system of justice has prevailed. I feel fully exonerated."

"Did you have any doubts about what the verdict would be?"

"I was confident that my attorneys could convey the truth to the jury."

"Will you be returning to the Department?"

"I hope so. I'll be talking with the President later."

"Mrs. Lindsay, this must be a great relief for you."

Danica smiled. "Very great."

"What are your immediate plans? Will you and your husband be taking some time off together before he returns to work?"

Blake answered for her, quickly but smoothly and flashing his brightest smile. "I believe we'll have to come down off this cloud before we can make any plans."

Jason cut in before the next question could come. "Ladies and gentlemen, the Lindsays are happy but tired. If you'll excuse us now, I think they'd like some privacy."

As though on a moving walkway, Danica felt herself being swept toward the elevator. She clutched Blake's arm and leaned close to his ear. "I need to get to a phone."

"We'll go back to Jason's office."

"No, here." She made no effort to hide her urgency. "Isn't there one I can use?"

Blake gave her a guarded look, then turned to Jason. "Danica needs to call her parents. Can we go down the hall for a minute?"

With a nod, Jason reversed their direction and led them through the crowded corridor to the small room they'd often used during recesses. He and Blake stood talking by the door while Danica picked up the phone and, fingers trembling, dialed Michael's number. When the operator came on, she said simply, "Collect from Danica Lindsay."

He picked up the phone after a single ring. "Yes?"

"I have a collect call from—"

"Yes. I'll take it.... Dani?"

She felt her insides melt, and she sank into a chair. "It's over," she breathed, putting her hand up to cover tear-filled eyes. "Not guilty on all counts."

"Oh, sweetheart, that's great! I'm thrilled! Congratulations!"

Danica wanted to say so much, but her throat was tight and she knew it wasn't the time or place. She spoke slowly and with effort. "Blake and Jason are with me now."

"And you can't talk. I understand. I'm just so happy for you. For *us!*"

She smiled through her tears. "Me, too."

"What are the plans now? When will I see you?"

"I'll have to ... let me call you later. I just wanted to tell you ..."

"Thanks, sweetheart. I'll be waiting. Everything's going to be so wonderful. I love you."

"Me, too," she whispered. "Talk with you later." Mouthing a kiss, since her back was to Blake and Jason, she quietly pressed the disconnect button, then dialed her mother's number.

When she finally hung up the phone and turned, she brushed the tears from her cheeks.

"Is everything okay?" Blake asked cautiously.

Danica nodded and smiled weakly. She knew Blake had to have heard that she'd made two calls, but she felt no compulsion to discuss the first with him, and she knew that he'd never bring it up himself in front of Jason. "Mom was ecstatic. She says to tell you how pleased she is and that she'll call Dad right away. She asked if we wanted to celebrate with them over dinner and I told her that we'd probably be with Jason and Ray." She sent an apologetic glance toward Jason, who promptly put her at ease with a broad smile.

"That's exactly where you will be." He rubbed his hands together. "This is a victory for all of us. Let's make it good!"

IT WAS MUCH, MUCH LATER that night before Danica was able to call Michael back.

"I'm sorry it's so late—" she began, only to be interrupted.

"Don't be silly, sweetheart. . . . You sound beat."

"I am. It's like everything—all the tension and worry and excitement and relief—was suspended and now it's suddenly fallen in on me." She settled back on the bed and threw an arm across her eyes. "We went back to Jason's office after I spoke with you, then out to dinner. I have an awful headache. But I am pleased for Blake."

"I saw him on television. He looked properly victorious."

"Oh, yes. In hindsight he saw that the verdict couldn't have possibly gone any other way."

"Back to his old self, eh?"

"Very much so."

" . . . Dani, when will you be up?"

On a burst of strength, she spoke more forcefully. "I'm leaving here tomorrow, as soon as I can get packed."

"Have you told Blake?"

"No. I'll tell him in the morning."

"Do you think he'll give you any trouble?"

"I don't think so. In spite of all his chest-puffing, he treated me with kid gloves today. He must have an inkling of what's coming. I'm sure he knew it was you I called this afternoon."

"Maybe I should fly down—"

"No, Michael. I need to do this myself. And there's really nothing that can go wrong. Even if Blake gives me an argument, my mind is set. I've given him more than he deserves. And I do have that ace in the hole."

"Will you use it?"

"If he gives me the slightest problem, you bet I will. He'll agree to a divorce, Michael. It's over. Our future's beginning."

Michael let out a long sigh of relief. "I love you so much, Dani. That future's going to be stupendous."

She smiled. "I know."

"I'll drive down and meet you at Logan."

"No. I'm driving the Audi up."

"From *Washington*? Oh, sweetheart, that's not such a good idea. It's a long trip, and in your condition—"

"My condition will be wonderful once I get done what I need to do here. Besides, I need the winding-down time. The drive will do me good."

"Let me fly down and drive up with you, then."

"No." Her voice softened. "Just be there waiting. That's all I need, Michael. I'll be there the day after tomorrow. Just be waiting."

"I will, love. I will."

THE FOLLOWING MORNING Danica was up early, packing her bags, listening for Blake, who'd left even earlier to play squash. She knew that he was meeting with the President later that morning, though she also knew that the outcome of the meeting was irrelevant to her own plans.

She had the Audi nearly packed and was bringing down her overnight bag and purse when Blake came in the front door. He took one look at her, at her bag and purse, then set his jaw and walked past her into the den.

She followed him, coming to a halt just inside the room. He had his back to her and was staring out the window.

"I'll be leaving now, Blake," she said quietly but with conviction. When he said nothing, she went on. "I'll be taking the Audi—"

"Don't, Danica." He turned. "Don't leave."

"You knew I was planning to—"

"But I thought, after all this and, well, you seemed so happy with the acquittal..."

"I am happy with it, but it's over. All of it."

He didn't miss the deeper meaning of her words. "It doesn't have to be. We could try to make a go of it."

She was shaking her head, smiling sadly. "It's too late for that. There's no point."

"We had something once—"

"But it's gone now. It's been gone for a long, long time." She was surprised by the soft, almost pleading nature of his tone, but it couldn't affect her deeply. She'd meant what she'd said. "I'll wait about a month until things calm down here before I see my lawyer. He'll be in touch with yours to discuss the divorce."

"I don't want a divorce."

She ignored him. "I'll probably fly somewhere where I can get it quickly. I'd like things taken care of before the baby's born."

"I don't *want* a divorce."

"Blake, this isn't your baby."

"I can live with that. It's the divorce I can't live with."

"You haven't got any choice."

"I certainly do. I'm your husband. Besides, what do you think it'll look like if you take off like this one day after the trial?"

"It'll look like I'm exhausted and need to recuperate at our house in Maine."

"And the divorce? What do I say about that?"

"You say that the strain of the trial was too much."

"Bull. It's got nothing to do with the trial. You had your mind made up when you first came down here."

She tipped up her chin a fraction. "You're right. I was going to demand a divorce before all this happened. Now I don't have to demand it. You'll give it to me. Quickly and quietly."

He eyed her strangely. "How do you know that?"

Taking that proverbial ace from its hole, she very slowly turned it over. "Because I know about you and Harlan, Blake. I was fooled for a long time, but now I know." She found some satisfaction in his sudden loss of color but no joy in furthering her point. Yet she felt it was necessary. "I only wish you could have told me yourself. I might have understood if you'd done that. Instead, you used me, even though you knew I had a chance for happiness elsewhere. I won't be used again, Blake. It's as simple as that."

Though his jaw was clenched, there was little force to his words. "Harlan got to you."

"Indirectly, I suppose." She saw no point in elaborating.

His voice cracked faintly. "It's over, Danica. It was over long before he was killed."

"But there've been others, and there'll be others again. And I have a new life to lead, one that I want, one that's waiting for me."

Blake looked at the floor, then slowly raised his gaze. "And if I decide to fight?"

"It'll all come out in court. I don't think you'll want another trial, particularly once you've considered what the testimony will entail."

He stared at her, then leaned back against the desk, which was as close as he could come to sagging in defeat. Sensing that there was little left to be said, Danica shouldered her purse and lifted her bag.

"Thelma can pack the rest of my things and send them on later. I'll be seeing the doctor in Boston tomorrow. After that I'll be in Maine.... I hope all goes well with your meeting today," she said softly. "I'm sure I'll hear one way or another."

For a final moment, then, she stood looking at the man who'd been her husband for better than ten years. Strangely, she felt neither anger nor resentment, but rather a kind of melancholy. He was so very handsome, so very talented. And they'd been so very wrong for each other.

Bowing her head, she turned and left the house, aware of the finality of it all, of the fact that she was putting a lengthy, if painful, part of her life behind her. Only after several moments' respite in the car did she feel composed enough to drive. She still had another stop to make, and thought of this one unsettled her more because, though it wouldn't immediately affect her future, its outcome did touch her heart.

IN A TWIST OF FATE that Danica took to be promising, William Marshall was available. He was sitting at his large oak desk, studying position papers his aides had prepared when his secretary buzzed him to announce Danica's arrival. Rising from his seat, he met Danica at the door.

"Well, girl, you did it." He smiled broadly. "You and Blake both."

"We did at that," she said quietly.

He shut the door and motioned to a chair. "Sit down, Danica. You shouldn't be standing around in your condition." He eyed her belly. "You're really beginning to look it now."

She put a reassuring, perhaps protective, hand on her stomach, but she didn't sit. "I can't stay long. I want to get as much driving done as I can today."

He frowned. "Driving? Where are you going?"

"I'm going home."

"*Home?*" He was standing before her, his eyes darkening. "*This* is home. I thought you'd realized that by now."

"Home for me is in Maine. With Michael."

William came close to exploding. "With *Michael*! Have you lost your *senses*? Your place is with Blake. You've stood beside him through this whole ordeal, and now that it's over the two of you should be able to patch up whatever differences you may have had. Blake still has a solid future in this town.... Besides, you can't leave him. You're carrying his child!"

She raked her teeth across her lower lip. "No, Daddy. I'm not."

He glanced at her belly again, then her face. "What in the hell are you saying?"

"You know. Think. How could this child possibly be Blake's when Michael's the one I've been with most, when Michael's the one I love?"

"It's *his* child?" When she nodded, he cursed. "I'll kill the bastard!"

"No, you won't. He loves me and he loves this child, and he's going to make both of us very, very happy. I'd think you'd be grateful to him for that. After all, I'm your daughter and this will be your grandchild."

"It was supposed to be Blake's!"

"No," she said sadly. "You *wanted* it to be Blake's, that's all."

"Does he know?"

"Blake? He's known all along."

"And he sat back and took it?"

"I was serving his purposes. That was all that mattered to him."

"Why wasn't *I* told?"

"It's wasn't your business then. It is now only because I want you to understand why I'm leaving Blake. Don't you see? *I love Michael!* Blake and I have nothing left. Nothing!"

"He won't let you go. He needs you here."

"He's letting me go. We've already talked and it's settled."

Turning, William, stalked to the far side of the room, then swiveled to face her. His eyes were hard, and her heart sank. She'd hoped that he'd yield, that he'd defer to her judgment for once. Obviously, he wasn't going to do that.

"You're being very stupid, Danica. Blake is in a position of power and prominence, both of which can rub off on you. He has it all over Buchanan any day."

It was one thing for him to put her down, quite another for him to do so to Michael. "You're wrong," she said in a warning tone. "You don't know the facts."

"Well, enlighten me!" he roared as he threw his hands out and paced back from the side of the room. "If you think you're so wise, tell me. And don't give me that hogwash about love, because it's flighty and feminine and it won't get you *anywhere* in this world."

"That," Danica responded angrily, "depends on where you want to go."

"You're sure gonna go nowhere, girl. You could've been on top with your tennis, and you quit. Now you're doing the same thing all over again. *What's the matter with you?* Haven't you learned *anything* in thirty-odd years on this earth?"

"I've learned plenty," Danica retorted, her eyes blazing right back at William's. "I've learned that you and I have very different definitions of what 'being on top' means, and that while your definition may be just fine for you, it's not for me. I've learned that I have options in life, that I can take the road *I* want rather than the road someone else wants me to take.''

Shaking all over, she paused only to gasp for air. ''There's only one thing I've ever really wanted in life. A family. A warm, loving, close family. I never had it when I was growing up because you and Mom were too busy with your career to even stop and consider my needs. I never had it with Blake because he was so involved with Eastbridge and...and...well, it just never came. I was ready to give up on my dream because you all kept saying that things like duty and responsibility were more important. Then I met Michael, and I learned that I wasn't crazy to want the things I did. I learned that by taking a road of *my own* choosing, I can have it all.''

Seeing her agitation, William patted the air. ''You're pregnant, Danica. You're being emotional. You're not thinking clearly—''

''*I* am. *You*'re the one who's missing the boat.'' Her eyes narrowed. ''Do you want to know what else I've learned? I've learned that you're fallible. You make mistakes just like the rest of us. Your judgment on some matters leaves much to be desired.''

William stiffened. ''I won't have you talking to me that way, Danica. I'm your father. I deserve respect.''

''So do I, and I'm going to get it!'' She had reached the point of fury where there were no holds barred. ''Do you have any idea why my marriage failed? *Do you?*''

''You gave up on it.''

''I did not. *Blake* did.'' She straightened. ''You may have thought that you knew him when you chose him to be my husband, but you didn't. And for ten long years I didn't know him, either. At first I thought I was doing something wrong. He spent more and more time out of the house, less and less time with me. I rationalized and tried to compensate, but it didn't work. Toward the end we shared little more than the same last name. *And do you want to know why?*''

''Yes,'' William goaded indignantly.

''Because Blake prefers men to women! He was having an affair with Harlan Magnusson! A full-fledged homosexual affair!''

William raised his hand and, for a minute, she thought he was going to hit her. Then the hand curled into a fist and lowered slowly. "I don't believe you," he stated very, very quietly.

"You don't have to believe me," she said, suddenly even more quiet than he. "Blake confirmed it. And it explains certain things—such as why Harlan was able to get that illegal shipment out of Eastbridge."

"Are you suggesting that Blake was sweet-talked into it, that he knew about it all along? You're skating on thin ice, girl. A jury acquitted him."

"And I'm not making accusations one way or the other. All I'm saying is that there always was a special relationship between Blake and Harlan. Now I understand its full nature."

William was not one to accept defeat graciously. Danica might be his daughter, but Blake had always been his man. "Maybe if you'd been a better wife Blake wouldn't have had to . . . to resort to something else."

It was the final straw. Danica was the one who wanted to hit now, and only by pressing her fists to her sides did she refrain from doing so. Every one of her muscles was rigid. She didn't so much as blink, though her voice was tremulous when she spoke. "I don't have to justify my actions if you're so blind that you can't see what I've done even during these past five months of hell. All my life I've tried to please you, but that hasn't been enough—not for you, because I never quite reached the top, and not for me, because I don't want to get to the top as you see it."

She shifted her purse on her shoulder and swallowed. "I'll be leaving now. I'm going to stop in to say goodbye to Mom. By the way, she doesn't know about Blake and I don't want you to tell her. Considering the fact that she's had one stroke, she can do without the added strain. Besides, she accepts me for what I am, and she knows that I'll be ten times happier with Michael than I ever was with Blake and, thank God, that means something to her."

Danica turned and headed for the door. She walked slowly, waiting, praying that her father would say something to heal the rift between them. When he said nothing, her shoulders slumped and she quietly let herself out.

ELEANOR INSISTED on driving as far as Hartford with her, and Danica was grateful for her company. She told her of the conversation with her father, omitting that one part about Blake, and about her fervent hope that one day William might see things her way. She told of her plans for the divorce, of her desire to sell the Kennebunkport house and move in with Michael as soon as possible. She told about her hopes for the future, her excitement, the dreams that seemed finally within reach.

And Eleanor was happy for her, which was some consolation for the pain Danica felt at her father's rejection.

The following morning, feeling more rested and alive with anticipation, she climbed back in the car for the drive to Boston and, after that, the final leg of what had been a long, long journey.

Chapter Twenty

ONE MINUTE THERE WAS NOTHING but a cloud of fog before him, the next she was there, materialized from the mist. Stunned, Michael came to an abrupt halt.

He wondered if he was dreaming because he knew he'd lived through this once before. Then the weather had been as inhospitable, the figure before him as striking. Now, though, it was the January wind that whipped through the ends of her sandy hair, and rather than a long skirt she wore jeans. Her jacket was as chicly oversized as the other had been on that March day nearly three years before, but this time it covered a rounded belly, inside which lay his child.

She was his dream come true. When he opened his arms, she came running, throwing her own around his neck, burying her face in the collar of his sheepskin jacket as he crushed her to him.

"Dani . . . Dani . . ." he murmured, defying the thunder of the waves by pressing his lips to her ear.

She was crying when he held her back, but she was laughing too, and she was beautiful. Unable to speak, she simply grinned at him while she brushed the tears from her face. He saw it then, the ring finger on her left hand. Taking it in his, he stroked its slender length.

"It's gone," he whispered hoarsely. "Your wedding band's gone."

She nodded vigorously, then laughed when she still couldn't stem her tears.

"You've left him?" he asked cautiously, knowing she'd been planning to but refusing to count on it until it was done. She nodded, and his voice rose. "For good?" She nodded again, and he spoke even louder. "And you're free?"

This time when she nodded, he bent his knees, threw back his head and let out a great whoop of joy. By the time he'd straightened, she was burrowing against him again. Wrapping her tightly in his arms, he held her until she raised her head and sought his gaze.

"I'm . . . so . . . happy!" she cried.

He gave her a crooked smile. "So am I. I was beginning to think you'd left your tongue in Washington!"

"Oh, no. I'm just happy! Kiss me, Michael. We've made it!"

He kissed her once, then again and again. She was laughing when he finally released her. Opening his jacket, he drew her inside, then turned them both and started walking slowly along the beach. When moments later Rusty loped in from the mist, Danica knelt to hug him, then returned to her man.

"Tell me, Dani. Tell me what happened."

She did, though she grew sober from time to time. "I really feel sorry for him, Michael. I read in today's paper that he'll be back as Secretary, but I don't envy him his future."

"You don't envy him because it's not the life you want. You've chosen your own, thank God."

She slanted him a cautious glance. "When I said I was free before . . . you know that it's only in the figurative sense just yet. I still have to file for the divorce, and I told Blake I'd wait a couple of weeks until things die down, but I'm going to get a quick one and he won't give me a fight."

"That's all that matters. . . . What about your father? Do you think he'll ever come around?"

Her expression grew more pained. "I don't know. Mom will work on him, and I know she'll be coming up here to visit whether he chooses to or not. I want him to, but it's up to him. I can't dwell on it, Michael. I've earned the right to our happiness."

He tucked her closer. "You certainly have." They were both silent for a while before he spoke again. "Do you remember that first day we met here on the beach?"

She'd been thinking of the same. "How could I forget? It changed my life. . . . You talked of pain then, of how sometimes strength comes from facing pain and dealing with it.

You were right. I think that's what's happened to me. I feel so much stronger, so much more *whole*."

"You were always strong, sweetheart. You'd been dealing with pain for a long time before I came along. The only difference is that now you see it, now you see the strength in yourself."

"Perhaps." She looked toward the waves. "You also talked about the ocean. Do you remember? You said that everything here was raw and truthful and commanded the same from us. You said that falling victim to the sea meant baring one's soul."

"I remember."

She turned into him then, sliding her arms inside his jacket and around his waist. "It can be painful, as it was then, or it can be beautiful, as it is now." Her voice grew hushed. "I love you, Michael. With my heart, my soul, everything, I love you."

For the longest time he could only drink in the adoration she offered. "I think I'm the luckiest man on this earth," he murmured at last. Unaware of the bounty of love his own gaze returned, he grew concerned when she began to tremble. "You're cold. Come on. Let's go back to my place for a warm drink." When she chuckled, he tipped his head. "What's so funny?"

"You said the same thing that day, and I remember thinking to myself that it'd be hot chocolate, just like your eyes."

"And I remember thinking that you had the most stunning violet ones I'd ever seen. I have to amend that. They're even more stunning now, all love and glow.... Well?"

"Well what?"

"How about that drink? You refused me that day."

"I was scared then. You were too attractive."

"Are you still scared?"

"Not on your life, bud." She broke away from him. "I'll race you there." With Rusty at her heels, she started to run, but the sand slowed her down and Michael caught up with her after she'd taken no more than three plodding strides.

"Ohhhhh, no, you don't." He firmly anchored her to his side. "A woman in your condition doesn't race."

She didn't argue because in her joy to be reunited with him she'd completely forgotten about her condition, and there was so much she wanted to tell him about that. "Michael, guess what?" Her eyes widened. "I heard the baby's heartbeat!"

His voice jumped. "You did?"

She nodded. "I saw the doctor this morning and he put the stethoscope in my ears and there it was."

Michael's eyes were round, too. "How did it sound?"

"Thu-thump. Thu-thump. A good, healthy little heartbeat. You'll hear it next month when you take me to the doctor." He grinned even more widely, but she had more to say. "And I can feel it moving now. It just kind of turns from time to time and there's this ripple inside me."

"I'm jealous. When will *I* be able to feel it?"

She laughed. "As soon as its little leg is strong enough to kick when you've got your hands on me."

"Mmmm, that's where I want 'em, babe. That's where I want 'em." Hastening his pace, he headed home.

AN HOUR LATER they were sitting on the floor before the fire having seconds of hot chocolate. They'd been talking non-stop about one thing and another since they'd come in, but the spell of the flames had taken over and they'd fallen into a warm and comfortable silence. Curving his body behind hers, Michael rested his chin on her shoulder.

"Hypnotic, isn't it?"

"Mmmm. Maybe it's the time, though…or the place…or you."

He pressed his lips to her neck and murmured against her skin, "I think all of those things. Mmmm, you smell so good."

She smiled and tipped her head against his. "This is what I've always, always wanted. A home, a fire, the man I love, our child…"

Michael slipped his hand under the hem of her bulky sweater and caressed her belly. "Mmmm, you *feel* so good."

Closing her eyes, she basked in the warmth of his touch. When his hand moved higher to cover her breast, she pressed her own atop it. "*That* feels so good," she murmured. A different kind of spell was taking over, well, not truly taking over because the other was still too strong, but mixing with it to make her float. She was still thinking about the heavenly sensation when she felt herself being lowered to the cushions Michael had quickly tugged from the nearby chair. Opening her eyes, she met his gaze.

"I've been waiting a long time for this," he whispered and reached for the hem of her sweater again. This time he drew it up and she arched her back, then raised her arms to help him. The sweater was tossed aside and his fingers went to the buttons of her blouse. "Tell me if you get cold," he warned huskily, but she knew she wouldn't get cold because, between the fire in the hearth, the one burning in her body and that in Michael's, she was melting.

He had her blouse open and eased it off, then reached behind her and unhooked her bra. It too was discarded and he sat back on his heels to look at her. His gaze traced fire along her profile, retracing it again and again over her swollen breasts and their pebbled tips, then again down over the curve of her belly. With hands that trembled, he very slowly drew the stretch band of her jeans down until the curve was bare; then, with awe in his touch, he inched his palm back up over everything his gaze had scaled.

"Beautiful . . . so . . . beautiful," he whispered as he continued to familiarize his fingers with every nuance of her altered shape.

Danica lay with hands by her head and her hazy eyes on his. A tiny sound came from her throat when he rubbed the tips of his fingers over her darkened nipples, and in the delight of the moment she lowered her lashes and let her head fall to the side. He touched her everywhere then, always slowly and with wonder, always with the same devastating effect on her senses.

She heard him move and felt him taking off her flats and the stylish patterned socks she'd worn. Then he was slipping the jeans and her panties down all the way and she was naked. She opened her eyes to see him before her bent knees, and she would have murmured a protest when he gently eased her legs apart had it not been for the worshipful expression he wore.

He looked at what he'd opened; then he placed a hand there and stroked her, and she did murmur, but not in protest, because she felt the heat and the tension that had begun to gather and she wanted him to relieve it as only he could. He had the key to her heart, and hence her body, and she knew he was feeling joy in pleasuring her and that enhanced her pleasure ten-fold.

Her knees fell farther to the side and he inched closer. He caressed her slowly, looking up along the creamy lines of her body from time to time to meet her gaze and smile. She smiled back while she could, but she was breathing more heavily and clear thought was fading fast.

"I love you, Danica," he breathed, slipping a finger into her. She arched at the sensation, then closed her eyes and bit her lip when he introduced a second finger and began to move both.

She whispered his name in a tattered gasp and closed her fists on the edges of the cushion beneath her head.

"I love you," he murmured again, and she cried out because his words, his fingers, his very presence, conspired to drive her to higher and higher peaks. Then she sucked in her breath, held it, and let it out at last in a series of fierce bursts.

Michael watched her, heard her, felt her moistness spasmodically hugging his fingers. Only when the tension had seeped from her and she lay limp did he remove them and slide up alongside her body. He stroked her face until, smiling shyly, she opened her eyes.

He spoke softly. "I've always wanted to do that, to watch you when you climax, but I can't when I'm in you myself because I can't think straight then." He smiled. "You've got so much passion in you and you let it out with the same grace, the same beauty, with which you do everything else in life."

Blushing, she managed to raise a hand to stroke his face and the light shadow of a beard on his jaw. "You unleash the passion," she whispered brokenly. "You unleash so much of what's good in me."

"Then we complement each other, which is how it should be."

She thought about that for a time, until her pulse had returned to normal. "I read a tea bag tag once—"

He rolled his eyes. "Oh, God—"

She lowered her hand to his chest. "No, I'm serious. It was soon after I met you, but I was thinking about Blake at the time. The tag said something about love being a magical bond, which makes one and one far more than two, and I remember thinking that Blake and I were so separate that there wasn't any possible way we could combine to produce something else, at least not emotionally. Maybe deep down inside I was fantasizing about you and about how I *knew* we could make something more." She began to stroke his chest, absently at first, then with more direction when the swell of his muscles titillated her fingers. "But it's strange. When we're together, when we make love, we're totally united, really only one, though there's no 'only' about it. It's when we pull apart, when it's over, that I feel like so much more because I've still got a part of you with me and I'm that much fuller a person for it.... Am I making sense or am I babbling?"

"A little of each, I think, but I love it." He was smiling as she lifted her head to kiss his chest.

"Take your sweater off. This is absurd."

Laughing aloud, he whipped the sweater over his head, then curved his arm along her back, supporting her while she moved her lips through the hair on his chest.

"*You* smell good. What have you got on?"

"It's either soap," he mocked in his deepest voice, "or eau de Michael. You'll have to be the judge."

"Not soap, but clean. I love the way you smell."

"Thank God for that," he murmured, sliding his hand down to cover her belly. "And one and one certainly does make more than two, if we count baby here."

"That was the obvious part," she breathed, dabbing his nipple with the tip of her tongue. "I was trying to be more... more esoteric."

"Esoteric." He arched his back, then cleared his throat, but his voice still came out sounding hoarse. "Good word, *esoteric*.... Dani, you're driving me crazy." Her lips were moving in lazy circles over his ribs, her breath warming his flesh, and she lowered a hand to his jeans and was cupping the firmness, which strained against the placket of his zipper.

"Take off your pants, then," she whispered.

"You do it."

"I can't. I feel weak, and you've made me that way." Leaning back, she grinned. "I'll watch."

With a low growl, he rolled to his knees, tore at the fastening of his jeans and pushed them, and his shoes and socks, off to the side. Then he lifted her up and against him, groaning when her breasts touched his chest. Sliding his hands down her back, he cupped her bottom and raised her hips against his. She had her arms around his neck, which was good, because moments later he was lowering them both to lie face to face before the fire.

He kissed her then, drinking deeply from her lips in long, lingering sips. She offered her tongue, and he took it readily, sucking, pulling it deeper and deeper into his mouth. Her hands were on him again, and she was using her fingers and her palms to extend what was already so fully extended. When he could take no more of her torture, he lifted her thigh with his and opened her to his gentle probing.

It was Danica's turn to whisper soft words of love, and she did so repeatedly as he sheathed himself in her warmth. She kissed him between breaths, stroked him where she knew he'd be inflamed and tightened herself around him as though she'd hold him there forever.

And there was something more beautiful to their coupling than there'd ever been before because there was no element of desperation this time, no fear of separation. Their love was unfettered and invincible, their future here, now and always.

Epilogue

BLAKE LINDSAY SERVED as Secretary of Commerce for another year. He was never quite as much at ease in Washington after the trial, and when he submitted his resignation just prior to the start of the campaign for Jason Claveling's active reelection bid, it was graciously accepted. He left for Detroit to take over the reins of a large but troubled automobile manufacturing concern. In time, given his keen business sense and his organization expertise, he was able to turn the corporation around.

Though he lived in the same city as his family, he·saw little of them. He never married again.

CILLA BUCHANAN NEVER DID WRITE a story such as the one Harlan Magnusson had suggested. Though she believed that he'd been telling her the truth, she'd lost her taste for that subject. There were other stories to write, which she did with much enthusiasm, but she had more important things on her mind as time passed. After living together for a year and realizing that their lives were much richer when they had each other, she and Jeffrey Winston were married—again.

Jeffrey was gratified that, of the eight companies and seventeen individuals indicted as a result of his investigation, twenty-two all told were found guilty of the charges brought against them. He went on to carry out other critical work for the Department of Defense, though was very happy to share what he could with Cilla at the end of each day. Chauvinist that he'd once been, he took an active role in caring for the child they subsequently had.

GENA BRADLEY PROVED TO BE as wonderful a mother-in-law as Danica had known she'd be. The two women shared a special bond, one that grew stronger with each passing year.

Michael's father, John, accepted Danica with remarkable grace. He seemed to see it as a victory that a Buchanan had stolen away a Marshall. Michael saw no point in reminding him that, in some regards, it had been the other way around.

ELEANOR MARSHALL MADE UP, in the years that followed, for all she hadn't done when Danica had been younger. Her health held up, so she visited often and was always there when Danica called. She quickly grew to love Michael and became Danica's and his champion, such that William, albeit begrudgingly at first, accompanied her to Maine for the birth of Danica's child. In time he seemed to accept what Danica had done, and though he and Michael never fully warmed to each other, he showered genuine affection on their child.

MICHAEL AND DANICA WERE MARRIED in March, three years to the day after they first met. It was a quiet ceremony, with only Greta and Pat McCabe present to serve as witnesses, but it was precisely what Michael and Danica wanted, and it was beautiful.

Two months later Danica gave birth to a daughter. Michael was by her side, holding her hand, telling her how much he loved her and their child, just as she'd dreamed. From the start he was a doting father, even more so as their daughter grew. And when, two years later, they had a son, his capacity for love seemed simply to multiply.

Professionally, they became a team, collaborating on many books as the years passed, though writing was far from their only interest. Michael continued to teach at Harvard one afternoon a week each fall, staying the night in Cambridge only when Danica could be with him. Danica, filled with the self-confidence that came from being a champion wife and mother, approached a cable television station in Portland and sold it on letting her host a program similar to that she'd done in Boston. Michael and the children were her biggest fans.

When she stopped to look back over those years, the times that were closest to her heart were those when she and Michael and the children were together before the fire on blustery winter days. The warmth, the closeness, they shared then epitomized everything she'd always wanted in life. She loved and was loved. She felt peaceful, fulfilled, and was very, very pleased with the path she'd chosen.

One of America's best-selling romance authors writes
her most thrilling novel!

TWIST OF FATE

JAYNE ANN KRENTZ

Hannah inherited the anthropological papers that could
bring her instant fame. But will she risk her life and give
up the man she loves to follow the family tradition?

Available in June at your favorite retail outlet, or reserve your copy for
May shipping by sending your name, address, and zip or postal code
along with a check or money order for $4.70 (includes 75¢ for postage
and handling) payable to Worldwide Library Reader Service to:

In the U.S.
Worldwide Library
901 Fuhrmann Blvd.
Buffalo, NY
14269

In Canada
Worldwide Library
P.O. Box 2800, 5170 Yonge St.
Postal Station A, Willowdale, Ont.
M2N 6J3

BPA—TOF-H-1

 WORLDWIDE LIBRARY